# CHILDREN OF STONEWALL

# CHILDREN OF STONEWALL

A NOVEL

BY

KAYVAN KABOLI

SIMPLE TALES LLC

ISBN-13: 978-1-7326806-2-3

Editing by Mandy Erickson

Cover design by Retta

# DEDICATION

In memory of all those who throughout history became victims of religious fundamentalism.

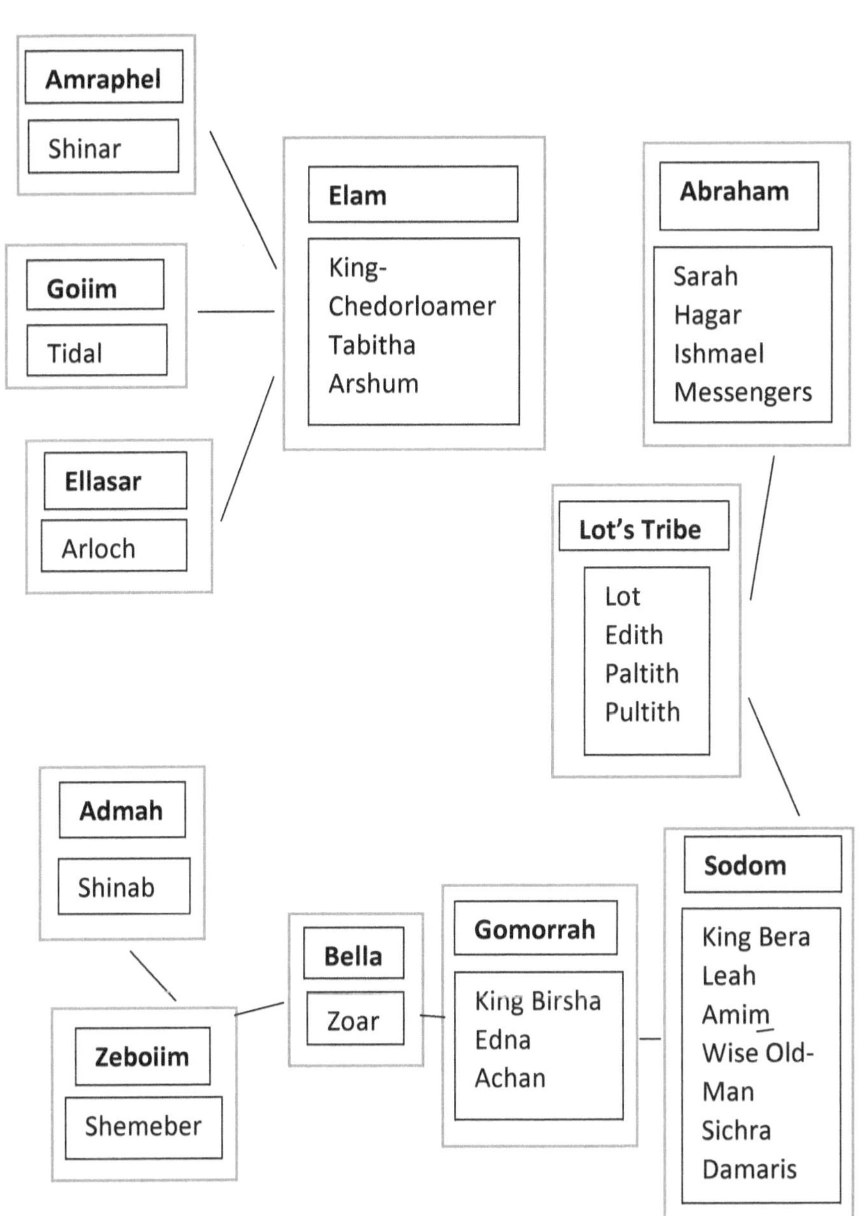

Amraphel
Shinar
Goiim
Tidal
Ellasar
Arloch
Elam
King-Chedorloamer
Tabitha
Arshum
Abraham
Sarah
Hagar
Ishmael
Messengers
Lot's Tribe
Lot
Edith
Paltith
Pultith
Admah
Shinab
Bella
Zoar
Gomorrah
King Birsha
Edna
Achan
Sodom
King Bera
Leah
Amim
Wise Old-Man
Sichra
Damaris
Zeboiim
Shemeber

## Table of Contents

# Chapter 1- His Excellency

I have set my bow in the clouds, and it shall be a sign of the covenant between me and the earth.

When I bring clouds over the earth and the bow is seen in the clouds, I will remember my covenant that is between me and you and every living creature of all flesh; and the waters shall never again become a flood to destroy all flesh. — Book of Genesis [9:13-15]

*Atlanta - Georgia*

John Wesley the Third stood up and walked toward the window. Outside, gardeners were busy trimming bushes. A reflection of the sun generated a beautiful rainbow arc in the large water fountain in the middle of the garden, as the water splashed upward forcefully. He stared at the rainbow. The more he gazed at the rainbow, the more he frowned. He always had a contradictory feeling about the rainbow.

Although the rainbow was no more than a reflection and the penetration of water particles in the components of the sunlight, he believed this game of lights and water was God's promise to Noah.

John knew the Book of Genesis by heart. After everything on earth was destroyed by flood and storm, God swore to Noah that he would never destroy the earth again. Then, he showed humans the rainbow as a symbol of his promise. But now, John felt, the most sinister of God's creatures had confiscated the rainbow as a symbol of their unity, choosing it as their flag. Alas, the rainbow, which should be the manifestation of the promise of God, was turned against God by Satan.

Outside, rows of tall pine trees outlining a carefully decorated garden created a distinct boundary between the end of the garden and the lush green view in the back. A spectacular view including the lake and rising grounds was on display, like a stunning painting, from the window on the third floor where his office was located.

He touched the cross on his chest for a second and walked back to his desk feeling a sharp pain in his legs. He slowly sat in his comfortable chair behind his elegant dark cherry desk. Dipped into his comfortable cognac leather chair, John Wesley the Third felt relieved.

His carefully trimmed white hair, always combed from left to right, decorated his high forehead. His reddish-triangular face with his defined nose and stiff, thin lips made him look somewhat agitated and suspicious almost all the time. His eyebrows formed with a few scattered pointy hairs above his small eagle eyes. He no longer had the strength to walk steadily. But his slow body movements and his careful steps gave him a magnificent look. He demanded that anyone who knew or was in contact with him should address him as His Excellency.

His manner and deeds were such that others, even those who did not want to, would address John Wesley the Third as His Excellency. He had ordered all maids, assistants, and subordinates to politely correct any speaker who would use a different title to address him as His Excellency. Although in his view, all men were created equal before the eyes of God, he considered himself undoubtedly deserving of such a title. He believed that years of work and efforts in spreading the light and love of God entitled him. His Excellency never showed modesty to please others.

John Wesley the Third lifted his hand from the book that was on the desk and placed it on the armchair, symmetrical to the other hand. At the age of 75, sitting in an uneven position even for a minute could have brought severe pain to his spine for an entire day. He looked at the book on the desk again. The book was his latest work about John Wesley, founder of the Church of Methodism in 1738, which detailed the history of Christianity at the Holy Club. In the book, His Excellency attributed part of his credibility to a direct family relation with the famous John Wesley. This claim created a somewhat controversial issue that was challenged by the Post Evangelicals, also known as Evangelicals Left, or Liberal Evangelicals. Recently, the topics surrounding the book, creating controversies, discomforted the high circles and heads of various branches of the conservative Evangelicals. The lack of sufficient support by fellow conservatives to decisively condemn Liberal Evangelicals annoyed His Excellency.

Opponents of His Excellency tried to challenge this claim from various angles, including the use of the principles of Protestantism in eliminating any mediator and deity's representation in the church. In one case, a member of the Liberal Evangelicals wrote an article, mocking the use of the title "His Excellency" from the church's point of view, and determined that any praise belongs only to the grace of God and His son. Of course, the great scholars of the various branches of the church at high levels carefully prevented the leak of this conflict to the public. However, after the publication of his last book, the stress and suffrages driven by engaging in those arguments opened the door to invasion by numerous diseases. Contrary to his doctor's opinion, he believed that excessive redness of his skin, muscle aches, and pains in his lower legs were a direct result of the nervous discomfort and a source of distress. His family doctor, however, had strictly prohibited him from the consumption of red meat.

His Excellency's carefully arranged office on the top floor of his luxurious mansion showed his utmost discipline and attention to details. The magnificent effigy of John Wesley, with long white hair extended to his shoulders, showed the founder of the Holy Club in the

18th century, preaching a sermon. It was placed in the best spot on the wall, right behind His Excellency's chair. Two lights pointed to the effigy from the lower corners, emphasizing its prominence compared with other items in the room.

He turned his scowled face back to stare at John Wesley's picture for a second. Then he picked up a large orange envelope that was on the desk and emptied its contents. His trembling hand was visibly shaking the corner of the front page as he held the bottom of the *Bay Area Chronicle* newspaper. As His Excellency put on his glasses, he looked at a yellow Post-it note, sticking in the middle of the front page. It read: "Look at the third column on the second page."

He opened the newspaper, turned the page, and placed it back on the desk. A circle, drawn by pencil, bordered the columns. The headline read: "Revisiting Sodom to explore the right story."

After reading the first few lines, John lifted his head, took his glasses off, then picked up the phone and dialed. When the call was answered, without an extra word, he commanded, "Arrange a meeting... not everyone needs to be present, only main bishops." Then he hung up the phone, stepped toward the door, and exited the room.

His Excellency would leave his room every day usually at this hour to visit his son, John.

The renovated three-story mansion with more than 15 rooms was nothing short of a palace. Servants and a chauffeur occupied three rooms located on the ground level in the back of the building. At this grand mansion, His Excellency could accept religious and political figures, in addition to performing various religious activities for his close followers, their families, and their caretakers. The third floor housed His Excellency's office, a bedroom, and two other large rooms that were used as a warehouse. His Excellency used these two warehouses to securely preserve important documents—personal, religious, and church documents.

John Wesley the Third opened the door and went to his son's room. His room was located right below his father's office on the second floor. On the semi-dark side of the room, a very sickly look small built teenage boy was lying on his bed. Noticing His Excellency's entrance, John hid a book that he was reading, pushing it under the blanket slowly. His Excellency unhurriedly closed the door behind him; as he walked toward the bed, John turned to him with a weary smile on his thin, jaundiced face. His Excellency came close to John's bed, placed his right hand on John's forehead, and asked: "My son, how are you today? Were you able to study? Are you happy with your teacher?"

While his right hand was still on his son's forehead, His Excellency put his left hand on the Bible which was on the small table beside John's bed. The boy nodded. John had long refused to utter a word to his father's questions. His Excellency then added, "The maid said that you still insist on going to the school, you can when you recover. I don't think that your illness has improved yet, John. Until then, you have to be homeschooled. You should know that the level of your homeschooling is much higher than the public schools. More important than that, you need to be independent, doing your routines, before you can go to the school."

It all happened about three years ago when John was ten years old. The alarm sounded clearly for His Excellency that the devil had arrived. The Evil sought to destroy the very family that had always guided people toward accepting the way of God in the church. Now this family was under attack. Satan targeted John, His Excellency's only child, who was the best candidate to pursue Christ's real values, side by side with his father.

For a moment, uncertainty and doubt encompassed His Excellency's state of being. He closed his eyes and prayed to his God, "O my dear God, whatever I did in my life was for you; it was for your dignity and greatness. It was you who guided me in the most decisive moments in most difficult times," His Excellency continued, as his hand was on the gospel of Jesus Christ; he repeated these words again in his mind. With one hand on the Bible and the other holding John's hand, he saw himself as the mediator and transmitter of a godly message from God to the son. The Holy Spirit.

***

The day he saw John in his bedroom's walk-in closet, wearing his mother's clothes, lipstick, makeup, and high heels, His Excellency felt a hard strike on his head. He stood silently, clutching his head in the spot where he felt the pain. John had escaped from the bedroom. The blow was not merely imaginary: he felt a swell under his fingers, and he was not asleep. His Excellency could no longer stand. It was impossible to hold on; he suddenly dropped to the floor right where he was. His eyes narrowed. He shut his eyes. The light was off, but a mixture of light from the stand and window in the bedroom crept into a relatively large area of the closet where everything was carefully arranged on the shelves. He felt himself breaking into a sweat. John Wesley the Third was suffering from high fever. He sensed rapid and strong heartbeats, mostly on his temples.

His Excellency opened his eyes only to see that the demons were sitting by his side. The siege was arranged. He had guessed that surely, someday, demons would come for revenge. He was unaware that so many demons existed. They caught him off guard and cornered him unexpectedly. It seemed that in a blink of an eye they metastasized immediately to stand side by side. Rows of demons stood shoulder to shoulder, blocking the doorway to the bedroom. He could finally see the bedroom from under the feet and tails of a few demons. Most looked the same, but several demons had different shapes and faces. Apparently, those were leaders, guiding the rest. It seemed they carefully plotted the attack, planning for months.

His Excellency gathered his breath in his chest and tried to shout: "Sara," he called to his wife. But no sound came from his throat. He sent his force back into his chest, but his mouth was shut. A devil was sitting on his mouth. The lower part of the devil was right on his face. He noticed that the devil sitting on his mouth was not dressed. Until now, John Wesley the Third had not thought about whether devils wore clothes or were naked when they would not appeared in the form of humans. But now, he saw that they were nude.

He had to escape from hornet's nest. He tried to look around. He saw others. They were also naked. He felt he was not able to breathe. He realized that his whole body was numb. If only he could move a little, make a simple motion, but he realized there was no chance of that. Satan sat on his face looking toward His Excellency's feet. Breathing became a struggle, and his face turned purple. The devil found out about his strive. The devil's vagina was compressed on His Excellency's mouth, and her anus and tail were pushing onto his nose.

At that moment, His Excellency realized that the devil sitting on his face was a woman. Until now, he had not thought that Satan had a gender. He always said in his sermons that the temptation of sexuality was from Satan, but he never wondered which gender. The devil moved her tail slightly, and a tiny orifice to breathe was opened. He inhaled through the nose. The air that went into his chest through the nose and into his lungs was odd. It was aromatic, not the bad odor of an anus. It was the aroma of the most exquisite perfume that His Excellency had never experienced. Overwhelmed by this mysterious, delicious feminine scent, blood rushed to his shaft, awakening his manhood involuntarily, and he gave into carnal lust. His Excellency tasted the sweetness on his tongue. John Wesley the Third was still feeling the devil's vagina, sitting on his mouth. He tried to save the whole taste by licking his own lips. Wanting more, he then tightened his tongue and brought it out, feeling the wall of the devil's vagina. Now the flavor, its fragrance and sweetness, had slipped down from the tip of his tongue to the bottom of his taste buds. He was in Paradise. How could the taste of heaven come out of a woman's vagina, from a devil, no less?

His Excellency opened his eyes. Demons still were everywhere. Now they were clearly dancing in frantic yet soft motions, swirling, spinning in superb and magnificent harmony. It was the proclamation of the Satan's victory against Christ.

The only sensation he felt was from his involuntary erected penis which was pressing against his pants. He felt numb again. From between their legs, tails, and hooves, he saw Sara. Demons were carrying her on hands over their heads toward the bedroom. Once more, His Excellency tried again to shout out, but he fainted instead. When he gained consciousness, he found himself dangling from the ceiling by his penis, the only point of the body that he still could feel. He turned his head to look down. Sara was lying on the floor, and several male devils were slowly moving, slipping up and down on her naked body. He felt his tears of sorrow pouring down on Sara and the demons. His Excellency looked at Sara, wanting to help her to ease her pain from the devil's sexual torture. He looked down at her face. To his surprise, Sara was neither sad nor did she feel any pain. She was apparently climaxing in her highest delight, immensely enjoying the torture by the demons.

"Lord," he cried out with all his power when he found his mouth free to shout. Nothing happened. Calling God louder again, he shouted, "Save my Sara as you did Abraham's Sarai, who was caught in Pharaoh's grips. I know that Abraham witnessed his wife's captivity through which Sarai was taken to be Pharaoh's love mate, as I do now see my Sara in devil's hands. Oh great God, most gracious, merciful God; you are the creator of all universe. You are the savior of all human beings. You saved Abraham's Sarai, now help me and protect my Sara from grips of these devils."

His Excellency thought about Abraham. Now, he thoroughly understood what Abraham endured when his Sarai was given to Pharaoh. When he arrived in the land of Pharaoh, Abraham knew that they would give his wife to Pharaoh, so he told Sarai to pretend she was his sister. Pharaoh's men sent a handsome bonus to Abraham in exchange for his sister. Trusting God, Abraham accepted the reward. Abraham believed that God would not allow any harm come to Sarai.

And when Pharaoh was about to own Sarai, God prevented Pharaoh from that shameful act by threatening to send a plague to him and his people. In fear of divine punishment, Pharaoh returned Sarai to Abraham and criticized him for his deceit of hiding the nature of their relationship. But Abraham did not lie entirely. Sarai was Abraham's half-sister. She was chosen to be his wife. Then Pharaoh gave Abraham all the bonuses and rewards that were promised and released them.

> When Abram entered Egypt the Egyptians saw that the woman was very beautiful.
> When the officials of Pharaoh saw her, they praised her to Pharaoh. And the woman was taken into Pharaoh's house.
> And for her sake he dealt well with Abram; and he had sheep, oxen, male donkeys, male and female slaves, female donkeys, and camels.
> But the LORD afflicted Pharaoh and his house with great plagues because of Sarai, Abram's wife.
> So Pharaoh called Abram, and said, "What is this you have done to me? Why did you not tell me that she was your wife?
> Why did you say, 'She is my sister,' so that I took her for my wife? Now then, here is your wife, take her, and be gone."
> And Pharaoh gave his men orders concerning him; and they set him on the way, with his wife and all that he had.—Book of Genesis [12:14–20]

His Excellency knew the story of Abraham; he had read it hundreds of times and correctly remembered every verse. He had assured people in the church about God's vicinity to his creations and of sending help in the time of need. His Excellency knew that God would save both his son and Sara. It was there that he became inspired by Lord to start John's treatment, even though, like Abraham, he had to be forced to send his only son to be slaughtered.

His child had to be cleansed of sin, at the expense of his son and the mother's life. If Sara had to be smashed under the devils' hooves, it was the price he was willing to pay. And so with all his existence, His Excellency accepted this commands from God right then and there, while he was hanging from the ceiling. He looked down again. There was nothing. Sara and the devils were gone. He found himself lying in the same place where the female devil forced herself on him. "How could it be?" he asked himself.

His Excellency had been split into two individuals: one hanging from the ceiling and the other lying on the floor, one from Earth and the other heavenly. From that day on, His Excellency knew that his heavenly being would convey God's commands to him. He opened his eyes and saw Sara staring at him with an anxious look. Sara asked him worriedly, "What happened? I called 911, and they are on their way. They will arrive at any moment."

***

His Excellency remembered so very vividly that entire evil affair. That cursed day passed in his mind in a blink of an eye. His Excellency and his family were attacked by demons. John Wesley the Third remembered it while he had one hand on the gospel and the other holding his son's hand. From the day that God commanded him, he confined his ten-year-old son to the house and subjected him to the harshest treatments as a cure.

Subsequently, Sara left His Excellency and began her campaign to protest her husband's and the madness of John's treatment. His Excellency knew that these were the sacrifices that God had asked him to make, as the Lord had called for Abraham to sacrifice his Isaac. His Excellency prayed, "O my God, whatever I did in my life was for you; it was for your dignity and greatness. It was you who guided me in the most decisive moments and difficult times."

His Excellency was fearful of repeatedly asking God, "How long should I witness my son's agony and torture? Reveal Isaac's replacement calf to me?" His Excellency knew that the Lord is the most omnipotent of earth and time. He knew that eventually, God would answer his prayers. He knew that he would once again embrace his Sara as God returned Sarai to Abraham.

Before leaving the room, His Excellency made the sign of the cross and prayed to the Father, Son, and Holy Spirit.

## Chapter 2 – Arthur

*Silicon Valley, San Francisco- One month earlier*

No code was executed on that day, and no test was being passed. Sometimes the most skilled programmer could not figure out where the problem was. This issue had confused Arthur and the project manager alike.

Staring at his phone screen, Art was checking trends on Twitter. Even before the election, checking Twitter hashtags had become one of Art's habits. Receiving streaming news on the subject of the presidential election and its surrounding excitement forced people to use social media. For Art, however, getting news was not the only reason for visiting Twitter frequently. When he was tired of coding or had a hard time finding a solution, he used Twitter to distract his mind. He had learned from experience that when he deliberately avoided the problem and relaxed his mind, the answer would suddenly appear.

Late on that afternoon, Art was struggling with a bug and needed a distraction. What could be better than the heated election stories? 2016 apparently was different from all previous historical election years. Since the announcement of the results until now, most hashtags on Twitter have been about Hillary's unbelievable defeat and the controversies surrounding president-elect Trump.

***

Art remembered the election night vividly. What a night it was! More than a month had passed. His boss, David, the owner of Tech2AI Company, had ordered pizza and beer for all the employees. They stayed until late at night to find out who the winner would be. A 90-inch widescreen TV, located in the corner of the hall, was divided into four windows. Each window was on a different news channel with its own projection for each state. One of the employees with a remote control was bringing the sound from one window to the other, announcing updated information. Every projection would create a frenzy among the crowd, bursting the salon to its excitement. In addition to the television, everyone with his own phone also informed others of updates from online news sources.

The coders' workstation, a long table in the middle of the main hall, was divided into two equal parts along its length. Sixteen computer monitors were arranged with two screens, back to back, facing in opposite directions, allowing coders to work without distraction.

On the election night, however, chairs were placed on one side of the hall so that half of the hall was empty, while the other half was full of excitement. Several whiteboards were installed on walls for the purpose of writing code examples, instructions, and notes. There were yellow and red Post-it notes on some parts of the boards. Along with each sticker, lines of codes written in colorful dry markers appeared to be from various coders in different handwriting.

It was madness in the hall when each network's anchorperson announced a new projection of the candidate's total Electoral College votes in different states. CNN's Wolf Blitzer with his always urgent tone, making any news sound like breaking news, would give the crowd an instant thrill by adding more urgency. Up until three-quarters of the count, there was an air of excitement in the large working area. There was no doubt that the Democratic nominee would win. Some were already starting to celebrate—toasting with their beer, and starting to get drunk. During the last quarter, however, the trend was shockingly different. A few states were determining the overall outcome of the election.

The crowd's mode of excitement, hopeful of a celebration, swiftly subsided. It was as if an ultimate tragic result were imminent. The loud laughter disappeared. The moment of truth was approaching. The pizza boxes were stacked on top of each other, with few slices left, along with the bottles and empty cans of beer and other beverages. Now, the eerie feeling of the inevitable was slowly crawling in. It felt like a severe hangover after hours of euphoria, like balloons that became deflated. The possibility of losing had frightened everyone, like they were seeing ghosts in the middle of the night. It had to be an error; it had to be a mistake. Unfortunately, there was no error. Trump's Electoral College vote chart that appeared below his picture had passed the required 271, then reached 304. Each window on TV displayed the same numbers, and there was no hope for any correction.

Few people grabbed their belongings and left in disbelief; few others quickly wiped their tears before anyone else noticed. It looked as if all their energy had evaporated. A couple of people stayed calm, showing no emotions as though they were wearing the mask of indifference and did not want to reveal their political position in public. It was clear that they were pleased.

Art, like most of his colleagues, had expected the Democratic candidate to win, but after the results were revealed, he did not find himself distressed. Art had not voted that day. He did not like Trump's campaign style or his manner. Disliking Trump, however, was not enough of a force to make Art vote for his opponent. Furthermore, it was clear to him that in the state of California his vote did not matter, because California always belonged to Democrats and it always would be a Democratic state.

***

More than a month had passed since that night, but the election fervor remained on news portals and social media. For Art, the issue that most occupied his mind was staring at him. The chief rival at the moment, the challenging lines of codes on the text editor, invited him to a duel.

Art turned to Twitter, distracting himself to let the answer come to him, but the solution had yet to light any sparks in his mind. Of course, this method of distraction had its own snags. Sometimes, a hot topic attracted his attention more than it should have, and he found himself spending more time reading the news than working. He blamed the articles' length and breadth. Art believed that journalism in the new era should adopt a new platform according to the speed of modern life. He was a real fan of brevity in anything.

Art felt that someone was watching him from behind. When he turned around, he saw David, the head of the company, also staring at Art's computer screen. Pointing to a line of code, David suggested, "That function must be called here. Otherwise, it won't work."

As if Art was caught doing something wrong, he situated himself in the chair correctly. The chair moans and jolted. "I tried it, but it didn't work. I have to go back to the function itself, maybe there is a mistake there," he said hastily.

David now stood next to Art, looked at the monitor, reading lines of codes closely. Because of the dark background for the text editor, fingerprints and some spots were visible on his 24-inch monitor. Art would not usually pay much attention to those spots, but now, with his boss standing beside him, looking at the screen, he did not wish his work ethic and discipline to be associated with an uncleaned monitor. David seemed to notice his discomfort and to put Art's mind at ease, he touched the screen with his index finger, pointing to a line and said, "I'm not sure. That function once called here and once there."

"I don't think so," Art replied highlighting the line that David suggested to prove that his boss was wrong, "We'll see," while explaining, Art held down the control key and pressed F5 simultaneously. In one-tenth of the second, the program was executed, and contrary to Art's expectation, a favorable result appeared on the monitor. David said, "Aha, you see? I was right."

Art mumbled something that David could not comprehend. David also could not tell whether Art was unhappy or pleased to find a solution, but in order to change the subject he asked, "Are you going to stay for the meeting tonight?"

The young programmer who had not yet recovered from the blow, baffled by his own mistake, answered absentmindedly, "I don't know, maybe. When?"

"Everyone will be here soon. You are already here, so, stay."

In the past, David had personally invited Art several times to attend his meetings with his friends at the company's office. But each time Art, though still had nothing else to do, turned it down with an excuse. Usually, at the end of David's discussions there was a collective meditation.

Art decided to stay. He felt he needed to ease the pressure; he was overwhelmed with codes that had been piling up in his head. Taking a break was proving effective. He thought maybe he would kill two birds with one stone. To attend a non-mandatory meeting would be a sign of gratitude to his boss and at the same time, he would relax his mind with meditation.

Lately, holding spiritual sessions and meditations had become very popular in Silicon Valley. Most of his friends who were working in tech companies in Northern California attended these spiritual sessions. He also heard that individual or multidisciplinary meditation sessions were fashionable and most managers encouraged staff to attend.

Apparently, the ancient spiritual world of Buddha and Hindus had tunneled several thousand miles westward to reach the rich world of technology in Silicon Valley. But Art had heard that David's meetings with his friends, which had taken place for many years, were fundamentally different from the rest.

The gatherings on Wednesday nights were not among the company's mandatory meetings. Topics of discussions were not work issues such as agile software development model or coding standards. They were about various philosophical theories. Essie, David's close Middle Eastern friend, and David started these meetings. After a few years, others from outside the company joined the meetings. Apparently, David intended to rent a larger space to accommodate a higher number of people for his Wednesday night meetings.

David's eyes sparkled when he heard Art's positive response and said, "Great. I would love to know your expert opinion about all the discussions and conversations. You know, my whole philosophical theory is based on artificial intelligence and similarities between the creation and computer programs. It's interesting for me to know what you think."

David's last comment about Art's opinion was, in fact, expressed wholeheartedly, and not just to please his employee. Art had been hired a year ago; he possessed keen ability to process and solve most problems quickly. His intelligence and solid character, ethics in both his work and personal life, helped him to gain David's utmost respect quickly. Essentially, David was far from being a strict employer and by no means had ever treated him just as an employee.

While David was walking toward his room, Art said, "Until then, I'll send today's work as a new version on Github to be stored. Then, I'll go eat and come back soon."

David answered from a distance with a somewhat higher tone for Art to hear, "You don't need to worry about food. Essie always brings sandwiches for everyone; he usually buys more than we need; don't worry, just stay."

***

On that last Wednesday night of the year, when other companies threw magnificent parties and spectacular shows with popular celebrities to please their valuable employees, Tech2AI concluded its regular meeting with meditation. Although Arthur was invited to several of those lavish parties, he did not feel like he could endure a loud and crowded environment that night. He decided to join David's gathering or, as Art would call it, "a philosophical party."

The soft sound of rain droplets hitting the window attracted Art's attention. David was busy comparing the similarities of the creation of artificial intelligence and of humans. Five people were sitting on somewhat uncomfortable chairs with glasses of wine and bottles of beer, listening to him. Art pulled a gulp of beer and looked out the window.

He stared at the magnificent rainfall outside under streetlights. David's voice in the background, like a distanced lullaby, felt peaceful. Art also felt covered, dry, and warm, watching the rain outside. It was hot. Apparently, someone had raised the thermostat. For a moment, he wanted to cool his face under the rain.

Art looked at David, who was trying to explain his theory to his audience passionately yet calmly. It was as if David's enthusiasm and calmness were in a sharp competition, sometimes overstepping each other, "Now, we are creating artificial intelligence that can learn and analyze if it is exposed to information. It means it can extract new facts from the same information that it's fed. Now, our artificial intelligence is creating its own robots and new languages."

David's office was decorated plainly. Melody, David's wife, believed that simplicity is the best design. With a simple oil painting hung right behind David's desk, she brought on the beauty of an orange-splashed autumn morning to the room. To decorate the other wall, David mounted a picture of Jim Morrison, his favorite singer from the rock band The Doors. David's choice was not opposed by his wife because of its harmony with shades of autumn painting.

Melody painted all walls with a mild lime color background, a color that would relax the eye while matching other objects in the room.

Sam, the company's project manager who had never missed a meeting, asked in his scratchy voice, "Well, what is the conclusion of your argument? I was involved in these kinds of discussions before, I mean, if you want to make the creation of human beings identical to what we are creating now, it's an inaccurate comparison. Your conclusion has a flaw. You cannot withdraw your desirable result based on what you said."

Sam ran his fingers through his thin hair, then locked his hands in front of his billowing belly. While it was unclear whether his blushed face was the effect of drinking wine or the excitement of speaking in front of the others, he continued: "I'm somewhat familiar with these technological hypotheses that want to incline man in the role of new God. But before we could claim it, there are still many theories that need to be proven. We still are nothing compared to the greatness of the true creation."

Essie was looking carefully at Sam, who was uncomfortable in his seat. Essie, an old friend of David's, was sitting beside Art, David, Sam, and Melody. Usually, the Wednesday meetings were much more crowded. Apparently, the concurrency of this night with the end-of-December parties in Silicon Valley and San Francisco left only these five individuals in that room. The meeting went on amid outside's freezing cold air and heavy rain from the red, impregnated sky.

David answered, "Of course, as you said, there is no comparison. My discussion is not about God and does not refer to any religion. Again, you are correct, many theories need to be proven and more evidence to be presented to conclude to that extent. No one claims that the nature of human creation and AI are the same. But think about it, when we have AI, we create the learning machine that can analyze and pursue its interests. We basically become a creator. You can't deny it, right? "

Sam remained silent. David continued, "And we also consider a safety factor for the sake of our security in our programs, for example, a shutdown switch, in case of emergency. I think we must go one step further and provide a mechanism to deal with the thinking problems of these machines. It's necessary if they need to remain connected to us, as their creator, in the event of an overwhelming accumulation of information and failure to find a solution. In parentheses, let me say that this is one of the issues we need to work on, on our future projects. But, going back to the subject, yes, I think there is such a mechanism in us for contacting the creator, and there is an emergency switch somehow installed in us. If we know how to access it, we can use it to find answers to many of our questions. This connection helps our search to reach the truth."

Essie, who apparently was looking down for a long time, focusing and listening to David, raised his head to make a comment but he changed his mind and took a sip of his red wine instead. David noticed Essie's gesture, so he asked, "Ah, did you want to say something, Essie?"

Uncertain about speaking, Essie mumbled and, while swirling his long thick mustache using his index finger and thumb, said with his unique accent, "I wanted to say that your theory is very abstract. You create desired functions on your machines. What possibly could be accumulated that might require either a special channel or a backchannel necessary to get in touch with you as its creator?"

Art looked at the bright light on the street through the window again. The rain was still falling heavily. He thought if the rain continued to fall as hard as it was then, in a few hours, it would be difficult to get through the streets. For a moment he regretted staying and agreeing to David's suggestion. He wished he was home sitting in his comfortable sofa drinking beer and watching TV.

David replied to Essie immediately. "I hope together we can create this emergency conduit or back channel in our own informative machine system to prove its necessity. But this subject goes back to the philosophical category of destiny versus the will. We had this discussion for many years. The concept of having this functional switch is useful when the default is not sufficient for our machines. It is possible that machines think and work on defaults forever without any problem. But let this back channel be our bypass default in case machines need to solve their problems. This is when it goes out of its default path and reaches relative self-control. What I am talking about is an example of free will versus fate or default. The majority of us, as human beings, have lived all our lives in default. I think there is a back channel within humans that can bypass default to reach free will and liberty."

Looking out the window again, Art saw that, fortunately, the rain was light. Melody, who was silent until that moment, turned to her husband and said, "Well, why don't we put all necessary functions in machines or robots or whatever you want to call it in advance? In this case, there won't be any need for the back channel. This applies to humans, too. Why didn't God, the creator or the master programmer who created us, provide us with everything that we needed? So we wouldn't have to search or meditate to be able to contact Him, to gain strength, and solve our problems?"

"Because millions or billions of possible variants of probable problems may exist and it's hard to provide all keys to every unknown possible lock. I'm sorry darling, but if you agree, let's talk about this important discussion in the next meeting. I would like to discuss this topic later. I kind of know both yours and Essie's opinion on this matter, but I would love to know Art's and also the opinions of the people who are absent today. It's late, and I'm afraid we can't finish this interesting discussion now. As usual, let's conclude our session with meditation. The weather might get colder, and our commute might be affected."

Melody quickly agreed with David, but she was not very pleased. She would have been happier if she could continue to at least make her point. David added, "You all are familiar with how we perform the meditation, except Art who is here among us for the first time. It took years of encouragement to convince Essie to believe finally...”

Melody held David's hand and smiled, as if she knew the jokes that regularly exchanged between the two old friends. “... First, we close our eyes; then we try to clear our minds, removing everything. This is perhaps the most difficult part of the whole process of meditation. At the same time, we must stop new thoughts. After we are able to keep our minds clear—and by the way, there are ways to achieve this, which I'll cover later—we bring the image of cleansing our bodies to our minds. We try to cleanse our body from head to toe, ridding ourselves of everything that may be harmful to our entire physical being, things like germs, bad bacteria, viruses, and any physical contaminations. The third step, if you are well advanced, is to connect and communicate with a source of existence, or universe, or a superior force. Finally, the last step is that everyone experiences a particular phenomenon which is completely unique and personal.”

Until that moment during the meeting, Art had a semi-warm feeling from drinking beer. He was drawn into his own thoughts when listening to David and others. But at the same time, he was growing impatience and could no longer endure the session. However, as David was guiding his audience, the meditation became attractive to Art. This was his first time, and he was a little uncomfortable with his lack of experience. He had heard and read a bit about meditation, but never seriously considered practicing it. Moreover, it was hard for him to focus and meditate in the presence of both the head of the company and the project manager.

David noticed Art's struggle and to ease his mind said, “Don't worry, Art. This is not something you can learn overnight; it takes practice and patience. It may take years before someone can master the techniques of meditation and reach the last stage to benefit from it. In fact, there is no end to meditation. I don't think even the Buddha himself had reached the last stage. By the way, if you lost interest and got bored, out of respect for others, please stay silent.”

Art agreed and replied, "Okay, it's interesting to me, I always wanted to learn, and now I think I would like to try it." Art responded as honestly and quickly as he could to just say something. Now all eyes were staring at Art, which made him more uncomfortable.

Until that night, Art had never seriously thought about meditation and had no intention of starting. But David's talk about the multiple stages of meditation prompted his enthusiasm. It was now a mental challenge. Art loved challenges and problem solving. This particular quality was the primary cause of his success in coding and computer programming. His challenge at the moment was not exactly the same as finding a solution in writing code. "Maybe it's not too far either," he thought.

During a short break, Melody and Essie started talking to each other. David and Sam were talking about a possibility of a new project in upcoming days, and Art, who did not want to be involved in their conversations, stood up and walked toward the window. The rain now was almost over.

Art felt the daylong fatigue in his neck and back. He thought, "Unless meditation rescues me, these discussions were useless. I might have been better off going to one of those parties, better than this dull atmosphere for sure."

Art was still thinking about the problems that he encountered throughout the day at work. He turned and looked back. David was busy talking to Sam, and Essie was still chatting with Melody. David again noticed a look of boredom on Art's face. He immediately stopped his conversation and told people to gather around. "Well, friends, if you agree, let's meditate. The sooner we finish meditation, the sooner we all can go home. It's very late as it is. It's obvious that Art is more tired than all of us. Art, come and sit down."

Essie whispered something in Melody's ear, and her laughter was the last sound that drew everyone's attention. Everyone sat on the chair as before the break. Before starting, to make sure Art understood the whole process and to be clear again, David said, "I repeat once again. First, clear your mind, then imagine you're cleansing your body. Hopefully, you will be able to get in touch with a higher conscience or whatever you call it. Be sure to be in a positive mood. It is quite normal to fall asleep. If that's the case, try to get a good nap." And with that, they started to meditate. David was guiding them through each stage of meditation, speaking softly and slowly, in short sentences, sometimes creating images to help the group.

Art could not focus. He could not quiet his mind; he was aware of the presence of others. It felt impossible to clear his mind, let alone cleanse his body. He repeatedly tried unsuccessfully. The first thing that came into his mind was what the hell he was doing at that moment in that place. If anyone had told him a week ago that he would participate in a group meditation, surely he would have laughed at that person. But now, he was sitting in this place, on a cold winter night, with people whom he barely knew, trying to clear his mind.

He considered himself a man of science and facts. He always had reservations with any unrealistic issues. He would make fun of such sessions, calling them ridiculous and voodoo mumbo-jumbo rituals. Not that he thought spirituality is completely synonymous with magic and trickery, but he believed that with the power of the mind, one could open the gate to the current physical sense only in this material world, obeying physical laws. Where would he draw the line between real and unreal world? In his question, he saw a contradiction.

A few minutes passed. Art had yet to clear his mind; different conversations intensified inside his head. He had obviously engaged in a self-mind debate. As if David understood Art's struggle, he raised his voice to gain Art's attention. Art heard David's voice sharper and louder, "Imagine that your mind is as busy as a stadium, like the Coliseum in ancient Rome, where the gladiators are battling. The excited crowd is cheering; now get them out of your mind, one by one. Start with the gladiators, then the emperor and the crowd. One by one, get them out of your mind. Now it is only you and the silence. The

Coliseum is almost vacant. See the empty Coliseum as your mind—a vast field of nothingness. Look at all the corners. There is nothing, only silence, and vacuum. And your eyes looking for something to delete, but there is none. Nobody is there."

In that moment of silence, Art realized that he was falling asleep. David's voice brought him back to alertness. "And now consider the same stadium littered with rubbish from food, banana peels, vomit, and there are blood spots on the field."

After another brief pause, David continued, "Now think that this stadium is your body. Clean it up. Now you feel that inside your body is getting cleansed. It gives you the feeling that all your organs perform at their best, all the cells and molecules that made up your body are in their highest form and function and harmony."

Art found himself woken up by David's voice several times; he would imagine the scenes David was describing. He could not remember how many times he had napped. Tranquility swallowed him whole. It was as if his cells were vibrating from top to bottom; he felt the bliss. The pleasant warmth encompassed his entire existence. Now David's voice was at a distance and Art did not understand what he was saying. He did not know whether what he heard was David's voice or a conversation in his own mind connecting to the source. He recognized some of the words, but others he heard as sounds he didn't recognize. Then it was silence, and he paid more attention to himself, his body, and state of mind. A moment of tranquility passed. He did not know whether he was asleep or still awake. Lethargy conquered his whole body. He heard David's voice again. As if to be heard, David had to speak loud, "Now you are connecting to a source of energy and existence outside of your body. Look now somewhere outside of you. You may have never seen it before."

David's voice was completely cut off. Art saw his being as a boiling fluid that left his body, and he suddenly felt a connection. He looked out. What was it? Where was he? He had no idea. Everywhere was red. He felt the heat. Art looked through the window. It was all red; he saw an open field on fire. He was losing his calmness. He was slipping into restlessness. It was not pleasant. The window now was a rocky cleft, with a gap slightly higher than the level of his eyes. He stretched his neck to look out through the gap. He saw red and fiery explosions. A blend of dusty smoke and redness merged with the Plainfield. He squinted to see better. Yes, there was fire rising from the ground, into the sky, bouncing back again. Art now could hear the big fiery stones crashing to the ground, shaking the earth under his feet and transferring a jolting wave through his being.

Now, Art could identify people in the Plainfield who were escaping the unknown. People were fleeing in every direction. The horror overcame Art. Men, women, and children were on fire burning to the ground. Unexpectedly, a face appeared through that same gap, looking inside. Art jumped back out of horror. The face was a man's, red but not burnt. Evidently, he was asking for help. The man pointed to the burning field behind him and said something that was not audible to Art. Then, hopeless teardrops flowed from the flushed man's eyes. He tried to spell out his words, one by one, as if he knew his voice could not reach to the other side. The man stretched his unusually long arm through the gap. Art shouted in horror and fell to the ground.

When Art opened his eyes, David and others were crowding over him. Lying on the floor, they could see he was shivering. The first word out of Art's mouth was "Sodom."

"Art, Art," David took his arm and shook him. "Wake up, what happened?"

Art's eyes were wide open. He was looking up silently. But they could tell he was not in the present. Art stared at David's eyes and said, "Sodom."

After a few moments, as if he just woke up, Art asked, "What happened? Why am I on the floor?"

David replied, "I don't know. We were meditating. Suddenly you fell back on the floor screaming. What happened? What did you see? Where did you go?"

Art, lying on the floor, pressed his head between his two hands. Sam was looking at Art frantically. Melody was full of sympathy, though she did not know what had happened. Essie stood beside David observing the scene quietly but anxiously.

David asked again, "What did you do? What was going on? Explain please."

Art remembered the scary scene, burning ground, and running children, elderly women and men. He closed his eyes again. Touching his shoulder, David shook him calmly and said, "Art, are you OK?"

"Yeah, I'm well," Art answered. He got up slowly. David fixed Art's chair for him to sit. Art situated himself and started to explain the horror. David, holding Art's hand, could feel that he was shaking with anxiety. David looked at Essie to see his raised eyebrows.

"Sodom?" David repeated the word with a tone implying a mixture of surprise and question.

Art asked, "What did that man want to tell me? Who was he? What was all that about? It was like a horror movie, but it seemed very real."

Noticing the time, David answered, "I do not know exactly, we'll talk about it tomorrow. It's late now. You better get some rest. I can give you a ride."

"I'm fine," Art said, "it was a terrible scene. I'm still shaking. Surprisingly though, I feel a jolt of energy in me. I don't feel tired at all. It's weird; I want to run all the way home. I'm hot. Everything is weird."

Art fell silent for a few seconds, and then said, "It felt very peaceful at the beginning of the meditation. I never experienced such a calm in my life before. I remember when you said to connect to the source and then everything was changed. Then, I saw those scenes. I have to get out of here now, it's very hot, and I'm burning inside. I cannot stand here anymore."

David listened to Art carefully. Melody and Essie were standing there next to David. After listening to Art, Sam went out of David's office to the main hall. He pulled his Android phone from his pants pocket and typed something on its soft keypad.

David turned to Art and said, "We never experienced such a thing before, all these time we had meditation sessions, not even once we had anything remotely similar. Your case is unique. In the process of connecting to something out of the body, whatever it is, everyone has a particular experience. It is personal and specific to oneself. Until now, I haven't seen anything like this. Apparently, you've been communicating with something, someone, a place, or a historical event. It shows how capable and ready you are for meditation. Has it happened to you during meditation before? "

"This was the first time I did a real meditation on guidance," Art replied. "I wasn't into this stuff; this is a totally new experience for me too."

"Sodom?" Essie asked, stressing the oddity.

David immediately stopped Essie and said, "It's too late now. Let us talk about this tomorrow. You, Art, and I…" David immediately realized that he forgot Melody and added, "If Melody also wants to come… what about first thing tomorrow morning?" David asked Art. Though his eyes were on Essie and Melody, his question was apparently addressed to them all.

"I need to work on the project that we stumbled into. How about after work?" Art said.

David interrupted him and said, "Forget about the project, your teammate will be there. I'll ask Sam to work on it as well. This is very important to me. It's more important than the project. I haven't seen such a thing before."

Melody said, "I can't come. I have an important meeting. I'll be busy all day tomorrow."

Melody, while preparing to leave, continued, "Let's go now, I'm exhausted, I have to get up early in the morning."

"Are you sure you don't want a ride?" David asked Art again.

"Yeah, I'm sure. I'm so energetic now that I can run through these cold streets until the morning."

Sam showed his head through the office's half-opened door and said goodbye to everyone, then closed it. Essie raised his hand as a sign to say goodbye, but Sam had already had shut the door.

David, Melody, Essie, and Art entered the street behind the building where they had parked their cars. As soon as Art's feet touched the sidewalk, he took a few deep breaths. Art inhaled San Francisco's late December night chilly air, deep into his lungs and said bye to the rest of the group. He could not stand still, even for a second. His inner force now transferred to his feet, he immediately started running.

Essie told David, "It looks like he is serious about running in the streets all night. What did you do to him, David?"

"If I was not so tired, I would run with him," said Melody, who apparently became excited by Art's vigor.

David turned to Essie and asked, "Do you want to go in my car or Melody's?"

Essie replied with a big smile on his face, "Of course, Melody's, what do you think? Am I crazy to choose your company over hers?" I'm not in the mood at this late to hear your philosophical mumbles." And he started walking with Melody to her car.

Utterly confused and still baffled by what he saw, David started his car and drove off.

# Chapter 3 – Michael

Art ran for several blocks at a relatively high speed after he left his coworkers. He could hear his breath and feel his flushed face, but there was no sign of fatigue. The man's face behind the stone gap appeared to Art from time to time, but the extraordinary energy that surrounded his body did not allow him to think about the details of that event. At that moment, what mostly occupied Art's mind was the excessive energy that exploded inside him. That energy, as he experienced during the meditation session, would rise and drop continuously. Any high tide drove him to the point of flying. He was still running. He asked himself, "Where did this energy come from that hurled me into this excitation?"

His blood, rushing through his veins, found his flesh and activated a strong sexual desire. He was unable to wait for traffic lights. Night came to its quiescence; only a few cars were in the streets, which allowed Art to jaywalk occasionally. After running through several more intersections, he saw a bar on the other side of the street.

He did not know precisely how long he was running. He had no idea in what part of the city he was. He had just left the office and ran. A strong force within him brought on a happy feeling. He felt connected to the trees, the lights, and the street and all the surroundings. He loved this city.

Since he left San Diego after high school to come to UC Berkeley, he fell in love with this city. He could no longer be comfortable in Southern California, where he was born and raised. His mother was the only reason he went back to San Diego once in a while.

Instead, Art had a strong affection for San Francisco. He liked this city wholeheartedly, in all its existence. This city was first made by gold seekers, then it matured in the hands of the dock workers. He loved the shores, the ocean—everything.

Arthur Stevenson could not have imagined living in any place other than San Francisco. The city was sacred to him, although he never believed in any religious concept such as sacredness. But at that moment, the word for him was synonymous with good feelings. Now, in an extraordinary burst of endearment and the moment of an overwhelming sense of belonging, he felt he built this city himself, with his own bare hands. Art felt he constructed its infrastructure brick by brick. He belonged to this city, and this city was made for him. He thought, "This eruption and burst of energy are not normal; it is definitely related to the earlier event."

Art walked toward the bar. Halfway across the street, he noticed the bar's window was beaming out a reddish light. As he approached the bar, he looked inside through the window. Not much was visible inside but the redness. Going to bars was not Art's habit, but he felt a strong urge to go to this specific bar on that particular night. He closed his eyes. Again, he saw the stone gap and the horrifying red scenery. He opened his eyes, walked toward the door, and entered the bar.

He stepped inside. As soon as his eyes fell on the bartender, a young man, Art felt a strange sensation. Not knowing what it was, whatever it was, though he tried hard, Art could not take his eyes off of the young man. The bartender was busy serving two customers. No one else was there. He lost track of time. Suddenly, he felt calm again. His pulse slowed down. The excitement of moments ago had lessened.

He sat at the counter not too far from two other men. Art followed the movements of the bartender, whose attention was still on the other customers. He waited until the bartender was done chatting with the semi-drunk men. Noticing the newcomer's gaze, the bartender came toward Art and stared back at him. His hazel-green eyes, on the other side of the counter, sent a tremor through Art's body. The bartender said nothing. They both looked at each other for a moment in silence. The man brought up a large glass from under the counter and filled it with beer from the keg. Then he turned to the shelf full of various bottles of hard liquor. He picked a bottle of vodka and placed it next to the glass of beer. The bartender placed the shot glass next to the bottle and filled it with vodka. He pushed a glass of beer to Art and placed the shot glass next to it. Their eyes were fixed on each other; there was no need for words. It seemed as though they had already exchanged thousands of words through their eyes.

"How did you know what I wanted?" Art asked.

Without any word the man just shrugged his shoulders; there was expertise in his gesture.

Like the man's silent response, Art said: "Then pour it in."

The man nodded his consent, raised the shot glass full of vodka and poured it into the beer glass. When he pounded the empty shot on the table, Art held the man's hand with the shot together for a moment. He then released bartender's hand and said, "Thank you."

The bartender stared at Art's bright eyes and said, "It seems you have crossed the fire, passing through the blaze, instead of being in the freezing cold. Your hands are burning." Then he reached out to shake Art's hand and continued, "I am Michael."

"I'm Arthur. My friends call me Art."

Art realized his excitement was re-ignited. He had thought it was diminished when he stepped into the bar. He felt the new energy, a completely different force, replacing what he had experienced the previous hour. They were still holding hands. Art was surprised by his own courageous act. He was never this forward with anyone. The calming and cool stream, flowing from Michael's hands to Art's burning palm, had the effect of an ice block, cooling Art's inner heat. Art closed his eyes for a moment and saw the red-faced man behind the stone gap. He opened his eyes and saw Michael's face in his place.

Michael's face was different from the man's face in the meditation. He could not have guessed exactly how old Michael was. "He looks older than me," said Art to himself.

His dark skin, light brown curly hair, and dazzling eyes, which emitted a different color from every angle, revealed Michael's multi-racial background. Art had never seen such a gorgeous yet manly face anywhere before. Art was uncertain whether he was dreaming or awake; he was mesmerized by the incredible beauty in front of him. For a moment, Art thought that it was the meditation that caused him to be fascinated by Michael's attractiveness.

His eyes and his well-defined cheekbones indicated he must have some Asian blood in him too. Michael was a combination of African American, European, and Asian blood, a mix that created a masterpiece. The genes giving him dark skin made his face a velvet canvas on which his bright eyes and not-too-light-colored hair and the delicate face of the Far East evidenced the diversity in the creation of man. His perfect jaw line was in impeccable harmony with his muscular body.

Art exhaled deeply, a sigh of relief revealing the depth of his inner peace and elation. Michael, still staring at Art, let his hand remain in the hand of a stranger who sat in front of him. Michael's calm face did not show any doubt. He apparently also felt the exchange through their hands. Michael realized that this strange and invisible stream, whatever it was, gave him a strong sense of ecstasy, a powerful emotion that he had never experienced before.

# Chapter 4 – David

*San Francisco, Southern California*

Art always wondered about Essie, an unattached, single man, with typical Middle Eastern features like bushy barrows and heavy mustache, who occupied a little space next to David's office. Art never understood Essie's function in Tech2AI, or his title and specific responsibilities. Even from the beginning, Art could never comprehend the bond between David and Essie. They seemed a world apart. Essie was always searching on different websites, reading and writing materials, and no one in the office knew what they were about. Several times a day, David or Essie would go to each other's office to engage in endless conversations.

When Art started working at Tech2AI, once Essie came to his workstation and asked Art's teammate a simple technical question about encryption. After returning to his room, Art asked his teammate, with whom was working a joint project, "What project this dude is working on?"

Art's colleague replied, "I don't know exactly, I heard Essie and David are longtime friends. They used to work together and have been living in Southern California years ago. They say now their friendship is deeper than their work relationship. Essie looks like Saddam Hussein but younger and leaner. Once, before you come here to work, I remember David said that in the early 1990s, Essie migrated from Iran to the United States. They were in the same college and got to know each other through a fiery philosophical debate."

Surprised, Art said, "Who talks about philosophy these days, let alone have it as a pretext to start a friendship?

"I don't know. Who cares? I don't know Essie much, but I know David. He is an honest man," replied the teammate.

David knew Essie even before he dated and married Melody. Everyone thought that the three of them lived together in the same house. Melody would come to the office after she was finished with her work and they would leave the office together at night. Stories of the three of them living together and other rumors, depending on the person's wild imagination, were circling, though Art never liked to believe them and refused to accept them. Sometimes, Melody's extra attention to Essie pandered those rumors. Melody was a charming, happy woman who emanated her excessive inner energy by her natural, joyful movements and laughter. Melody's abundant attention on Essie made most male employees, particularly Sam, jealous. Art was a witness to Sam's envy, which took the form of his expressing dissatisfaction with Essie's uncertain position in the company. Sam could not hide his dislike, especially his facial expressions, when he heard Essie's occasional and unwarranted comments on various work-related issues.

Art had had no specific encounters with Essie before the meditation night. Melody's attention to her husband's best friend had never bothered Art, which was another reason why, like other men in the company, he did not have a judgmental view about Essie. For Art, Melody's cheerfulness, laughter, and high level of energy was a positive aspect that she would bring to the office's dull atmosphere and nothing else.

***

David and Essie's friendship had started years ago when both were college students in Orange County in Southern California. Young David had been fascinated by Eastern culture and philosophy. In his early 20s, David experienced his first trip outside the boundaries of his birthplace. He took a journey in search of meaning that was supposed to develop a concept more than a vacation or getaway. Over the years, Eastern awareness, stemming from the influx of spirituality's culture, wisdom, and yoga, had swept away the West. David, fascinated by Buddhism, traveled to India.

David had read exciting stories about young Americans, such as Ram Dos and others fond of spirituality, who felt the need to be in a place full of mysticism. India was a magical land that had attracted many enthusiasts. People from all over the world would travel to find mysteries of tranquility and peace. India, this great cradle of democracy—with its diversity of tribes, languages, and religions—had summoned David to its magic. The birthplace of Buddha and all those gurus who could emit spirituality from their eyes became irresistible for emotional and kindhearted David.

David finally decided to go to India, along with several other young friends, with the dream of finding people on the other side of the globe who could show him the way to the Garden of Eden. Alas, everything went wrong from the beginning. David was stricken with a severe case of food poisoning the very first day. It seems that this specific virus infiltrated his stomach lining so deeply that it was impossible to get rid of it easily. David vomited almost all of his being on that journey; everything but the virus came out. Local doctors did not seem to care much about his wretched state. David's condition did not raise a flag, as misery was a common reality, affecting all living souls equally.

He had already heard a lot about the poverty, the plight of overpopulation, yet wished to visit the country. David loved India. He had a contradictory feeling while lying in agonizing pain the whole week, out of his wits. On one hand, a journey that he had desired all his life was wasting away before his eyes. Wishing not to lose any more days, he wanted to stop time and get well, to continue his journey to find the ultimate state of happiness and tranquility. On the other hand, the hairy masters and gurus with their laughter and large stomachs, and their speech of peace, only made him more nauseous. Disgusted and whipped by the wrath of reality, he came back home.

Long after his return from that horrible journey, every word of ancient wisdom, Eastern culture, or yoga brought to David's mind only the memory of the disease, hungry children, well-fed gurus with chubby faces, and the trash on the street.

David knew that his view of India was severely altered, and maybe if he had not been poisoned, the bitter memory of that trip would have been a pleasant one. David still wished to visit the great Eastern country, but because his physical health could not be guaranteed, he avoided planning another journey.

David encountered his second experience in understanding Eastern philosophy. This time, he did not go anywhere—a part of that culture came to him. He met Essie in a philosophy class in college. Later, David told others that the universe had placed Essie in his path to reach the destination he had always wished and to make up for his failed trip to India.

In college, David came across Philosophy 101, which covered Western philosophy from Socrates to this day. In that class, David received more than what typically a student was given because of one particular classmate with a strange name. He remembered when the professor called that name for the first time, he looked back to see whom that name belong to.

At that time, it had been a few years since Essie had come to America as a refugee. Essie was a passionate young man full of emotion and clamor. In debates, he tirelessly argued his views to the opposition on various topics, regardless of the subject matter. At first, David's attention was drawn to Essie during a debate between the professor and young foreign student on Plato's ideas. David jumped right in. The professor tried to explain Plato's views on the weakness of democracy in administrating of the society in ancient Greece. Opposing Plato's ideas as an idealist, Essie emphasized democracy as the only possible way to guarantee justice and freedom for all in a society. The professor, who had found this a good opportunity to open up views of the great scholars of ancient Greek on philosophy and politics, intentionally was provoking Essie by pushing Plato's point of view. Essie, passionately, unaware of his raised voice, was throwing examples of dictatorships everywhere at the professor's face.

The professor seemed to be happy with the heat of ongoing arguments. He was usually dealing with boring classes with a bunch of sleepy students whose primary motivations were passing a few units to satisfy general education requirements. Essie was pouring icy cold water on snoozing students' faces. On several occasions, David jumped into the discussion, despite the fact that his knowledge on the subject was not as rich as Essie's. David challenged Essie based on his understandings of the history of philosophy that he had learned from the textbook.

"But people are not always right in choosing their rulers," said David.

"Democratic elections in a few countries may have resulted in disaster because of people's poor choices, but lack of democracy caused hundreds of countries to suffer under dictatorships," Essie responded, fluttering with a slightly formal accent.

David said, "But Nazism was a dictatorship that destroyed Europe for six years."

The professor used the opportunity from a moment of silence and spoke, "Each of you expressed only a part of the truth, but we're speaking about Plato's idea. We should remember that Plato and his teacher Socrates defended the rule of aristocracy at a time when democracy was the participation of the ignorant mass in government.

That kind of democracy brought the society to its demise, so much so that the people's court voted for the execution of Socrates to punish him for his views. Meanwhile, how Plato defined aristocrats was very different from our classification today. Plato believed that it is ridiculous if each citizen takes turns for a period of time to be placed in ruling positions of the government. Plato, like his teacher, believed it would be disastrous for a country the day that a merchant or businessman rules. The government affairs should be carried out by people who are specialized in the matter. Of course, democracy in ancient Greece was quite different from the form of many countries today."

After that class, Essie and David continued in a heated debate which took a few hours. Essie called in sick to work that day, and David canceled all his appointment. Their friendship started from that day on. They both were passionate about various ideas, especially in politics and philosophy. Later, when they knew each other's history more, their friendship reached a new level. However, the new bond between them did not stop their heated discussions. Sometimes, one would hurt the other by using harsh language to win over the debate, and neither seemed to be restrained in that way.

***

His friendship with Essie opened doors of a new world to David that originated from a rich culture with few-thousands-year-old history. This time, through Essie, David learned the rich Eastern culture and satisfied his inner need without having to go on a journey.

David's interests and dreams constantly tested his family's patience. The only child of an upper-middle-class family, David's future should have been nothing short of a decent and better-than-average life. However, David's mother had a different view, as she repeatedly reminded him, "You suffer from lack of self-confidence. You are worried and underestimate yourself among your friends. You are more than what you think you are. You're a handsome man, and every girl desires to be with you. You do not appreciate your value."

"What's a big deal if girls compete over a man? What's next then? First, they want to die for you, and then they want to kill you," David would reply jokingly.

"What next? What experiences do you have with normal pretty girls? I remember your disastrous marriage with that Hungarian girl. It seems you received what you asked. So in the future, wish for more because the same thing you said and I quote, 'What's next?' happened to you because of that Hungarian girl."

David's mother was somewhat correct. In elementary school and later in high school, David mostly befriended immigrant students from India, China, and Korea, or those whose parents were immigrants. Years later after high school, David had a short-term marriage with a girl from Hungary. His social behavior about dating and the circle of friends had left his mother astounded.

David was an only child. With no siblings and no playmates, he often played with his imaginary friends for hours. Sometime, he would request that his mother let him have a play date, but the mother was too busy attending her own social meetings. At that moment, David had no choice but to fill his time with his imagination.

After college, David's friendship with Essie and his brother, Amir, infuriated his mom more than his marriage to the Hungarian girl. "Who are these people that you are wasting your time with? Especially the one who looks like Saddam Hussein?"

His mother referred to Essie with his thick mustache hanging over his lips and his habit of swirling it with his thumb and index fingers, a habit that disgusted her even more. Because of the hostage taking of the U.S. embassy staff in Tehran that lasted for 444 days, David's mother had a grim view toward the Iranians. His mother would constantly remind David of American hostages who suffered because of his friend's countrymen.

After a quick divorce from Katrina, his Hungarian ex-wife, David doubted himself on every aspect of his life. His father had died recently. Everything Katrina was pretending to be collapsed after the wedding. The whole adventures with Katrina including dating, moving in, and marriage until divorce lasted no more than a year. Soon after they were married, David realized that they really had nothing in common. Several big and small defeats in both love and work worsened with the death of his father, and all that disrupted David's existential views and his beliefs.

The story of one afternoon that he spent in Mount Soledad was David's favorite. He was always telling his friends when he was asked about the real beginning of his spiritual life. It was one of those melancholy autumn days when a storm of colors is created from tree leaves on the ground. David had separated from Katrina several weeks before. The day before, he had been fired from his job that he had no interest in working at from the beginning. For a long time, he was looking for a proper excuse to convince himself to submit his resignation to his boss. He was hesitant and could not easily decide how to finish it. The idea of searching for a new job frightened him. He did not want to reach out to his mother for help. On the other hand, after Katrina, he had no motivation to keep that job anyway. He initially applied for the position as a technician upon Katrina's insistence for its steady paycheck.

The same day that David decided to step up and resign, his name was called through the loudspeaker in common area. David was not sure he heard it right. He realized from the foreman that he had to go to the human resources office. When David arrived there, he realized they had already decided to fire him. Later, every time he remembered that moment, he burst into laughter. But when David heard his dismissal, he was so upset he could not sleep that night. Although he was going to resign, he didn't like being fired. He always struggled with a fear of rejection and not being liked by others, and that day at work he had been rejected professionally. Maybe his mother was right. Perhaps that was the reason behind his desire to date and befriend only foreigners. At least, there was less chance of being rejected due to his look and light hair color.

The next day, David remained in bed late. He could not sleep all night, thinking about the rejection at work. He looked at the clock. It was twelve, and he was not even hungry. Suddenly, he felt that he was being suffocated. He lived in Orange County at the time. David jumped into his car and after a while found himself pushing on the gas pedal on southbound Interstate 5, driving without any destination. David had no idea where he was heading. He only knew he had to push on the gas and keep moving to avoid suffocation. David would cross the Mexican border, entering Tijuana, if it were necessary. He did not realize how he ended up on the road leading to La Jolla. Perhaps it was due to the traffic ahead that slowed him down to the point of stop-and-go. Again the same kind of suffocation that David felt in his apartment attacked him. Only speed was the relief. He saw cars driving on the right lane close to the shoulder. He turned his signal and situated his car in the moving lane toward La Jolla Village Drive. Lowering both front windows, he sped up for a while until the brake lights in front him warned of another upcoming traffic jam. He looked around. The thought of stumbling on a narrow road to La Jolla gave David the same nauseating feeling. He had driven on this route before. The green light to the left-only lane was the only path where he felt he could breathe. It led David to an open road that led him to Via Capri St. He found himself on an uphill, zigzag road leading to Mount Soledad. It was strange. He had driven all the way to be on this steep, narrow, snake-like road, heading up without a specific destination. Drowned in his thoughts, he felt he was ascending to the sky, being pushed by forces unknown to him.

David reached a crossroad at the highest point of Via Capri. He first examined the left. From a distance, a big cross glowed like a giant white monster. He turned left and parked his car in a designated parking area. He already had a better feeling. When he got out of the car, a cool breeze caressed his cheeks. He walked toward the gigantic white cross. The wind continued stronger, now touching and refreshing his face. It reminded him of his childhood, and how he loved the touch of the breeze on his face. He went ahead and reached the cross that was located in the center of a large platform in a small square. Some tourists were taking pictures of the big cross and themselves from different angles. There were captivating views from all around the square, overseeing the ocean and I-5. David spotted a bench and walked toward it while looking at the spectacular view of the ocean and land. He felt a pleasant sensation throughout his body. He sat down on the bench and looked at the ocean. A sign on his left was showing the height of over 800 feet from sea level. Low waves in a quiet ocean were like thin white threads growing close to the shore, then fading away. On the right, he looked down at the land and the narrow roads passing through houses. Cars, like small toys, were moving slowly on slim roads. The sunshine was using its last strength to press its warmth on David. The wind was gradually getting stronger. David closed his eyes and tried to meditate. Tourists around David were talking and screaming out of excitement, which he found somewhat disturbing. It was difficult for David to focus on meditation.

Just as he was meditating, a mystical feeling took over his entire existence. A wave of warmth swept through David's limbs from top to bottom. He felt that he was communicating with forces and phenomena around him. Perhaps he had contacted the same tourists' spirits who had disturbed him with their laughter and happy emotions a few moments ago. Whatever it was, a strange, pleasant, and different feeling was crawling into his mind and body. This was the second time that David experienced this kind of feeling. He had gone through the similar sensation in LAX for the first time a few years ago.

A couple of months after his father passed away, he took his mother to Los Angeles airport to visit her sister in New York. David's aunt had long married a Wall Street banker. After David's father died, his mother's loneliness had raised his aunt's concerns, and she insisted that she visit her in New York for a few weeks. The September 11th attack has not happened yet, and people could accompany passengers all the way to the front of the plane into the terminal. After his mother entered the jet bridge that connected the terminal to the plane, David sat on a chair for a few moments and closed his eyes. He was feeling sad inside, grieving his father's death and distressed for his mother who was now alone. Suddenly, David experienced the same feeling that he was now feeling on the top of Mount Soledad. He felt he was connected to all the people. It was as if an invisible string created a network, linking him to all beings in that place. It looked like he was them and all the people were him, connecting to one sole. A warm inner sensation had given him a weird, tranquil awareness. He opened his eyes and saw a young couple. The young blond bearded boy was caressing a cute young girl who was leaning on his shoulder and staring at David. The guy asked: "Dude, you seem too relaxed, what did you take?"

David just responded with a smile.

***

The airport experience had happened years ago, but it was carved into David's mind. After the death of his father, David, an advocate of scientific thoughts throughout his life, threw himself completely into the ocean of Buddhism and Eastern beliefs. Despite his willingness to connect with Eastern philosophy from his early 20s and the horrible experience in the journey to India, it was difficult for him now to understand those concepts. Essie's views also were totally different from what he was looking for in Buddhism.

He tried hard to graft what he believed in before onto what he was learning now. On this path, the more he forged ahead, the more futile the result was. How could he change his system of thought? Though he felt a higher power must be behind everything, it was not easy for him to change his thinking, which had been institutionalized within him for years.

David did not know what to expect from meditation. What should he see or experience? The more he searched in books, the more interpretation varieties he found. David expected a clear concept from the meditation, like what he had learned from Kant or Machiavelli, which were explicitly explained philosophy and politics. But instead, he was receiving complex statements, like bad translation texts, from Hegel's writings.

Finally, a simple meditation instruction helped him: "There is no definite explanation. Just close your eyes and try to think about nothing and focus on your breaths. This was the hardest and most important part. Ejecting unwanted thoughts is like a war that initially seemed to be impossible. But with recurrence and practice, one can prepare his mind and become ready to concentrate, only if he does not fall asleep." More practice helped David achieve relaxation through meditation. That simple guidance helped him more than searching through pages of books.

Sitting on the bench at that moment in Mount Soledad, David felt the same sense of tranquility as at the airport. Still on the bench, he was flying over the water on top of the ocean. The breeze was still caressing his face. He opened his eyes and saw two seagulls with their wings wide open against the wind, suspended in the air a few yards to his left. Seagulls were able to remain in the air with a small twist to the left or right without bringing the wings together. At first, David thought he was really flying, but looking at the sun brought him back to reality. The lower part of sun's circle stuck to the end of the ocean on the horizon. Two Asian tourists ran to where David was sitting, pointing their camera to the sun with long-focus lenses. Serenity was more than just a pleasant feeling for David; it was a real quality that was sitting inside and occupying his entirety. A need resurrected within David and provoked a strong desire for a mate, a person who could love him unconditionally and in return receive his unlimited love. When he saw the tourists who were standing on his right, staring at him, David realized that he had made his request out loud.

# Chapter 5 – Simone

*San Francisco*

Melody's office was located on the eighth floor of a stylish building on Mission Street, which she had always said was the right place for work. Her office had three fairly elegant rooms: a conference room, a lounge area, and a small kitchen where a refrigerator, microwave, and a small oven were provided for future employees. The reception area in front of the entrance and Melody's office were the only areas that were furnished and decorated. The whole office took almost half of the floor.

She found the office after a lot of searching and visiting places with real estate agents—almost a month. Melody had been working toward this point for ten months, from launching the startup to moving into this building. This was the first time in her life that she was highly satisfied with the success of her own work. Beside Melody, the founder and CEO, only one more person was working for Roma Skincare Products.

Simone, a young girl whom Melody hired only one week before, quickly became familiar with innovative Roma Skincare Products. In a very short time, she launched two promotional campaigns on Twitter and Facebook. Melody was pleased to see that Simone was trying her best to handle the company's various affairs. She was satisfied with her choice of hiring.

Melody was busy interviewing several applicants since moving into this building. For the most recent interviews, Melody allowed Simone to have a seat during the sessions and used her input to evaluate candidates. Simone's contribution during the interviews raised Melody's level of respect for her abilities, although no definite decision was taken as the result of those meetings.

Tech2AI, owned by David and Melody, was the largest shareholder of Roma Skincare. Melody had some of her friends aboard with less than ten percent of company's stakes. David was opposed to renting a place of this size for a newly established company. He had suggested that she use a couple of rooms in Tech2AI in the beginning, then expand the office as the business grew. Melody, however, preferred to start her business in a distinct and stylish place. She fatefully believed in recognition of her products in the market and swift growth of her company. For several years, she had been working on a facial mask and skin rejuvenating creams.

Melody refused to respond to Simone's numerous questions about the ingredient of the facial mask and other company's skin products. It wasn't just about keeping her property a secret; she felt emotionally attached to her products. Those products were too personal to allow her to share their details with someone whom she did not know well yet. The idea of the startup came to Melody's mind when Essie told her an observation from Iran.

***

Two years ago on an August morning, David, who had spent all night preparing for project presentations had left home in a rush, without taking his laptop. David asked Essie to stop at their home and bring his laptop before coming to the office. When Essie rang the bell,

Melody opened the door wearing a blue mask. Essie was shocked for a moment. But he gathered quickly that the person in front of him was in fact, Melody. Melody laughed at Essie's bewildered face and invited him to come in.

"What happened? Did I look so much different with this mask that you didn't recognize me?" Melody said while moving inside ahead of Essie.

"For a moment, I thought that a strange man is in your house," Essie emphasized on the word man to annoy Melody.

As Essie was looking around, he watched Melody walking toward the bedroom and said, "You changed the decoration here again. Every time I come here, something is changed. Where are you going? I came to get the great master's laptop."

"It's in the bedroom. He was working late for his presentation. I'll bring it right now; pour yourself a cup of coffee."

Waiting for Melody to come back, Essie went to the window and looked at the backyard. He stared at the roses and geranium flowers planted around the courtyard. A gentle breeze was shaking branches and flowers. A joyous feeling came over Essie as he viewed the backyard garden. He always praised Melody for her artistic talent, especially in design and indoor decorations. Melody had won Essie's admiration for her taste in almost everything. She used special mist tubes that she had bought from Home Depot and installed them herself to maintain a high level of moisture, leading to the heavenly garden in the backyard.

Essie looked back baffled. He had lost track of time. When Essie noticed Melody's presence, holding the laptop in her hand, he realized that he had not been there mentally for some time. He tried to remember his thoughts, but Melody's voice, asking something, was preventing him from focusing. The smile faded away on Melody's lips when her wobbly voice could not bring any reaction to Essie's motionless face. He was looking at Melody silently. She did not have a mask on anymore. Apparently, while he had been away mentally, she had been able to dress, make her hair, and put on some make-up. Essie tried again to see how long he was standing in front of the window. He looked at his phone, but it was no use as he did not remember checking the time before.

Recently, he had been losing track of time, without knowing what his last thought was. He also would wake up in the middle of the night without knowing where and who he was and what he was doing there. In that condition, he would feel an invisible, unknown hand had shaken his shoulder. Only passing time could bring him back from the void. Recently Essie had been experiencing this condition during the daytime too. His doctor believed he was likely suffering from psychological damage caused by tortures he had endured in prison and hardships that had taken place earlier in his life.

When Essie returned to the present from depths of his void, he smiled back and said, "You're not blue anymore."

"It's a while. Where have you been? I was calling you but looked like you weren't here and could not hear," said Melody with a concerned look.

To change the subject, Essie said, "What does this blue mask do for your face anyway?"

"It keeps the skin fresh yet tightens the face's muscles; it is basically an anti-aging mask," replied Melody.

After seeing Melody's smile that he believed to be a permanent part of her face's feature, joyful Essie told her about a kind of mud and soil with holistic and therapeutic properties that he knew in Iran.

"There is a kind of mud that is used by women in Iran traditionally, and I think that it does more than the blue mask. It is colorless, or better to say it has the color of the dirt, but it is all natural and has no harmful chemicals in it."

Then, Essie typed some words in Farsi on his phone's Google search box to show the product's name to her. Melody was craning her neck to see what he had found. "I will text this website's address to you. Go ahead and search more about it," said Essie.

Thinking about creating a unique product brought a smile on Melody's face. She asked, "What else? Do you know more traditional substances in this line? How about hair growth, your hair looks so healthy, what do you use?"

"You won't believe it," he said immediately. "My hair began to fall out a few years ago. The first thing that I did was to stop using shampoo."

"What do you mean, how do you wash your hair then?" Melody wondered.

"I don't know if you know henna? It's a powder that when it's mixed with water, it turns to a paste form—well, almost paste. It has many benefits and is used mostly in India, Iran, and the Arab countries. I use it just like shampoo. As you see, it fortifies my hair and keeps it black."

Melody's eyes sparkled, and the excitement appeared on her face. After a pause, she said, "I always thought that you color your hair. As for hair growth, do you know how much money is in this line of business?"

Later Melody came up with her own mask product based on that mud. She found out that the similar substance can be found in a hot spring in Reno, Nevada. By mixing that mud with a few other herbal substances, Melody created her own formula for skin care, a product that Melody felt she always owed to Essie.

In the case of henna, it did not go the way Melody had thought. There were many obstacles to transforming henna into a product that could replace commercial shampoos on the market. However, she was still developing a shampoo based on henna that could be used on a daily basis.

***

To Melody, her relationship with Essie was the most valuable of all of her friends and family members. Melody's product was so special and emotional, she could not share it with Simone, as she was an employee whose acquaintance did not exceed more than a few weeks.

# Chapter 6 – Timothy

*San Francisco – "Get Cool" Bar*

"**A**pparently, today is busier than usual. What's up?" The young man in front of the counter asked Michael, who was serving customers.

Michael brought up the two full glasses of beer from under the keg and placed it on the counter in front of the two customers. Then, he turned back to Timothy and asked "Tim, didn't you go to work today? Usually, you're not showing up this early."

Michael's help, Suzan, a middle-aged woman with short red hair, was busy tending customers as well, spinning around, taking orders, and serving patrons. They would help each other if one of them was overwhelmed. Right above the liquor racks on the corner of the ceiling, two 70-inch luminous LED flat-screen TV were showing two different networks' programs. One of the televisions was showing president Trump's inauguration replay in the presence of several pundits on CNN. Political experts were examining the new president's speech, which he had delivered a few hours earlier that day. The other TV was broadcasting a live basketball game between the Golden State Warriors and the Houston Rockets. Tim's favorite team, the Warriors, was winning. Tim's eyes were slipping between both TV screens, dividing his attention between the exciting basketball game and the captions of Trump's fiery speech, threatening the world, emphasizing on his America-first slogan.

Tim, whose eyes just followed a three-pointer by the Warriors' guard, replied, "No, I was working today, but I went out early to complete a special report. I'm working on a report that requires interviewing executives of some tech companies. It's not an easy task to schedule appointments with these people."

Michael did not respond. Tim pulled his phone out of his pocket and looked at it. A buzz had alerted him about a new text.

After a brief pause, Tim continued, "Michael, can I talk to your friend directly? My article that was published yesterday made an excellent impression on many readers. People keep leaving comments, some cursing, but mostly they are positive and applauding comments."

Michael, curious and suspicious of Tim's question, did not hear the customer sitting next to Tim ordering Scotch. He directly stared at Tim's face and asked, "What friend? What are you talking about?"

Tim turned his eyes from the TV that was showing the game to Michael and answered, "It was very interesting, about your friend's vision of Sodom. I did not name anyone; I just wrote the story."

Michael frowned; the depth of lines on his forehead became deeper and entangled while he threw a dirty look at Tim. Tim was familiar with this mood and look. As Michael's face became more flushed with anger, his whole body informed Tim that a storm was imminent. Michael could not control his anger. With an irate voice he asked, "How did you allow yourself to do this? The story I told you about ... our conversation was just a friendly chat."

Michael returned to the customer who had requested his Scotch many times already and said, "I'm sorry, right away." Then, he asked Suzan to take the customer's order.

Michael's phone vibrated in his pocket. He pulled it out and pushed on his ear. It was Art. From what Tim could see, it was apparent that the bartender was on the verge of an eruption. Michael just listened; after the conversation ended, he placed the phone back in his pocket. Tim remained silent. It did not take too long for Michael to burst in rage, taking Tim's collar by two hands and pulling him in front his face. Tim's beer glass fell on the ground and broke loudly. Everyone was startled. Michael blushed as if all the blood in his body had rushed to his face at once. Michael still had Tim's collar in his strong hands, and their faces were inches away from each other. "You are a deceitful man. You said you didn't name anyone, but Tech2AI's name was mentioned in your article. Why did you use the name? That was why I left you. You could never stop lying, and I could never get used to your lies."

Suzan noticed the intensity in the air, hastily placed the Scotch in front of the customer sitting next to Tim, then she held Michael's hand said, "Michael, Michael, calm down, calm down."

Suzan's voice and the customers' frighten faces, looking at him with concern, brought Michael back to his senses. Tim used the opportunity to pull himself back from Michael's grip. Now angry with an equally flushed face, Tim stared at Michael's eyes and with a deep, broken voice replied, "I said, I did not name anyone, I didn't say whether I mentioned naming any place or not. Maybe I was wrong to name anything at all, I'm sorry. But you have to know that I never lied to you when we were together. This was your excuse to leave me."

Michael, who seemed a bit calmer, turned his back on Tim, and said, "I don't want to see you again."

Tim grabbed his briefcase and moved toward the exit door as the rest of the customers in the bar watched. He pushed the door open and walked out.

***

Tim had never gotten over his separation with Michael. He was in love with Michael with all his being. In the past six months, Tim had tried to fill the void inside him with others, but Michael's image and thoughts of Michael never left him alone. Everywhere he went, he would see Michael, walking with him in the park, watching TV while holding hands, lying on the couch together. Tim even started a serious relationship after breaking up with Michael, but every time, it was Michael that he would see on the bed, hugging and kissing him. Even the next morning, in his imagination, it was Michael whom he had the breakfast with.

Michael was more of a listener than a talker. According to their friends, they were opposites in how they engaged in conversations. Michael was a man who needed to be squeezed to spit out a word. On the contrary, Tim was nothing but mouth. He enjoyed talking forever. On every subject, he had an opinion. For Tim, expressing his view on a subject of his interest was as if he was making love with words. Even writing did not diminish his insatiable craving for talking.

Tim had started his career by writing in a blog, and he now had a column in the prestigious *Bay Area Chronicle* newspaper. He was recognized for his articles addressing social issues. Michael believed that if Tim wrote more and talked less, it would have had benefited his audience twofold: First, it would put Tim in a higher position as a writer, and second, it would give his audience the option to hear his opinions.

Tim was active in the gay community. He barely missed a meeting, session, or party. Sometimes, he would go from one party or gathering to another, whether he was invited or not. He tried to be present with Michael everywhere. But Michael's desire was not the same. Tim considered his life complete at the age of 27. With a flourishing career and the peace of mind to have Michael on his side, all aspects of his life seemed to be moving in the right direction.

Timothy H. Henry, the son of a prominent lawyer in Northern California who owed his national reputation to the controversial Pooch Lister trial, saw life as a paved road, on which his splendid chariot was galloping. Because of his family background, he was ahead of many friends and classmates throughout his school years. His father, Stewart Henry, had provided the best educational opportunity for his only child.

Publishing the first-hand information of his father's client's controversial trial helped Tim run one of the most viewed blogs. It also boosted him to a position as a high-profile journalist, which brought him thousands of followers on Twitter. Unlike his critics and rivals, Tim's boss at the *Bay Area Chronicle* believed Tim's success was the result of fluent writing on interesting subjects, rather than his father's contributions. Michael also believed in Tim's superb writing style.

Their breakup, as Tim claimed, did not happen overnight. Michael had felt emotionally neglected by Tim for a long time. While this was bothering him, Tim was failing to address it, trying to sweep the problem under the rug. Michael, bashful and a little timid, was a very self-conscious man who did not like to interact with people in a social setting, a fact Tim never much cared to understand.

They knew each other from high school. Then, years ago, their paths crossed again in a gay bar. Michael immediately recognized Tim. Tim's memory of Michael was hazy. However, Tim remembered the skinny boy who was not hanging out with anybody in high school. Tim would never have guessed that Michael was gay too.

That day, Michael was in the bar on the insistence of one of his friends. When he bumped into Tim, he immediately recognized the loud, talkative boy in high school. It took a while for Tim to recognize Michael. Tim's attention was mostly drawn to this young, handsome, masculine body standing in front of him. Michael was talking, but Tim did not hear a word; he was fascinated by Michael's charm. The bar's dim light was also a culprit, delaying Tim's reaction to Michael's approach. In awe of so much beauty in front of him, Tim stared at Michael for a little longer. He knew he had seen that face before, but he still could not place it. Even after remembering Michael Joyce, his former classmate, Tim still did not want to say anything and kept his gaze on this young, vibrant body, sizing him up and down.

"Wow, how could you be the same Michael from high school?" Tim said, then hurriedly shook Michael's hand. Embarrassed by his own abrupt comment, Tim added, "Dude, sorry I'm checking you out like this. But I can't believe that this body belongs to the same tiny Michael who was getting out of everyone's way, not getting any attention."

"After graduating from high school, I started working out," Michael said, as Tim continued squeezing and holding onto Michael's hand.

That visit led to the beginning of their relationship. Sooner than Michael expected, Tim asked his new date to move in with him. Michael was not ready to move in with him just yet. Tim did not ask again for several months, but eventually, he insisted again. Michael accepted, and they moved in together, renting a new apartment.

"Do I really love him?" This was a question that Michael had repeatedly asked himself. The answer was bothering him, because Michael knew he was not committing wholeheartedly. "Yes" was the answer to his own question every single time, over and over. Indeed, Michael believed that he loved Tim. But he knew love would not come from conviction, and that would annoy him.

"Why shouldn't I love him?" Michael engaged in a self-debate, using reasoning to respond to himself, comparing pros and cons. Michael could not vividly see the qualities for which he should have loved Tim. Undoubtedly, he admired Tim's diligence, creativity, and excellent writing skills, but were these features really enough to love someone? Then he would casually convince himself, "Why not?" And again he would fall into an endless loop of debating himself.

In his subconscious, the more Michael tried to convince himself that he loved Tim, the more he found himself doing the opposite. Michael knew Tim's character had a big flaw and that raised alarms.

"Am I attracted to him because of his family connections and social status? Maybe I am." Over the course of four years, Michael constantly denied that he was interested in Tim's family's social status. He had repeatedly fought against his paradox, and he emerged worn out every time. One day, in a heated battle of self-discovery, Michael finally submitted and declared, "No, it cannot go on like this. I'm not like this; at least I know myself."

It was months after the separation that Michael eventually realized his reason for putting an end to his relationship with Tim. Michael had begun to list the factors that could not be the cause: "Definitely, it's not his talkative and excessive manner. It's not Tim's extreme sociability."

No, undoubtedly these were not the reasons for ending their four year relationship. Tim's extroverted qualities could be a small problem or even a positive factor in any relationship between two people. Not that Michael personally liked those qualities, but now it became clear to him that those could not have been the real cause of the breakup. One day, it became clear to Michael that he could never explain to Tim:

*When, after a few years, you cannot basically convince yourself decisively that you love your partner, either, there is no love at all, or that is not perfect love. If you cannot count reasons for your love, at least to yourself, and honesty is part of your character, benefits of high living standard and the high social status that comes out of this relationship become psychological stress that blurs everyday life. Of course, you need not a reason or logic to evaluate love.*

Michael's new finding was like a light in a dark room. Before that, he was struggling to make sense of his feelings to himself, let alone explain them to Tim. "Yes, that's it," Michael repeatedly was reminding himself. Michael's decision was a shock to Tim who never found the reasoning convincing.

Michael felt guilty because he could never clarify his findings to his former partner. Because of his guilt, Michael allowed Tim to visit him in the bar occasionally. Now, for the first time, Michael sensed that

Tim took advantage of his amiability, abusing his trust. Michael decided to end the connection with Tim, once and for all.

"I do not want to see you again." Michael finally said it.

When Tim stormed out of the bar, the harsh cold wind slapped his face vigorously. His heart was cooling down with every step forward—his mind too. In the past six months, Tim had always been looking for an answer to explain this unexpected separation. He was torn apart; he had no idea why Michael left him. Now, his unease and broken heart became instantly calm and cool, like the impact of the cold wind kissing his hot face. With his article, he indirectly introduced Michael's new love as a superstitious person, though without naming his name. Tim never had any intention of taking vengeance, but now that the last tie between him and Michael was severed, he did not regret publishing his piece at all.

# Chapter 7 – Sodom

*Sodom Territory – Palace of King Bera*

Art found himself in the same underground, looking through the stone slot–type window, observing everything that was going on outside. He did not expect to be at the same place in his second meditation session. Art thought about his first time: witnessing those scary scenes had shaken him. He was eager to find out what awaited him the second time. He had started the meditation in his boss's office with only David present; David apparently was more interested than others in their group in knowing the result. This time Art reached the state of his total relaxation much faster.

The relaxation that came over him as the result of earlier meditation was replaced with deep anxiety from remembering his first experience. From the same opening, he looked carefully out, expecting to face horror, fires, children, and women running out of fear, and men perishing in the city square. But to his astonishment, there was no sign of fire, shouting, or moaning. Instead, he saw a beautiful, lovely, sunny day. People of the city were busy on the street, walking with their children, who were playing joyfully. In the distance, life on the plain and the hill was streaming to its fullest, and the sunshine was stamping its mark of happiness everywhere.

Art thought about exploring the location where he was standing. He took his eyes from the stone gap and looked around. He squinted and then rubbed his eyes. The place looked like a long chamber or basement underground, and a cool breeze was blowing from behind. Apparently, the small stone gap allowed the flow of cool air, connecting inside to outside. On the walls of the long zig-zag corridor whose end Art was not able to see, torches were mounted at different locations. Art moved toward the end of the corridor. His earlier fear dissipated by seeing a normal, sunny day, and now his mood was transformed into excitement to explore the area. He slowly moved toward the end of the basement, which veered to the left.

Inaudible voices were coming from afar. He paused a little, then walked ahead slowly. He passed by a torch and stared at it for a few seconds. The fire was real. He felt the heat on his face. He crossed the torch, and when he reached the end of the corridor, he stood for few seconds. Art cautiously stretched his neck forward and turned his head to the right, and quickly to the left. On his left, there was another corridor with torches on the upper parts of the wall. He entered into the new pathway, and now he could hear the noise louder than a few minutes ago. The voices were still unclear; they sounded like mumbling or people talking simultaneously. He stepped forward gently so that the echoes of his footsteps did not inform his presence. Those mumbling voices were getting louder every moment.

When he reached the end of the new hallway, he could clearly picture a large enclosure on his right where a number of people were chatting. He peeped through a hole in the wall prudently. It took a few moments for his brain to process the scene behind the wall.

Art's jaw dropped, and his brows were raised in astonishment. He was surprised to see men in a kind of a Turkish bath setting or sauna type of environment. Under the gentle lights of a few torches, in every corner of the sauna, naked men were kissing, making love freely. By no means Art was able to comprehend the time and place of these scenes. He thought, "Am I dreaming?"

Watching these scenes aroused Art. As the laughter of a couple came from another point, his eyes slipped from one corner to another, then around the room.

Art heard a sound from behind. He looked back. It sounded clearly like a conversation between two men that were coming toward him from the very pathway he had taken to arrive where he was. He saw two silhouettes coming in his direction. Art checked his surrounding quickly. There was no place to hide. "Should I be afraid? Do I have to step in and go inside?" Questions flashed through his head.

Two shirtless men, holding hands, were approaching from behind. Having dressed where he was standing, Art could not have been normal among them. He looked at himself to check his own outfit, but Art could not recognize his own body. Being two feet from the light of the torch, he should've been able to see his hands and feet, but he could not. The two men were about 10 feet from where he stood. Now, Art felt his heart in his mouth. Sweat ran on his forehead and behind his neck. The two men advanced closer to him. Art tried to squat on the darkest spot between the two torches, hoping he wouldn't be noticed by the two men. They were one step away.

Art, who had lowered his head, realized that they were standing right above him. He raised his head. One of the men was staring at him. Art knew his eyes and face. It was the one whom Art had seen through the stone gap in the fiery mayhem the first time he visited this place. The man's right hand was wrapped in a piece of cloth. Apparently, Art was invisible to the second man, as he had been surprised that the first man stopped so suddenly to stare at the ground. The second man did not know what the first man was looking at.

# Chapter 8 – Peter Jr.

*Georgia, Atlanta – His Excellency's office*

His Excellency, sitting at his desk in the office on the third floor of his house, was deep in his thoughts. He was looking down at the fingertips of his two hands which were touching each other. On the other side of the desk, Peter Jr. pulled out a newspaper from his briefcase, handed it over to his Excellency, and said, "The New York Times has published a detailed report on Church Militant, stating that they have rapidly increased their number of members and amount of donations during the recent presidential elections. This specific Catholic church in Michigan strongly supported Trump."

His Excellency stretched out his right arm, took the paper from Peter Jr., and leaned back in his comfortable leather chair. He slowly took his glasses out of his breast pocket, placed them on the bridge of his nose, and began to read the article. For a few moments, the office was immersed in silence. Peter Jr. gazed up at John Wesley's picture on the wall right above His Excellency's head.

Peter Jr. quickly lowered his eyes when His Excellency tossed the newspaper on the desk and began to talk. "The Militant Church is a joke. Its position is certainly not the Catholic Church's view. Their leaders in Michigan have made a lot of noise to promote their church. Many people are responding to this hustle and bustle nonsense. Don't take them seriously. Public arguments between the Pope and Trump shows the opposite of this so-called American Catholic Church positions. The Pope clearly stated that Trump is not a Christian."

"What do you think of the situation, in general?" asked Peter Jr. nodding in agreement. He added, "Groups like the American Family Council and Family Research Association have also gained in popularity. In general, right-wing groups are growing across the country. What's our overall stand?"

During Peter Jr.'s comments, His Excellency stayed silent, looking back down at his moving fingers again, indicating that he was drowning in his thoughts. Then, His Excellency replied with a sneer, "The last two groups you named are connected to us directly. The problem of alt-right, as liberals call it, it's another matter, and all of this has nothing to do with the article you showed me. Why are you mixing them up?"

Then, His Excellency turned his head and stared out of the window. After a while, he just said, "Trump," and went mute again.

Peter Jr. did not understand whether His Excellency had a question or was going to make a statement or maybe more would follow. Hesitant to say anything, Peter Jr. decided to remain quiet. John Wesley the Third was still staring at the horizon through his office window. His Excellency, the head of bishops at the Baptodist Church, doubted he would continue to speak. He did not know if Peter Jr. would understand everything he intended to say. Furthermore, he was not sure if that would be fundamentally right, to explain his analysis clearly to his subordinate. Peter Jr. was an intelligent, honest man. His Excellency had trusted him, but the complex issues in the past year seemed so intricate that His Excellency doubted Peter Jr.'s ability to grasp the whole picture, let alone follow what he was about to say.

To His Excellency, Peter Jr. was a coordinator, adviser, personal assistant, butler, and secretary combined. John Wesley the Third met Peter Jr., a pastor in Jacksonville, during a church business trip. Peter Jr. had been introduced to his future boss by one of the city's well-known politicians twenty years ago. Ever since that day, Peter Jr. tried very hard to stay in close contact with His Excellency. Finally, he moved to Georgia upon the head of bishop's suggestion.

Peter Jr. had been involved directly with the Church and Technology Project two years after its launch by His Excellency in 1995. Peter Jr.'s proactive attitude in discussions and his performance in carrying out the project's initiatives lifted him to the position of His Excellency's right hand.

***

The Church and Technology Project was a comprehensive conservative Baptodist Church program in which the church prepared itself to face the overwhelming advancement of Silicon Valley. Through this project, the church first recruited the talented young and faithful members who had entered the new computer world in the mid-1990s. Then, various well-resourced Evangelical churches paid all these members' tuition and fees at the best tech universities in the country. Since then, the Church and Technology Project had sent hundreds of these young graduates to the largest tech companies in Northern California to work as hidden members of the Conservative Evangelical Baptodist Church. Years earlier, His Excellency, despite being still young, had successfully united two of the most popular conservative churches, Baptist and Methodist, together. His full-hearted and brilliant efforts had spawned the creation of great Church of Baptodist.

The Baptodist Church could not afford to stay in the dark on what was being declared one of the most important inventions since the Industrial Revolution. And Silicon Valley was the epicenter of the new era: the internet age. The media were full of news about various amazing projects that were being led by tech companies. Working directly under His Excellency's supervision, Peter Jr. became one of the main organizers and coordinating agents of the church in Silicon Valley. In addition to addressing numerous issues, he was in charge of new recruits, relocating them, and later receiving and analyzing countless reports from them. He also had to keep the faith and spiritual values of these tech geniuses at the highest possible and practical level.

In 2014, Peter Jr. wrote the renowned doctrine of His Excellency, based on the conclusion of agents' reports from the tech world. The doctrine, which had been written under His Excellency's direct guidance, engendered a huge clamor among Conservative evangelical circles around the nation: "Artificial intelligence in Silicon Valley, the highest and most ruthless attack on Christianity and the church since the crucifixion of Jesus Christ."

His Excellency presented his doctrine during a speech in 2015 to summoned leaders of different branches among conservative churches. He introduced artificial intelligence as the most dangerous attack on human creation by God in general and Christianity in particular. He called for raising church leaders' awareness and designating a special budget for this issue. In this lecture, His Excellency had described the orientation of tech companies toward artificial intelligence as not an accidental process that was simply the result of knowledge and research. He believed artificial intelligence projects were instead organized, purposeful, and fully informed, and were targeting the heart of religious beliefs in the twenty-first century.

In His Excellency's view, numerous AI projects had begun many years ago to develop and create ultimate thinking machines parallel to human beings; they are not only about making computer programs easier to function.

In the same speech, His Excellency reminded the church leaders about the perfect harmony between the tech world and homosexuals in the attack on family values, as well as a political and civil system that has been established for many years in this country. He warned against the conquest of the latest social and judicial barricades, namely, the legalization of same-sex marriage in the Supreme Court. To His

Excellency, the progression of artificial intelligence would be the last nail in the coffin of the church, which will guarantee the destruction of religion and Christianity in society.

His Excellency, in his famous thesis, did not intend to frighten believers by showing many aspects of these terrible facts. In addition, to the shaking hearts of the conservative church leaders, he presented the solution to the grave and real threat posed by the union of tech and sinners. His Excellency pointed out many strengths of the church such as the wealth, resources, and power of belief that in his view was connected to the divine source. He called upon the church authority to act now: "If we do not move and act today, it will be too late tomorrow."

The head of conservative bishops at the Baptodist Church outlined his plan: "In the first place, all agents based in Silicon Valley companies will be transferred to companies that are specifically working on artificial intelligence projects. Secondly, the church should raise the discussion of the threat and dangers of creating AI and the fact that it might eliminate the human race by defeating human intelligence. We must plant and fertilize these types of discussions within the tech world as much as possible."

His Excellency knew through reports and news that such debates had already begun among the heads of tech companies. "One of the ways of managing this chaos is to persuade and encourage the views of those company owners and presidents who expressed doubts about the unleashed development of artificial intelligence. Then, their views need to be spread among the public view."

His Excellency said, "Choosing and investing in the best presidential candidate in the 2016 election is one of the most important challenges of church intervention in politics. If properly executed, it can compensate not only for our recent failures but also will bring new victories for followers of Jesus Christ."

In that speech, he did not mention the details of church involvement in the upcoming elections, but His Excellency undoubtedly cheered an active and effective intervention in the selection of the right candidates that could compensate for the country's lost faith which had plunged into the abyss of Satan during the past eight years.

That doctrine and that speech laid out the foundation and direction of the conservative church activities for the challenging years to come. In addition to eyeing current events in San Francisco through Peter Jr.'s reports, in the past two years, His Excellency personally focused his work on political events across the country: ascending Trump, Congress, and ultra-right movements.

The nation's political situation and putting Trump in the White House were issues that the His Excellency had doubt Peter Jr. could comprehend completely. His Excellency sometimes believed that the development of events and Trump's decisions created such crises that analyzing them correctly and making the right decisions would be difficult even for himself and the church leaders.

John Wesley the Third, therefore, hesitated to answer Peter Jr.'s question, "What do you think about the situation, in general?" He could not just tell Peter Jr. that "you better be in charge of your tasks and do not ask anything about the strategic analysis and decision."

How much could he inform Peter Jr. on the agenda? He wondered, "Does my subordinate have the capacity to digest the decisions and actions that the church has been involved in at the highest level of political affairs?"

After a long pause, staring at Peter Jr., His Excellency said, "Our support for Trump is different from that of others. Trump knows well that without our full support, the presidency would have been a dream for him, as it was the same for George W. in 2000. Do not make a mistake; Trump is different from George W., a lot different. The era and time are very different from the past. Today's situation is very dynamic. When Donald accepted our pre-condition of choosing Mike Pence as his vice president, he secured our total support. We found the best ticket to be present in the White House. We have also come to the conclusion that the conservative Church of Evangelicals had never, in recent history, gathered this much political and religious power in one place: the White House."

# Chapter 9 – Smith

*San Francisco*

Melody was at her desk in her office, interviewing an applicant who was nervously waiting for the first question. Melody was scrolling pages of the applicant's resume up and down on her computer screen. She was not sure what to ask. Melody knew general interviewing methods and some questions to ask. A few hours earlier, she had searched for typical questions to be asked in a job interview, but they all seemed very cliché to her.

She also believed and told David, "All interviews are almost useless unless the employer gets a chance to examine the actual knowledge and ability of the applicant in practice. Otherwise, it's just about feeling and how much the interviewer cares about the interviewee's manner and look. An interview set is a stage of sales. The interviewee, the seller, comes in with a resume as a sticker, describing its commodity to the interviewer who is the buyer, and then the bargain begins. The interviewer's job is to find out to what extent the label is an accurate representation of the applicant's product, which is almost impossible. Yes, education is essential, but indirectly. I've read somewhere that nearly all formal education which teaches theories to students do not correspond to what actually works in a job. Other than education, the rest of the label stickers are series of exaggerated, unverifiable claims by applicants."

"Why did you quit your last job?" asked Melody.

The applicant was a round-faced girl with a gentle makeup. She had a coat and a skirt on and became a little more tense when Melody asked about her previous job.

She answered, "I did not like the work environment there. Everyone was aggressive, and there was a lot of pressures, not that I'm complaining about the workload, but the competition was getting to the point of an unhealthy..."

Melody interrupted her and said, "Well, one must be resilient to any environment..."

Melody ended her sentence unfinished. It seemed the type of advice one gives to her little sister. The founder of new skin care company hated the process, but there was no choice; she needed to finish the interview. "Is this girl honest in her answer?" Melody asked herself, "If she is honest in her statement, why am I giving her advice? If not, why is she using a lie against herself? She could only think of one possibility as her motive, to convince me that she is an honest and truthful person."

Melody did not like the complexity of human beings. "Why shouldn't humans ..." she became aware that apparently she's been interviewing herself.

The phone rang. When Melody pressed the button on the phone set on her desk, Simone said from the reception desk, "Your husband is here."

Melody responded, "Tell him to wait for a little, I'll be done shortly."

"So far, I've just asked one question from this girl," Melody said to herself.

David and Essie were sitting outside in the waiting room, right across from Simone. Simone was behind the reception desk and was checking out David and Essie stealthily. David was busy with his phone, tapping on its screen and pausing to read texts. Essie was holding a magazine and was busy reading while toying with his thick, full mustache. Once in a while, Essie would take a glance at Simone secretly, then go back to being lost on the magazine pages.

A buzz was heard from David's phone. After a couple of seconds, he poked Essie's arm with his right elbow and showed him his phone screen. Essie was checking out Simone at the moment but quickly looked at David's phone and read the text. On the screen that his friend held for him angled for a better view, Essie read, "They broke into my apartment. They came in and trashed everything."

Essie sent a question to David just by gazing at him along with raised eyebrows. David could decipher his old friend's look: he was asking whose text was.

David, who apparently did not want to mention Art's name loudly in the presence of Simone, pointed to the sender's name. Squinting, Essie looked at the screen again and then into David's eyes. David stood up and said, "I'll go visit him. Tell Melody I had to go. I'll meet you guys at the office," and walked out quickly.

Just seconds later, Melody's office door was opened, and the girl whom Melody interviewed came out and quickly walked out of the office. Behind her, Melody appeared with her usual smile under the door frame, with her two arms stretching upward, as if she was holding the frame from an imminent fall. Melody, first, turned to Simone and then, to Essie and said, "Hey, what did you do with my husband, where is David?"

Essie looked at Simone, then stood and walked toward Melody's office saying, "Something came up, and he had to run." Then, both Melody and David disappeared into Melody's office. Simone's eyes followed them both with her eyes until the office door was closed shut.

***

When David arrived at Art's apartment, the door was half open, and the lock and handle were broken. David opened the door slowly and went inside. Art and Michael were sitting at the kitchen table. The kitchen lay in a small corner of a large suite. The whole apartment was a relatively large room, and the closet at the end led to the bathroom. Right before the closet, there was a queen-sized bed.

David asked, "Hey guys, what happened? Was anything stolen?"

The furniture in the living room and everything else was shuffled around. The mattress was torn, half hanging on the ground. Books were ripped and spread out across the floor. A small bookshelf mounted on the wall was almost empty, and some ripped pages were dangling off the shelves.

"Only my laptop is missing; other than that they didn't take anything else," replied Art.

Michael was holding Art's hand, caressing it. David found a chair to sit in and asked them, "What about money? Nothing else is missing?"

Art replied, "I don't keep money at home. It's not clear what they were looking for."

Astonished, David looked at them and asked, "Have you called the police yet? Did neighbors see anything? Breaking the door must have made some noises, did anyone hear anything? When did this happen?"

Art replied, "I don't know. I wasn't home last two days; I was at Michael's."

Michael said, "I knocked at some of the neighbors' doors, but no one answered. The next-door lady is usually very nosy, but now she's not answering. I called the police, and they're on their way here."

David stood up, walked toward the door, and kneeled to look at the fragments closely. He said, "Do not touch anything; maybe fingerprints can be found."

A shadow appeared in the corner of David's eye from behind the door. He gently stood back up, raising his head, and saw the apartment door was opened. He saw a tall, bulky African American man in suit who covered the whole door frame entering the apartment. David was frightened for a second. But the man took out his badge and showed it to David. "Detective Smith, and this is Hun, my assistant," said the man, pointing at his colleague behind him.

Smith's heavy build and presence completely hid his partner. David did not pay much attention to the other policeman. He smiled and shook Smith's hand and introduced himself. Detective Smith looked around and asked, "Is this your apartment?" It was unclear who that question was for, as the detective was facing the wall when he spoke.

Not hearing any response, Smith turned to David and asked him firmly this time, "Do you live here?"

David said, "No, Art does," pointing toward the kitchen.

Detective Smith went to the kitchen and saw the two young men sitting at the table. He turned back and looked at David again but did not say anything. Hun, Smith's assistant, was carefully examining the mess around the apartment. Detective Smith approached the two young men and asked their names. Hun wrote their name on a tiny notebook as they introduced themselves.

"Arthur Stevenson ... Michael Joyce."

Smith turned to Art and asked, "What do you do and where do you work?"

David, who was behind Smith, said, "He works in our company. He's a programmer; writes code for software."

Smith turned back and threw a meaningful look at David, showing his displeasure that David responded instead of Art.

Smith continued, "Did you have a fight with anyone recently? Or have you gotten involved in any controversial issue?"

Art shook his head with a no answer. Smith then asked Michael, "What's your job?"

Michael replied, "I am a bartender. I work at the Get Cool Bar."

"When did this happen?" the detective asked.

Art replied, "I don't know exactly. Sometime yesterday."

Smith turned to Hun quickly and asked Art, "What do you mean? How don't you know when this happened?"

"I didn't come home the night before. This evening, when I came home, I saw the door was broken, and everything was on the floor. My laptop is missing. Nothing else is stolen, if you want to know."

Hun, who was silent until that moment, asked, "Did you have any home insurance?"

"No, as I said, I had nothing valuable here," replied Art.

Hun asked again, "Did you stick the thing on that wall?"

Everyone turned to the direction that Hun was pointing. A small pocketbook was glued to the middle of the bookshelf. Hun went to the bookshelf and examined the spot on which the pocketbook was pinned. Addressing Art, Hun asked, "Are you a religious person?"

Art, who was surprised by this personal question, looked at David and Smith. Michael glanced at Hun. David stepped forward and stood beside the rest.

Art said, "Not so much, why do you ask?"

Hun pulled up a pair of thin plastic gloves from his pocket and put them on. The assistant detective removed the pocketbook from the bookshelf and came back to the kitchen area and said, "Besides some torn pages of books, this is the only thing on the shelf… I mean… it was taped on the back of the shelf."

Hun, who had captured everyone's attention, gently held the little book with two fingers and showed it to everyone. What Hun was displaying was a pocket-sized Bible. With a gesture, Smith asked Hun to show both sides of the Bible. Examining the Gospel's backside, Hun opened a page which was bookmarked with a yellow square sticker. Then, he read two lines that were highlighted on the bookmarked page.

"[19:24] Then the LORD rained on Sodom and Gomorrah sulfur and fire from the LORD out of heaven;

[19:25] and he overthrew those cities, and all the Plain, and all the inhabitants of the cities, and what grew on the ground."

Everyone was silent. Michael asked, "What does that mean? What is it trying to say?"

Hun raised his head and slowly checked all four people around the table, one by one with a smile. The smile created two tiny wrinkles around Hun's round mouth and positioned two small lines in place of his eyes. It was not clear what Hun had in mind by his facial expression. His gesture and face was an indication of victory. He apparently was proud of his discovery.

As much surprised as Michael, Art said, "Is this a message or a warning? By marking this book on a page ..."

Smith corrected him and said, "The Gospel. It's not a book."

"... I'm sorry, the page of the Gospel has been marked as a sign, and the verses apparently refer to something," Art continued.

David put his hand through his hair, jumped in and asked Art, "Wait a minute. Are you sure that this is not yours?"

"No, I never had a Bible at home. I do not understand what this is doing on my bookshelf."

Smith, who suddenly seemed to have remembered something, turned to David and asked, "What is the name of the company you guys are working at?" At the same time, he searched for something on his phone.

When David tried to respond, "Tech ..." Smith completed his word, "2AI. Isn't it?" And then he held his phone screen to David's face.

"Have you seen this?" Smith was showing Tim's story that had been published in the *Bay Area Chronicle*.

David stayed quiet for a moment and looked at Art. Then he said, "I did not see it. If I may, I need to leave; I have an appointment."

"Of course," Smith said, "but before you go, tell me which one of these gentlemen is the subject of the story?"

"I don't know what you are talking about? I didn't read that story," David replied.

"So be sure to read it. It's about your business," Smith said with a sneer on his face, "It's good advertising for your company as well. In any case, I'll go to your workplace later. In the meantime, if you have not, read it. And when I'm there, we'll talk about it."

Then, Smith turned to Hun and said, "Call the forensic team to come here."

Detective Smith then turned to Art and said, "Until our job is not done, you cannot stay here." With a smile that had a specific meaning for Art and Michael, Smith continued, "If you can, go to your friend's house."

# Chapter 10 – Stonewall

*San Francisco – David's Office*

"We don't know what we've got ourselves into. Strange things are happening around us that is by no means accidental," David said. Turning to Art he continued, "Your experience visiting Sodom is not just an imagination. I didn't expect such a phenomenon from meditation. We never had such strong connection to any kind of source before."

Essie said, "If you remember, once I showed you a book from a physiologist ... I don't remember the name ... it was about going back and dealing with events in the past, confronting negative effects," and with a sneer continued, "I remember it was the time you dragged me into this mumbo jumbo."

Essie could not hide his grin after the last phrase. He knew about David's resentment if his spiritual thoughts fell into the mumbo jumbo category. Essie always enjoyed irritating David a bit.

Indifferent to Essie's comment, David said: "You can say whatever you like. Yes, I remember that book very well. I read other books by the same author. It mostly was about regression and regression therapy. But Art's experience is different; he's been able to contact someone in the past, someone other than himself."

After listening carefully to these longtime friends who were at least 20 years older than him, confused Art said, "I don't know much either. I haven't read much on the subject at all. Have I ever lived in Sodom in one of my past lives, if there is such a thing? Was I the person whom I met behind that stone gap? Was the person who stopped and watched me later in fact me watching myself in that basement corridor? It is all exciting and confusing at the same time."

"Not necessarily; we don't know exactly. There are many questions left unanswered about regression therapy as well. Our only way to find out is to go back and to make the connection and to observe. But my concern is your mental and emotional health. What do you think, Art?" David asked with a concerned and serious look.

"I haven't had any bad feeling after coming back," said Art. "Only during my visit, I got a bit scared and anxious being in an unknown place and seeing all those weird stuff. So far, though, I can come back easily when the pressure gets too much. "

Essie said, "I wish there was an expert on this subject that we could consult with."

"There are no specific expertise or certain known measures to explain this subject. It's not a medical or technological field," said David, then added, "Essie, you know well about a series of events that led me to understand the strong effects of meditation. If you remember, I had repeatedly shared those experiences with you before. Perhaps you were tired of listening to it. However, with all that happened to Art, I feel he deserves to know that as well."

David continued: "When my father died, the emotional conditions triggered a strong need to approach the world of spirituality. Before that, on my journey to India, I had a terrible experience pursuing spirituality. Then, with my father's passing—since that was my first close encounter with the death and dying phenomenon—I decided to engage myself in Eastern philosophy. I wanted to be able to somehow adapt my intellectual frame of thought to the phenomenon of my father's death. Before that, I had believed only in a scientific, factual approach to everything, and I was a total nonbeliever in metaphysics and supernatural views, not to mention religion. The more I read, the more confused I became. I didn't know what to expect from meditation, almost like someone who would expect effects of drinking alcohol from smoking marijuana. I had gone to discover a world with a totally different mindset and expectations. And the more I was trying, the less progress I made."

David saw that Art was listening with all his focus. He continued, "I think you could enter the trance better than all of us. There is no explicit guidance and explanation. Just close your eyes and try to focus on your breath. Avoid anything that is coming to your mind. And as you may have experienced yourself, it's not easy at first, but with practice, you will get better. This simple technique helped me more than many books did. But what I wanted to convey is that this path is completely personal, and there is no definite general guidance that can work for all. Everyone connects to the source and reaches a certain destination in his own way. Maybe one will never get to the end, or there might not be an end at all. In general, you must be careful of any negative impact on your spirit and psyche."

Art seemed thrilled: he felt energetic again, and stood up and walked across the room. He was facing the main work hall, showing his back to David and Essie. Then, he turned back and with a quiet but decisive voice said, "Now it's time—let's start. I'm ready."

David and Essie exchanged looks. David had never seen Art in such a state. It was as if despite his age and youthful appearance, Art had suddenly matured into greatness. His majestic eyes glistened like stars; his long hair was covering his shoulders, giving Art a distinguished look. David had never seen Art like this before. He always considered Art a handsome young man, but now it seemed that his beauty surpassed the physical state of man into a spiritual state of gods. David and Essie had noticed the beginning of his transformation days earlier.

***

David: "Did you notice changes in Art's overall look? He's been changed so much."

Essie: "Yeah, he became more handsome and attractive."

David: "He looks like Jesus Christ ..." David ignored Essie's loud laughter after the comparison to Jesus and continued in a higher tone, "Seriously. Look at him. He looks just like paintings and images that are shown in churches or in movies."

Essie, who was still laughing, said, "First of all, you need to define which of those imaginary images of Jesus is in your mind. I've seen at least four or five completely different images in books, magazines, and movies. One of them even had an African-American look. Now, that you referred to the look of Jesus Christ, I must say that our Art is much more handsome than all of those pictures."

David was annoyed by Essie's comment, which was challenging him even about the conventional appearance of Jesus. He said, "Now you're debating me on Christ's look? There are different images, but in general, the common denominator of all is a slim and innocent look with fairly long hair. You can pick any color that gives him a celestial appearance."

Essie laughed again and mocked the word "celestial," which led David to retreat from his claim.

***

When David saw Essie staring at Art, he started to say something about his appearance but changed his mind and instead said, "Before we start, I wanted to check one or two issues or questions with you guys. First, is the collective meditation helpful for Art to gain power? Or will only two or three of us suffice? There are so many unknown aspects, and we have no clue what they are until we practice them and find out. Secondly, Art, can you recognize their language? Can you understand what they say?"

David's last question made Art to pause and think. Then, as if pausing between every word would help him tap into his partial memory, Art answered, "I'm… not sure …"

David added, "Don't pressure your mind to recall now, but when you are there next time if you could remember and focus on that."

Art suddenly stopped David and said, "I might have understood some words. I can't recall the meaning now, but I could comprehend them. Unless you guys were talking simultaneously during the session and it overlapped, and all talk intermingled somehow…"

David interrupted Art and said hesitatingly, "What you should know is that you're an exception. You have to believe this very important fact. I never imagined that this could be possible." As if David suddenly overcame his doubt he continued, "Don't you feel any change in yourself too?" And then he looked at Essie.

Essie's nod was an endorsement of David's observation. He was staring at Art. Art, who apparently had been embarrassed, mumbled few obscure words that were a mixture of shyness and modesty.

Art's enthusiasm was fading, and his restlessness was evidence that he was becoming tired of theoretical talks. Finally, he demanded, "It's better to leave discussions for another time. We can have better understanding later when we have more evidence. So, let's start."

"Right," David replied. "I intended to say that we all know the story of Sodom and Gomorrah only as it was written in religious books. We don't really know whether it's true or just a story. Some ridiculous stories that …"

Essie burst into uncontrolled frantic laughter. He tried to stop laughing and talk at the same time: "Ridiculous? Wait … to hear its Islamic version … you would not believe it."

Essie took his dark big framed glasses off, trying to wipe his tears dripping down from the corners of his eyes, rolling on his cheeks and then through his mustache. Then he explained, "In the Islamic version, supposedly, flying elephants bombarded and destroyed the city of Sodom, dropping rocks on its people who were committing abhorring acts of sin."

David and Art became infected with Essie's hysterical laughter and started laughing themselves. David very seldom witnessed Essie's loud laughter. Art was a little confused because he always thought Essie was too serious of a man and somewhat quiet.

Essie jokingly went on to say, "Now I understand David's concern. Art, if suddenly you saw a squadron of elephants in the air, carrying rocks with their trunks, throwing their loads on enemy's positions, know that you are watching the scene from the Islamic point of view. Basically, Islam is obsessed with stoning sinners. Excuse me, guys, you think I lost my mind, but there are so many things about Islam that you don't know."

"The historical timing is crucial," David said. "There is no doubt that it is critical when you get to Sodom." It was unclear whether David was mocking Essie or was serious in his remark.

Essie undoubtedly knew that he did not make sense to David and Art. Nevertheless, he enjoyed the conversation to the last drop of words.

To recenter, David said, "Okay Essie, I'm sure you will tell us later. But let's go back to our subject, we've put together a few topics: That today, Art will continue his journey, I hope ... I mean we'll try ... Then, we will find out if Art can understand their language. Also, whether the number of people in meditation has any effect on Art's abilities, and finally if Art has the power to choose where and what period he arrives. Or it is completely random? So far, these are all the unanswered questions that I gathered. I think as Art said earlier, only the action will we know answers."

Art was impatiently waiting to start the meditation, listening to the discussions of two friends who had been debating each other for years. Art had hoped the conversation would not become a long one. He knew that once they started a debate they would not give up easily. One of them would always come up with a witty remark or something interesting to say to have the last words. But now Art was not at all interested in wasting another moment.

Art had the answers to some of David's questions, but he did not know why he had not shared them with David, Essie, and others in the group before. Art did not tell them that he had gone on trips to the past alone by himself. In the last few times, he had not always descended into Sodom. Art never knew where he would travel to. It seemed as though his ship had landed somewhere in time, and he was simply an observer. Art did not know where he was at that particular moment or why. When he could connect to that unknown force, he would go straight to the designated path. Art had done this many times privately. He had not told Michael because he was afraid Michael would stop him. Recently, Michael was fearful of Art's changes. Fear of being harmed and losing Art had made Michael too sensitive. Therefore Art decided to meditate and connect secretly. When he returned from his meditative journeys, Art would crave for more of that strange, powerful feeling.

On one occasion, Art felt that his strong desire to meditate might sprung from a desire to be more powerful, a power that was conquering the totality of his being. Whatever it was, and whatever the cause—whether it was curiosity or the sense of being like Superman— Art fell in love with it. He wanted to possess that power within himself more and more. The beauty of this extraordinary power was not just the ability to travel back and forth in time during the meditation. It was an explosion of energy when he came back in the present time, a strange and fantastic source of energy that was quite real and potentially more potent than anything Art had ever seen or felt his whole life.

But why did he hide this amazing experience and energy from the group, a group that had given him this power? Art had no answer to this question, so he justified his action by telling himself, "No, of course, I didn't receive my powers from this group. They only showed me how to reach it."

Among the crowd, only David knew that eventually, group meditation would lead to something bigger. He was sure of its benefits. He was searching for it for years. David had a different purpose—peace and tranquility—and sometimes he had somewhat reached his goals. But he knew the inner world would be far beyond what he and Essie had experienced. It was David who knew years ago that the seed he had patiently planted would someday become a tree that would bear fruit.

Although Essie was the one carrying the theoretical load for the group, he did not mostly believe in David's philosophy. Contrary to his mystical Persian background, he had believed only in the law of science for years. Apparently, he now was witnessing the very phenomenon that he denied for so long. Interestingly, the impossible fruit of that elusive tree manifested itself in Art. Art was the great fruit of a tree that could be generated only in an unknown inner world.

On one of his solo meditations, Art landed in a place other than Sodom. He felt strong energy and realized immediately that he was in a new place. It was a place in time closer to the present and familiar, though he hadn't been there before. He arrived there in the midst of chaos in the street. Police cars were everywhere, some still occupied, with broken windows. There were barricades. It was an utterly uneasy atmosphere. He saw trans people having the street under their control, while some women, cursing loud, were throwing rocks at this particular bar and breaking its windows. A chill ran through his spine. He was at Stonewall; it was June 28, 1969. He knew and had heard a lot about the uprising in that particular place. He had heard various narratives, but now Art was witnessing the event up close and personal.

Art knew that the Stonewall event, a rebellion that occurred in New York's Greenwich neighborhood, was not the first incident in the long history of discrimination, repression, and violence against gays, lesbians, drag queens, and transsexuals in America. Art had studied history to some extent. He had read that Stonewall was ground zero and a pivotal moment in the American LGBTQ community's movement, organization, and eventual achievement of civil rights. He also knew, three years before Stonewall, police had cracked down on a transgender community at the Compton Cafeteria in San Francisco, and seven years before that, in the Cooper Donut shop in Los Angeles, transvestites had also been severely attacked.

This was the famous Stonewall. Art was at gravity central in the history of LGBTQ rights. His heart trembled and tears came to his eyes. Art had different feelings toward Stonewall than toward Sodom, perhaps because he knew and heard more about Stonewall than he did about Sodom. He had heard only vague stories from the Gospel, and of course, always doubted the reality of such religious tales. And in case of historical events, if they did occur, they weren't accurate as narrated in Old Testament. He became sure, only later, when he heard tales of events from King Bera directly. But Stonewall was an entirely different historical landmark. Only 50 years had been passed. It was a turning point, a beginning to an end, an end to LGBTQ silence.

New York was passing through the last year of its sixth decade in the twentieth century. None of the LGBTQ groups had any rights to express themselves, nor did they hope to relieve pressures that were imposed continuously upon them under the judiciary system aegis. There was not even a place to find the desired mate if one sought to lessen life's stress. The only possible site in New York was a poor area where the Stonewall Bar was located: in the Greenwich Village neighborhood of Manhattan, at Christopher Street between Sheridan Square and 7th Avenue South.

Stonewall Bar was a meeting place of LGBTQs who could find one another, have a drink, and enjoy time without fear of being harassed by the police. At the time of Stonewall riot, it was unimaginable even to dream of enjoying the partial rights that the LGBTQ community achieved years later. The institutionalized rights would not be possible without fighting tooth and nail.

It was an election year, and the candidates were promising to clean up the city for good. And so the Stonewall Bar was exposed to police invasion and brutality—the bribes would have to give way to the higher purpose for the police. Destitute youth from Christopher Park, on the other side of the street, were also visitors to Stonewall Bar, as they hoped to receive food and drink from well-off queer patrons. Whenever Stonewall was attacked, those homeless young men living in Christopher Park would also be given their share of violence from defenders of so-called law and order.

Those occasional assaults had been going on for a decade. The bar patrons knew that the police attack on Stonewall would be a usual, repeatable event; however, at least Stonewall offered a place where they could be themselves when the police weren't raiding.

Usually, the night of a police attack, the bar manager would receive a tip in advance. A double tab with a baton on the door was the sign, and then the dim lights inside the bar were lit completely. Those who tried to escape through the window were beaten up severely and thrown into a police wagon. The new well-off customers paid their way out of trouble with the police. Those who were standing too close to each other would separate, trying to get past the invasion by adhering to the required status quo.

But on that night in June 1969, the raid was carried out without notice. It was not due. Usually, the raid took place once a month. But this time they came early. The attitude of the police was different too. They began to frisk individuals inside the bar. Outside, several women were thrown into police paddy wagons. It was said that the bar owners did not pay the usual bribe to the police. Suddenly a loud crash was heard outside. It sounded like a heavy item like a piece of rock or a bottle crashed on a piece of metal, like the body of a car. Then another fell on a police car. And then, immediately afterward, there was the sound of smashing beer bottles.

Inside, the crowd began to push the police. A few fell on the ground after receiving hits on the head by police batons. The crowd was gathering outside, adding to the number of people already inside. It did not take long before between 400 to 500 people gathered passionately in front of the Stonewall Bar. A young man shouted, "Pay them ransom for god's sake." And everyone threw pennies to the paddy wagons, venting years of anger and frustrations. First, there was the sound of coins raining down, then it turned into a flood. Now, it was police who took the beatings from the young men and women. Police asked for backup, but it was too late.

The riot had begun. It seemed as if the pent-up pressures of a decade of bullying and abusing was exploded on that night of June. Lesbians were punching the police officers. The street that night was taken over by gay men, lesbians, queens, transsexuals, bisexuals, and anyone considered a queer.

From the very next day, a new movement was born, which was not the only result of the Stonewall riot. Decades or centuries of suppression had formed this movement. The so-called normal society had viciously suppressed innocents whose only crime was to have a different sexual orientation by default. Yes, Art had heard everything before, and now he saw it up close. He felt the violence firsthand, the violence that had lasted for years and perhaps for centuries.

Hitler in Germany had sent homosexuals along with Jews, leftists, and members of opposition groups to death camps. The soaps that were made in Nazi's concentration camps consisted of a mixture of flesh and skin from all prisoners including queers, Jews, and others who were tortured to death. Homosexuals elsewhere had been victims of the Abrahamic religions—like Judaism, Christianity, Islam—or any other beliefs that owed part of their empowerment to bashing LGBTQs. Different branches of Abrahamic religions fueled their vehicles by passing through the highway of suppressing, harassing, and killing LGBTQs for centuries. Slaughtering LGBTQs in all corners of history was always justified by synonymizing their names with sin, pedophile, anti-law, violator, or Satan itself.

And Art was now able to travel to the depths of history to see each and every one of those crimes and injustices and add to his power every time.

# Chapter 11 – San Francisco

"There lies new San Francisco,

Sea-maid in purple dressed,

Wearing a dancer's girdle

All to inflame desire:

Scorning her days of sackcloth,

Scorning her cleansing fire.

See, like a burning city

Sets now the red sun's dome.

See, mystic firebrands sparkle

There on each store and home." —Vachel Lindsay (1879–1930)

Art no longer needed David's guidance to meditate into a trance, but if he was in the group meditation, he would usually accompany the rest. All three, like previous meetings, adjusted their posture on their seats to find a comfortable position. They closed their eyes and David started his words slowly:

"Empty your mind. Do not think about anything. Inhale deep lungful breaths, hold, one, two, three, and now exhale. Your mind is clear ... Now, imagine that you feel lighter. You're placed on threads like spider webs. These webs are connected to the universe with the source in its center. Webs became light on the spots you are connected to. Now you are connected to the main central charger through these wires that are attached to each point of your body. You're getting energized, both physically and spiritually. Every single moment, with each deep breath, you connect more to wires and webs and thus to the source. Now that you're connected to your real world, go and discover."

Time passed. Silence ruled momentarily. Both windows in David's office, one on the street, and one on the main hall, were shut. However, the silence was broken periodically by sporadic sounds from outside. On the other side of the street, a giant crane was hovering over the building like a big fluttering flag. Art had seen these high-rise cranes in different parts of the city recently. Throughout the day, the sound of dumping steel beams on the ground and sharp hammering were the signs of adding new stories to the existing buildings around the city.

Art heard the sound of howling wind blended with the intermittent bangs. He opened his eyes, then he looked down, and suddenly Art felt he was going to lose his balance. He raised his head and saw the whole city beneath his feet. He could see that there were only a few tall buildings that, like pillars, connected earth to the sky.

Art found himself on the tallest crane. He looked around. On the horizon, smoke was rising from different spots of the city. He looked more precisely and recognized the Golden Gate Bridge. He was sure now that parts of the city of San Francisco were on fire. Sounds of explosions were added to the previous bangs and crashes. Then he heard the recurrence of gunshots and a storm of machine guns, alternating.

Rocket-like shots opened his eyes to the reality of what was going on in front of him. He saw helicopters approaching him on his right;

one crossed over his head. Seconds later, two jets flew over the Golden Gate Bridge toward him. He looked at the horizon. He could not recognize if it was morning or dusk. Art knew that it was not nighttime yet, but he could not see the sun. He looked up. Over his head, there was dark smoke. He felt the heavy air hard to breathe. Stellar, flickering blasts crashed into different streets with a formidable sound. He stared at the streets below, under his feet. Sandbags in the middle of the streets reminded him of the guerrilla war movies. Two other fighter jets crossed over his head with a terrifying sound; seconds later a large building, with a giant billboard, crumbled on itself. It was hit by one of the fighter jet's missiles.

San Francisco, his favorite city, was under attack. Art wanted to defend this city with all his heart and power. A small buzz on his left forced him to turn his head. A large, motionless flying drone was in the air, recording him, a red light blinking on its underside. Art quickly stretched his arm toward the drone, as if he was trying to grab the flying object. But the distance between Art and the drone was about ten feet. The drone's upper rotor blades stopped rotating abruptly. While still hovering in the air, the drone's lights went off.

Art looked under his feet again but did not see the crane. He was suspended in the air. He felt powerful. Art targeted the unmanned aerial vehicle with his palm at a 90-degree angle to his stretched-out arm. The UAV approached him. For a moment, Art thought he was the one moving toward the drone. Without repositioning his body, he looked down at the building under his feet. No, indeed, the drone was being forced to move toward him. The drone was within his reach. Grabbing the overheated drone, Art detected a small camera underneath. He snapped it off quickly, which caused a scratch on his finger.

Art sensed he could move freely in the air. He could not believe it, but he was flying. He turned back to see that the UAV fell to the ground. Throughout his life, he had always wanted to sit on the highest point of the Golden Gate Bridge. He flew toward the bridge. Through the smoke and the fog, he looked down, checking streets underneath. He detected flags and banners on the streets, showing different designs of the rainbow. Some buildings and shops were in flames. Through smoke and haze, Art identified the armed forces with special uniforms under his feet, carrying semi-heavy weapons. He descended a little. Art could not recognize the type of guns and uniforms. He saw the forces pointing their weapons at a specific building across that street. A tank was ready to shoot at the same target too. In front of this building, he saw barricades. A sizeable full banner with colors of the rainbow was mounted on the upper floors of the building.

Art stopped approximately 50 feet above the ground where the armed forces were. He felt a supernatural power within him, which he could transfer to every part of his body with ease. He held his arms and hands close and parallel to his thighs on both sides in a vertical stretched body position, then closed his eyes. His two fully opened palms, facing down, targeted the tank and armed forces underneath. Palms still facing downward, his stretched arms began to rise slowly without bending. As his hands rose, tanks and other weapons ascended into the air. Some soldiers that did not let go of their weapons rose but seconds later threw themselves down. It seemed Art was holding the tank with his left hand and controlling other weapons and rocket launchers with his right hand. He pushed his left hand down and moved his right hand to the side on his right. The tank hit the ground hard, and other guns and the rest flung in the direction according to Art's hand movement.

Art opened his eyes with a loud scream. He looked down to check the outcome of his actions but instead saw David and Essie squatting on the floor of the office while he was holding the chair's armrests firmly. It was evidence of chaos in the room. The two framed pictures on the walls had fallen, and the glass had shattered to pieces. David's desk had been moved, and papers and folders were flown everywhere. Art saw David's pale face, and apparently he was talking. Art could not hear any sound or word. Then, slowly David's voice grew louder, "Art, Art, can you hear me? Wake up."

Art was there and aware. With a smile on his lips, Art's face was exhibiting an epic look, a combination of calm and power. He adjusted himself in his chair and looked into David's eyes. He felt a burn in his left hand. He peeked at his left palm. Art saw the same scratch while removed the camera from the UAV. He smiled again and looked out the window. It was dark.

Essie asked, "What happened?"

Art did not know where to begin. He felt a closer connection to these two men. When he started to narrate the story for them, the doorbell rang. Art stayed quiet. David pulled out his phone and pressed on the vibrating Bell app. The app opened, showing the front door camera. Outside, Detective Smith and Melody stood together, waiting for the door to be opened. Their simultaneous arrival at the door, a coincidence, forced them to exchange a few words.

"Shit," said David and then showed the phone to Essie and Art.

It was 7 o'clock in the evening. There was no one at the company except for the three men. David stalled and did not know what to do. Essie whispered to David, "Who is he?" And when he found out the visitor who was standing close to Melody was a police officer, quietly told him, "Do not open."

David turned to Art to learn his opinion. But at that moment nothing mattered to Art. His head was resting on the chair, his body stretched out diagonally. He had his eyes closed and was recalling scenes in his meditation. His whole body was on fire, bursting with energy and full of a strange feeling that was moving all over his body.

The doorbell rang once more, and David's phone buzzed. David sent a text to Melody stating, "I won't open. Don't talk to the person standing next to you. Just say nobody is in and go to our usual restaurant. I'll see you there."

David saw Melody pull out her phone and quietly read the text. After a quick look at the camera, there was a brief conversation between Melody and the detective. Then Melody walked toward the elevator with detective following her.

David said, "I hope Melody was able to convince him."

Essie turned to Art and demanded, "Well, young man, tell us: What happened? It seems you had too much adventure in Sodom."

Art sat upright in his seat and responded, "I didn't go to Sodom. This time, I was just around the corner."

Art described everything to David and Essie. They were listening to the whole time, wide-eyed with their jaws dropped in astonishment.

David said, "We don't have time now. We'll be talking about this later. Melody is waiting... I'm speechless. Really don't know what to say. I'm not sure where we're heading with this."

David left the office after being assured that Smith was not waiting outside the building. He asked Essie to meet up at their usual dinner restaurant. It was few blocks away from the office. Essie was the last person who was supposed to leave the office. As he was waiting for David to leave the building and before going out himself, Essie monitored Art's overall condition. Not many words exchanged between them, but Essie noticed striking changes in Art. Art was not the same as before. Essie noticed a confidence that did not exist in Art before, not even yesterday, not until now. He detected a clear glow in Art's face and eyes simultaneously. In his adventurous life, which had taken place in many different countries, Essie had seen many sparks in people's eyes, but the fire in Art's eyes was from a different world altogether, a kind of energy he had never seen.

Essie asked, "Are you okay, Art? Where are you going now? Do you want to join us at the restaurant?"

"No thanks, David asked me, too, but Michael is waiting for me. I'm going there... haven't seen him since this morning."

Art stood up. Essie looked at him again. "Yes, I'm not mistaken," Essie said to himself. "Something has changed, either his shoulders have become wider, or his posture has improved."

Art, too, realized that something within him had changed. When he stood, he thought for a moment that he could fly. The room spun around his head. Essie jumped to catch his fall and grabbed his hand. Touching Art's skin, Essie's hand burned and was pushed back by an unexpected spark. Art also felt it but did not react, and instead said, "It must be a carpet static. Are you okay?"

"Yeah, but that was a hell of static. Are you ready? Let's get out of here," Essie said and moved toward the door. As David had instructed, when Essie and Art reached the ground floor, they left the building through the back door. That door was precisely across from the main entrance. Behind the building, there was a smaller street where tenants usually parked their cars. After saying goodbye to each other, they walked in opposite directions.

On the other side of the street, Officer Hun was sitting in his car, hiding, trying hard not to be seen. With his phone, Hun took several pictures of Art and Essie before they separated.

***

After exiting the building and parting from Essie, a strange and powerful feeling encompassed Art's mind and body. They were the same senses that came over him at David's office when he returned from Sodom for the first time. The only difference was that he felt much stronger forces within him now. His body began to vibrate and pushed him forward. On his way to Michael's apartment, he could not have imagined fitting in a car or bus at the moment. None had the capacity to fit him at that time. Running was the only option. He had to run. And he did like the first time he had found Michael. Only running could lessen the chance of an internal explosion. He thought about Michael. Michael was the one who made him cool and calm for the first time. He knew Michael was not working that day and was now waiting for him in his apartment. He kept running without noticing anything in his surroundings. Pedestrians, some surprised and some panicked, rushed out of his away, passing him cautiously.

Art ran through all the streets, one after the other, without any sign of weakness. At every step he was covering a longer distance. A few times between steps, he felt that he had glided, and in few instances, he did not feel the impact on the bottom of his feet at all.

"Am I flying?" Art asked himself.

He stopped. He was on the ground. There was an overwhelming force inside, boiling. Art was standing on a quiet street. He did not know how many miles he had run, but Art knew he would not be far away from Michael's apartment. Not more than a few more minutes remained before he would reach it. Oddly, traffic lights at every intersection turned green on his arrival. Was he in total control? He knew only that this mysterious energy within him needed a channel, as something was about to burst inside.

Art was almost sure that the distance between Michael's apartment and his workplace was less than 15 or 20 miles. He knew his fast heartbeat was not caused by running, but rather because of the accumulation of his inner energy. He did not feel tired at all. He was starting to consider his power as supernatural, likes when he was in the sky, above the troops that were about to attack the building with a rainbow flag.

Art did not want to test his power, but he could tell that with a tiny push of his pointing finger, he could smash the platform where a lion's head sculpture stood. "Lion?" he asked himself, wondering if he had seen that sculpture before. "Where am I?" He was in a side street. Art put his hand on the platform, admiring the details, but suddenly the statue exploded as if the pressure of his hands was too forceful. Startled, not knowing what to do, he started running again.

Not long after, he found himself in front of Michael's apartment door. Having lost track of time, Art did not remember how he entered the building. "Is he sleeping?" he asked himself. He knocked on Michael's door, which created a few dents on its wooden body. Michael expected Art earlier but went to bed not knowing when Art would show up. Woken up abruptly and scared from the loud knock, Michael opened the door wearing only underwear.

Art stepped in quickly, held Michael's hands up, pushing him against the wall and kissed his lips hard, as though he wanted to release all the excess energy onto Michael. Stunned, Michael knew that Art was coming, but not with this bold entrance. Michael kissed him back. After a moment, he knotted his hands around Art's body and kissed him even harder. Michael was a few inches taller. Art gently placed his head on Michael's shoulder and embraced him entirely and passionately.

Art felt of a stream of serenity that slowly poured into his mind from his love. This feeling of calmness did not diminish the power inside. Art cooled his mind, but his excitement was reaching an alarming level. He felt the love with all his being. Michael's pure existence was an ocean of relaxation, drowning and soothing him every second. And Art slowly moved down Michael's body. Michael's legs were wobbly, but he could not imagine allowing any movement, even the smallest one, to put an end to this moment of pure pleasure.

Art should have been able to control his power. This journey was different from the others. What happened to him? He did not know. He did not experience any of these feelings before. Unlike Sodom's trips, Art was not only an observer this time; he was able to interact with his surroundings. That was a huge difference.

Now both men, hand in hand, standing and facing each other, stared into one another's eyes. In Michael's eyes, Art saw serenity and peace as he had seen an hour before, flying in the sky. He held Michael's hand and guided him to the bedroom. Now, they both were standing face to face again, their hands hooked together, looking deep into each other's eyes, lifting any veil from one another's soul, showing the purity of their loving hearts. An offering of one's heart to the other, a mutual love, a shared feeling.

They lay in bed. The kiss was not the only connecting point for expressing a deep feeling of love at that moment. They intertwined with each other, one soul in two different bodies. Art became a burning flame and Michael in return, like an iceberg, welcomed his fiery fever. With every move, Art was experiencing the motions, being calm and high simultaneously. They twisted with each other like two snakes. The intensity was so high it reached the point of two becoming one.

Art's body cells were not cooling because of Michael, for Michael was a seamless fire himself. The feeling of cooling relief was not at all physical. This was soothing soul process in which their inner and outer beings were reaching equilibrium.

Now, at this very moment of joy and happiness, Art found himself on top of the Golden Gate Bridge, in the clouds, feeling the refreshing wind gently touch his face. It was as if he was looking at the horizon where the ocean stops and the sky begins. With a loud cry of joy, they both experienced the bliss of their immense love for one another. Art's inner fire was now of different intensity. The sexual excitement had subsided, but the love between them became a thousand times higher. Art put his head on Michael's shoulder and felt blessed.

# Chapter 12 – Déjà Vu

*San Francisco and Tehran*

Unlike Art, who rushed toward Michael's apartment after the two men parted ways, Essie stopped for a moment and looked around. He felt something was not right. Hun, sitting in a parked car across the street, dropped his phone on the passenger seat and slowly lowered his petit body until his head was below the dashboard. Several cars passed in the street between Essie and Hun. An oversized truck, with length and width almost too large to fit in that street, slowly drove by Hun's parked car. The regular traffic and a few pedestrians, walking casually toward Essie, temporarily dissipated Essie's suspicions.

When Essie felt that something was wrong, he thought, "déjà vu," about thirty-six years ago in Tehran. Everything felt the same: he had been trapped and was almost on the verge of being captured. It was an incident that he never forgot. After so many years had passed, he could still review the details of that day vividly.

***

After the revolution in 1979, Essie, then in his last year of high school, became involved with one of the newly formed political groups like thousands of other youth in Iran. Not too long after Shah toppled, the honeymoon phase of celebrating freedom was over. Things changed quickly. Universities were closed, bookstores were set on fire, the Islamic police expanded massive arrests of young activists, sending them to jail, and waves of executions began. The Iranian regime's security forces rapidly identified and eradicated any opposition groups' members and supporters.

Security forces had been able to identify Essie's apartment. They had invaded the place where Essie and several other activists were living. One person, who was in the apartment at the time of the raid, was arrested. The Islamic police patiently encircled and besieged the entire neighborhood to capture the rest of the team.

Unaware of the situation, Essie was walking toward the apartment. But he had a gut feeling that something was off. He had no idea that security forces had invaded his apartment and arrested one of his friends. He sensed a misplaced feeling of his surroundings. Essie thought he would check the secret sign, the vase behind the window that each member was supposed to check before entering the building. If it were there, then all would be clear. He reached the corner of the street where the apartment building was located. After passing by several buildings, he could check the vase on the third floor across the street. He saw the vase, but the presence of a man who was sweeping the street drew his attention. It was unusual for a city worker to clean the street at that time of the day. Usually, early morning was the time to pick up trash. Besides, sweeping streets was not in their job description. He had already stepped into the main street and still had doubts about whether he was in danger. But he could not take the risk of going back. He suddenly remembered that two or three streets before coming to this intersection, he saw a couple of suspicious guys standing around.

Now, his concern about falling into the trap of the security forces grew stronger. What he did not know was that his captured comrade was unable to take the vase away from the window. There was no other way to go but forward. The police would rather capture Essie in the building than arrest him in the street. He stood still. He wanted to close his eyes to think, even just for a few seconds, but it was not wise. He was aware that the police were monitoring him. He did not want to be arrested under any circumstances. He had experienced prison already. He would have preferred to take bullets on the street than to be subjected to interrogation and torture. He said to himself, "Come what may. I have no fear of the bullets, so come and get me." Then he stepped onto the street to cross to the other side.

Essie looked around. Nothing was on his left, not even a car from far; but on the right, a small pickup truck was approaching. Two couples were walking in opposite direction on each sidewalk, and one woman was holding her little girl's hand. As Essie walked into the center of the street, he heard loud music, growing louder by the second. It was coming from the approaching pickup truck. The driver was enjoying the music, illegal according to Islamic moral code. The driver, unaware of the situation, was absorbed in his music. When the driver saw Essie trying to cross, he naturally accelerated. There was no such a thing as pedestrians' rights in Iran. When the pickup had almost passed him, Essie grabbed onto the left end of the truck and jumped into the bed. He then lay still. Seeing Essie's move, the man pretending to be a city worker dropped his broom and pulled out his gun. Other undercover police released several shots in the air, trying to catch the driver's attention. Agents appeared from different buildings and ran after the truck. The driver thought that the Islamic moral police were trying to arrest him for possessing illegal cassette of singers from the Shah era. Scared and trying to avoid arrest, he pushed down on the gas pedal and sped up. He was not aware of his unwanted guest lying in the back of his truck. Security forces were now firing openly at the pickup truck. Everybody was running away, jumping inside open buildings or stores. A bullet hit the truck's rear window behind the passenger seat and shards of glass flew out. The pickup truck managed to flee the scene, taking Essie as its load and unwittingly rescuing him from a deadly encounter.

***

Essie sensed the same unusual, undercurrent situation now as he had experienced in Tehran. Essie's mind reflected on that evening thirty-six years ago until he reached the restaurant where David and Melody were waiting.

Detective Smith, like Hun, was sitting in his parked car across the street in front of the restaurant when Essie entered the diner. Earlier, when Smith received Hun's text on his phone, he wrote back to him, "You do not need to pursue any of them. I emphasize, do not follow them."

After entering the restaurant, Essie heard the buzz of his phone. He read the text and replied with a short one. David and Melody were sitting in the corner booth. Everywhere it was dim. The restaurant was lit by lamps shedding dim light over each table, and several big screen TVs were showing exciting sports competitions.

The feeling of being watched and the fear of captivity took Essie back to his old world of paranoia. He checked his surroundings and was skeptical of everything. Essie glanced everywhere, looking at every table. All seemed normal to him. Several families were sitting in different booths, eating or waiting for their meals. Two young men sat in the corner, waiting to order. Their nerdy appearance did not raise any suspicions. When the hostess asked him, "how many?" Essie pointed, and walk to the corner both where his friends were sitting.

David and Melody welcomed him with a smile. Melody kissed his cheek and said, "David has told me what happened to Art while meditating. What do you think? It's becoming like fantasy fiction. Don't you think these journeys are Art's pure imagination? Now he sees things that have no historical references."

"I don't know. It's getting too strange. If those are dreams, they're affecting him in reality too. After David left the office, I saw he was in an unusual condition. Art had a tremendous boost of energy that he could not understand either. I'm struggling with it myself; maybe I'm losing my mind too. Besides, the ground was shaking hard in the office, and all papers were spread around. We cannot ignore that."

David did not hear a word. He apparently was roaming in his own world of bewilderment. The latest events in his office had completely confused him. He could not understand what was happening. He was mesmerized by the glittering light inside his glass, which was merely the reflection of the lamp's light above their table. He could hear Essie's whisper in the background but was thinking about what Art had narrated just a while ago in the office. San Francisco in fire and blood? He saw Melody who was holding his hand. David heard his own name and awakened.

"David, where are you? Aren't you listening?" asked Melody.

"No, I'm sorry, did you say something?"

Melody continued, "Did you hear what Essie just said?"

Essie stared at David's muddled face for a few seconds. The waiter was approaching them, so with a shush to David, Essie implied they should not speak.

"What would you like to order please?" the waiter asked Essie.

"Just a coffee, dark please," Essie answered. The waiter's fake smile could not hide his disappointment.

Essie asked to see a picture on David's phone. "Did you save the snapshot of the detective on your phone?"

"Yeah, I have the recording," replied David.

"Can I see it?" said Essie.

David played the video showing Smith's face as the detective stood in front of Tech2AI's entrance, waiting for a response to his ringing the bell.

Essie said, "If I'm not mistaken, I saw him sitting in his car right here in front of this restaurant when I came in…" then he added some meaningless words. David asked instantly, "What are you saying, Essie?"

"Someone beating the raven with the stick." Essie had translated an expression from Farsi literally word by word into English, which essentially made no sense. Usually, Essie made jokes like that to amuse David and Melody. But at that moment, Essie's tasteless joke only added to David's confusion. Melody smiled to Essie so that he would not feel out of place with this untimely joke. But what Essie had translated for his friends meant that they were being watched by Smith who was sitting outside. Melody found it amusing now that she understood the joke and started giggling.

"It's impossible that he could have followed me. I was cautious, and I checked my tail all the time," David said uneasily.

Essie was still laughing with Melody over his joke, and once his giggle transformed into a smile, said: "Not you, but surely this lady was followed," and pointed to Melody.

Alarmed, Melody abruptly stopped laughing. With a concerned face, she looked at David and Essie. Then, she asked, "What are you guys talking about. What is it that I don't know?"

"Do you remember that I told you Art called me to go to his apartment because his apartment was broken into and trashed? Two police officers came there while I was with Art and Michael. Detective Smith knew about the *Bay Area Chronicle*'s article too. They found a Bible that wasn't Art's, but apparently marked a specific verse in it …"

Essie immediately cut David's words off and said, "Whoa, whoa, whoa, wait a second, what Bible? You never mentioned the Bible before," and knotted his eyebrows.

The more David described the story, the more the lines on Essie's face changed. David knew this state of Essie's mood: it was a reflection of the analysis in process in his brain. It was Essie's habit to toy with his mustache when he was deep in thoughts. But now he was flipping through his black mustache with fingers from both his hands while staring at the table. Melody, worried about Essie, held his shoulder and asked, "Are you okay, Essie?"

"Yeah, I just feel that nothing is normal around us anymore and we are getting into more than Art's meditation stories, which sound like fiction. What I'm saying is that… dangerous things are forming around us in the real world."

He turned to David and continued, "That's why we need to be more disciplined and get more organized."

David asked, "What do you mean? What should we do?"

"The first thing we should do is to create a specific communication system to exchange information between us. Art is in the center of the action. He needs to be in this systematic circle. Melody too," Essie said.

"Tell me more in details, please. What exactly do we have to do here?" David asked as he looked at Melody, noticing signs of anxiety on her face.

Essie responded, "One of us," he turned to David, "which is you, David, should update a messaging or communication app, informing all of us about events like this on a daily basis. Of course, we should all participate in this, but you need to sum them up. Art needs to inform us about everything that happens to him, everything that he thinks might relate to this issue. We have to become more sensitive to and skeptical about our surroundings."

Peace of mind was slightly discernible in David's face after he listened to what Essie said. David knew that Essie had gained much experience in such matters when he was fighting the regime in Tehran. Hence, having Essie in charge of security relaxed David somewhat.

David turned to Melody and sarcastically said, "Fortunately, we have someone who can teach us with his long experience in skepticism."

Melody, as a sign of protest, threw a napkin onto David's face and babbled a series of words in response. The napkin fell on the floor after striking her husband. Trying to grab the serviette from under the table, David bent down but could not reach it easily. He was struggling to reach it, stretching his arm out and ducking his head underneath the table. Suddenly David realized that both Essie and Melody were silent. When David brought his head up and sat back on his seat, he saw Simone, standing beside the table. Melody was frozen: she didn't expect to see her assistant at that time and at that place. It was obvious that Melody wanted to say something but she could not. David also did not say anything about Simone's presence. Finally, Melody asked, "Simone, what are you doing here? How did you know that I'm here? What happened?"

At that moment, Essie got up and stood beside Simone, held her hand, and said, "I asked Simone to come over and pick me up."

Melody's face flushed with anger. She could not digest the scene in front of her eyes. The smile on David's face disappeared when he turned to Melody and saw his wife's face. Melody said, "What? You and Essie? Since when are you two together? Had you already been together for some time? How long?"

David quickly realized the situation. He knew his wife perfectly well. He knew that Melody was distraught because she felt they kept this a secret. David was well aware of Melody's code of ethics which was exclusively personal. He knew his wife considered this type of secret a stab in the back. David jumped in, and holding Melody's hands said, "My darling, are you ready? It's too late; Essie and Simone are going somewhere. We'll have to go too."

Melody gathered herself, trying to keep her composure. Only David could recognize the state of his wife's mind. David stood up and waved to Essie, imploring him to leave without letting Simone see his signal. Essie expected some adverse reactions from Melody regarding Simone, but he had no idea Melody would be so out of line, to be this annoyed at seeing them together. Essie pulled on Simone's hand and said goodbye without hugging Melody. Helping Melody to recover, David asked, "Are you ready?" Then he jokingly, with a calm tone said, "Up until now I thought you get upset only if I keep secrets from you. It was only me that you cared about. It's strange to see your sensitivity toward others, my love."

Melody was silent. Though she was calmer than a few seconds ago, she avoided looking directly at David's eyes. David, waiting for Melody to gather her stuff off the table, continued to stand by her.

They walked toward the exit door with Melody walking ahead. David looked at Melody's elegant figure from behind. He had mixed feelings. He found himself too much in love with Melody. David became surprised by an emotional flood in himself. It was as if Melody was the cause of his heartbeat at that moment and the possibility of losing Melody's love to someone else gravely upset him. "It's impossible, it's not possible," said David to himself.

*When you, as a king of your world, in absolute security of your castle, think your queen loves only you, and this confidence exists because you deserve the integrity of that love, not because there are no rivals around, your attention to her love is reduced gradually. And only when you doubt the integrity of her love do your emotions erupt along with the kind of worry that conquers your mind and heart.*

Of course, David did not doubt Melody's love, but her excessive sensitivity to what had just happened made him think otherwise.

Outside, Melody was recovering from the attack that enveloped her just minutes ago. Sucking in the fresh air, she turned back and looked at David who was thinking and gazing down on the ground. She said, "Is your car here?"

"No, I walked here. Let's go in your car. Tomorrow, I'll manage a ride to the office."

David forgot to check if Detective Smith was still there. Before Melody pushed the start button in her SUV, David moved forward and placed his lips on hers, a move that surprised himself. While kissing her, holding her arms tightly, David felt an eruption of his unusual emotions again. The taste of that kiss was different. Then, he sat back in his seat, and neither of them exchanged any words until they reached home.

On their way to the house, David was thinking about Melody's past, and how they met. Melody drove the car all the way to the end of the driveway. The sky was red. Melody opened the garage door and went inside. David hesitantly stood outside. He wanted to meditate and shake different thoughts out of his mind before going in. David had a hectic day, which exhausted him both mentally and physically. He closed his eyes. Suddenly David heard Melody's screams from the inside. The garage door was still open. He quickly ran into the garage and then inside to find Melody. She was standing in the middle of the living room trembling with fear. The window to the backyard was open. To calm Melody, David rushed to her, hugged her, and asked, "Are you okay? What happened?"

"When I came in, I turned on the light. I saw a man run through the window and jump out into the backyard," said pale Melody, who was shivering severely.

David asked, "Were you able to see his face?"

"No, it happened very quickly. I saw his back. I think he had a mask."

David pulled out his phone to call but hesitated and stopped.

"Call the police," Melody said anxiously.

Still having his arms around her, David said: "No, it's unnecessary now." And put the phone back in his pocket. He embraced Melody again, wanting to merge with her.

# Chapter 13 – Council of Conservative Bishops

*Undisclosed location*

Twelve men dressed in black designer suits were sitting around a magnificent, dark knotted walnut wood conference table. The table's grandeur and the purity of its wood had given the large room a luxurious significance. It was as if Mother Nature had grown this specific walnut tree with its different knotted curves in a unique way to make this table suited for this very conference room. The grand chairs were equally plush. There were two doors, one in front and the other at the back of the conference room. A red velvet curtain covered the glass wall, hiding the conference room from the hallway.

The thirteenth man, His Excellency, wore a white suit to distinguish himself from the rest of the men. He had been leaning back in his chair, tilting his head down toward his chest, as if he was taking a nap. The untold code of conduct forbade the twelve men to make the slightest noise. They were sitting silently in their chairs.

Peter Jr., sitting in the comfortable chair on the right side of His Excellency, could not hide his unease. He felt out of place and did not understand why His Excellency insisted on his presence around the table with those prominent bishops. Peter Jr. looked to his right and then across the table, watching all bishops, one by one noticing their equally bewildered looks. Then he turned his face to His Excellency while putting his left hand on the table.

His Excellency slowly raised his head like a heavy statue and looked at Peter Jr.'s hand. The head of the bishop's sharp glare doubled Peter Jr.'s discomfort, to the point that he quickly withdrew his hand. Then, without looking into His Excellency's eyes, he hastily said, "The technician has arrived. He is here now."

Peter Jr. apparently had tried to keep his voice low, but the silence in the room and everyone's attention on him magnified his voice so loudly it was as if he had spoken through a loudspeaker. He was struck by the echo of his own voice. Peter Jr.'s boss bent his head down to his chest again and touched the cross in his hand. Peter Jr. also touched a golden cross that hung by a gold chain from his neck. Some around the table mimicked them, touching their crosses. His Excellency, without any movement in his seat, slowly lifted his head and said, "Tell him to come in."

Feeling relieved, Peter Jr. quickly jumped out of his chair. As he was instructed earlier by his boss, he dimmed the light of the conference room before bringing the guest in. In the conference room that was so bright a second ago, the bishops' faces became hardly recognizable.

It did not take more than two minutes before Peter Jr. and Sam entered the room. Sam's eyes took a while to adjust to the shadowy light. There was no additional seat available for the guest. Peter Jr. sat down on his chair and asked Sam to stand between him and the person to his right, guiding him with his hand. He did as he was instructed.

Sam looked around. As his eyes adjusted it was easier to observe the room and people sitting in their chairs, but he could still barely see their faces. He only saw men, mostly old, in chic suits, sitting around a carved oval conference table. Sam noticed the only man who was wearing a white suit sitting in his elegant chair at the head of the table. Sam stealthily noticed that the man in white suit authoritatively pointed to Peter Jr. to start.

Peter Jr. leaned forward on his seat and solemnly started his short introduction, "Dear honorable gentlemen, as you know, I urgently called this meeting upon His Excellency's suggestion to give you an overview of an important report that we have received from our contact in San Francisco. Because of the significance of this issue, and on the instructions of His Excellency, we asked him to come here and tell us his observations himself."

Then Peter Jr. nodded to Sam who was staring at him nervously. The droplets of sweat were descending on Sam's forehead, dripping onto his chubby cheeks, where, joining other droplets, they flooded his chin and neck. Sam wiped his chin and the top of his lip with the soft handkerchief in his hand. He then loosened his white-and-blue diagonal striped tie to let badly needed air into his lungs. Sam felt his entire body was soaked in wet under his white shirt and dark blue suit.

Sam opened his mouth to say something, but no sound came out. With a mild cough, he tried to pull the words out of his throat. But the words, disobeying his cough's command, created a severe struggle inside and brought more redness to his cheeks. Once again, he gathered all his forces, focused on his throat, and opened his mouth.

"As I wrote in my report, strange events have occurred in the company where I work. The company's chairman holds weekly discussion meetings, concluding with a meditation session. One of the attendees, Arthur Stevenson, who is a homosexual, claimed he has seen strange things while in a trance. At the end of the session, he fell to the floor, crying and screaming. He told everyone that he had gone to Sodom and been in contact with someone there."

One of the bishops on the other side of the table asked, "Are you sure it wasn't a show or entertainment? You said that the person was a homosexual. How about others, are they, like him, sinners?"

Sam answered, "No, I don't think it was a show, probably he was not aware of this place Sodom. And no, the other three people were not gay, they are straight."

Another bishop, who was sitting stiff and motionless asked, "Then what happened, where did that person go after that?"

"No one had gone anywhere as long as I was there. I was the first to leave."

The same man asked, "Why did you leave? It was important to stay and hear what they had to say."

"I was tired and didn't feel good plus I didn't think that they've had more serious subjects to talk about."

Another bishop—Sam could not discern where his voice was coming from—angrily replied, "You didn't think so?" And with a firm voice continued, "We do not send you there to think. The church was never in this much danger since the Renaissance. And you say that you are guessing no other serious conversation were there to report?"

His Excellency nodded to show his approval of the last statement. It was one of his famous lines in his presentation that he said in a speech a few years ago. "The church was never in this much danger since the Renaissance."

Sam looked at Peter Jr. and quickly glanced at His Excellency timidly and said, "I'm sorry."

Another voice asked, "How are these meetings conducted, and who are the other three?"

"One of them is David, company's owner and president. Usually, his wife attends and sits next to him. The third is David's longtime friend. He is an immigrant from the Middle East. His name is Essie."

Peter Jr. demanded: "Which country in the Middle East? What is his specific job in the company?"

"I think he came from Iran. He's a close friend of David's and his wife's for years. I never see him working on a specific project at the company. Once or twice, he got involved and contributed to an application's logic and design before development. He has a room at the end of the hall, and he is always busy researching there. His research, however, is not on technological issues. He doesn't have that much knowledge about computer programming."

Peter Jr. asked again, "Is he a Muslim? Is he close with the person in question?"

After brief contemplation, Sam said, "I don't think that he's a Muslim. He is an Iranian post-revolutionary in exile who fled his country. He's a mysterious and very quiet man who does not speak much to anyone. Art Stevenson has no real relationship with this guy. Once, he was talking with David, speaking against the Iranian regime and religions in general. I have gathered that he was participating in insurgencies years ago ..."

"That is enough," said Peter Jr. whose tone indicated boredom. "Enough was said about that foreign Muslim; tell us more about that deviant guy."

Sam said, "There's not much to say about him. He's a normal young man ..."

Peter Jr., who had asked the most questions so far, interrupted Sam and asked emphatically, "Normal? Since when a sinner, who has sexual engagement with his own gender, considered normal?"

After talking with an obvious streak of anger in his tone, Peter Jr. threw a sharp look to his right. Sam who, like butter was melting under a laser gaze by bishops, especially, His Excellency, lowered his head and looked down in shame.

Sam was shocked by Peter Jr.'s reaction and replied with dismay, "My apologies, by normal, I meant no significant aspects. He is not even that special in his line of work. Once, I advised David to fire him. I don't know why the company owner is interested in him. It was the first time he attended David's weekly meditation sessions."

Raising his right hand, His Excellency declared the adequacy of Sam's presence and with a look at Peter Jr., ordered him to escort Sam out of the conference room. Peter Jr. stood up and showed Sam the way out. They both went out from the back door. They turned to the left and walked through a relatively narrow corridor. After a short distance, Peter Jr. stopped and opened the door on his right into a room. He went inside, guiding Sam to follow him. Inside the empty room, there was only one ordinary wooden chair at the center.

"Wait here for me to come back," said Peter Jr. with a friendlier tone than just seconds ago.

Sam said, "If I may, I have to go. Tomorrow I have to be at work early in the morning. I have a plane to catch in three hours."

"Wait for me to come back; don't worry about the ticket. We're going to arrange your return. We have a few guaranteed seats available on every flight in the United States. If one is not available, the airlines will kick someone off the plane for us."

Worried, Sam looked around in that empty room where he was standing and said, "Okay, I'll be waiting."

In the conference room until the return of Peter Jr., who managed to come back quickly, absolute silence was an unspoken rule. Peter Jr. returned to his seat. His Excellency hesitantly leaned forward after a few seconds, put his two hands on the table, shifting his weight slowly, stood up, and said, "We have arrived in a new era. Send this message to all your subordinates and church believers in your congregations. The mission that had been given to Jesus Christ from Abraham is now on our shoulders. We have to be prepared. Satan is at our door, threatening our roots. In this battle between God and Satan, the devil has targeted Jesus Christ. We're all in danger—Judaism, Christianity, and ..." with mumbling, he hesitated to name the third religion, "and those who claim having inherited Abraham's divinity. We all know that, except us, the rest, even those so-called Christians, are not saved. No matter how much they claim otherwise, it is Jesus who will eventually succeed in all."

Then His Excellency made the sign of the cross. And so did all bishops around the table.

# Chapter 14 – Samuel

*San Francisco – Tech2AI*

Sam was inside the main hall, his eye on David's office. He supposedly was monitoring two programmers who were working on a project. Sam positioned himself so he could have the best view of David's office while trying to inspect various projects. Since returning from the bishops' meeting, he had not been able to get any more detailed information about the ongoing meditation meetings. He was under pressure specifically from Peter Jr. That was not a pleasant situation, and he was not at all happy about it, especially as he had not been well recently.

For the last few days, Sam had thought about making an appointment to see a doctor, but his workload and writing reports for Peter Jr. kept him from picking up the phone and calling the doctor's office. Sam got up every morning with unbearable pain, a strange burning sensation all over the soles of his feet. It was as if he was walking on needles; after a couple of hours, however, the burning sensation would subside mysteriously. He had searched online for the cause or the cure but had not found any definite answer. The persistent problem worried Sam, causing him to be hesitant to start anything new in his life. He was not the type of person to like new adventures to begin with, but his reluctance became worse after his recent physical condition.

Sam was very lonely: he had no one in his personal life. At age forty-eight, he lived alone in a one-bedroom apartment in San Francisco. Sam had never married. He believed that he was not a virgin, but in reality, he had never experienced sex with anyone. Sam had never been in a relationship as an adult, whether with the opposite or same sex, that could lead to a love story. All his dating attempts, including those dates who were introduced to him by acquaintances or rare accidental encounters, had failed. His religious beliefs forbade him to have sex in exchange for money.

Sam was the only child in his family. At the age of twelve, when he realized that his playdate was a girl, he fell in love instantly, a state that he later considered his first love. Before the big revelation, Sam thought that his playmate in the church was a boy. But it was all lost when, after that summer, the girl's family moved away and he did not see her again. Sam had never forgotten about that experience. In his adulthood, however, he did not seriously pursue anyone he was attracted to due to his shy nature and stocky, nerdy looks. His chubby red cheeks made him too embarrassed and insecure to approach anyone of the opposite sex. Instead, Sam devoted his whole time to religious and school studies. He now had gotten accustomed to his loneliness, refusing to participate on those rare occasions when he would receive invitations to parties.

Years had passed quickly. Now, with thinner hair that hardly covered his pink scalp, making his face look more round, he appeared almost 65. Sam—short, stocky, and soon to be bald—became slower and less active in his daily routine. He was avoiding fast-moving maneuvers. Once Essie jokingly asked him, "With your body language and your soft speaking manner, you'd have been well suited to work in the field of diplomacy. Why did you choose technology?" Sam only smiled in David's presence but did not like Essie's jokes at all.

Sam never liked Essie and would have avoided him whenever he could, as if this stranger who came from the other side of the globe suffered from a contagious disease such as leprosy. Sam was careful not to bump into Essie, and if he was forced to exchange things like paper or food, he avoided touching him. In case Sam had any contact with the Middle Eastern man, he immediately washed his hands with soap and water.

Sam always wondered why Melody felt so close to Essie. Why did she laugh at his lame jokes? Why did she always kiss him on social occasions? Sam could never understand why David would allow Essie to be so close to Melody. Sometimes in the Wednesday meetings, Sam would find himself staring at Melody longer than he should have. Sam liked this attractive, overjoyed, and energetic woman. At first, Sam convinced himself that he did not have any feelings for his boss's wife. But over the time, unleashing his imagination, Sam not only dreamed out but also satisfied his needs while awake with Melody's images. Sam had framed a photo of Melody and himself in a Christmas party and put it on the lamp stand by his bed. At that end-of-year party at the restaurant, Melody took pictures with all the employees, including Sam. She had her arm around his neck, kissing his cheek.

Melody had filled the place that the twelve-year-old girl from his childhood had left open. The story in Sam's mind later changed so that Melody was initially the same girl he played with, loved, and lost in the church, and now she would return to his arms if she found out that he was the same boy.

Sam would wait for Melody every night. He knew her schedule in the evenings. After she finished work, Melody would come to David's office to go home or to a restaurant with her husband and Essie. When Sam felt overcome with the impossibility of being with Melody, he disappeared from the world into the darkness of his lonely apartment, sitting on his sofa, staring at the reflected street light on his wall for hours.

Although Melody was a few years older than Sam, he thought she could be an ideal spouse who would have made him happy in all aspects of life. Sadly, Sam also knew that he would not win Melody's heart if something happened to David. Essie undoubtedly was a serious competitor. But in his imagination, if such a day came, Sam would take Melody's hand and leave this forsaken city for good. Sam did not know where, but even if he had to go to a deserted island to be alone with Melody, he would do that in a heartbeat. Sam despised this city. He hated San Francisco.

But the Baptodist Church, to whose cause Sam had devoted himself, had made other plans for his life. Since the mid-1990s, with the advent of the computer world, the Conservative Church, with the eloquent guidance of His Excellency, decided to prepare itself for human intervention in the critical war against creation. Sam was one of the earliest scouts recruited to be deployed to Silicon Valley. When the artificial intelligence phenomenon became the first word in Silicon Valley, the Council of Churches, in line with the fundamentalist viewpoint, was proud of the decision it had made nearly 20 years earlier. The council knew that in order to control the process and the growth of technology, it had to have the knowledge, and in order to gain that knowledge it had to penetrate the field. Hence, by choosing the best young people among believers and providing a high level of training in cutting-edge technology, the church slowly infiltrated into the heart of large companies, especially those that were active in developing artificial intelligence.

Sam's report on a few sessions of meditation that were the source of published material in *Bay Area Chronicle* convinced the council that they had planted one of their best in the most important, though not the largest, artificial intelligence company.

Apparently, neither the article nor reports on what was happening in Tech2AI had anything to do with the technology and AI. But the central council, and especially His Excellency, believed that the published piece and reports on Art, despite their non-technological appearances, were definitely related to AI technology.

***

Sam could see inside David's office that his boss, Art, Essie, and Michael were talking but he couldn't hear what they were saying. As Sam was monitoring ongoing projects and tests in the main hall, he had no chance of joining the discussion in David's office. Sam saw that Essie had an eye on the main hall where the coders were busy. He could not figure out if Essie was looking at them or just staring while he was listening to others. It was frustrating for Sam that regardless of his many attempts to get information, going to the office for different reasons, he was not successful. As soon as Sam walked into the office, they refrained from talking.

They waited until Sam left the room. With a face that was a mixture of confusion and curiosity, David asked, "Who is this guy, do you know him, Art? Where did the story come from?" Art was holding Michael's hand, sitting next to him while watching his phone.

"I know him," answered Michael, and while glancing at Art with a guilty feeling, he continued, "His name is Tim. He is an old friend of mine, a journalist, son of the famous lawyer, Henry. He heard the story from me, he once came to the bar, and I told him the story. I should have known better. I am sorry; I had no idea he was going to publish it." Art looked at Michael while he was talking.

"Several other papers and websites have published it too. The story became viral and shared on social media very quickly," Essie said in a relaxed manner.

David turned to Essie and said, "Since this morning, a few journalists have called here and asked for an interview. Apparently, it made some noise. Why do stories like this become favored by so many? Do you think breaking into Art's apartment was connected to this? Why did the police follow us, instead of pursuing the intruders? Melody was so scared."

Essie asked immediately, "Where is Melody now? How is she?"

"She's okay. She's gone to work," said David.

"What is obvious," Essie said, "as I said before, something is happening around us that is becoming more and more complicated. There are many unknown issues, but we cannot wait and let them attacks us. Furthermore, we don't know where we're being targeted from and why. They might target one of us soon. We should be ready."

David and Michael started to talk simultaneously, but both stopped to allow the other to speak. David said, "Go ahead, Michael." But Michael stayed quiet as a sign of respect to him and with his hand gesture asked David to continue.

David said immediately, "What can we do? We still do not know any individual or individuals who are assaulting us or why. Essie proposed to use a communication system among us to exchange all info. What else can we do?"

Essie said, "I also thought a lot after I heard what happened in David's house. If the events that happened to you and Art are connected, we're facing an organization or people who are planning systematically. Therefore, we have to work systematically, too. We need to be organized, perhaps designating a secret place to gather. Another thing we can do to help guarantee our security is that we should raise the issue in the public arena. In this way, we'll increase the cost of attacks for our enemies."

David, nodding in agreement with Essie's proposals, interrupted him and said, "How can we trust any of the reporters to make this issue public? Can we do it with control? I mean, is it in our power and on what pretexts?"

"Yes, trust and control matters, so we strictly will work with Tim, Michael's friend..."

Michael jumped in disagreement and corrected, "Former friend—don't count much on this, I will never talk to him again."

Essie urged Michael and asked, "But you need to understand that this is our only chance to know our attackers. Believe me. I have experience in these matters. When an issue becomes public, it at least benefits us to show where we stand. And yes, the risk is that the attackers will increase their activities, but we no longer stand alone. Luckily, now we have found good support through this article and its echoes on the weblogs. But most importantly, the attention of the gay community has been raised in our favor. I believe we have to add Tim to our group. Even I think we need to publish Art's latest vision and make it a red flag. By doing this, we warn people about the future of San Francisco and even the entire country, with regards to the issues that these days are happening everywhere..."

Michael jumped in with a tone in his voice that was a mixture of anger and discomfort. He said, "Don't even think about it. I won't talk to him, ever. Think about another way to raise the public awareness. You said that you were considering other ways. I threw him out of the bar last time and said that I no longer wanted to see him…"

Art was only observing their conversation. David stopped Michael calmly and told him, "You don't have to ask him. I think one of those reporters who left me a message was from the Chronicle. I can call him. I think we must all agree with Essie. He is more experienced in these matters than all of us. I've heard stories from him about years of fight and politics."

Michael hung his head down, and after David finished, he said, "I don't have a problem if you want to invite him, but do not expect me to be ..."

Before Michael finished his plea, Art took Michael's left hand in his right hand while staring at him romantically. Michael looked at Art's eyes silently, then looked down again.

"We all need you, Michael, but most of all, I need you to be with me, by my side ..." Art said. "After a short pause, Art continued, "don't worry about anything."

"We're facing something that you may not have fully understood, my friends," Essie said. "This is an actual phenomenon in the realm of reality." He paused for a second and continued, "I myself, don't believe that I'm saying this, but what happens to Art is not a dream."

Essie saw surprise in all three listeners and continued, "Art, tell everyone yourself what had changed in you." Then Essie looked at everyone and emphasized, "No one can understand how real this phenomenon is, no one but Art."

Art, unprepared and shy, was not ready to talk, but he was forced to gather his mind and himself completely, mumbling a few words and finally said, "Ah ... Essie is right. The first time I saw those scenes in meditation ..." At this moment, Art turned to Michael and held his hand again. "The same night that I met Michael, I thought I was probably in a dream, and the energy eruption in my body might've been influenced by the state of trance that comes from…for example from a hypnosis session. But the next sessions, especially the last one, made me certain that some real changes have in fact happened to me."

David was so thrilled that could not stay calm in his chair. He immediately asked, "What changes? Tell us more precisely—what changes are you talking about?"

David's excitement to finally find answers to his endless questions would not give Art any chance to reply. He had no patience to wait for even a second to receive Art's response.

When David finally paused, Art first tried to say something to explain, but after saying a few words which sounded like, "I…hum …just …," he stopped. Instead, Art brought his hand under Essie's chair, grabbed the lower part of one leg, and effortlessly lifted it from the ground with Essie still sitting on it. He held it for few seconds without any discomfort. David's eyes popped out. Michael gripped the handles of his chair with two hands as if it was he who was suspended in the air, instead of Essie. Essie, who was sitting on his chair about two feet above the ground, became uneasy, but he did not reveal any surprise on his face. From the top, Essie looked into the main hall where programmers were busy. His eyes were looking for Sam, but he could not find him. Essie then said to Art, "Okay, that's enough. Put me down."

David said, "It's fantastic, it's unbelievable. How is it possible? Where did you get this power from?"

When David had become a question machine again, Michael asked, "Essie, how did you find out that Art has changed?"

Essie's chair was on the floor now. While he was repositioning himself, he said, "I did not know this much, but after the last meditation, Art burned me badly," He raised his right hand and showed a mark on his wrist. "This was caused by an accidental touch with Art's hand. It is a kind of burn that happens when stored static energy is released in contact between plastic or metal and human skin. Touching Art that night was a powerful electric shock."

After a brief pause, Essie continued, "I guess this little performance is a small drop in the vast ocean of his powers and the change that happened to him, right Art?"

Art only nodded a few times. Essie went on, "Now you understand how important this issue is. Knowing Art's power, now we can rule out the coincidental nature of these attacks around us. We have to keep our guard up and constantly evaluate events by understanding connections between them. We have to be ahead of our opponents. If not ahead, we should be not too far behind. Michael, you must believe that the greatest danger is not for us, but is for Art. He is the main target of those attacks."

This time, Michael stretched out his arm and held Art's hand. Both looked romantically at each other for a moment, and David noticed their heads were turning to kiss each other. David stood up and closed the shutters of the wide window.

Sam was sitting in a chair at the far side of the window from outside, facing the wall as if he was checking his phone, but in fact, he was filming the entire episode—all that happened in David's office. When David closed the shutters, Sam pulled himself away from the window, stood up, and quickly went to the restroom. He locked the unit door inside the men's room and took out his phone, turning the screen on and putting its volume on silence mode. Sam tapped on a video file and watched the scene where Art had raised the chair on which Essie was still sitting. Then, by tapping on the sharing icon, he brought up the Telegram app and sent the video file to a user account called GDNN. Sam waited until the entire clip was uploaded. Before completing the upload, he flushed the toilet.

Outside the restroom, he bumped into Essie and dropped his phone. They both panicked. Sam's face was more flushed than his usual red color. Essie bent down and picked Sam's phone off the floor and looked at it. Essie saw the telegram's application and the file that had just completed uploading. No snapshot or preview was showing, and the image indicated only that it was a regular file. Essie stretched his arm and offered the phone back to Sam. Essie was astonished by Sam's nervousness and said, "I'm sorry, I didn't think anybody was here. By the way, Telegram is a great app, and it is one of the few apps that are not yet filtered in Iran. This app has several million users in Iran."

Sam, who had not yet recovered from the shock, just snatched his phone back. Sam could not come up with something to say to Essie. He had not heard a word of Essie's last few sentences at all. What he heard was Essie talking about an application.

Sam said, "Excuse me," and bypassed Essie and went toward the sink to wash his hands. Surprised by Sam's weird behavior, Essie went inside the restroom.

# Chapter 15 – King Bera

*Sodom territory – King's Palace*

Art's heart was now palpitating so strongly he could hear the sound of its beats in his left ear. The stony steps under his feet felt firm. He slowly started climbing the steps one by one. He did not comprehend how he had come to be in that place. He hesitated for a moment and looked up. He saw a slightly opened door at the highest point, from which a little sliver of light was illuminating the dark area where he had been standing moments ago. Art turned back and looked down to see a space slightly below, a relatively large area with barrels arranged in a row against the wall. At the other end of the area was an unknown pathway. Art was surprised that he had not noticed the barrels at the bottom of the stairs, which was at ground level. A voice, coming from the above, caught his attention.

Curious, Art climbed the stairs. He peeped with one eye through a one-inch opening in the door. It seemed there was a corridor on the other side. He realized that the place underneath must have been a basement. With the palm of his hands, Art pushed the heavy door slowly and craned his head out to look left and right. The corridor was empty. He heard sounds coming from the right. Art tried to open the door fully, but the loud screeching from the door hinge prevented him. He opened the door just enough to squeeze his body into the corridor. "I have to decide," Art asked himself. "Which side should I choose? Why am I here?"

Suddenly, he remembered. He had been on the same path several times in the past. Art did not recall how he had arrived in the dark area of that basement. Forcing his mind to remember the past was useless, and it only diminished his energy, forcing his mind into a loop, circling the path of dreams and nightmares. His fear of not being able to rescue himself from that loop in the semi-visible depth of his mind paralyzed him. It took him far from brightness to the shadows, where it was hard for him to find a way out. And now he felt like falling into that whirlpool.

Luckily, a loud cry jolted his mind, and Art was awakened back to the moment. Two armored guards, armed with swords, noticed Art. They pointed him out to each other and rushed to attack him. Focusing on his mental power, Art found no trace of fear or anxiety inside himself. He closed his eyes for a moment, and when he opened them again, the two soldiers in front of him were drawing their swords out of their sheaths. Art stretched out his right arm. With the palm of his hand, he signaled them to stop. Suddenly, both guards were frozen on the spot. Although vigilant, the guards were perplexed that they had no power to move. Art walked passed them toward the end of the hallway. He reminded himself to be present at all times, to avoid plunging into his thoughts and memories. His inner wisdom told him just to observe and stay vigilant and to do nothing more.

When he reached the end of the corridor, he found another hallway off to the right. On the left, the direction he chose, was a large area. Art looked back.

No one was following him, as the two guards apparently were still in a frozen state. He stepped forward and saw a large platform inside a chamber which included a luxurious royal seat. A ballroom with a stage featured tall columns and statues. It linked to the end of the corridor through which Art had entered earlier. When he approached the royal throne, he noticed a hand on the right armchair holding a grail.

There were little burn patches on the fingers that were twisting around the grail, which contained a red liquid. When Art stepped forward, the man sitting on the throne turned and stared at Art in astonishment. Art immediately recognized him: he had a curly lock of hair on his forehead, a thin mustache, and a sparse beard. A few healed wounds were visible on man's face. The man instantly stood to face Art and demanded, "You ... I know you, who are you?"

Art knew he was the same man whom he had seen through the slot initially in his first visit to Sodom, the same man who had seen him in the past and somehow connected with Art. But more importantly, Art realized that he understood what he was saying. Now, he could answer David's question regarding communication with people in his visits to Sodom.

"My name is Arthur; we have seen each other before."

The person in front of Art was silent. Art thought the man did not understand him. While Art was absorbed in his thoughts, wondering about why he understood that man and the same did not happen for him, the man answered, "Yes, I remember, in the cellar and on the day of the plot. I thought I was losing my mind. My companion in the cellar did not see what I saw, and then you disappeared. It seemed that you do not know me. Where did you come from? What are you doing here? How did you cross the guards' barrier? It does not seem like you are with conspirators."

Growing more comfortable now that mutual comprehension was not an issue, Art replied, "I am not from around here. I came a long way. I guess here is Sodom, and no, I'm not a conspirator. I have no bad intentions."

"I see through your words that you are not an inhabitant of the great Sodom or our allies, neither belong to a territory..."

The man's speech was interrupted by heavy steps that were approaching quickly from the very path that Art had taken. The two guards, now free from their paralyzed state, arrived at the platform, holding their swords. The guards were following another man, the warrior in command. The man in the throne raised his hand as a sign of peace and said, "There is no threat here."

The head of the guards, breathing hard, gazed at Art and told his master, "Forgive me, Your Highness, we did not see how this man came here. We will remove him immediately."

Art, excited and pleased, said to himself: "So now others can see me too."

"No, I know him … that is, I do not know him exactly, but I saw him before. I am safe here, leave us; I want to talk to this young man a little longer."

His Highness then raised his hand, silencing the commander and pointed the way out. Then looking at Art, he introduced himself, "I'm Bera, king of Sodom. When and where did you come from? What is your purpose?" To which Art replied:

"It's a long story …"

# Chapter 16 – Mark

*The United States Disciplinary - Barracks – Kansas*

The guard turned the key, opened the cell, then looked at the two inmates inside, one sitting in his chair and the other on the bed. "Mark Stevenson, you have a visitor," he announced impatiently, waiting to put handcuffs on the prisoner.

Mark looked at the other inmate surprisingly then sluggishly stood up and asked, "Now? Visitor?" and exited the cell.

The way up to the visitation room, Mark thought about what had been happening and who came to visit him now. All these years, his sister, who lived in another state, was the only person who came once a year to visit him. Mark had no recollection of anyone else wanting to visit him, and, of course, he had no expectation either.

When they reached the visitation room, the guard took off Mark's handcuffs then directed him to go in. There was a man in a dark suit with a gray tie sitting in one of the chairs with his briefcase on the table.

Mark cautiously walked towards the man who stood up when he entered the room. The man stretched out his arm for a handshake, and said, "Mr. Stevenson, I'm Joseph Grigard, attorney at J & J law firm," and sat down again in his chair.

Without any words, Mark shook the attorney's hand and sat down in a chair, facing him from the other side of a table. Without hesitation the lawyer informed him, "Our firm has taken your case to help the defense counsel, and after a review, we found many discrepancies during your trial. The trial counsel's negligence during the investigation and interrogation as well as the testimony of witnesses could help the defense counsel reopen your case. You have been tried in general court-martial, and you have the rights to retain civilian counsel. We would like to request a retrial; of course, your consent is needed. You must sign these official forms to reopen your case."

The lawyer opened his briefcase without showing any distinguishable emotion or any kind of excitement. He then took out some folders and put them on the table.

Mark's surprised face clearly illustrated his struggle to comprehend the lawyer's words. The conundrum of this firm's interest in helping him occupied his mind, and the lawyer's explanations did not help solve it. After watching him bringing out the sheets from his suitcase with utter calmness and formal indifference, Mark demanded, "Who hired you?"

"Our direct client is an organization called In Search of Lord LLC. The entire cost of the reopening of the case and possible future retrial are fully covered by this client."

"And why, why do they want to help me?"

"I do not know about their relationship with you, and frankly I'm not interested to know that. I was assigned to this case merely to serve as the head attorney to re-open your case."

The attorney's cold manner infuriated Mark to the point of explosion. Enraged, Mark subdued his anger, and with calm but trembling voice asked, "Team of lawyers? I don't know this institution that hired you. Why after seven years are some people suddenly interested in this? I'm not going to sign anything; everyone knows that there is no free lunch. Until I know what their motives and interests are in my case are, I absolutely won't sign these papers."

His words echoed in the visitation room. Mark stood up to end the conversation. The lawyer calmly and carefully put the papers back inside his fat black briefcase the same way that he took the papers out. Then he said, "I told you I have no idea about the incentives, but if I were you, I wouldn't reject their offer. What do you have to lose but years in prison? Do you have any other hope? However, in case you change your mind, contact me at this number to expedite your case as soon as possible."

With these his last words, Joseph Grigard handed his business card to Mark who still seemed baffled by this unexpected proposal at that time of night.

Mark took the card and walked back toward the guard who was standing at the door. Only after taking a few steps, Mark heard the lawyer's voice, "In the meantime, if you change your mind, I want you to take time to recall the incident and the details of the day that led to your court-martial. The smallest details can play a significant role in the reversal of a sentence that leads to your freedom."

When Mark heard the lawyer's last comment, he paused briefly but did not turn his head back to look at him. He continued walking toward the guard to have his handcuffs put back on. He felt rays of thrill all over his spine. The word freedom, which was spat out of the attorney's mouth, had created a tumult in his mind. "Is it possible that I could get out of here one day?"

One question was gnawing at his mind, though: "Who were these people and what is their purpose to send a lawyer here?" He wished to end this nightmare, but what would be the payback?

He could not have access to the internet certainly at this hour of the night. He thought to call his sister and ask her to search online for the institution's name, In Search of Lord LLC, but he put off the idea because of the two hours' time difference in California. He had never initiated a phone conversation with his sister in the seven years of his imprisonment. Mark's hope to live outside the prison wall had been resurrected by the lawyer's visit that night.

Mark could not shut his eyes that night. He vividly remembered the scene of that nightmare seven years ago. No part of it was forgotten, not even tiny details. He could see victims' faces over and over again and his own wicked action, like a film that was repeatedly reeling before his eyes. Almost immediately afterward, he had come to himself and regretted his deed instantly. It was too late; the trigger was pulled. At that moment he felt as if it was not him in charge of his body and mind.

It was two years since he was transferred to Kandahar from Bagram Airfield. In command of a battalion in the U.S. Army, Mark exhibited self-courage and boldness beyond human ability, performing very harsh operations. The Taliban's activities had been increasing in recent months and rebuffing their unexpected attacks required more information from local people. Lack of familiarity with the region and the impossibility of contacting indigenous people without a translator had pressured not only Mark but the entire U.S. military command in Afghanistan. Several interpreters who had recently been recruited and employed in the States by contractors and deployed to Afghanistan only added to the complexity of the situation. Mark had repeatedly requested an interpreter in Pashto, a dialect used by Taliban and people in southern Afghanistan. But those who were deployed as interpreters, after passing successful examinations of the Pashto language in the United States, knew only Farsi and English. To use new interpreters, the communication still needed an interlocutor for the final translation between Pashto and Farsi.

Ghader was one of those rare translators who mastered all three languages—Pashto, Farsi, and English. He was an educated young man who grew up in Kabul, the capital of Afghanistan. His father was a deputy of agriculture ministry in Najibullah's government, the last

Soviet-backed president before the withdrawal of the Red Army from Afghanistan. After the collapse of Najibullah's government in 1992, large cities in Afghanistan plummeted into chaos wrought by various Mujahedin forces that had previously united and fought against the Soviet Union's military intervention. Almost Ghader's entire family was killed in the bombardment of Kabul, which was carried out by Gulbuddin Hekmatyar's Islamic Party forces, influenced by the Muslim Brotherhood ideology. Gulbuddin Hekmatyar was supposed to accept the prime minister position after the collapse of Najibullah's communist government, in unison with other Mujahedin forces known as the Peshawar Accord. Intrigued and pushed by Pakistan, Hekmatyar opposed the Peshawar Accord and decided to take over the entire government. With intelligence and military support from Pakistan, Hekmatyar killed thousands of people in Kabul by launching rocket and missile attacks in the capital. Through a family friend, before Najibullah's ousting from power in April 1992 and the onset of civil war in Afghanistan, Ghader's father managed to send him to a powerful northern commander, Ahmad Shah Massoud.

Despite the massive bombardment of Kabul, Gulbuddin Hekmatyar could not capture the capital, and the disappointed Pakistani army redirected its resources and capabilities to strengthen the Taliban. In 1996, the Pakistani-backed Taliban managed to defeat other Mujahideen forces and capture Kabul and two-thirds of Afghanistan. Mazar-e-Sharif, under the control of Ahmad Shah Massoud in northern Afghanistan, was one of the few areas that were protected from the Taliban's incursion and, thus, Ghader was able to remain in a safe area.

After the U.S. attacks to Afghanistan in December 1991 and the exodus of the Taliban from the capital and many strategic areas, Ghader quickly embarked for U.S. military bases. He passed various exams and security challenges and was recruited by the U.S. Army. Ghader's adventuresome reputation in helping various military operational units even reached the different Pentagon circles in the States. Each U.S. military division and battalion commander in

Afghanistan had called for Ghader's transfer to the units under his command.

It was two years since Ghader's release and transfer to the States had been approved by U.S. military commanders both in Afghanistan and the United States, but a shortage of quality interpreters in the region postponed his discharge. Mark had been able to gain knowledge on local movements, Afghan groups, and political forces mostly because of his talks with Ghader. Reports and materials from the army's internal channels were no match for the quantity and quality of information that Mark had received from Ghader. Mark was so dependent on Ghader's ability to obtain the local enemy's whereabouts that he would not even plan for operations without consulting with him first. It was through Ghader that Mark found out the Iranian regime helped the Taliban in transferring their troops, despite a great deal of propaganda and reports. The lack of a clear understanding of Middle East and policies in Washington had dampened the military's command abilities in Afghanistan. But Mark was able to avoid many disasters with the help of indigenous news and, in particular, Ghader to understand what was happening on the ground. In the course of his close cooperation with the interpreter in every situation, Mark was fascinated by the integrity and loyalty of Ghader to the coalition forces. A special bond grew between the two. Ghader became the son that Mark had lost years ago.

A constant recollection of that event was the punishment that Mark imposed on himself. But after a while, he started to feel a numbness. He lost his ability to inflict self-harm by remembering that damn night. Like the scene of a movie, he could see pulling the trigger in slow motion. His finger pulled the trigger twice.

Later, Mark remembered which one was killed first. They were together, under the same blanket. No precision was needed. Their heads and faces were attached on the lips, kissing. Mark did not need to move his Sig-Sauer handgun too much. Bang, and immediately two inches to the right, and a second boom.

Everyone was asleep in the shelter, but Mark was awake. He had had a maximum of two or three hours of sleep at night. He was thinking about the situation of his forces in the upcoming battles. The Taliban had increased its presence. Mark's sleeping area was away from the soldiers' barracks. He always would go to the barracks to check everything in the middle of the night. When he stepped in through the doorway, his attention was drawn to a rustle coming from one of the beds. He saw a shadow on the left and in the middle of the shelter. He first thought that an animal found its way in. He opened the gun's cover and pulled his Sig-Sauer out of the holster. He moved ahead slowly and reached near the bed where the sound was raised. Below the blanket, he saw two moving bodies. The little motions underneath the cover were similar to the slow movement of arms and hands. The blood rushed to Mark's face. With the left hand, he pulled the blanket off and without knowing why he pointed his handgun at them.

He saw two men, kissing each other. In the dark, he immediately recognized both, their now terrified faces. Ghader and Jonathan. They were staring at Mark, who was now pointing the gun at their heads. Mark's whole being was boiling within his chest, and his heart was pumping fire through his face. There, in the bed, was Jonathan, a 22-year-old man who had been deployed to the unit less than a month ago. It was hard for Mark to comprehend what he was witnessing. Mark had fought to keep Ghader in his unit. And now he was seeing Ghader with a young newcomer in bed. This was unthinkable for Mark. A handgun was still pointing toward two living targets, like two immobilized rabbits, staring into snake's eyes. He pulled the trigger. Bang, bang, and everyone in the barrack sprang with horror. When they turned on the lights, soldiers witnessed Mark kneeling on the floor beside a bed with sheets soaked in blood.

***

His Excellency was reading the court-martial transcript in which Mark received a sentence of 40 years. He reached the part on the transcript where Mark confessed to a double murder on record in trial counsel's presence.

Trial counsel: "You want us to believe that you shot and killed the two innocent men under your command in Afghanistan because you went mad. Your defense counsel says that insanity was the reason. Tell us, what were you thinking at that moment?"

Mark: "I wasn't thinking about anything."

Trial counsel: "You did not think about anything, or you don't know what you were thinking about, or you don't remember what you were thinking about?"

Mark: "I don't know. I don't know."

Trial counsel: "What did you see when you took the blanket off the victims?"

Mark: "The Afghan interpreter of the unit and one of the new soldiers in our battalion."

Trial counsel: "What was it they were doing? The scene that you saw, please explain."

Mark: "I have already told you guys, they were in bed under a blanket together doing god knows what they shouldn't do. They were sleeping together."

Trial counsel: "Do you mean they were already asleep?"

Mark: "No, they were awake."

Trial counsel: "What were they doing?"

Mark: "They were kissing."

Trial counsel: "Well, what did they do after they saw you?"

Brand: "Nothing."

Trial counsel: "What does that mean? They just kept on kissing each other?"

Mark: "No, they both looked at me."

Trial counsel: "Well, then, what did you see in their faces, horror, embarrassment, or what?"

Mark: "No, I…I looked at them but, I… saw Art, my son."

Trial counsel: "And you shot them."

Mark: "Yes."

Trial counsel: "Twice."

Mark: "Yes."

Trial counsel: "On whose face did you see your son?"

Brand: "Both."

Trial counsel: "And you shot twice."

Mark: "Yes."

His Excellency put the copy of the court transcript on the table and thought to himself, "He shot Arthur, twice."

# Chapter 17 – Essie

*San Francisco – Restaurant*

Essie's behavior was odd. Simone realized during the short time she had been dating Essie that some of his acts seemed even more out of place. She could see that Melody was the reason Essie was timid the night she showed up in the restaurant. Simone also did not understand Melody's reaction at the time.

In fact, Melody was not the only one who had been shocked that night in the restaurant; David became uneasy and surprised by the awkward situation as well. David had expressed his dissatisfaction with a short comment, but Simone quietly observed Essie, who intentionally refused to hold her hand while leaving the restaurant. She wanted to believe that perhaps Essie was too shy to show affection in front of his friends.

Simone, a young, vibrant girl, was trying not to rock the boat about Essie's reserved and coy manner. She understood that it was hard for him to kiss or hug any girl in public. Simone demonstrated a level of understanding regarding Essie's timid behavior about the display of affection in public. A girl as young as Simone considered his social manner in the context of cultural difference.

Essie had spent most of his life outside of Iran. Notably, in the past 25 years, he had lived in California as a U.S. citizen. Essie had his own particular behavior in response to various phenomena that did not even resemble those of other Iranian Americans. Essie could not believe the reality of Simone's friendship and affection—it was like a new breeze on his old dried soul. After separating from Soheila, his ex-wife, it seemed unlikely that he would be with another woman again, let alone experience any intimacy. After he was assured that Simone's attention and glances at him were not just the usual curiosity, many assumptions formed in his mind. Usually, Essie would discuss his hypotheses about any occurrences with David, his buddy with whom he had shared everything for almost 20 years. Essie could not name a reason why this time he kept Simone a secret. Essie had even shared his most private matter involving his ex-wife with David, whom he loved like a brother.

Like everything else in his life, Essie tried to analyze Simone's motivation to date and possibly become romantically involved with a man about 20 years her senior. The first reasonable possibility was his close relationship with Melody and David. This could give Simone an opportunity to be closer to her boss. In Essie's calculation, that could have hurt Simone; it was a double-edged sword. Indeed, Melody's reaction to the newly formed friendship between Essie and Simone did not seem to serve its purpose.

The other possibility was that Simone simply liked him and wanted to experience dating someone with an unusual look, weird accent, and uncommon appearance, a person who had won the trust of a successful couple.

But from the beginning, Essie found Simone to be very smart, detailed oriented, and shrewd. It was discomforting to accept that this vibrant thirty-two-year-old girl would think about a long-term relationship, so the final analysis was that Simone just was feeding a temporary attraction to an older man. Essie never had the chance to experience a normal life. Right in the midst of his transition from adolescence to youth, the storm of revolution in Iran uprooted everything along his path. He said to himself, after exhausting all speculation, "Why should I question and analyze her interest so much? Maybe there is no mystery in everything anyway."

***

"What does Essie mean? What is your last name?" Simone asked him the first time they went out. Essie chose the finest restaurant, which he thought was suitable for their first dinner together. He reserved a table in that restaurant for its popularity, ensemble, and ambiance. All the tables were decorated with modern and stylish furniture. Essie had often noticed how this restaurant was always full and had the urge to try it at least once, but every time he thought, "I would look pathetic going in and sitting without a companion in that pretentious high-class environment." And now, Essie seemed satisfied to be there with a beautiful young lady in an exceptional milieu.

The flickering light of small candles on the table had added to the beauty of Simone's slim and attractive face. Essie remembered Melody's opinion about the right light glinting from the proper angle as the main components of determining a beautiful face. He did not like thinking about his own look under this light; undoubtedly, the illumination of his mustache could not be an appealing scene. Essie had to dissipate the negativity. He turned his attention to Simone's face. He saw the reflection of the shimmering light in her bright eyes and was stunned by the harmony of her face's features. Essie wondered if the harmony between her hairstyle and her petite body was all coincidental, or the result of having a good hairdresser. The restaurant's ambiance and the presence of young couples all around poured warmth into Essie's heart. He felt the excitement that his body had craved for a long time.

"Essie is short for Eshagh, which is Isaac in English. My full name is Eshagh Sepehri. I was not pleased with my nickname at first, but what can you do when friends start calling you that, and it stays with you forever?"

Essie was surprised how candidly he offered so much information without any inquiry from his audience. "Questioner or interrogator, what's the difference?" He thought, "In any case, information should not be given more than is asked for or needed." This experience was gained when Essie was involved in a full-fledged war with the Islamic regime after the revolution, a struggle that led to the destruction of a generation, his generation. Those were the same years that he miraculously had been saved from horrendous and deadly incidents and fled his country perforce.

While Essie was wandering the corridors of time, their waiter brought a bottle of wine. He returned from his memory to present a little too late. Essie noticed that he regrettably had Okayed the wrong bottle of wine with no presence of mind. Even though he had tried very much to enjoy Pinot noir, he always preferred Merlot. Even his second choice would be Cabernet. Essie had not much knowledge and specialty in wine, but even the movie *Sideways* could not convince him that Pinot had a better taste and effect than other wines. These few sips once again showed him that he did not like the wine. He had no other choice but to swallow it at that moment. Simone realized that Essie was somewhere else mentally and said, "What were you thinking about just now? Where were you?"

"No, I was tasting this wine ..." And he explained his opinion to her about that movie and the type of wine that he liked. The combination of restaurant ambiance, her presence, and the youth sparkle emitting from Simone all brought a pleasant feeling to Essie that he had not experienced for a long time. Drinking wine on an empty stomach doubled the effect of good feeling and made him talkative in an unusual way, so that sometimes his speech would elevate to an oration, "When someone speaks of a fugitive, we imagine someone who has committed a crime, someone fleeing from justice. But after the revolution in Iran, for many, the meaning of the word fugitive became totally different."

Then, Essie moved on to a different subject and continued, "Revolution, the word *revolution* for people in the West, portrays images of historical events that they have either read about or seen in movies or documentaries which the narrations and stories are in line with the author or filmmaker's point of view."

Simone was very surprised at the start of such a subject without any prelude or background, but she continued to listen to Essie's lecture.

"The French and Russian Revolutions have been examples of the normal course of life's transformation in those countries that quickly and irreversibly changed everything at the time. What has been seen and heard from the two revolutions is mainly the establishment of guillotine frameworks in France and execution squads and labor camps in Russia, later called the Soviet Union. We see little real analysis of what actually happened there that has gone beyond comparison with these two historical examples. Of course, the usual process in people's lives under the monarchic rule of Louis in France or the tsar was not normal and forced social classes in the society to unite. What was taught in political science classes is not a narrative of people's lives, but the inevitable social encounter."

Simone looked around. Surprisingly, she had listened to Essie's semi-speech and other than the big words which she did not understand, received a wave of warmth from him. But she felt they came from a pure heart. Simone still was wondering why Essie had initiated such a topic. Despite her careful attention to his words, Simone could not comprehend parts of Essie's argument. The field she had studied at her university was entirely different from the subject that Essie was talking about. As Essie had guessed, her information was from movies she had seen. Simone touched her brunette, ironed hair; pushed it from her forehead to behind her right ear; and focused on

Essie's talk. Simone's move, playing with her hair, made Essie even more enthusiastic in his talk. He took a small sip from his glass of wine and continued:

"But do not be fooled, the revolution in Iran was very different from the two classic examples that I just mentioned. My friends and many others, who were killed, learned this crucial fact but too late. In the midst of the revolution of 1979, at age sixteen, I became a devoted political activist. I was restless. Nothing could ground me. Waves of unrest took me to the streets, like millions of other high school kids. In the absence of any legal political party or existing social-political background and activities in the community, various new political groups popped up like mushrooms. I chose one of the groups that claimed to emphasize more in justice and freedom."

Simone was surprised that Essie was telling his own personal history as if he was talking about the main character in a story.

"Iran was shaken with a big bang, and people started panicking. It was such that my youthful tendencies, along with the activation of my adolescent hormones, shaped my direction toward a variety of political, cultural, and sporting activities. A baby eagle, ready to fly, suddenly spread its wings and after flapping, found them taller and stronger than he thought they should be. At that time, alongside the other birds, I saw the power that could contribute not only in determining the fate of my fellow citizens but the whole of humanity on earth. I really believed and thought that way."

Simone said, "Wow, I am so sorry, I don't know what to say. I'm speechless."

Simone was taken by his tale—not just by the story but the direction that this supposedly romantic dinner was heading. She showed a little unease, which made Essie realize that he was perhaps becoming a bore and the sole speaker.

He looked at the young couple sitting next to their table. Because of tables' proximity, apparently, they were as surprised as Simone by the sort of romance that Essie had presented to the girl sitting before him. Now really embarrassed, Essie tried to change the subject and talk about Simone's interests. But Simone asked, "It seems though that this young, eager flapping bird was not able to fly as high as he wished in the sky of his dreams. Was he?"

Essie had repeatedly analyzed the reasons for the fall of those little birds in his mind. He added, "When you get absorbed in issues and events that you've been involved in for many years, the line between fact and fiction becomes blurry. You no longer know if what you are saying is a myth or reality or your mental transmutation of both. The contradiction had divided the society between the Islamic fanaticism and the secular modernity. And in the vacuum of established and influential political parties, this paradox threw strata of the people in a vortex of death. This whirlpool undoubtedly would place an ancient civilization on a dark landscape. Despite his tendencies to guide the country in the direction of modernity, Shah made colossal mistakes. He shut down political arenas with excessive force for decades, and unfortunately, only clerics had the opportunity to utilize traditional communications networks, such as mosques, and therefore had been able to maintain their traditional organization."

Certainly, Simone wanted only to continue talking about Essie and his life experiences, not another lecture or political analysis. But it seemed impossible to stop Essie from enlightening Simone with his views and analysis. He was just warming up.

"It didn't take too long for Islamic extremists and fundamentalists under Khomeini's leadership to brutally suppress their inexperienced rivals, and spread their dominance with violence throughout the country..."

Essie suddenly realized that he might have gone too far again and after a moment of silence said, "Forgive me; I don't know why I'm talking so much tonight. It may be the effect of the wine. Pinot may not have been a wrong choice after all. Many of these events are personal experiences that if you haven't lived them have no meaning to you. It is all based on knowledge of what happened. Without knowing them, all these words seem pointless and abstract. Sorry, I know it may perhaps feel that you were listening to gibberish. Thank you for your patience, which I know it comes from your kindness. I promise not to ever talk about these subjects again. "

Simone replied, "No, not at all. And I don't say it because of my kindness. True, sometimes, I had no idea what you were talking about, but your words made sense to me. I don't know how to say it, but it made its mark on my heart. I like it when you talk. Even if I don't really comprehend what you mean."

Actually, Simone was not lying. Essie's words, despite their complexity, made their way into her mind and soul. It was not a night that Simone had imagined before coming to the restaurant. She never had a date like this before, either. But the more he talked, the more Simone was becoming interested in knowing this strange, coy, honest, talkative, pure-hearted, Middle Eastern man. Simone never had a thought that she would kiss him, let alone make love to him that same night.

Hours later, when they both rolled over in bed, each had a different feeling, transmitted into his and her soul by kisses and fusion of fervor. Sensation and climax were a new form of communication that interconnected them.

Essie was like a honeybee, sitting on various layers of Simone's petals, drinking from her sweet nectar. And a moment later, with another short flight, he lay on another petal and on another, almost saturating his insatiable thirst. Essie realized that he had found his long-lost intimate.

Simone, like a queen trusting a strange knight, opened the gateway to her castle. She had reached a new climax in a marathon of sexual ecstasy. And then came the calmness, drowning all the passion and excitement of a full night. Essie had a smile on his face like a conqueror, but ever so momentarily.

His mind was actively analyzing: "What's happening to me? Is my smile for swimming in the sweet sea of honey? Or is it for a sense of strength in my oration that brought such a sweet result?"

Whatever it was, he saw the truth and assured himself that he had never talked about his past in order to reach glamorous and magnificent lovemaking like this. At that time of the night, he could not calm his revived body. He felt young, and as if a mysterious lock had been opened inside, he turned to Simone and pulled her back into his arms.

# Chapter 18 – Motivation

*San Francisco – David's Office*

"Wow," Tim expressed his feelings by exhaling from his chest. He seemed to be genuinely affected by the exciting story that Art was telling the group. David, observing him, could not determine if Tim's excitement was genuine or sarcastic. Michael was the only person there who knew Tim very well, or at least he thought he did.

This was Tim's first attendance at the group meeting. Simone also was present, alongside Essie, who sat between her and Melody. An unpleasant, repulsive tension between the two made him feel crushed. Simone told Essie of how Melody's manner had changed for the worse. Although she knew that this conflict was unlikely to jeopardize her job security, Simone felt uneasy. She was worried about her sour relationship with her boss. There was no possible way to end this battle peacefully. Simone could not talk to Melody nor would she want to, and at the same time, she could not continue working in the harsh environment. Essie felt somewhat guilty to have jeopardized Simone's position, but mostly he was disappointed in finding Melody unreliable. He remembered how impressed Melody was with Simone—so much that she talked about Simon's bright future with Roma Skin Care. But now Melody's petulant and antagonistic behavior in regards to their relationship was baffling Essie.

An unpleasant feeling had encompassed Essie's mind: "Why should it be like this?" He had no answers. Yet Essie dared not start a conversation with Melody about the night at the restaurant or about his relationship with Simone. He feared the outcome of that conversation. Essie had never experienced this type of dismay before. He was trying to gather his mind and focus on Art's adventurous story about his recent trip to Sodom and about King Bera, the most powerful man in the region who told the story to Art. Essie simply could not concentrate.

Essie was astonished to admit he was fearful regarding the situation between Melody and Simone. "It cannot be fear," he thought. Essie had dealt with worse fears: he had struggled to survive, had faced imprisonment and fights; in almost all these situations, he had overcome human fear. And now, he was puzzled as to how a simple conversation with Melody over a trivial subject became so complicated. Essie was in horror of Melody's possible emotional outburst toward him. His relationship with Melody was sincere. That was all. After his separation from his ex-wife, Essie had been able to cross through an emotional abyss only with Melody's total support. He never had doubted her friendship and never doubted Melody's love for David. Essie believed that David and Melody were one soul in two bodies, and he always felt he had a solid connection with them. Essie felt very close to Melody, and he never worried about the purity of his heartfelt feelings toward her as well.

If only Essie could consult with David on this issue, he certainly would have received support. But he did not dare. His fear was spinning off into uncertainty—he was about to enter a tunnel with an unknown endpoint. David's friendship was too precious for Essie to lose. Of course, he loved his brother Amir too. But David had become more than a brother to him; he was the only confidant and the most trusted soul that Essie knew. David was everything to him. Essie's mind was frantic with the possibility that he was hurting David with all these nonsense relationship issues.

In fact, David was the only one who could fully focus and listened to Art's detailed narration. Art, as the narrator, was really present. Art was the speaker, and David was all ears. Unfortunately, the rest of the group was mentally and emotionally in disarray. Tim and Michael were also somewhat muddled. Perhaps Michael was under more pressure than Tim, thinking and evaluating the situation as he unwillingly was forced to be in Tim's company again.

Tim's admission into the group put Michael in a challenging position, a situation that he did not wish to be in at all. While they were sitting in a circle as a group, Art was the speaker, and Michael positioned himself close to Art on the left. He wanted to hide from the pressure of Tim's constant gaze. Tim was looking at both Art and Michael from where he was sitting, on Art's right side. He would sneak a peek every once in a while, moving forward in his chair, pretending to reposition himself for comfort but only to look at Michael. Michael was not comfortable. He detested what Tim was doing. Tim was shifting his gaze like the lens of a camera between Art and Michael, trying to study them both together. Tim was desperately but hopelessly watching Art, who now had the key to Michael's heart. Tim was searching: what exceptional character had made Art so special to Michael? Why Art? What was so remarkable about him? Tim was still in love with Michael.

Indeed, a critical necessity brought the whole group together at that moment. Each person's presence was crucial in various degrees. They all feared a looming storm whose clouds were already forming with thunder. David couldn't care less about his earthly belongings, the future of his company, or all of his assets. In fact, the recent developments brought on by Art's addition to the group concurred with David's philosophy. His meetings had been going on for many years, and at last, Art's revelation, his power, and ability to connect to the past, most of which David was unaware, was the answer to David's lifetime quest to answer philosophical questions around human creation.

The presence of a stranger at midnight who broke into their house was from unknown forces. Melody sensed David was encountering a big challenge and she was ready to do anything to help. David was her center and her strength. Her heart belonged to him, and she did not doubt that if needed, she would protect David as a virtual shield against all threats, regardless of any danger.

Essie was in a situation similar to David's. In addition to seeking a solution to his own puzzle, he found a chance to help the group. He felt indebted to David for his kindness and now by devoting all his expertise to improving security for everyone, perhaps he could minimally repay years of David's generosity. His experience could be considered a great asset to the group's protection, especially for David and Melody. Essie had no one else in the fifth decade of his life but this couple. He knew the special bond between them was utterly unbreakable. Of course, Simone's recent presence in his life was a colorful gift that was refreshing his soul.

There was only one Art for Michael. There was no Art before and after his visit to the source of his mysterious power. Michael had seen only Art, ablaze, who overnight traveled to the corners of history, Art whose body and soul had fused through years of challenges and became hard like steel. On the very first night Michael saw a fiery flesh that had entered the bar, hours later he had embraced him in bed. Michael discovered that Art's soul was also an extension of his steely body. Before he made Art's acquaintance, to Michael, the meaning of love was a misunderstanding, a wrong address, a corrupt omen, and a self-cheating hobby. In search of true love, Michael followed many illusive paths that ended in agony and pain. This time, Michael had no illusion. He knew that he was not hallucinating. He had found love. Michael knew he finally found his true love, his soul mate. And he was there to protect Art with all his being.

*If there is a choice, it is not endurable for a true lover to spend a moment elsewhere, far from his other half.*

Other than that place, next to Art at that moment, where else could Michael be?

And Art was the only one who was roaming the clouds in another world. Not because he had gone to Sodom. Like a chemical reaction that transforms materials into an entirely different substance, Art's journeys had transformed him into a new being. Art was the main reason everyone was present in that group. The recent adventures that seemed to Art a strange dream or a science fiction movie had changed him altogether. No wakeup call was ringing to explain all of these stories as spectacular dreams. All of these events were just as real to him as Michael's love. His world had changed, and with that, his soul and body had also been transformed.

"What am I?" Art had recently asked himself over and over again. Whenever the answer "I do not know" was flowing into his mind, Art instantly would push it away. Not that he did not know, but he was in the process of knowing. This process required self-knowledge, self-confidence, self-examination, and inspection of his surroundings. Everything around him was also in the process of changing. Michael's presence was the first revelation in his life. Art had never fallen in love before. He did not know what love meant. He never knew what it was to fall in love head over heels. Before his visit to Sodom and subsequent acquaintance with Michael, Art had no deep connection with anyone, nor did he live with anyone. He did not even have a minimal experience that would add up to anything resembling love.

Art did not doubt himself and his sexual preference. He knew he was gay even from before his teenage years. Before that, in his childhood, his behavior was not like that of other boys either. Art remembered how his behavior would make his father mad. He now had an image of his father in the dimness of his dreams, an image that had been carved into his mind and memory.

Neither his preference for toys nor his manner was like that of other boys. Art despised violence. His father was in the military, a guy who identified himself as a disciplinarian. Of course, Art did not have a clue at that time that he was the reason his father was agitated all the time. All Art could see was his dad's state of despair in dealing with Art's manner. What was wrong? He was just himself, without any pretenses, spectacle, or unusual requests. His only wish was to make his father happy, which always seemed impossible. And after a while, the father was gone. No one, not even his mother, wanted to talk about him. He suddenly just disappeared, vanished without a trace.

But his father's absence created a hole in Art's heart, and it became larger and larger every day. Art blamed himself. He was convinced that he was the reason for his father's bitter face. Art was certain about his intuition. There was no doubt that he was the one who upset his father. And his certitude was not far from the truth.

Art never forgot the day he was invited to one of his classmates' birthday party. Like a stream of water that carves gaps ever deeper on rocks, the passing time engraved the images of that event in his mind. Art was in the sixth grade. His father took him to a place called Tumble to celebrate the birthday along with about 20 other kids. It was at a shopping center in a San Diego suburb. In a two-hour period, a crew of four or five teenagers led several activities: running fast, throwing balls, aiming targets, and passing obstacles. Art was almost always the last to finish among the boys. Standing next to the rest of the parents, Art's father was looking at the kids playing games. Art's heart was crying every time he noticed father's harsh and disapproving gaze. His pleasure in playing games was dissipated by father's sadness. After the first few rounds, his father turned his back on Art and engaged himself in talking to a mom of one of the kids until the activities were nearly done. The woman was giggling. Art became annoyed. His father threw a half glance at the kids when the birthday boy blew out the candles mid-song. Then he continued his talk to the woman. A few weeks later, his father disappeared. Art had no doubt that he was the culprit behind mother's sobbing.

"What am I?" The void was resurfacing in Art. He could not find any answer for this forever lingering question. The void was nearly consuming him until one day Art saw the light. It was a glorious afternoon that his mother sat him down in his chair in front of her and demanded, "We need to talk."

Art's heart fluttered in his chest. "Is he back?" he wondered. "If so, where is he? Is mom leaving me too? If yes, why?"

Art was on the verge of crying, so his mother said, "Art, you are a very special boy. You are an extraordinary person. You should be proud of yourself; I'm proud of you, too. Many people don't understand this. Often, among different groups of people, there is only a small section that has special characteristics. And you and others like you are those special souls. You will realize it later, but you must know and remember that you're a perfect boy even better than..."

At this moment, his mother cried and hugged him. Art's mind was at ease now that his fear of losing his mom subsided. He hugged his mother back ever so tightly. Art knew that people cry in time of happiness and he knew this was one of those times.

Art was now comfortable in this group. For the first time in his life, he was among people he loved, solid friends whom Art could protect and receive their support and protection in return—straight folks whom he could trust.

Art stopped talking. He was the sole speaker, talking to the group about his conversation with King Bera. He looked out the window. Art liked that window in David's office as it reminded him of the stone gap that he had seen in Sodom for the first time.

It was now sunset. Art loved the sunset. Love had become his core characteristic. Recently, he loved everything around him—people, nature, and everything else. He had found the source of love. He and the source were one, and love was the center. Seamlessly, Art became love itself. Art felt that he had known the people in that circle around him for many years and could understand them completely with all his heart.

The silence lingered, then suddenly awakened everyone. David turned and looked at Art. Essie came back from his thoughts and asked, "Art, would you please repeat the last part?"

"The story that King Bera told me was very interesting. It was different from everything that has been said about this subject so far," said Art.

As if he came back from his daydreaming by the silence and Essie's words, Tim moved his notebook on his right thigh and asked, "Who said what and how different it was?"

Art smiled and replied, "Does my voice sound like a lullaby to you guys? I said King Bera, King of Sodom, the one I had contacted from the beginning, explained to me in detail the events that happened in that region. His stories were completely different from what has been written in the Old Testament and Gospel or other versions of the story in other religions books. Now just try not to be shocked as I tell you guys what I heard from him…"

Simone prompted, "How did you explain your presence, how you got there, to King Bera?"

After Simone's interruption, Melody turned to David with a dissatisfying look, as if she was telling David silently, "Why the hell is she asking any question?"

Art responded, "I did not get into the details. I sensed that given previous visits and my coming and going at will, he partially accepted this unusual relationship as a fact and did not push too much. He avoided asking too many questions himself."

Then Art said to David, "The king himself told me that they also have a ceremony like our meditation, a collective performance, a named minds connection. Actually, theirs were more advanced than our sessions." Art turned to Simone and answered, "Perhaps King

Bera had a better understanding than I thought, and accepted me as who I was there. A passenger who would definitely travel to other dimensions. He wanted me to tell the world what really happened."

For a moment, Tim stopped taking notes, jumped in, and asked, "I'm sorry that I'm suggesting this, but is it possible that all of this that you think you saw, was actually a dream or imaginary...?"

David stopped Tim by raising his arm and said, "We have already gone through this step. Today it's your first time attending this meeting. You and I spoke earlier about the special circumstances that we are in. Too many incidents are happening, and without your help we can't know what they are. That's why you are here—to help us discover who exactly is targeting us. Essie suggested that it was you who accidentally published Art's first trip to Sodom." David looked at Michael when he mentioned the word "accidentally" and continued, "You can raise public attention. We also decided to invite you here to continue writing Art's stories. We believe this will increase our safety factor."

Essie continued David's argument and expanded, "Of course, you need to refrain from naming your source. Because of Michael's acquaintance and his approval, we made sure that we could count on you. There is no need to name Art in any of your stories whatsoever."

Michael gazed at Essie. It was clear that he was not pleased with Essie's comment. Instead, Essie's remark brought a broad smile to Tim's face. Apparently, Essie had somewhat convinced Tim. Presenting another show by Art to prove his power was the last thing David wanted.

Art continued, "King Bera told me that the Valley of Siddim was a land of plenty and every piece of land was fertile. Their silos were full of agricultural products and, after dividing them among all the citizens, they had no place to store surplus. Prosperity was a shared value in their cities and villages. Welfare and comfort were a given fact among residences, and people filled most of their time with various performances and games. There was no such a thing as slavery in their territories. It was not tolerated under any circumstances. There was no limit on love and friendship. What King Bera said, at first, reminded me of the utopia. Isn't this the ideal society that human beings sought throughout the history and are still seeking to find?"

David said, "As I searched into historical texts, which were mostly fed by religious sources, I confirmed what you said. But there is still no clear evidence of those stories. Each of the five regions, cities, or provinces was under their own king's control. They were enjoying living in the fertile, vast, and flat area of the valley of Siddim. We all know that the Old Testament was written by Moses. In fact, every story from the beginning of the creation to the start of the New Testament is the product of Moses' mind. Some of those stories that were closer to his time may have been taken partly from the actual historical event. Of course, all of them went through the first Abrahamic religion's prophet mental filter."

Michael: "With this account, if Moses were a homosexual, then we would have Adam and Steve now in the Gospel, instead of you know, Adam and Eve."

Michael's comment garnered a burst of laughter from all the participants. Essie continued Michael's theme and said, "But apart from the joke, Michael is right. The Old Testament is the source of all documents and events. The majority of scholars believe that Moses wrote it. History is defined by the person who authors it. We really can't prove the veracity of any of these stories, even the life story of Moses himself. Why did he leave Pharaoh? Did he really grow up in the palace, or did he simply organize poor people to take over the power? He might have had extraordinary power like our Art. We are not sure about Moses, but at least we are confident that Art has seen these events with his own eyes. Art's power proves that he's not bullshitting."

Tim said, "I always had this question why all the Abrahamic religions are hostile to gays so much. They have persecuted gays throughout history."

Essie responded, "Think for a moment. Moses begins the story of human creation with Adam and Eve. So the desire between man and man, or woman and woman, would destroy the foundation of his religion, and, consequently, Christianity and Islam, each of which copied from the Old Testament. They had to be in denial of homosexuality. Probably ... or for sure ... Moses must have known about the existence of gays, but it's not clear why he denied the legitimacy of being homosexual. He's been so unfair in the story of Sodom and Gomorrah. He knew Sodom and Gomorrah were unique regarding prosperity and governing their people. These are questions that Art might be able to find answers for in his future visits."

Art continued, "But the story of King Bera began just like any other story with a 'But.' King Bera described that one day in his chamber, where I met him, he received a message that some few hundred people had arrived at the city gate and sought permission to enter…"

# Chapter 19 – Lot

> Abram took his wife Sarai and his brother's son Lot, and all the possessions that they had gathered, and the persons whom they had acquired in Haran; and they set forth to go to the land of Canaan. — Book of Genesis [12:5]

## *Sodom – King Bera's palace*

Sitting on his throne, King Bera was accepting people one by one. They were led in by the guard's commander as their name was announced. It was the day that King Bera set aside to speak to his people about their problems. The throne was in the middle of the platform, separated by ten steps from the lower part of the chamber where there was a queue of men and women. A messenger passed by the line of people, walked toward the guards, then whispered something in the commander's ear. The commander immediately interrupted the man who was talking to the King, asking the king for permission to talk. King Bera looked at the commander and nodded.

"My king, I have just received a message that a group of unknown people have arrived behind the East Gate and they are requesting permission to enter the city."

"Do we know who they are? Why are they here? What is their purpose?" the king asked.

"No, my king, we have yet to find out why they are here. They are asking for permission to enter the city and remain here forever."

The king paused for a few moments and said, "Who speaks on their behalf? Do they have a leader or a commander?"

"Yes, his name is Lot," the head of guards responded.

"See if they have any immediate needs to be fulfilled until I personally speak to him. Tell him to be ready tomorrow when you go and bring him to me—not to the palace, elsewhere in the city where I can see him without him knowing who I am. Do you understand?"

"Yes, my king, as you command," the commander replied.

King Bera turned to the man next to him and informed him, "Our men, who are watching all areas around here, have been reporting unusual movements the last few days. We have to determine who they are and what they want."

The next day, the king and several of his companions visited Lot without their armor or any military equipment. Lot, who had come to the city's gates with his people, had been brought inside the city. Two young women accompanied Lot who claimed to be the head of the tribe. The accompanied women were said to be Lot's daughters. Because of Lot's insistence, the guards allowed his daughters to be present at the meeting as his advisers. After Lot and his daughters paid homage to the delegation that came to represent the city, Lot began his request to enter the city as an inhabitant: "We have come a long way. We crossed the desert to reach here. Your city shines like a bright star in the darkness. We want to live among the people of Sodom peacefully."

King Bera asked, "Why should we let you into our city when we do not have any information about your identity? List your reasons for us; then we may consider your request."

Lot replied, "We are who we are. I am Lot, and these are my daughters. Our food supplies and our herds are depleted. We have no chance of survival outside these city walls. We have heard about the surplus of food supplies in Sodom. The renowned fertility of your land and your felicities have reached beyond your borders."

One of Lot's daughter added, "There are many beautiful girls among us who could bring joy to your community."

The king looked at the guard's commander, raised his brows, then turned to the girl and demanded, "What is your name?"

"My name is Paltith, my lord," the girl answered with a smile on her face. Rolling her eyes, she indicated that what she said created interest in the audience.

King said, "Paltith, have you heard the name Chedorlaomer and the city of Elam?"

After exchanging a look with his daughters, Lot replied, "No, I don't believe we have heard such names before."

"You must know that we do not allow slavery; we do not have slaves in this city," King Bera, staring into Paltith's eyes, continued. "The territory that I just named is not too far from this place. Your offer may be attractive there, and slave owners can be good partners to deal with you."

Lot prompted, "Of course, we do not have any slaves among us either. My daughter did not articulate what she meant."

"Right, we will examine your request, and in the meantime, if you need anything, ask the guards at the gate. Your requests will be provided."

***

Art continued the story. "This Chedorlaomer, the King of Elam, whose name King Bera mentioned, carefully monitored the status of the regions of Sodom and Gomorrah along with their allies. As David said, Sodom and its allies were living in a very fertile land in the plain of Siddim, an area close to the present location of the Dead Sea in the Middle East. Above the valley of Siddim, Elam's territory, along with several other smaller areas, had neither flat land nor natural resources. They were at high altitudes, and their primary source of revenue was trading slaves—attacking other territories, capturing slaves, and plundering. The other resource that Chedorlaomer had under his control was a mountain river that irrigated the plain of Siddim. River flow was vital for the survival of these five cities in the plain: Sodom, Gomorrah, Bella, Zeboiim, and Admah.

"The wealth of the five territories in the plain and their governance system had attracted Chedorlaomer's attention. Sodom's community governance and its free lifestyle, which was similar in allied territories, were a threat to the slavery system in Elam and Mesopotamian areas. Chedorlaomer considered the ruling structure in Sodom as the leading cause of the unrest and occasional riots in the areas under his control. The news about the way people lived in the valley of Siddim made ransoms and tax collecting difficult for Chedorlaomer's soldiers, something that was infuriating the king of Elam."

Tim asked, "Well, why didn't Chedorlaomer attack those cities in the plain? He could have sorted out all his problem at once."

Art answered, "He would have if he could, but he had reasons to be afraid. The allied territories in the plain had an excellent defense arrangement. Also, Chedorlaomer was concerned that the dissatisfaction among his people, the slaves, as well as his warriors, would create a backlash if they went to war. For those reasons, he could only send spies and saboteurs regularly to Sodom and other territories in the valley of Siddim."

****

Amim, the king's senior advisor and lover was in the delegation that accompanied King Bera to visit Lot and his daughters. Holding Amim's hand, the king commanded, "Inform the royal council members to hold a meeting in a few hours in the assembly hall."

While stepping alongside the king, Amim—with broad shoulders, a firm and sturdy chest, and equal height—squeezed Bera's hand, signaling that the order would be executed immediately. King turned to Amim with a smile and said, "Think about the conversations we just had with them. I count on what you think about these people. Meanwhile, make sure representatives of our sister cities are present at the meeting. They have to go back and report to their authorities afterward."

With a nod and another hand squeeze, Amim expressed his agreement. He parted from the king by taking few steps and waved at the guard standing in disguise at the corner. The guard came forward, and Amim ordered him, whispering, "Send a message to the wise old man that we'll have a meeting in the palace in few hours; his presence is needed in the council hall. A carrier will be sent to bring him over."

The guard bowed to obey and then disappeared.

***

When the guard reached the school gates, he saw children of different ages playing in the schoolyard. In a corner off to the left, isolated from the rest of the area, an old man with a white beard was speaking to students in a gazebo covered with foliage. The girls and boys were sitting on the ground in front of the wise old man, listening to his lecture. The guard stood aside and waited for the old man to finish his teaching session.

The wise old man: "... Yes, as I said, there are so many things that we do not know, and the ones we know have come from our forefathers. That is why by learning and passing them to our children, we convey the knowledge of our ancestors to the next generation."

One student asked, "But in inscriptions and stories transmitted from our fathers to children, there is no answer to the question of where we came from."

The wise old man looked at the boy and with a smile answered, "Of course there isn't. If there was an answer, for sure, you would have heard it from me long ago. It should be noted that not too long ago humans like us found the knowledge and the maturity to get food from the earth. We became farmers after being hunters. Humans developed tools made from hard and soft metals, out of rocks. We are the first to become a state rather than a tribe; many around us are still living in the same way as our ancestors..."

Another student asked, "What is the difference between a tribe and the state?"

The wise old man replied, "We no longer need to get our food from hunting. We do not fight with our neighbors for food and spoils. Instead, we make deals with them. We manage our internal affairs through a division of labor. Some defend our borders, some work on the land, and you are learning. We still have a long way to go. So it's very important that you, as future wise scholars, learn and think as much as you can. Someday, you will be teachers and wise persons of future."

Another student, with a thunderous voice, asked, "Where does a dead person go?"

The wise old man touched his thin hair and answered, "We don't know that either. There were tribes before us who ate their dead to find out where one goes after death. Perhaps this was an excuse— perhaps they were hungry—but whatever the reason, except getting a full stomach, there is no answer to this question. I have heard that in distant regions they still eat good people after death to inherit their goodness. There are many other stories that we will talk about later. But now let's get out of here before you eat each other." The students burst into laughter. "Don't forget, learn and think as much as you can. That is one of the most important tasks in our community."

The students stood up and scattered. The wise old man looked at the guard who approached him and said, "Well, it seems that I am summoned. There must have been some news in the palace. What is it?"

After paying tribute to the wise old man, the guard replied, "I do not know, my lord. I just came to tell you that your presence in the palace is needed."

***

## Council Room

In the first row of the advisory council around the table were King Bera and Amim and three others: the wise old man, who had a habit of toying with his long white beard, and two women named Leah and Sichra. Leah was the commander of the army, and Sichra was responsible for all affairs outside of Sodom. King Bera sat at one end of the table and Amim was next to him on his right. Leah and Sichra faced each other at the table, and the wise old man sat in a chair at the opposite end from King Bera. In the second row, four observing advisers including two women and two men representing Sodom allies were also present. They were sitting next to the wall, listening to city leaders who gathered at the council room.

King Bera began the session. "As I briefed you all by messenger, a group of about 1,500 people including men, women, and children, along with their herds, have arrived at the eastern gate and are seeking shelter in our city. I met their chief personally, and I heard his request. I want to know your opinion on their request."

Leah wiped the sweat off her neck from under her black, braided hair. She paused for few moments after King Bera finished his words, and asked, "How do we know that their presence is not a new trick from Chedorlaomer? Recently he has increased his efforts to sabotage and distract us. We know that there were conspirators among slaves who recently escaped from Elam. We often receive refugees who seek shelter, but the number of Chedorlaomer's men among them has increased lately."

"We do not know the nature of these people's request to stay," said Amim. "But we can see that their appearance is not similar to those who live in Elam."

The King turned to Sichra and asked, "What do you know about them? You're more familiar with affairs outside our borders."

Sichra immediately replied, "Apparently, they were separated from the larger group. We found out this from those who received our help outside of the gate in the last couple of days."

The king said, "We will not make a final decision here. We'll wait for our allies to offer their opinions on this issue. Perhaps they have received similar requests at their borders. What do you think, wise old man? Today, you are unusually quiet."

"I do not have a positive view of these people, my king. They are in considerable numbers. If some of Leah's concerns are correct, their entry can be disruptive. I believe that, even after our allies became aware of the situation, they should not be allowed to obtain permanent inhabitance immediately. We have to talk to each one of them and find out the truth about their past. After gathering enough information, then we can evaluate their requests."

The king nodded in agreement and said, "What is certain is that we can use their labor for sure. But neither can we grant them immediate permanent shelter, nor can we hold them behind our gates forever."

"If they do not have equal rights, then we have treated them as slaves," said the wise old man. "It does not matter if we keep them outside the city. So far, they've been living this way. Of course, the cold season is fast approaching, but then again we have to be cautious."

The king looked at Leah and said, "Leah, go with your men to give them what they need, and collect as much information as you possibly can. Then, review the gathered information with the help of wise old man." The king turned to Sichra and continued, "Go to our allies in person and talk to the respected kings and find out what they think. Amim will accompany you on these trips."

With a surprised look on his face, Amim said, "But my king, I'd rather be with you, in case any problem arises."

King Bera put his hand on Amim's shoulder and said, "What problem? Do not forget that Leah has the inside and all the borders under her control, as the head of defense." Then he looked into Leah's eyes, waiting for an answer.

Leah, who was staring at Sichra, turned to the king and said, "Of course, that's not a worry."

***

## *Elam Territory*

Chedorlaomer's rugged body was moving in an up-and-down motion as he rode his white stallion, its long white mane waving with every step. He looked at two of his guards who were a one-horse-neck distance behind him. The proud horse was looking around, pounding his hoofs on the ground in harmony with his ride, as if he knew his master was a king.

The guard to the right of the king caught up to him by striking his heels on the horse's underbelly. After drawing the king's attention, he said, "My lord, we have received reports that a group of people have arrived at the gate of Sodom."

Chedorlaomer asked, "Who are they and what do they want there?"

"We do not know yet, but will send a few men tonight to find out their origin and purpose."

The king reduced his horse's speed without pulling on the harness. It seemed the white horse was aware of his rider's intention to let the other reach him from behind. The king then demanded, "Find out who their chief is and tell him to come here."

After the guard heard the king's command, he pulled his horse's harness, made a full turn to the opposite direction, then broke into a furious gallop. Chedorlaomer galloped too by jamming his heels into the horse and darted forward, leaving his guard behind. The guard who was riding on his left saw Chedorlaomer's hand as a sign to follow him. With a loud "Hey," and a strike at the horse's belly with both heels, the guard sped up, reaching the king's horse far ahead.

# Chapter 20 – Faith and Liberty Conference

*Washington DC – Omni Sheraton Hotel*

The crowd in the Omni Sheraton hall was reaching full capacity. The White House had already announced that President Trump would take part in the "Path to Majority" conference, held by a group called the Faith and Liberty Alliance along with Vice President Mike Pence. Before the White House, the Faith and Liberty Alliance informed its members through a press release:

"Following the biggest and most successful campaign of the Faith and Liberty Alliance—with 1.2 million face-to-face conversations going door to door, 10 million phone calls, sending 22 million letters to physical addresses, and the persuasion of 30 million voters in 117,000 churches—we secured a victory for the conservative candidate Donald J. Trump. And now we are proud to announce that the 2017 Path to Majority conference will be held for two days starting June 8, 2017, at the Omni Sheraton Hotel in Washington DC."

His Excellency founded the Faith and Liberty Alliance in 2009 in Atlanta, Georgia. Then he asked other Evangelical churches that had the same conservative views to participate in this alliance that was designed explicitly for a grass-roots movement.

It was not the first time that His Excellency, an exceptional visionary, saw the need for the existence of such groups in society. Several times in the past, to advance church purposes, he had started similar organizations that were effective at various levels. But his main motive to create the Faith and Liberty Alliance was to oppose the presidency of Barack Obama who had been elected in 2008. All efforts by the Baptodist Church in defeating Obama had failed, and the head bishops of conservative churches recognized the need for a more fundamental and organized surge to defeat the liberal Obama in 2012.

His newly formed alliance did not have the desired result on election: Obama won. But His Excellency blamed Mitt Romney and his Mormon church for that failure, not the newly established group. The Faith and Liberty Alliance undoubtedly bore its fruit in the 2016 election year. The religious and political ideas of His Excellency had started emerging in 2014. The coalition was able to bring many different conservatives in the political, social, and religious spectrum under one umbrella, aiming at the primary objective, eliminating LGBTQ rights, with the slogan "Preserving family values." By investing in Trump, the coalition could achieve its goal by embracing all right-wing ideas and groups, thanks to the real estate mogul's anti-Mexican rhetoric and questioning of Obama's place of birth. His Excellency chose the opposition of same-sex marriage among extreme right wingers. The goal was to make LGTBQ issues a common target. The head of bishops at Baptodist Church believed that the anti-Latino rhetoric could not have posed much danger to the polls. His Excellency, however, was strongly opposed to anti-black slogans and campaigns.

His Excellency did not attend the conference personally. While he was in charge of organizing the June 8 conference, he sent Peter Jr. to Washington DC that day. In a message to Ralph, the public relation representative who was appointed by the Baptodist Church, His

Excellency had emphasized that Peter Jr. was the one who had the first and last words above all.

Trump, standing behind the podium, was super excited to see passionate people applauding his energetic yet soft speech. Through Peter Jr., His Excellency personally had directed the conference management team to make sure the crowd continuously cheered to pump up Trump with their emotional applause.

President Trump, as His Excellency expected, began his speech with the following sentences, "You did not leave me behind, and I will never leave you, you know this well."

When His Excellency heard Trump's speech live from the television, he realized that the movement that he started eight years ago was now flourishing. He also knew perfectly well that Trump had his own agenda separate from the church's goals. It was more upon His Excellency's skills and resources, not Trump's, that this cooperation and collaboration could further blossom. Though the conservative church was always worried about Trump's speeches and unexpected controversies, His Excellency, unlike the others, knew that Trump's narcissism and ego, rather than specific goals, was the main motivation behind his talks and deeds. Furthermore, reelection in 2020 would be an indispensable requirement to keep Trump grounded and tame under the authority of the Baptodist Church.

His Excellency played his cards with Trump carefully. Despite having the upper hand, he never pressed the president more than needed. The conservative church closed its eyes and said nothing when candidate Trump held and waved a rainbow flag at the Republican Convention. His Excellency was cautious not to publish an article on any of the sites attributed to the conservative church against the rainbow flag scene at the convention.

One of the critical key issues was the presence of Peter Chill, a gay billionaire investor alongside candidate Donald Trump. Although it was a controversial issue that could engender crisis, His Excellency, unlike his colleagues in the leadership of the Baptodist Church, believed in allowing Trump to use Peter Chill's card in his campaign. Peter was the right person to impress, though only for a short term, Silicon Valley and all those sinners in San Francisco. He was used as a cushion for their frequent attacks.

His Excellency was aware that Peter Chill dreamed of declaring his homosexual orientation at the conservative Republican convention. Chill wanted to be remembered as the person in history who, with his boldness, raised the conservatives' political and religious capacity for tolerance. But Peter would soon painfully feel Christ's slap across his cheek when he watched Trump's speech at the Path to Majority conference. Peter must have understood that holding the very conference meant not only that the church did not forget his sins of opposing God and his son, but also that he would lose his place among the LGTBQ community. He would be burned by both sides.

Of course, the Baptodist Church did not close its eyes on all of Trump's foolish decisions. The church, adamantly, refused to give Trump the feeling of having unconditional support from the house of God.

During Anthony Scaramucci's nine days as White House communications director, the Evangelical Church took advantage of Mooch's stupidity in his interview with *The New Yorker*. In that interview, Mooch submitted to his ego and used an unprecedented profanity to respond to his opponents. By publishing an open letter, His Excellency forced Trump to disgracefully expel Mooch, who bragged in the media about his friendship and support for LGBTQ. His Excellency, in an open letter, officially ordered Trump to wash Mooch's mouth with water and soap and personally put his belonging in a box, escorting him to the White House exit gate.

The leaders of Baptodist Church believed occasional harsh criticizing, like the one about Mooch, would remind the president that there could not be a free pass to do anything he wanted. Ousting

Mooch from his position in the White House garnered public opinion and support among most liberals who were disgusted by his vulgarity and egoistic manner. In addition to holding the flag of morality and human values, the Mooch example was a perfect one to restrain Trump's heady acts and policies.

The church knew well that Trump was not at all a reliable person; the church did not want to tie its reputation to Trump's faith and personality. Meanwhile, guiding church members and forcing followers to follow their leaders' recommendation in the next election proved to be difficult tasks for His Excellency.

Trump had the possibility of winning voters' trust among the extreme right in a few states, regardless of the consequences of his words, deeds, and actions. But His Excellency knew that the level of believers' thoughts and values undoubtedly was different from those of the few percent of voters in the alt-right. It would be difficult justifying and encouraging church members to support Trump in the 2020 election with frequent controversies that could directly jeopardize conservative values.

On the other hand, the widespread participation of church followers would be a decisive factor in the next presidential election in 2020 or the mid-term congressional election in November of 2018, a factor which required the president to act in line with the church's values. Even with the possibility Trump's impeachment, the church would continue to maintain its power, perhaps increase it, by replacing him with Vice President Mike Pence. From the very beginning, the conservative Baptodist Church had precisely calculated all probabilities. In the event of the president's removal from office, the vice president, who was a full-fledged believer, would be a better replacement.

Now, the presidential speech at the Faith and Liberty Conference was ultimately gaining Christianity's power in politics, which culminated in the fruits of His Excellency's efforts. This great victory was not possible for the Baptodist Church without Trump in the White House.

As the smile on His Excellency's lips penetrated into the greater parts of his face, Trump's sweet voice was what the bishop wanted to hear from the TV at the moment: "You fought hard for me, and now I will fight hard for you..."

# Chapter 21 – Melody

*Southern California*

Melody was the universe's response to David's request at Mount Soledad. Or at least he thought that way. David had told Essie that he met Melody only a few months after his exceptional spiritual experience at Mount Soledad in San Diego, when he was looking down at the Pacific Ocean from an 800-foot elevation.

Melody was a woman full of energy who could make her audience joyful, the first to be approved by David's mother. She changed David's life entirely: for the first time in his life he learned the concept of self-confidence. It was because of Melody that David saw his own inferiority complex, though his mother had told him many times. Melody revealed to David his most prominent characteristics and how to use them in day-to-day life.

People who suffered from any kind of negativity considered Melody pretentious and therefore closed the possibility of any warm relationship with her. Skeptics would ask who could laugh from the bottom of their heart in this dark and despicable world. Genuine laughter, however, was one of Melody's most significant features, even though she had suffered two severe breakdowns in her life. She had two disastrous marriages. Melody always believed that the universe constantly was testing her purity.

Her first husband was a sex addict. Her second husband's sickness was not the same as the first, but far worse. Melody always would say, "I wish he were a womanizer too," as her second husband's sickness shattered her dreams beyond repair. Her first marriage lasted only two years. Melody's life in la-la land with an over-spending sex addict did not only generate a mental illness, but it had grave financial consequences. During that time, Melody was giving her husband all her paychecks to deposit in the bank, unaware of her husband's habit of cashing the checks to spend on mistresses and prostitutes. In the end, what had hurt her the most was feeling like a fool, realizing that her family and friends all knew about his many affairs while she was in the dark. She was being blindly in love and trusting carelessly. This very shame of her ignorance shocked Melody's soul to her core. In the end, what was left was her work at a travel agency that failed as the internet grew.

Melody was a natural salesperson due to her vibrant spirit. She could connect with everyone quickly, transferring her good feelings to the other person. Melody could create trust with any buyer, friend, or acquaintance, a trust that she always honored with her sincerity.

*Some remain in the past and devastated, after such a nasty case. But a frenzied and stormy spirit can throw herself out of a dark and depressed crypt in search of fresh air.*

After the separation from her first husband, Melody had no desire to socialize or even talk to anyone. She needed a change. Melody resigned from her work and enrolled in college.

*In such situations, a positive change is usually the right path out of this dark crypt. And relative peace is the first station after wandering outside of that dark place.*

Melody regained her calm during a few years of loneliness. Unconsciously fearful of repeating the bitter experience of the first marriage, she turned down proposals to meet with the opposite sex, whether he was a classmate, colleague, or friend of friends.

After earning a bachelor degree, she found a job selling medical equipment and busied herself with work and sport. A thirty-year-old woman at the height of physical condition, she was slowly recuperating from her loneliness and reclaiming inner joy. She also would avoid hanging out with female friends as it required attending parties and meeting guys. She was enjoying her solitude, spending time at the gym and reading books.

The solitude, contrary to what people misinterpreted, provided peace of mind for her and it was not because of depression. Melody often refused her older sister's frequent invitations to attend family parties. She knew that Mimi, her sister, had plans to encourage her to go on dates. She did not doubt her sister's goodwill, as she had not suspected anyone before, but the fear of being cheated on again prevented her from participating in any social gathering. The most significant blow was the betrayal of her trust. Had her first husband told her about his wish to be with other women, considering separation, she would have understood. But he repeatedly denied any interest in any other woman. He had even threatened to commit suicide if they separated, at the same time he was engaging in affairs. It sickened Melody to think about her husband sleeping with other women, but it was not as catastrophic as her feeling of being a fool. The concept of being cheated on and lied to was the primary source of sadness.

One night, she accepted Mimi's invitation for dinner at her home after Mimi's insistence and a promise that she would not face a big crowd. When Melody arrived at Mimi's house, she found that she was not the only guest. Mimi and her husband, Ben, had invited a man named Jim. She pulled Mimi to a corner in the kitchen and asked, "I told you before that I'm not interested in being at your parties."

"There is no party here. Jim is Ben's colleague, and he asked Jim to be with us tonight before he knew you were coming," said Mimi.

Melody received Mimi's explanation with disbelief but agreed to stay for dinner. After her ex-husband, Melody had become skeptical of everything. That night in her newly remodeled kitchen, Mimi had not told Melody the truth about her careful arrangement to get her sister to meet Jim. Melody was supposed to meet with a man who was 20 years her senior. Jim, a soft-spoken man with his gentle manner and calmness, calmed Melody's worries and brought a sense of assurance, restoring her lost trust in the opposite sex. Melody did not speak to her sister that night. She said goodbye and left after dinner, dessert, and a little chat.

The day after, Melody dodged many of Mimi's questions about the night before. Then she received a phone call directly from Jim. Melody was surprised to find a calm tone in Jim's voice even on the phone line. She rejected Jim's invitation to go out for dinner with an excuse. The next day, Melody called her sister to complain about sharing her phone number with Jim without her permission, but eventually, it was Mimi who convinced Melody to accept Jim's invitation.

Years later, Melody still remembered that night in a fancy restaurant in La Jolla. Even after all the events of the following years, she still felt its calm atmosphere. Jim's behavior that night as a gentleman treating a lady became an example for Melody to persuade David to follow. Melody believed all boys in school should learn Jim's brand of how to put a woman on the pedestal to make her feel loved.

That night Melody permitted Jim to build a bridge, transferring soft and soothing sensations to a woman who had been hurt by her first and only love. Perhaps it could be a beginning to heal Melody's soul. The warm rush of the white wine was another reason for Melody to bring down her psychological guard against Jim, a shield that she had maintained against men over the years.

Dates between Melody and Jim became more frequent. Apparently as the number of visits between them increased, Jim's excitement to enter into wedlock with Melody grew. Jim introduced Melody to his friends, couples whom he had known for years. Some of them were even older than Jim. Melody found calmness in the circle of Jim's friends without a trace of any excitement. Melody sought to find out why an emotional relationship with the opposite sex did not create any excitement in her but had no success. Melody's bigger surprise was the fact that the lack of excitement in this new relationship did not bother her.

Quicker than expected, their relationship evolved into marriage. Jim was in a hurry to start a new life with Melody and she was happy to hasten the process as well. She wanted to make permanent the feeling of restored peace that had sprouted in her heart since dating Jim.

The first two years were a combination of serenity and storm. Melody was creating the storm, and Jim would abate the whirlwind masterfully with his calm. Melody's past bitter experience made any of Jim's moves suspicious. And it was Jim who poured peace onto Melody with his tolerance. Jim conveyed the message of love to his young wife with thousands of spoken and unspoken emotional languages. In the old and new circle of friends who mostly were couples in Jim's age range, the women were more worried about the presence of the young, bubbly lady than vice versa.

But the age difference still did not reassure Melody's suspicions. Each time, Jim responded with his fatherly type of caresses to Melody's delusive and unsubstantial accusations of his desire for another woman whom he might have glanced at, whether a neighbor or someone in the street. With a kiss on her hand or eyes, Jim assured Melody that the period of distress caused by the betrayal of her ex-husband had come to an end and that she should not be worried any longer.

Though barely, Melody finally restored her lost trust. Now this recovering woman understood that by choosing Jim, she chose calm over excitement. She realized that her preference for an older man was a response to her fear of the next husband's possible desire for another young woman. This finding gave her reassurance that could justify the acceptance of the big age gap between them. In Melody's situation, marrying a much older man did not represent the lack of a father figure in her life but rather the fulfillment of peace of mind for possible mistakes by a younger man. And with that conclusion, Melody regained her peace.

Melody's second marriage could have healed all inflicted wounds by the first marriage on her soul and mind. In dealing with his wife and various events, Jim's intrinsic peaceful manner was leading Melody to the recovery road every day. Even Jim's voice was a kind of meditation for Melody which not only reduced her emotions and innate energy but also put off her volcanic eruptions. Melody had been convinced that Jim's eyes, as opposed to her ex, were not wandering after other women. And she almost had found herself in peace. In fact, over the course of several years of living with Jim, Melody was on the way to go beyond peace, until one day when she encountered an unforgettable scene, an occurrence that she never could imagine in her darkest nightmares.

"God, how can you possibly bring such a disaster to me? How is it possible that I am a witness of such a catastrophe?" Melody would repeatedly ask later.

It was impossible for Melody to comprehend. This new incident created a new and much deeper scar on the remnants of past injuries that could not leave room for recovery.

*How could you think about a remedy to heal your previous wounds when you were stabbed in the heart bleeding or fell on the ground by a bullet in your throat? At that moment, all you do is try to wheeze and grapple with whatever you can grab, not descending in a quagmire of mind so you can be meaningful for yourself.*

And once more, maybe worse than the first time, Melody was placed in the same situation.

The incident happened in Mimi's house during a big party. It was a hot summer evening and Pico, Mimi's Jack Russell terrier, was thrilled to see many guests, especially children. The host had desperately sought to quiet Pico's excitement, which revealed itself through uninterrupted barking and jumping up and down alongside the pool. The scent of various newly bloomed flowers, after the lessening of the late July heat, excited the life inside everyone in the little courtyard's garden. It was unclear whether it was the flowers' scent that made the dog excited, or the unexpected presence of that many people, or the smell of freshly mowed lawn, or the children chasing each other around the pool. The guests were sitting inside the living room or out in the backyard with glasses of wine or bottles of beer in hand, chatting with each other. Inside the kitchen, Melody was helping her sister and the maid, preparing snacks and appetizers to be served to guests. As usual, Melody had an eye on Jim to see to whom her husband was talking at the moment while she was busy working in the kitchen. Melody was totally relaxed. Work could keep her remarkably calm, but at the same time, a slightest doubt or wrong thought would take her to the point of outburst. Her mind was like an unpredictable locomotive, stopping at the random stations of thoughts, moving from one subject to another. Sometimes she let her imagination fly so high it would cross the boundary of reality into fiction, especially when conspiracy was a possibility.

*Who can you trust, when you are betrayed by closest relatives?*

For Melody, the environment for conspiracy was ripe in any circumstance, and this was not a life she had imagined for herself. Until that moment, Melody was on her way to overcoming her fear of being played with. She had no idea her skepticism would become a proven fact in the following minutes.

Melody just had finished arranging small cookies in a crystal diamond-shaped bowl and handed it to Graciela, a maid who worked for her sister at parties. Having seen Jim previously in the backyard, Melody looked out through the window again. To widen her viewing angle, she leaned toward the window. She could not see him. Melody walked into the living room from the kitchen and nodded to some of the passing guests. She felt anxiety in her stomach and tried to stay calm. Melody had experienced this condition before, only to find out that each time she filled her mind with vain feelings by overreacting. Melody walked into the backyard. She felt the pressure of men's gazes on her body from every corner. Mimi, who never said nice things about her in the past, always defined her slim body and slender waist as eye-catching, which of course she attributed to her young age. Her sister reminded her: "Wait until you get pregnant, then you will understand what beautiful body means. After childbirth, all beauty, firmness, and freshness of a woman will go out with the baby. But before delivery, you can make any woman at any age jealous."

Melody's uneven, short bleached-blond hairstyle that was longer on one side of her thin face had given her a unique charm. The same slim face highlighted her eyes and little pointy nose. Her head and the length of the neck was in total harmony with her face and shoulders. Men's hungry, laser gazes were not strange for Melody. In any circle, she could distinguish men's eyes easily from admiration or lust, as well as that of their wives, whose jealousy levels varied depending on how close they were to their husbands. Only in a few cases could Melody establish a close friendship with married women who had come with their husbands in these venues.

Melody could not find Jim in the backyard. She entered the house again. There was no more sound of happy kids, playing and screaming, like before merging with other guests' chatters, creating an annoying hullabaloo. She recognized the kids' hum coming out of the corner room on the first floor. She hesitated for a few moments. She thought Jim was in the bathroom. Mimi walked past her and asked, "What are you looking for?"

"Jim," Melody replied.

"I saw him around a few minutes ago," said Mimi.

Melody walked toward the noisy room to check inside and opened the door. She saw Jim lying on the floor on his back in the middle of the room; some kids were crawling on him. She was relieved for a moment. She went inside. Jim moved and tried to sit up while one kid was trying to climb up on his back. When another kid moved away, Melody took a look at Jim's crotch. She saw a bulge in that spot, under his gray pants. Melody walked toward him quickly and touched Jim's penis. She found it fully erected. Jim stood up and straightened his pants. With rushing blood into her face, Melody asked loudly, "What is this? Why do you have a hard-on?"

"We were playing, and the kids jumped up and down on me, and it happened," replied Jim.

"What do you mean happened? Aren't you ashamed of yourself?" said Melody furiously.

"Don't make too much noise; we were playing. The kids were enjoying the game. Didn't you?" Jim asked, turning to a couple of them behind him.

Melody just realized that the kids still standing there, watching the couple arguing loudly. She instantly turned back and took a step toward the door, but before getting out, she turned back again and told Jim, "Get out, before I call everyone here."

Jim flattened his pants out again and went out. Melody followed him and entered the hallway connecting the room to the kitchen. Something had closed her entire throat, and she could neither breathe nor swallow. She ran toward the front door.

Outside, Melody continued running without knowing which way to go. A gentle breeze touched her face. Apparently, she had gone a couple of blocks. It was hard for her to breathe. Her throat was still clogged. She looked at herself, up and down. She had grabbed her cell phone. Repeated coughs caught her by surprise. First, she brought up a lot of phlegm and then retched a couple of times. Feeling dizzy, she crouched. It was hard to stand. Melody took two steps and sat down on the ground.

It was right in front of her eyes. The disgusting scene, Jim's erection under his pants among the children, was not fading away from her mind. A coarse snail was crawling beside her left foot, aiming toward the vegetation, leaving a shimmering path on the ground along its path. On the other side, a little cottontail, standing on its hind feet, stared at Melody for few seconds then disappeared behind shrubs. Melody pressed her head between her two hands. She found herself in a dark street, sitting on the sidewalk. She did not know how much time had passed. She stood up and looked around. It was completely dark. She was in a small street: on one side, rows of tall trees, like uniformed soldiers, were standing in front of track homes. Behind the rows of trees, uneven bushes and shrubs were growing without any order. Melody could not recognize the place and did not remember which way she had come.

Melody started to walk toward bright lights that were glowing from the main street. Moving toward a small intersection, she saw headlights that were approaching from the right. She walked faster to reach the car before it entered the intersection. Standing in the intersection, she waived with her right hand to the car standing by the stop sign. Always afraid of strangers, Melody could not believe that she was asking one for a ride. The driver slowed down. Melody approached the car on the passenger side. The driver rolled down the passenger window. Melody cautiously lowered her head, looked at the driver, and said, "Excuse me ..."

"Are you okay? What happened?" the driver asked, looking into Melody's eyes.

"I'm lost and don't know where I am. Can you help ... giving me a ride?"

The man turned on the inside light to see the woman's face more clearly and to be seen. Melody seemed to be afraid.

"Yes, I can give you a ride, if you're not dangerous, I hope this is not a setup," replied the driver, smiling.

Melody climbed into the car. She was surprised to find herself sitting next to a stranger yet feeling relaxed. She never thought she would be that bold. After putting the seatbelt on, she turned to the driver and said, "I'm grateful. Please take me to a street over there to find out where I am."

The driver's face was somehow giving her peace of mind, and she did not know why. She settled herself in the seat and felt tired.

"How did you get here?" the driver asked.

"I don't know; I was just running," Melody replied.

"You don't seem to have the right outfit or shoes for jogging."

"I wasn't jogging..."

To change the subject Melody said, "I am Melody," and extended her right hand to the driver. She was startled at her own daring behavior. Melody never could easily communicate with strangers, especially with the opposite sex. Even thinking of doing what she just did would give her the shakes.

"I am David, nice to meet you," the man said.

Meeting David and having a short conversation with him, a stranger, brought much relief to the anxiety she had a few moments ago. Seeing Jim with the children upset her as she remembered the scene in the middle of the room. She covered her face with both hands. David looked at her and said, "Are you okay? What happened? Do you want to go to a specific location?"

Silence reigned in the car. Melody could not get her voice out of her throat. What could she tell this stranger on this dark street? To tell him that his second husband happens to be a child molester? Where would she want to be at this hour of the night, home? They had bought a house recently, but the thought of spending the night with Jim under the same roof gave her nausea. She could not think right and lost her focus. She finally answered, "I don't know."

They reached the main street. David pulled over and stopped the car, then looked at Melody. Melody was staring ahead now somewhat calm.

"Hey, I'm not in a hurry, but we cannot sit here all night," said David.

"I don't know what to say. Please don't think that I'm crazy. Something happened to me that I cannot explain," Melody said.

At that time a police car flashed its lights behind their car and shone the spotlight into David's car. David picked up his phone under the dashboard immediately and brought up the Google map. He quickly gave the phone to Melody and asked her to stare at it. Melody looked at David confused; she had not noticed the police. Meanwhile, the policeman came to David's window, indicating for him to roll it down completely. David nodded as he turned to the police officer and looked at the bright flashlight in his hand.

"Do you need help?" asked the police.

"No, officer, we were looking for an address when the telephone signal dropped."

David then turned to Melody and said, "Honey, do you have signal now?"

The police pointed the flashlight at Melody's face.

"Yes, it's searching," Melody, understanding now, hurriedly replied.

"What is the address you are looking for? Maybe I can help," the officer asked.

"No, officer, that's okay. Now that we have the signal back, GPS is the easier way to find it."

The skeptical policeman looked at David, then asked Melody, "Miss, are you okay, is everything all right?"

And then the officer turned his flashlight toward the back seat. Papers and folders were spread around.

For a moment, Melody hesitated whether to tell the police about Jim's deed in her sister's house. The officer pointed the flashlight at Melody again, waiting for an answer.

"Yes, Officer, everything is okay."

The officer returned to his car after saying good night. David's astounding flushed face seemed a little uneasy, thinking about his quick reaction to hide the truth that he had picked up this woman two blocks away. By lying, David felt he protected Melody from a seemingly unpleasant issue that she was concealing from him. Melody, who temporally came out of her state of sorrow by the police presence asked, "Why did you lie to the police?"

"I don't know; I do not know at all. I didn't want to put you on the spot to answer the police's questions. For a moment, I felt that you were not in a good condition."

Melody lowered her head down and kept silent.

"Now I know where we are, not too far from my sister's home." Melody guided David where he should go.

When they were a couple of houses from Melody's sister's house, Melody noticed that the last guests were just saying goodbye. Melody said to David, "Don't go farther, please. Just stop here."

David pulled over and stopped. They both felt less formal now than when Melody commanded him to stop the car. In Melody's voice, David could detect a tone of pleasant, long, intimate acquaintance. They were both caught off guard, surprised by the mutual trust that had built up.

David paused for a moment and then addressed Melody, "I don't know how to say it but are we going to see each other again?"

Melody, observing the scene in front of her, stretched her neck and pretended she did not hear the question. Guests were leaving Mimi's house, and Melody was still staring ahead. Though Melody was delighted to hear David's question, she did not know what to answer. A strange feeling vibrated throughout her body from head to toe. Contrary to her expectation, she trusted this man, sitting behind the wheel, a stranger that she had just met thirty minutes ago. It was over with Jim, after she saw that horrible scene in her sister's house and then left.

A car approached from the opposite direction and passed them by. She turned to David and looked at his face in the light of the passing car. It was a sincere face, with bright, upright hair, flat on top, trimmed on sides and back. His small nose and eyes were not clear in the dark, but had a reflection of the brightness. In Melody's quick glance, the glare in David's eyes was not a color; it was the light, emanating from his soul and radiating toward Melody. After all the tumult of that night, Melody should have been crushed. In the past, such an incident would have depressed her beyond repair. How could Melody give a positive response to David's eyes? But she did, and surprisingly, it was not hard.

She was not able to think more. There was enough adventure for one night. She suddenly felt tired. Like a low battery level in a phone, Melody's lower energy level rang in her ears. At the same time, her phone rang too. It was Mimi. Melody did not take the call and tapped on the button to silence the ring. She said to David, "What's your number?"

The numbers coming out of David's mouth, were inserted through Melody's fingers and then tapped onto the phone's dial pad. When the tenth number was entered on the flip phone, Melody's thumb did not pause to press the green button, and after a while, David's phone vibrated and rang.

Melody opened the door and went out. There was only one word to describe the night with David: "Bye." David nodded at the passenger window with nothing but the dark of the night behind it.

Just a few months ago, on the top of Mount Soledad, overlooking the ocean in the caressing breeze, in a tranquilizing trance, along with flying birds and two tourists, David had sent his wish to eternity to find someone to love and be loved in return. And now, although she had disappeared from his view, Melody's scent assured him that tonight was not a dream.

***

Mimi was the family's eldest child. Her mother was the only one who called her Mary-Ann. Mimi hated being called by her real name. She even would get more repulsed by her mother's biblical explanation about the history of the name. When Mary-Ann was eleven, Melody was born, and one year later, a brother was added to the family. Almost all of the duties, especially taking care of Melody, fell on Mary-Ann's shoulders. In Philadelphia, where she lived with her husband and children, the mother had devoted herself to the Church of Jesus Christ. When Gladys was not busy with her religious duties, she would do charity work with friends, promoting her church to shine the light of Jesus on doubters' heart. Gladys genuinely believed that only her church was the true representative of God on earth. She believed that her family were directly descended from the Puritans. Mother was so busy infusing the love of Jesus into the spirit of the nonbelievers that she left the family and father on their own. Pursuing and identifying the dark-hearted, Gladys and her friends were approaching the circles of immigrants, foreigners, and the deprived to show the way of obeying the holy shepherd as faithful sheep. To Mimi's mother, the home was nothing but an extension of the church.

Contrary to what Mimi would have thought, her mother did not leave home duties unsupervised. By issuing orders, she was conveying specific responsibilities to each member of the family so life would continue as normal as possible. To Mimi's bad luck, in the absence of her father, she was the only caretaker at home. Her father avoided being involved with her mother's religious affairs. He was rarely present at home. What Mimi would later recall of her childhood and adolescence was taking care of two kids and all the chores at home. Changing diapers, cleaning, and cooking killed Mimi's desire to live in the house. She could not wait to leave the house and start a new independent life. She believed as a teenager that it was not fair for her to undertake all responsibilities of the household all by herself. Unlike many people, Mimi remembered her adolescent years very clearly. They were all archived one by one in her mind and she would review them throughout her life deliberately.

Mimi recalled her parents fight only once. She never remembered hearing or seeing a voice or scene of their lovemaking. One night Mimi could not fall asleep; she heard her mother's voice, shouting and demanding that the father wash his private part, a request that obviously outraged her father.

"Go, go wash it. How long do you want to live like an animal?"

"Oh, did gospel say about this or just the pastor in your church explained about men's sexual organ?"

Mother shouted, "This is the only thing I ever want you to do before coming to bed, and you act mulish."

"Why do you think you're better than the rest of the people? And to you, those who don't think same as people in the church are animals?" the father shouted back.

"It's not long ago that I had the condition. I've been told that most likely it came from you."

"Who said that, the church pastor or the bishop? What else about sex is discussed in those religious gatherings?"

Then something like a vase or bowl smashed, and then the loud conversation followed for some time. Eventually, they both silenced. Other than that, Mimi did not remember any type of relationship between her mother and father, whether sexual or non-sexual or social.

Two years before the end of high school, Mimi prepared an independent living plan for moving away from home and family. That was possible now that her siblings were older. She had no plans for continuing her education. She saved some money from babysitting and working as a cashier in the neighborhood grocery store. But when the time came, the girl who was supposed to accompany her to California backed out. Her friend's change of heart did not make much effect on Mimi's decision. She just had to take off and go to the West. With her savings, she could survive until she found a job. She was not as into the glamorous Hollywood lifestyle as her friend was. Mimi was not delusional about her looks and body. Her long face, small eyes, very thin lips, and long nose, which underwent plastic surgery years later, did not attract any boy in high school. Unlike her classmates, she was not trying to catch the attention of the opposite sex. To her surprise, she was somehow indifferent to the presence of her male classmates. Under the pretext of attending college in California, she won her mother's promise to pay for some of the cost of her settling in the new place. Mimi packed her bags and moved to Pasadena, a city near Los Angeles with a list of connections that Gladys collected from her church group.

Years passed. She started at a real estate office as a secretary. Not too long after that, she passed the California Real Estate Salesperson exam. At the same time, she met Benjamin and moved to Anaheim. Apparently, for the first time in her life, everything was going well— until she received her sister's request to move in with her in California. She did not respond to Melody's letter for a while. Mimi was not in a hurry to re-create the past. Any memory from years earlier, Philadelphia, her mother, and the church, irritated her. Even the thought of what she had put behind would have lessened her energy. And now, 19-year-old Melody was honestly asking and sending her messages that she could not explicitly refuse to answer. Finally, she agreed to Melody's request. Melody could be helpful with clients in real estate transactions.

When Melody moved to California, Mimi was six months pregnant, but later miscarried. It did not take long for Melody to develop anxiety from Ben's shameless gazes. She tried to hide in her room when he was at home. Melody would spend most of the time out of the house, and when Mimi needed help, if Ben's presence were also required, she would excuse herself. One and a half months after arrival at his sister's house, Ben found the courage to express his desire for Melody. Mimi, clueless about the situation, had asked Melody to help Ben collect signs that advertised open houses on the weekend. In the beginning, Ben did not say a word while driving. Melody sat next to him and was busy tracking Mimi's signs at every intersection. After passing through a few streets, Melody felt Ben's right hand on the back of her left hand. She pulled her hand repulsively as if a lizard had touched her skin. Frightened, she pretended to be still looking for signs. Ben, looking ahead on the road, did not speak a word until they returned home. Melody went to her room and did not come out until the next morning. When Melody told her sister in the kitchen about what happened in the car, Mimi calmly said, "You have to move out. It is better to find a place to live for yourself."

Melody's tears rolled down on her cheeks as she heard Mimi's response. It was hard for her to grasp what Mimi said. Melody was looking at the side of Mimi's face, which did not indicate what she was thinking at that moment. Mimi was staring out of the kitchen window onto the backyard. A hummingbird, facing toward the kitchen, was flapping on the same spot for several seconds. Mimi could not see the little bird. Mimi's look seemed to be lost in infinity. Melody could not tell whether she believed her or not. Without any word, Melody left the kitchen. The next day, Melody moved out to a place whose address had been given to her by one of her mother's acquaintances; it was linked to the church.

***

"Where did you disappear all of a sudden?" asked Mimi, when she saw Melody get out of David's car and enter her house. Melody's silence made Mimi uneasy, so she asked angrily, "Why are you behaving like a crazy person? Couldn't you take your family quarrel somewhere else tonight? What happened between you two? I've never seen Jim that upset before."

"Didn't he tell you what happened?" Melody asked.

Mimi replied, "No, what happened, where did you go?"

After Melody explained the scene she had seen to her sister, Mimi said nothing, but her face showed her refusal to accept Melody's claim. Mimi doubted her sister's allegation, but did not want to take a definite position at that time. Mimi used the family quarrel issue as an excuse to start a conversation. Melody had guessed her sister knew. Mimi had found out from Jim, but she pretended that she had no clue. Melody became furious later when she realized that her sister already knew. "Why do I have to be played all the time in my life?" It was a question for different points in her life, and she never had an answer.

Melody believed that she was not suited for this world. She also believed that what kept her sane in the midst of such deceptions was her heart that sincerely wished the best for everybody. Her open and honest character was the weakness that would always leave her defenseless against others, at least temporarily.

"Okay, now go home see where he is, and discuss the matter between the two of you," said Mimi.

The answer was so insulting that for the second time that night blood rushed to Melody's face. She could not fathom what was coming out of her sister's mouth. Anything but that, she thought, can't you think of any other answer but "go ahead, get along and solve the problem?"

If her sister had said that she questioned Melody's judgment, it would not be difficult to accept. But suggesting that she get along with a child molester meant she had no problem being in the same boat with the devil. In Melody's view, Jim was a criminal and nothing else. If all the universes came to Earth to convince her to think differently, she would disagree firmly. Not only had she seen it, to be sure, but she had also touched his erect penis. What was later more surprising for

Melody was that most of her friends and acquaintances echoed Mimi. Melody's view of life was thrown into turbulence, and she evaluated the community around her with a new benchmark.

Another blow came two nights later. Mimi insisted on a meeting at her house to review the situation with her and Ben one more time. First, she refused. But then, after Mimi's persistence, she decided to go. It did not matter to her anymore. Upon arrival, she realized that the meeting had already been set up, and once again she had been played. At the door, Melody decided to go back, but she did not want them to think that she had retracted her claim. Melody went inside. Ben and Jim were lying in chairs, wine glasses in hand, on the poolside, and Mimi, pleased and delighted, was doing her chores. Melody had not seen Jim for two days. Two nights ago after leaving Mimi's home, she had sent a message to Jim that she did not want to see him again.

Melody suddenly felt lethargic as she walked toward them. She could not even say hello to anyone. She never liked Ben. To her, Ben was an unintelligent man, a clown, a low-class individual who would hang around in parties with his excessive buffoonery. The fact that someone like Mimi could agree to marry an idiot like Ben was bugging Melody.

In the past few days, Melody remembered Jim's great interest in the film Lolita, starring Jeremy Irons. "How were my eyes were shut to this fact, or at least, how did the question not pop into my mind?" Melody thought. Sometimes, human blames self for failing to see the obvious truth for how ignorant one can be to miss such clear signs.

Ben said hello. Jim was silent, sipping wine out of the glass in his hand. Mimi joined them, trying to ease the air with a few fake laughs. Only Mimi and Pico were moving, Pico wagging his tail. For the rest, the atmosphere was so dense it was hard to breathe.

"Would you like a glass of wine?" Mimi asked Melody.

"No, I have to go. I'm gonna drive," said Melody.

Melody didn't notice how the subject came up, but it turned into a full-blown argument. Jim cried out in anger and called Melody a crazy bitch in need of psychotherapy. Mimi tried to calm the atmosphere and repeatedly invited Melody to have a peaceful reaction. Pico was moving his head from one person to the other with his ears upright as if he wanted to take part in the conversation. Disappointed that he wasn't getting attention, Pico grunted and then flattened his neck on the ground, pointing his eyes around. Apparently the hostile atmosphere in the crowd affected even Pico's behavior.

Jim denied the facts completely and questioned Melody's mental health. Ben, listening to all sides in silence, seemed to be pleased, smiling as if he was watching an erotic movie. Mimi hated Ben's state of mind in these situations. Eventually, when two sides came to a dead end, Jim stood up, pointed to the direction of the house's front door, shouting to Melody, "Get the fuck out of here."

Shocked, Melody tried to conceal her surprise. She did not know how Jim felt so bold in her sister's house. She was speechless. How dare Jim could throw her out of Mimi's house? Melody expected Mimi to do something: throwing him out was one option, perhaps the only option. If not, she could at least put Jim in his place and tell him to apologize for his profanity. But to Melody's horror, Mimi did not even say a word. Mimi just lowered her head. Melody stood up, gesturing that she wanted to leave in the hope of making Mimi ashamed and possibly forcing her to say something. But Pico was the only creature that broke the silence. Jim stood behind the barricade formed by Ben and Melody's sister and repeated his vulgar words to Melody, "Get the fuck out of here now."

Melody turned back and looked at the three of them before stepping into the building from the backyard to leave. The image forever was recorded in her mind. She walked out of the living room and went to the front door. Pico, with his flickering tail in harmony with his walking body, was escorting Melody to the end.

Her phone vibrated before she reached the car. She went into the car and saw a message from David on the screen: "How about a cup of coffee?"

This was the first message she had received after that night. She paused, doubting whether to answer now or later. "It's too late; I have to go to work tomorrow," she finally sent.

She sent the second message instantly, not wanting to convey rejection by her first message. "How about tomorrow? in the afternoon."

"Okay, I'll call you tomorrow at five o'clock," replied David

She sat in the car trying hard to hold back her tears. Standing outside her house, Mimi was watching Melody from a distance, expecting her to stop and talk. Melody would have to pass in front of Mimi's house where her sister was waiting. Melody decelerated but did not stop. She stared at Mimi's eyes while slowly passing her. Melody neither saw any regrettable sense in Mimi's look nor any guilty feeling. Surprised, Melody saw a sense of victory in her sister's eyes. Melody was confused. She could not comprehend the meaning of that look. She felt like throwing up. With a heavy heart, she pushed her foot on the gas pedal and drove away.

Mimi, on the other hand, was staring at humiliated, escaping Melody from the peak of her castle. She was dancing ambitiously within as if she finally and victoriously conquered and defeated her enemy's stronghold. The weird sensation had overtaken her body. Mimi's nipples tickled in that semi-hot summer's night, and a sexual feeling like the creeping snake passed through her lower abdomen. Something was becoming alive in her. The little girl, Melody, whom Mimi had always hated, weak, aggrieved and crushed, was running away in front of her eyes. Mimi felt that if she wanted to, she could lift her foot like a giant and put it on Melody's car and squish it. The whirlwinds of sexual thirst turned to an uproar in a heartbeat. At that moment, she craved to squeeze someone to the point of crushing.

Mimi went inside and entered the kitchen. She looked out to the backyard, where Ben and Jim were still sitting. With a bitter face, Mimi turned away with hatred. She went upstairs to the bedroom, locked the door, and lay down on her abdomen on the bed. She put her right hand between her legs and depicted a scene in her mind. Mimi imagined herself, on top of Ayla, her half-fictional love, covering her petite body by her own massive, tall frame. She found her clitoris with her middle finger of her right hand and started to touch herself, as a guitar player uses the string bending technique so that the outcome's echoes vibrate. Sometimes she entered the same finger into her orifice slightly and pushed it up to the top of her vaginal wall. The right hand was the only option. Her left hand could never bring her to a climax.

Although the windows were closed, she tried hard not to make any noise. But it was impossible. Now, she was completely devouring Ayla. Mimi squeezed her to the point where she moaned hard from the pain. With her eyes, Mimi told Ayla that she should not make a sound. Mimi put her left hand on Ayla's mouth whose eyes were begging for a sip of breath to stay alive. With shush, Mimi warned Ayla that she had better be careful not to make excessive noise. And then, Mimi took her mighty palm off of Ayla's mouth and replaced it with her lips over her lovers'. Ayla's nostrils flared. She could feel the deep breathing of Ayla on her left cheek. Mimi's big breasts were pressing against Ayla's. She loved Ayla's breaths when they were close to each other. Mimi threw her entire weight on her, who was being crushed like a chicken under her oversized body. Her finger now entered Ayla, moving not so gently. She felt her body and vagina as the same as Ayla's. Mimi felt she could not stop screaming coming out of her throat so she covered her own mouth, pressing it onto a pillow. Breathing became difficult. Her thirst-quenching satisfaction was expelling from the depths of her existence into her throat in the form of howling.

After few seconds, she became calm. She also felt that Ayla was breathing normally. She lifted her face off the pillow and took a deep breath. This was one of the best orgasms she had ever experienced. Mimi was not sure that a real lovemaking with Ayla could have brought her this much joy. She told herself, "No sexual orgasm can compare with the one I just had."

*When years of compiled rage are accompanied by sexual despair and find their way out, the climax is volcanic.*

"Ah Ayla, my beloved friend, I wish you had the same desire as I did. Oh, what if you were here beside me, and I could touch your heaven-scented hair. You wouldn't deprive me of touching your silky skin."

Mimi no longer had the desire to squeeze and crush Ayla's bones. She fell into a deep sleep with memories of her sweet beloved Ayla.

In the backyard, Ben and Jim raised their heads and looked at the window of the bedroom, which overlooked the courtyard. When they heard the whining sound, Jim asked, "What was that sound?"

Ben replied, "It's nothing. Sometimes, at this time of the night, coyotes and dogs challenge each other by howling."

# Chapter 22– King Birsha

After Tim's first three Sodom stories ran in the *Bay Area Chronicle*, he was considered unlike any other journalist in the organization. He was promoted from his previous position and was now a celebrity. His connection with David and his friends, and Essie's insistence on using Tim to spread the stories of Sodom foretold by Art through a prominent Northern California newspaper, had shown this newcomer journalist to be adept among controversial authors. He did not need to be recognized by his father's court cases anymore. Now Tim would feel his colleagues' looks, a mixture of envious and admirable stares, when he walked into the newspaper office. Tim had secured a cozy corner office on the top floor with a nice view, away from the crowded newsroom and other departments.

Soon after Michael threw Tim out of the bar for writing his first piece, his initial unpleasant feeling was replaced by a superb sense of victory, like winning a lottery jackpot. Tim was saddened by Michael's outrage, and for several weeks it left a dent in Tim's soul. Michael's unfair judgment almost made him regret his hasty action in writing someone else's story without permission. Although it was an instinctive reaction of any writer to grab a good story, Michael's anger and the subsequent ban on visiting him in the bar had put Tim in a lousy position. But David's invitation to the circle, then granting access to the incredible source of stories, put him in an exceptionally advantageous situation.

With such a feeling that he never experienced before, Tim poured his daily cup of coffee and a glass of cold water before going to his comfortable office to start typing the next segment of the Sodom stories. He put his briefcase down on the floor next to his chair, took a sip of his coffee, sat behind his desk, extended his arms forward, locked his fingers together, and cracked his joints. Tim placed his fingers on the keyboard and started typing...

***

## *Gomorrah region – Birsha's Palace*

King Birsha was lying down in bed between a woman and a young man. His left hand was under the woman's neck, and his right hand was playing with the young man's hair. The king turned to the woman and said, "Edna, I've been told that a messenger has come from Sodom to inform us that soon Sichra and Amim will come here to see us." Then he turned to the young man and continued, "Achan, if you want, you can also be there."

Then, the king stretched his neck toward Achan and placed a kiss on his cheek. Edna gently turned the king's face toward herself and said, "They have already arrived at the palace, my king. I arranged for them to go to your chamber now. There is no need for Achan to be there."

Achan frowned. He obviously was hurt by Edna's comment. He turned his head to look at the wall. But the king turned Achan's face back toward himself and said, "Let's hear from Achan." After saying that, Birsha moved toward the young man and put his lips on Achan's so that he had to pull his left hand from under Edna's neck.

Achan said nothing, but Edna got up and took her gown from the floor and put it on. "They are waiting for us; we should not keep them standing there too long," said Edna, as she was stepping out of the room.

***

King Birsha and Achan entered the chamber hand in hand. Edna was sitting on the king's throne and was talking to Sichra and Amim who were standing beside her. Edna did not stand up when she saw the king entered the chamber and continued talking. Then she ended her conversation with an opinion: "You have to see where they came from and what they really want."

The king stood in front of Edna, staring at her with a frown, without paying much attention to the homage that Sichra and Amim were performing. Edna rose and walked toward Achan and stood beside him, trying to take his hand, but Achan pulled his hand away quickly. Sichra and Amim noticed what happened between the king's close companions. Then the king sat on the throne and asked, "Sichra, how is my brother, Bera, doing? It's quite a time that I have not seen him."

"Very well, sire," Sichra said, lowering her head slightly to show respect, "King Bera has sent his salutary greetings to the king of Gomorrah and wished you well. King Bera also gave us the mission to personally inform you about the development of current events in Sodom. Numbers of people, whose intentions as well as their identities are not known, have arrived at Sodom's eastern gate. They seek Sodom's inhabitancy forever."

King Birsha said, "Is it possible that they are connected to Chedorlaomer?"

Amim responded, "We are investigating. King Bera also wishes to know if you will allow some of them to relocate to the great region of Gomorrah after the approval process is completed."

King Bera had asked Amim to raise this issue in a meeting with King Birsha and inform Sichra about the request on the way to Gomorrah.

King Birsha first looked at Edna and then said, "If King Bera thinks this is a good deed, I will accept. Why not?"

Both Sichra and Amim nodded to show respect to King Birsha. The king turned to Achan and continued, "Tonight, we will hold a celebration for our dear guests in honor of their presence. A grand celebration is what we have missed in a long while."

"Oh sire, with your permission, may we travel to the other three regions to deliver King Bera's message?" Sichra requested immediately.

With a deep sigh, Achan walked to Amim and Sichra, put his arms around each of their necks, and said, "Oh, how unfortunate. I was very eager to enjoy time with both of you and the king tonight."

The king rose and took several steps forward while thinking. He turned to the guests and asked, "How's our great wise old man? Has he sent us any advice or guidance?"

Sichra replied, "The old man is still wise and healthy. He has a blessing time with his students. He teaches all day but says he's still in the process of learning."

King Birsha said, "We would love him to come here and spend some time with us. Not a day passes without us thinking about him, and our hearts miss his rich poetry and his great stories. I hope he has not forgotten us. I will ask my brother, King Bera, to let the wise old man live here with us for a while."

Sichra replied, "Incidentally, because he knows about your taste, he asked me to send you special greetings ..."

The king jumped in and interrupted Sichra, "Didn't you bring me anything from him? Didn't he send anything?"

Sichra answered, "Yes, I was trying to say that he told us to offer the great king of Gomorrah a story. If there is an opportunity now, I'm honored to convey his message and then with the king's permission we will be discharged from your service and on our way."

King smiled and said, "I'm all ears."

Sichra looked at Amim and then Edna, who was standing very quietly, looking down without any movement, as if she was more eager to listen than King Birsha was. Sichra said, "In ancient times, there was a handsome king whose poetic taste made him the favorite of hearts, especially among young lovers, both men and women. Nothing was lacking in the king's life, and he had achieved everything he wished for. Happiness was the king's state of mind in his day-to-day life."

"One day, a stranger came to the palace and requested permission to enter, but he was rejected by guards who sent him away. The stranger came the next day and days after, and every time he faced the palace's closed gates. In following weeks, the stranger continued to not only pursue his will but also insisted on visiting the king himself, refusing to leave the place.

"The news about the stranger's persistence reached the king. The king's advisers considered the stranger in the best case a madman, whose cloth was a patched garment, wandering around the city as if he was astounded by an unnatural phenomenon. Days passed, and the stranger did not withdraw his insistence to meet with the king.

"The king eventually ordered him brought to his chamber. The raggedy man came to the palace, and the moment he saw the king, he fell to his knees and was unable to breathe. Then, he raised his head and composed a poem describing the king which caused disorder in the chamber. The king's poetic nature was pleased by listening to the beautiful poetry of the strange man. The king, pleased by his decision to allow his entrance to meet with him, asked about his demand. The king asked if he wanted a bag of gold or a horse or a graceful outfit. When he faced the strange man's silence, he offered some other attractive suggestions. The advisers who supervised the meeting were worried about the king's insistence. After a while, the man asked to whisper his wish into the king's ear. The king looked at his advisers, who showed their opposition in their fiery eyes. Against the advisers' wishes, the king allowed the stranger to approach the throne.

"The man advanced and neared his head to the king's ear and whispered something. After a few words, the king closed his eyes and listened submissively. It was a short whisper. No one knew what the stranger said to the king, but the king was no longer the same after hearing his words. The stranger left the palace. From then on, it was as if no king inhabited the king's body. Without a word, he decided to leave everything behind for good. The king turned into a raggedy man himself, the same as the stranger, and left the kingdom forever.

"News spread about the king and the stranger wandering around, begging for food or working in different areas, barely staying alive. No one ever knew what that stranger whispered in the king's ear that day, making him so selfless."

Sichra stopped talking. King Birsha took a step toward Sichra and said, "Well, then, what happened next?"

Sichra replied, "The wise old man spoke only to this part. He said he would narrate the rest of the story later."

The King, drowned in his thoughts, stayed quiet. Edna broke the silence and said, "The old man is just old, and there was no particular meaning in this story, and if so, we'll know it later."

Achan went to the king's side. Birsha put his arm around his waist while still thinking. Sichra and Amim bowed down as a gesture of respect and left the king's chamber. Edna stood up in front of the king and asked, "Why did you accept the possible admission of shelter seekers?"

Birsha, who seemed to just awaken out of the story, said, "Sodom is our ally, and we need to help them if we can. We are in an alliance with four other regions as well. Without each other, we are nothing. Without our allies, against Chedorlaomer, we are like chickens against a hyena. As far as we know, our secret of resilience remains in our alliance. But I envy their organization and their structure. We need to learn from them. I wish we also had a wise old man to guide us."

The lines and muscles on Edna's face twisted. She felt that she was explicitly the target of the king's words. She unleashed her anger and shouted, "What they all do together, I'm able to do alone. My lord, what happened to us that you're stinging me with your words? We do not have the wise old man, but we try to grow the wisdom in ourselves. Envy for something that is not beneficial to us will act like a poison from within, which will lead us to devastation. Here, efficient individuals are at the top key positions, and I am the one who is watching them. When you and Achan have a playful time in the bed, who do you think is in charge to make sure that the security of our palace and the masses are being impeccably provided for? Who do you think foiled Chedorlaomer's three conspiracies to set fire on our public passages? It was I, not the wise old man. And you never say anything about who strengthened our defense against the enemy. And you, Achan, you must know that I know your secret, I know where you spend your nights getting drunk in the city."

"Do not be disturbed by my words," said the king, whose body language was an indication of his regret for his extreme emotion toward Edna. "If I said something, I meant for our establishment to be in a better position, even though that you said it is fully under control."

Achan interrupted the king and said to Edna, "So you knew, yet you commanded the guards not to open the palace gate for me?"

The king looked at both of them in surprising, then asked, "What do you say, Achan?" Edna, what is going on? What does he say? "

Edna said nothing. Then the king put his arms around their necks and brought their heads closer together. The King placed a kiss first on Edna's cheek and then on the Achan's. With his hand on their shoulders, King Birsha pushed their faces so that his lovers' lips were touching. Edna and Achan's lips remained unmoved and separated after a few moments.

# Chapter 23 – James

*Undisclosed Location*

"This is one of the series that the newspaper has published about this issue. I don't know what their intentions are in playing this childish game. They are questioning our entire belief system. The latest issue has officially declared war against us. We have to think about a plan of action before it's too late. The situation is changing rapidly," His Excellency said.

One of the bishops sitting around the table picked up the newspaper. The table had a beautiful cherry finish with burnished brown wood; the five French-style armchairs were elegantly hand carved. The door in the right corner was closed. A large cross was mounted on the wall right behind His Excellency's seat. A circular lamp hanging from the ceiling above the table illuminated most of the table and its surroundings, but its height was only about two feet from the table, so it lit up only the chests of the bishops. Above the light's level, just the shadowy figures of the men present at the meeting could be seen.

The one who picked up the paper said, "There are hundreds of stories, jokes, nonfiction, and fiction, published against the history of Christianity every day. Some of them even find their way to the most important liberal newspapers or are shown on TV networks as documentaries. Why should we take this one seriously or pay special attention to it? What is the difference between this nonsense and those other absurdities?"

Peter Jr., on the right side of His Excellency, repositioned himself on his chair. Due to the sensitivity of the situation in recent weeks, Peter Jr. had had several phone conversations with Sam, sometimes twice a day, in addition to text correspondence. Peter Jr. gestured his intention to respond after hearing the bishop's question, but with his boss's hand movement, he re-positioned in his chair and remained silent again. After a careful assessment, His Excellency knew that he himself should lay the foundation for this small group, which will be the backbone of the future decisions and actions. In addition to his instinct, which was a result of more than 50 years' experience organizing conservative Evangelical groups, there was evidence indicating approaching significant events. His Excellency strongly believed that the current challenge ahead was more critical than all past religious and political events in his life. For this reason, he devoted his energy to analyzing and planning to confront what he believed was a monster rising against the light of God. Planning any action would be worthless if the other bishops, sitting in front of him, could not grasp the depth of the subject and the importance of the events. In his opinion, the men in this room were considered to be the true representatives of Christianity and God, although His Excellency did not entirely agree with views of some of them. Before showing a video, the head of bishops decided to convince them that the impending crisis, the imminent storm, should be taken seriously. In the video sent by Sam, Art was demonstrating his power. His Excellency had kept the video to shock the bishops as his final, winning card.

Before coming to this meeting, His Excellency wondered would have happened if he were not totally aware of the situation—what would have happened to Christianity in general and to the future of the Conservative Church in particular. Now, he felt that the cross of responsibility that Jesus carried was on his shoulders, carrying the historical mission of all those who had been sacrificed in Christ's path. After clearing his throat, His Excellency addressed the audience:

"We are under attack. Yes, what you said about lies, fake stories that are published every day against the church, is correct. Basically, what brought us together to form the central council of the true Church of Baptodist was based on the attack from the so-called progressive thinking which began to target the heart of Christ's instructions. We have been working together for many years. Now, not only throughout the nation but also in many countries around the world, we have a network that can thwart a conspiracy against the church. The reason for today's meeting in our small group, with fewer attendees, is to respond to and clarify what James had asked."

"The article that was just published on this," His Excellency pointed to the newspaper on the table in front of James, with a gesture of disgust, "is just the tip of the iceberg, coming out of a city that has long been the nest of the devil. We know that the heads of major tech companies in Northern California are systematically organizing meetings similar to ours..."

James interrupted His Excellency to point out, "But, we cannot be sure about this. There is still no clear evidence about these meetings."

The interruption not only upset His Excellency but also collapsed the thread of thoughts and words in his mind. For a moment, his facial lines were knotted, especially in his forehead between his two eyebrows. In his view, James's disrespect was unforgivable. His Excellency expected everyone in this room to respect his superiority as much as Peter Jr. did, but they considered themselves to be equal with the head of bishops, not lower. James, the main rival of His Excellency, always emphasized that the separation of the Protestant Church from Catholicism had been based on the removal of a boss or a person as a middleman between followers of Christ and God. In opposition to His Excellency, James was always lecturing on the role of the Pope and the hierarchy of the Vatican Church as a distraction from a real connection with God. The heads and leaders of the Evangelical Church, either those who were directly affiliated with His Excellency in the Bapdodist church or those in other churches, were not pleased with his placing himself at a higher position than the others. But few of them dared challenge the head of bishops on his views and actions.

His Excellency had convinced everyone on different issues by his doctrine that was backed by substantial proof. From his point of view, ultimately, practical results were the criteria to determine right from wrong, not the talk of blabbermouths. And what better outcome could have shut critics up than President Trump at the White House?

His Excellency resumed his speech, "Oh, James, my good friend, never doubt that for many years, they have not hesitated to make all efforts to dim God's light in the hearts of His servants. The growth of liberalism under the name of neo-Evangelicals or the more absurd left Evangelical is only the product of Silicon Valley's enduring endeavor and that sinister city." His Excellency specifically refused to mention San Francisco's name.

Peter Jr. knew well that his boss's greatest interest in the Old Testament was related to that part of Abraham's life, which was linked to Lot's stories. Peter Jr. had repeatedly heard with his own ears His Excellency's theory that the creation of Silicon Valley as technology's Mecca was not coincidental at all. He believed the presence of the largest technology companies that over the last few years have become wealthy was purposefully mastered in and around the sin city, traditionally a sanctuary to those sinners who promote homosexuality to counter God's creation. To the head of bishops, support of Hollywood in the expansion of homosexuality was a significant part of tech companies' constant effort. John Wesley the Third also believed that the battles that have been highlighted in recent years over financial issues such as unauthorized downloaded movies and the fights between tech companies and Hollywood were all fake and nothing but a show.

His Excellency continued, "James, don't doubt for a second that now AI, or artificial intelligence, is being designed and introduced as an alternative to the God's creation. There is no coincidence that tech companies and sinners are in the same boat with this." Then, he immediately turned to Peter Jr. and nodded.

"Yes, we have enough knowledge about your theories," James replied, "but we have to be careful not to rush. Creating controversies will cause a backlash. Our enemies will burn us in this digital era of media and the internet."

As James was speaking, Peter Jr. pulled out his laptop from his handbag next to his chair, put it on the desk, and opened its monitor. After a few inputs on the keyboard and clicks on the pad, he rotated it for the audience to see the screen. Then, Peter Jr. played the recorded video clip that Sam had sent from David's office. The audience became uneasy in their seats, and two bishops started whispering.

"Where is this place? Is that a robot raising the chair with someone sitting on it?" asked one bishop who was sitting across from His Excellency.

Another asked, "Are you sure this movie has not been edited? You cannot trust any video, photo, or document these days."

His Excellency replied calmly, "It's a startup company that is researching AI technology in San Francisco. Our agent has sent this video to us. There are still many questions unanswered."

His Excellency and Peter Jr. knew Arthur was not a robot. They concealed the fact that he was the same person whom they had talked about in the last session. But neither His Excellency nor Peter Jr. spoke about that fact. His Excellency saw that the bishops were partially upheld by his theory, but it was much less than what he and Peter Jr. had expected.

# Chapter 24 – Pride Parade

*San Francisco – Market Street*

"It could not be more beautiful than this. What amazing weather, what a day," David said, inhaling the air deeply.

Indeed, a mellow sunny day on Sunday afternoon in June was nothing short of a pleasant, satisfying day. The colors of the rainbow were splashed on the Market Street, yet there was no sign of any rain droplets as the sun was sneaking a peek behind the clouds in the sky. Despite a cloud-free sky, the seven vivid colors had been poured everywhere.

The annual Pride Parade was at its peak, decorated by rainbow flags, loud and proud, along the streets leading to Market. Laughter was not only spreading the joy in the air but also injecting pleasure to everyone and anyone who was marching or watching the parade. It was one of those days that a man would become thrilled just to be born and alive, and the wave of thrill overflowed to every single organ inside the body and materialized into life.

Three couples, David and Melody, Simone and Essie, Michael and Art, had come to see the parade to shake off the stress of recent incidents. Standing behind a barricade at the intersection of Market and First streets, they were watching various groups of marchers in the parade who offered their energy and inner feelings to the fullest.

Before the events and adventures of the past few months, meditation would have relieved David's stress from daily problems. But now, every meditation session, in addition to strengthening Art, had become a font of new adventures. But this beautiful day cheered this particular group, which was going to be identified as the center of gravity in future confrontations and emerging crises.

The music, crowd applause, and slogans, streaming into handheld speakers, kept David from fully understanding Melody's comments. The musical parade was just exhilarating; it combined marching men and women dressed in costumes with colorful makeup, sometimes half-naked, walking along the street. Many signs with slogans against Trump, in different heights and sizes, were particular characteristics of the Pride Parade in that day. These slogans, conveying different messages—from invitations to resist, to defend the democracy, to shield refugees and asylum seekers—were seen on banners, carefully decorated boards, and even handwritten on cardboard.

David turned his head to look right beyond where Melody was standing. He saw Essie in a hot spot, standing between her and Simone; on one hand, he was paying attention to Simone, and on the other hand, preventing any incident with Melody. Simone was staring quietly at the parade. David sent a text to Essie and signaled for him to check his phone. Essie pulled the phone out of his pocket and read the message, "What's the matter with Simone? She is super quiet today."

Essie looked at David's curious face. By raising his eyebrows and shrugging his shoulders simultaneously, Essie intimated that he had no idea. In fact, Simone had a strange feeling. She had contradictory emotions that she was not able to deal with. Simone was standing beside a man, her relationship with whom she did not know the exact nature. Of course, she would understand that apart from the needs and curiosity of a woman of her age, certain parts of her relationship with

Essie were a paradox. Simone was surrounded by contradiction. She grew up with it. Simone had intelligence and talent that were clearly obvious from very early childhood. She graduated with the best results from one of the best universities in the country to live a better life.

Despite trying hard, Simone had not been able to forget her family and sick brother. She had sent financial assistance to her parents and brother, whose specific illness could not be determined by any doctor. It was a rare disease: one of his brain glands could not produce the appropriate hormone. Her mother had taken her brother to various specialists in the hope of treating him, but there had never been a definitive cure. Simone's father had lost both his hands in an accident when he was working as a young technician in a machine shop many years ago. The company owners settled the compensation by paying a considerable amount of money. Over the years, her father's compensation was spent on the boy's hormone therapy. Simone took on the burden of providing for the family despite her desire to live well. Simone never mentioned any of her family or financial problems to Essie. Melody also did not know about Simone's challenging situation.

The contradiction was ingrained in the fiber of Simone's existence, so she was in harmony with it. Although contradiction and harmony are opposites, they had been coexisting in Simone's mind for years. Just like this moment that she was watching the annual Pride Parade alongside this mustachioed yet kind man. This was the first time that Simone had come to see the San Francisco Pride Parade, and she had no idea what she was doing there. Simone had never felt close to gays, nor was she there for fun.

At that moment, she was more concerned with the transfer of her family from Minnesota to Monrovia, a city near Los Angeles, where a medical research center called the City of Hope was located. Her brother's rare disease attracted the doctors' attention at the medical research center, but the City of Hope would undertake only part of the high cost of the treatment. Despite the Obamacare feature that prohibited insurance companies from denying coverage for preexisting conditions, insurance had refused to pay for the difference in cost. And so it was Simone who, in addition to her ever-increasing living expenses in San Francisco, had agreed to pay the hospital bills on top of paying for her family's cost of living in Southern California.

Simone was staring at the various groups passing by without sharing any joy, like the other spectators. She was drawn into her sad world, busy with calculating how to deal with the emotional contradictions in her financial and working conditions. Simone had never thought about Melody's adverse reaction to her relationship with Essie. Melody's thoughts and actions did not make sense to this clever girl who was utterly rational with a calculating mind. Almost all of Simone's decisions were based on a precise calculation, the opposite of what Melody believed and practiced.

It was fascinating for David to see more names in the tech industry in the parade with their logos that day, marching and celebrating among various LGBTQ groups. In the last several years, David had been planning for Tech2AI to attend the annual parade in June, but each time he missed the registration deadline, postponing the plan to the next year.

David turned to Melody and said, "We'll be there next year for sure. I'm talking about Tech2AI."

Melody said nothing and only watched a group of women and men in Native Americans costume passing by. They had decorated their heads and backs with long red, green, blue, orange, and yellow balloons. The spectacular exotic movements by one of the Native men attracted Melody's attention. The crowd started to cheer them loudly as they were dancing and passing by.

After years of living with Melody, David was fully aware of Melody's mood and character as well as his own problems. Watching the parade, he saw that Melody was undergoing several emotional challenges simultaneously.

Her experience of marrying two men who had betrayed her trust, her growing up in a religious family where the mother was more interested in attending to religious duties than to her children, and her only sister's betrayal in support of her ex-husband turned her into a distrustful person. After many years, Melody had come to the conclusion that she was betrayed by the "trust" rather than the two men of her life. Absolute and unconditional trust lowered her defensive shield and made Melody vulnerable to others. Unfortunately, almost everyone who came close to her took the maximum advantage of her pure soul and total trust.

David saw that despite her intrinsic passion, suddenly something would make her sad, but soon she bounced back to her default, natural, high-level of excitement. David understood these changes to some extent. After deep wounds on her tender soul from the past two terrible experiences, David could partly understand Melody's mood and behavior, and her overall condition. He did not react much to her provocations, hoping to improve the scars on her delicate heart over time. But sometimes, David would fall into the abyss of anger in the face of Melody's distrustful, sarcastic, or straightforward accusations. David's anger would turn a spiteful circle of distrust and distress into an endless loop. And a life that could have been a successful and ideal example of love between two souls would have been stuck in momentous turbulences and pitfalls.

The line of police cars, covered entirely with rainbow stripes, crossed in front of the cheering crowd. It was followed by groups of masked individuals, dressed in strange but lively costumes. A flood of various topics about recent incidents swarmed David's mind, and even the diversity of the parade participants could not allow him to enjoy the present. But the sudden sound of the audience clapping brought David back to the parade. He looked to his right and saw Art and Michael.

In contrast to the general sense of the street and crowd, both Art and Michael were standing in their spots quietly, looking at the passing marchers without any words. They held hands, through which they felt they were sharing their soul with each other. Their silence, however, was not calm, for each fell into deep thoughts for a particular reason that they were not interested in sharing with one another.

The day before the parade, Art received a phone call from his mother that had shaken his very being. It was about his father. "Father?" For many years, Art had closed that case, laid it at one of the lockers in his mind, and threw away the key to be lost in the ocean of his sorrow. During these years, his mother also helped him forget about his wounds. And now, Art was in an awkward situation speaking to his mother about him. "Mother must have had a good reason," he thought.

*Opening an old wound is not something a mother can do to her child easily. Especially a woman like her who was everything to him.*

"A lawyer called yesterday and said that your father's case is being reopened. They asked me to let you know and prepare letters with you in support of your father for the court and the judge," said his mother.

Art remained silent on the phone line. He could not say anything; it was as if words had stuck in his throat. His mother seemed to hear Art's breathing from the other side of the line. She was sensing Art's condition over the phone. His mother knew that the connection was not lost. The silence lingered. For moments, neither his mother offered an additional explanation nor did her son ask any questions. After all these years, hearing about his father again was like a bullet that penetrated his heart, and this was probably one of the goals that the Lord LLC had been considering when they reopened Mark's case. Art, however, did not know any details at that moment. His mind was frozen, and he was unable to ask any questions.

During those years, Art had developed various feelings about his relationship with his father and especially in light of his criminal act and imprisonment. Initially, when Art was a young adult, he heard the news from different sources, but for fear of confronting reality, he curtailed his curiosity. When Art realized that his father had indeed killed two young people in Afghanistan, the hatred toward his father encompassed his entire existence. For a while, the sense of hatred along with the adolescent hormone impregnated Art's mind, and again this was the mother who came to his rescue. Art then tried to forget everything, and he did. After that, he did not feel anything when he remembered his father or the incident for which Mark was currently in prison. Art buried his father and all memories in the corner of his mind. And now, with this news, the same nasty feeling that he had during puberty reappeared. This time, though, it was an unpleasant feeling without the hate—a reemerging, painful, aggravated wound whose odor disgusted Art. A sensation, like a bitter memory from the past, that would resurface in life and begin to gnaw at him from the inside.

Art thought about how just days ago he was walking on clouds, glimpsing joy and power, especially when he would come back from the depths of a long and far-reaching journey to Michael, telling secrets and trading needs. And now, with this new story, suddenly Art fell from the height of the clouds to the dungeon of his sorrow—unlike the Arthur who had been raised to fight hard against the disdainful darkness of crypts and dungeons to reach his potential enlightenment.

"Didn't they say who paid the attorney fee?" Art eventually broke the silence and asked his mother.

"No," she answered, "but the lawyer expressed much hope that he has a good chance to be released, and our letter of support would be beneficial. I have the lawyer's contact information if you want me to send it."

Without further comment, Art said goodbye to his mother and hung up the phone. From the moment the conversation ended to now that he was watching the parade alongside Michael and other friends, Art could not keep his focus on other topics. Again, like his teenage years, Art placed himself in the role of the judge, jury, prosecutor, and attorney, and he started the conversation with himself. He was looking at the parade's marchers while shaming himself for writing an imaginary letter in support of his father, who had killed a soldier and an Afghan translator in cold blood. No, he could not protect a murderer, even if that person was his father, who killed two gay men for their sexual orientation. If Art was supposed to do anything, he would have to keep his father in jail. But how? How could he deal with this inner paradox that was based entirely on anger and hatred?

Art looked at Michael. Michael was standing beside him and, like Art, was drowned in his thoughts. He stared at Michael's profile, admiring his strong, manly features. But Michael seemed to be far away from him. Their sweaty palms caught his attention. Art did not know if it was the result of his own thoughts about his father or something that Michael was engaging in his mind. Michael did not even notice Art's gaze. He was quietly looking ahead at the people in the street, and Art had no idea what his love was struggling with in his mind. Michael's face was not showing him any sign. Usually, the distance between their thoughts and spirits had been so close that they always felt one another's looks. But now Michael was in another dimension.

Michael remembered Tim and the calamity that he had caused once during the Pride Parade. After that damn day, every year, if Michael came to this place, he could not escape that memory. Michael had no plan to come this year, but when he saw Art's state of mind after talking to his mother, the bartender took the day off and welcomed David's suggestion to see the parade. Michael had enjoyed the annual parade before Tim's outrageous act.

Michael and Tim had never been part of the parade before, but that year, Tim urged Michael to participate in the parade along with his friends, with whom he had recently been heavily involved. Despite his insistence, Tim did not succeed in persuading Michael to get along with his new friends. Michael was not a shy person, but he dreaded public attention and in fact fled from it.

Tim had not come home from the night before and instead invited Michael to the party with his friend by sending a text message. Michael made an excuse and did not go. The next day, at the same spot where he was now standing with Art and other friends, Michael was waiting for Tim and the other club members he had joined recently. Michael saw Tim who was coming with his team from afar. When they got closer, Michael noticed that Tim was acting funny. He clearly was not himself. Tim had promised that he would not use another substance for getting high other than alcohol. But Tim's leaping and dancing raised Michael's suspicions. He could see that Tim must have been using other non-alcoholic substances. Michael decided to leave the place to show his dissatisfaction with breaking his partner's pledge. But he hesitated and did not leave.

Tim and the member of his club were in front of Michael. Tim saw Michael and ran to hug him. Before Michael was able to react, Tim embraced and kissed him behind the three-foot barricade which was intended to separate the spectators from the parade. Michael expected Tim to immediately join his group after the kiss and just continue walking, but he was surprised and was caught in Tim's arms. Tim asked Michael to join them. Tim, who was not in a normal condition, grabbed Michael's hand firmly and pulled him without knowing what he was doing. Michael, who was by no means prepared for such a move, fell forward on the bars and then landed on the ground. He looked up only to see everyone was laughing and shouting, while Tim was still insisting that he join them.

Another group on unicycles, wearing colorful masks, was approaching where Tim stood. Tim was not giving up and did not let go of Michael's hand. Michael got up and tried to go back behind the barricade. Although Tim was shorter than his partner, he locked his hands around Michael's waist from behind and lifted him up, swirled, then placed him back on the ground with a turn, facing the parade. Michael, who saw all the spectators' eyes focused on him, froze and was unable to do anything for a moment. Then, he flexed his arms and with a move easily released himself and pushed Tim away. Tim lost his balance and fell hard. With the impression that Michael attacked a member of the parade group, a few people in the crowd screamed and attacked Michael. As the tumult grew, the police intervened and lay

Michael down on the ground to cuff him in what Michael later called Tim's travesty. It all happened very quickly. Although this incident was not the cause of their separation, the trust between them, especially Michael's trust, weakened. Even though Tim regretted the whole commotion wholeheartedly, he criticized Michael's refusal to accept his apology as an overly rigorous reaction.

Music, laughter, and crowd's liveliness brought all of them back to the present time. The parade that should have been anything but a place to daydream turned into a mental cloister for each of them to review their personal issues. Essie was the only one who was observing his friends' conditions as well as watching the crowd vigilantly. David looked around like a person who just woke up. He saw Melody smiling at him. A few steps away, he noticed Essie staring at him in the hope of receiving a message. Then, David cast a glance at Art and Michael who were whispering to each other.

David felt his phone vibrating. It was Essie. He had sent a text suggesting they go to a coffee shop or restaurant. David looked at him and nodded in agreement. Pointing to Art and Michael, David implied that Essie should ask them to join in. Melody asked David about the message. David showed her Essie's text.

David saw a big smile on Melody's face. Apparently, she was tired of being there. She flashed her agreement as well. Another incoming text vibrated David's phone. Essie said that Art and Michael wanted to stay. David sent a text to Art directly, "Art, you guys, please come with us, if you want to see Essie and me healthy and alive again."

After a few moments, Art, who was standing on the other side of Simone, looked back at David. David sent another text, "Please."

When David saw the smile on Art's face, he realized that Art understood the humor.

The six of them elbowed their way through the crowd to reach a coffee shop and went in. It was jam-packed. Just at that moment, several people stood up from a table. Art immediately sat down as he was standing closest to the table. The rest of the group did the same. They needed one more chair.

Essie said, "What do you guys want? I'll order."

There was a long line at the cash register. The soft music that was coming from loudspeakers, mounted on the ceiling, was Essie's favorite. It was a relaxing piano sonata. Essie quickly took a spot in the line and told David to text all the orders. Melody joined him in line. Melody's move put Essie in an uncomfortable position. Essie had no doubt of Melody's action as a heartfelt gesture, but at the same time, he did not want to stay alone with Melody as the chance of speaking about Simone was looming. Essie thought it was too early to talk about that subject. He did not know himself where he stood with Simone. On the other hand, he could guess Melody's feelings well enough.

Essie had thought correctly. In fact, Melody was expecting more from Essie. He was their longtime friend and the way he handled his secret with Simone, whom he just met, was bothering Melody. She felt close enough to Essie that she felt she shouldn't be kept in the dark about dating her employee. But Melody was not sure whether it was time to say anything. She wanted to ask him directly but hesitated. What could she ask? She started a conversation in her mind, "What can I say, 'Why did you meet a woman and start going out with her?' Isn't this his personal matter? What is my business in this? Who am I to ask him about this personal matter? Isn't he just a family friend? Why shouldn't he have this right to date whomever he wants?"

The mind quarrel caused Melody to remain silent. The line was moving slowly. Melody felt Essie's unease. To start a conversation, she said, "Essie, did you know that for years, even for a while after moving to California, I was not comfortable among gays?"

Essie was shocked and looked at Melody. He looked around to see if anyone was paying attention to them. The crowd in the coffee shop seemed to come from the parade. He was afraid someone had heard Melody.

"Why? What was it that bothers you?" Essie replied, whispering in response to Melody's statement.

From his phone's buzz, Essie guessed that David sent the orders. He turned to Melody and continued with a chattering tone, "Let me confess something, me neither. Sometimes, I feel quite uncomfortable."

They reached the cash register. The cashier's braided black hair hung on her shoulder over a green short-sleeved shirt. She was ready to take their orders. Essie asked Melody, "What would you like?"

Melody said to the girl, "I like your hair," and after the girl smiled and thanked her, she ordered, "I want a medium decaf cappuccino."

Essie gave the rest of orders, and both went back to join their friends. David was talking, and as they approached the table he became silent. Melody said, "What were you talking about?"

While sitting next to Simone, Essie put his hand on her shoulder. Simone had tilted her head and touched Essie's hand. Then Essie stretched his head forward and said with a very low voice: "Hey guys, do you know what Melody and I were just talking about?"

Surprised, Melody became pale, and pleaded, "Essie!"

Essie had the attention of the rest of group now. They were waiting for him to continue. Essie went on with a whisper, "Melody was just saying that she wasn't comfortable among gay people before. I told her that I also have the same feeling sometimes. Of course, I don't know whether our reasons are the same or not."

"Why do you whisper?" said Michael with a short laugh. "We all have to bring our ears closer to hear you."

"I grew up in a religious family," mumbled Melody, who could not yet believe that Essie had shared her personal confession with the group.

Art interrupted her and said, "Hey, you don't have to explain any feeling you had in the past."

Melody now blushing, continued, "Not all of my family, it was just my mom. Because of my sister's heavy build and boyish appearance, and in order to keep her—us—alert about homosexuality, my mother constantly warned us about God's anger. You can't believe how many times we heard our mother's speeches about the revelation of God's fury in case of even talking to a deviant person. And years later, during my previous marriage."

David winced at this moment and jumped in, "Honey, you know that these are not all related, and you don't have to bother yourself by remembering the past."

Although there was a hum amid the music in the background of the coffee shop, everyone in the group could discern the sudden silence that fell on their circle.

Essie's name was called from the corner of the counter where ready orders were placed; Essie went to pick up the orders, followed by Simone, trying to help. After returning and handing over the orders to all, Essie took a small sip of his hot coffee and said, "But let me tell you my own reason. To be honest, this is the first time I came to see the Pride Parade in person. How can I say? Despite the fact that I have no personal and religious problems or barriers, seeing an event like today makes me feel a bit uncomfortable. I don't know how to explain."

"It's funny, I didn't know that," said David, who among all, paid the most attention to Essie.

"No, we have never talked about this subject with each other, but I understand the reason well. Although the Iranians are not religious people in general, Islam has implanted some of its nastiest concepts into people's mind," Essie said. "It's hard to declare which Abrahamic religion is worse compared with the rest in regard to condemning gays, but I think if Islam is not the first, sure it ranks the second. It is not easy to explain how these concepts work little by little from childhood, in spite of growing up in a secular family."

"To be clear, I'll give you another example: Iran has launched systematic propaganda against Israel and Judaism in the past forty years. Even my friends and I in opposition groups, who were totally against the regime's whole ideology and structure, would have been thrashed in the subject of anti-Semitism and failed to take a decisive position unlike the other issues such as human rights abuse or separation of 'mosque from the state.' It took us a few decades to find that the negative and poisonous propaganda of anti-Semitism also affected us deeply. What I want to say is that the human mind and beliefs are adversely affected if manipulated by a significant amount of systematic propaganda."

Art asked, "What do you mean you feel uncomfortable?"

Essie, "I don't know how to put it. When, for example, in public, such as at today's parade, I refrain from looking at gay men kissing each other."

"Dude, maybe you're in the closet too," said Michael with a laugh. "We used to be a bit like that before we came out."

They all burst into laughter so hard that people around stared at them.

"No, he's not," Simone said, laughing. "I would know if he were. Believe me; I would know." And with the corner of her eye, she looked at Melody who was looking down onto the center of the table. Everyone but Melody laughed again.

Then, Art looked at Michael and said, "We are invited to a party, and we have to go."

After Art and Michael left, the atmosphere became heavy again. "We're going too; I have to do some stuff," said Essie.

David held Melody's hand. After Essie and Simone left, David said, "I hope you are not upset that I interrupted you and didn't let you finish your story about your ex."

Melody replied, "No, I'm okay; you did the right thing. I know that Jim's dirty act has nothing to do with homosexuality. He was sick. But put yourself in my position. Imagine that a little girl like me who was bombarded all the time with the horror that homosexuals rape kids, as Essie said, like growing up with propaganda all around me in my childhood, and then to see Jim's dirty act... even after so many years, that clearly poisoned my mind..."

David squeezed Melody's hand and said, "I know. I fully understand what you're saying. But your explanation may have caused misunderstanding. Besides, Jim wasn't gay; he was a pedophile. Mixing these two is what religions are trying to achieve."

Melody felt relaxed. She took out a small mirror from her purse and retouched her makeup. Then, she looked at David. His eyes were closed. "How long was he meditating?" Melody asked herself. Sometimes Melody would think, like Essie, she was going through a time lapse. The coffee shop had become less crowded, and only a few people were staying in the line. The classical music was still playing.

***

That night, David had a strange dream. He dreamed that his attention was drawn to a heavily built half-naked woman. He found himself alone with the woman. David did not know where they were. He only knew that she seemed to be a German woman. The light was dim in the room. He approached the woman who was now completely naked. David felt uneasy. He had a guilty feeling that was bothering him. What if Melody saw him in that room with a naked woman? Severe anxiety passed through his heart and stomach when he imagined the possibility of Melody's presence, seeing him with the strong German woman whose firm breasts were in David's hands. He was now rubbing them slowly. He was afraid of kissing her. His hands that were over the woman's breasts slipped lower onto her belly and then stopped between her legs. Nothing was there. It was smooth and flat. David was surprised. He felt a desire to hug her when he saw Melody's face on the opposite wall.

David woke up disoriented and found Melody lying next to him. He still was feeling nervous. He closed his eyes again and thought about the strange dream. David tried hard to find the cause of such a dream. He went through the events that might have had happened in previous days. He tossed and turned but found it hard to fall asleep again.

# Chapter 25 – Wise Old Man

As Essie was walking one step behind Simone in a department store, he pressed the phone to his ear to hear better. "Hello, hello? David, can you hear me well?"

"Where are you, Essie?" David responded from the other end. "There's too much noise there."

"Where are you?" Essie answered David's question with his own question.

David replied, "Where do you expect? I'm at the office. I haven't seen you today. Why aren't you in the office? Where are you calling from?"

"Did you see the last segment of Tim's story today?" Essie ignored David's question, again, to ask his own about the story, about which he had called David in the first place.

David answered: "Not yet. I went to the Chronicle's website today and read a few lines, but something came up and I couldn't finish it. Our friend is really doing a nice job writing these stories."

Essie, whispering to avoid the attention of people passing by, said, "Yes, I like Tim's writing style too. I called to say that this part is about your favorite subject. Read it."

While David was on the phone, he began to enter the URL into the browser's address bar on his monitor's screen. Since he had previously opened the webpage, after typing a few letters, the full URL appeared. David pressed enter and began reading. He did not pay attention to what Essie said while he was reading on the screen. After a few moments, David heard a loudspeaker on the other end of the line. He said, "Essie, you didn't say where you are, but apparently, you are in a department store. Since when do you go to a shopping mall to walk? I thought you hated shopping."

Seemingly, Essie had not heard his friend's comments. He said goodbye and hung up. A smile appeared on David's lips for a moment, then he continued to read the story…

***

## *Sodom – King Bera's Palace*

Leah kissed Damaris's lips and lay beside her. As she put her head close to Damaris, a tuft of Leah's hair fell on her face. Damaris blew Leah's hair off her forehead playfully.

"Do you know that your lower lip is thicker than your upper lip?" Leah asked Damaris, then put her left arm under Damaris's shoulders and pulled her toward herself.

"How is it that my little body has this much capacity for so much love?" said Damaris. She cuddled under her lover's powerful arms and into her body with her eyes half closed. "A love that grows stronger with every rising sun. I must ask the wise old man this question. Every time I think about you, I tell myself, it's impossible to take in more love as my body and soul will overflow like a reservoir reaching its highest capacity. But every day, I'm filled with your love, more than the day before."

Leah caressed Damaris's small and delicate face and said, "If you want to compare, I must tell you that I am drowning in the sea of your green eyes. How can you carry the entire sea in your eyes?"

"When I think of a day that you don't exist, my crying eyes would be overflowing, and my tears would destroy everything in its path. Why should you have to be away from me?"

"I told you that I have to go on a mission," Leah replied, her teary eyes showing her outburst of love and emotion. "It's about the people behind the city gate, waiting to be allowed to come in. We've found out they had been separated from a larger group whose chief's name is Abraham. We will go with one of them to visit that group to confirm their allegation. Don't worry; I will return. It's imperative to verify claims about their origin."

At that moment, a loud horn sounded from the outside. Leah pulled out her hand from under Damaris's shoulder and said, "Get up, the public minds connection ceremony will begin shortly. We should not be late; we have to be in the palace."

Damaris said, "Why is it happening again so soon? We did that just a few days ago."

"Yes, it's on the night that the moon is in its largest and brightest shape," said Leah, putting on her clothes. "The full moon happens only once a month. The wise old man says that this night offers the best condition for the greatest connection between thoughts and minds."

Traditionally, at the end of the fifth continuous horn, the people of Sodom, wherever they were, would close their eyes to immerse themselves in their thoughts. The minds connection was a ritual that the wise old man had been practicing for years. After he shared his idea with the king, it became an obligatory ceremony for all the people of Sodom. The king, who was fascinated by the idea, had ordered that a common subject be announced two days prior to the day of public minds connection ceremony. During the ritual, the masses would think about the common subject while the sixth horn was played. The wise old man had realized that the aspirations of individuals were materialized in their calm and collective thoughts and through repetition. Sodom's rulers had used the minds connection ceremonies to increase agricultural production, improve public health, defeat enemies, and better the welfare and comfort of all members of the community. Only guards in the city and those positioned in essential posts were excused from attending the ceremony.

"So why aren't we able to connect our thoughts with everybody from here? Only two of us," said Damaris, frowning as she turned her head.

Leah replied, "Of course we can, as all people of the city do it in their homes. But the king asked me to be with them tonight, as he has invited the refugees' chief along with his wife and daughters to attend this event. There will be a celebration afterward. I want you to be with me there."

Meanwhile, the second horn was played. "We don't have much time, we have to hurry," Leah added.

At the palace, King Bera was sitting on his royal throne, observing his surroundings. Apart from several standing guards in the hall, the rest of the people, including advisers, and their families were sitting in a large area under the royal platform, waiting for the ceremony. The royal platform was above the huge hall, looking over the large chamber beneath. Two unoccupied seats were placed between the king and the wise old man for Leah and Damaris. Lot and his wife, Edith, with their daughters, Paltith and Pultith, were seated on the right side of the king respectively, watching the crowd in the chamber with surprised looks.

Paltith had a rounder face compared with Pultith's, and that was the only difference between the two sisters' facial features. Both had ringlet hair, red like rusted metal, covering their foreheads. Two locks of hair hung from both sides of their faces.

Leah entered the royal place and walked toward the king, hand in hand with Damaris, who was considered one of the most beautiful girls in Sodom. Lot's daughters looked at the newcomers and then at each other. The king saw Leah, stretched out his arm, and took her hand which was offered to him in return. King Bera pointed to Lot and his family and with a smile, addressed Leah and Damaris, "Tonight we have guests who will accompany us at the feast."

Nodding and paying tribute to the guests, Leah went toward the wise old man, placed a kiss on his forehead, and said, "The greatest wise man of all time, how is it that the moon is cast in red tonight? Shouldn't it be in its brightest state?"

Damaris added immediately, "It seems as if the color of the moon is like the color of my heart, bleeding for your journey tomorrow."

"What a beautiful metaphor, Damaris, is it your own poem from your pure love, or have you heard it from someone else?" asked the wise old man, nodding as a sign of satisfaction with her poetry.

Leah replied, "Damaris has recently impressed me with her amazing remarks."

King Bera said, "Love is always miraculous for lovers, no matter where, when, or what expression is used. Yet, beautiful Damaris, we all have our obligations and duties which we must diligently accomplish. Our people live a unique way of life that no one has ever experienced or lived before. Why don't you tell her, wise old man?"

The wise old man, toying with his beard said, "I fully agree with our noble king." Then he turned to Leah, and slowly whispered in her ear, "I have heard many things about Abraham, the tribe's leader that the refugees behind the gate were separated from. Talk to him and get to know him, then tell me after you return. I will be much delighted to know about Abraham and the circumstances surrounding his large tribe."

The loud sound of the third horn signaled outside in the city. The king said, "We have to get ready." Then he turned to Lot and continued, "Usually, the wise old man tells us a story after the ceremony before the start of the feast." The king turned to the wise old man: "Are you ready, the ultimate wisdom?"

The wise old man replied, "My king, I tell only the tales that I have seen or have heard in my life. I do reiterate them, sometimes truly, and sometimes with a few changes. We must know that many stories have existed, almost one for every living human being. Some tales have been told, and many have never been heard. If you had traveled as much as I did in my youth and had seen people as many as I have, just like me you would also always have a story to tell. I hope that I can bring joy to you all tonight. The story that I am about to say after our ceremony may sound more interesting to Damaris than the rest of you." Then, the wise old man caressed Damaris's smooth, dark shiny hair with his caring hand.

Soon after the wise old man finished his talk, Lot's wife, impressed with his wisdom, could not take her eyes off him. She was leaning forward in her seat to see him and hear his speech. Edith's attention to the old man made her husband uncomfortable. Astonished, Lot, leaning forward, blocked his wife's gaze and made her aware of her behavior.

The fourth horn was blown, and the king raised his hand to quiet the crowd. The clamor was silenced and King Bera, in a clear voice, suggested, "Let's be ready with the fifth horn to go deep in our minds and thoughts, and with the sixth to imagine what we have been told before. Our guests are here tonight for the first time to observe our ceremony."

Lot took this opportunity to stand up, holding his bowl of mead, and make a short speech: "We're honored to be here tonight, and I'm glad to...."

The fifth horn's continuous sound rose outside interrupted Lot's toast and forced him to sit down. The crowd in the chamber, and every location in the city, closed their eyes, trying to silence their thoughts. Only those who needed to be aware remained alert.

The sixth horn was heard, and the whole city became still. During the years since the ceremony had begun, people of Sodom believed in its effectiveness and felt that they were performing their duties. But like all societies, there were people with a variety of thoughts, tastes, and beliefs, who did not believe in what the wise old man and the king admired and believed.

The wise old man measured the efficiency of the connection of minds with its results. As announced two days earlier, for that particular ceremony, the image that people were supposed to cultivate in their thoughts was an invisible shield to protect the entire city of Sodom. All living creatures within the city would be protected with this shield. The wise old man and the king chose that image to be visualized because of the increasing threats by Chedorlaomer and the new migration crisis outside the city gate.

The seventh horn, which announced the end of the ceremony, awakened all from the depths of their thoughts. The seventh horn woke up the rest who were still in their inner world. Finally, the wise old man opened his eyes and said with a smile and deep voice that carried a sense of tranquility, "At last, I think one of these times I will not be awakened to return from the peace that was created in my mind. But think about it—who is considered to be awake and who is asleep? Are those with their physical eyes open awake, or are those whose thoughts are connected with their eyes closed awake? Which one is real?"

The King raised his bowl of mead to the wise old man. All the attendees followed the king and raised their bowls. King Bera said to the wise old man, "Without you, surely we would not have been as happy and prosperous as we are today. By 'we,' I mean myself and the people of Sodom. I cannot say anything on behalf of our sister cities: Gomorrah, Admah, Zeboiim, and Bella. But I'm sure that sharing our experience, strength, security, and happiness has been extremely effective in their lives."

The old man also lifted his bowl to the king, everyone drank the mead, and the celebration began.

Attendants brought in foods, drinks, and snacks. All elders and city officials were present in the ceremony. The wise old man took over the lead and, as his voice ascended while the voice of the audience descended, started to tell his story.

"One day, a raw bean along with its friends, sitting in the corner of the cellar, was picked up by the chef in the palace and placed in a bag to be taken to the kitchen. That day, the bean found the end of its destination in a giant pot on the fire, half full with water. The bean thought with the fire underneath the pot, heating constantly, it would not be able to withstand much longer and its multi-month life from the time that it was picked off from the farm would end soon in the boiled water. It could already sense that its external shell was being softened. The bean thought it would be a good idea to think of something and do whatever it could in its power to save itself.

"The bean could not climb the wall of the boiler. Every time it tried, it fell into the deeper boiling water. The contact with the burning hot wall was no longer possible. The only possible escape was the skimmer, which reached into the pot once to stir the contents. It was the only chance for the bean, as it was growing completely soft.

"While the bean was thinking desperately, the ladle entered the pot. The bean gathered all its fading forces to connect itself to a point on top of the ladle. When it was lifted, the bean could reach the top of the pot. When its freedom was within reach, the chef noticed the bean, sticking to the top of the ladle.

"The chef removed the bean from the ladle with his two fingers and held it in front of his eyes. After a few moments, looking at the bean, the chef said, "Do not be afraid and don't run away from me. Do you think I want to torture you? No, on the contrary, I want to let you serve a bigger mission. After I'm done, you can play a role in helping human life. Do you remember when you were drinking water on the farm? It was for this day. Of course, I do not doubt that you are not the first bean that found the courage to escape. You won't be the last either. But let me tell you a secret. Just like you, I got off the ground. But my soul was boiled and it cooked in this body. First I resisted, but I was cooked. When I passed through a few levels, I learned to become a chef. I was turned into a cook who now teaches you a lesson. You should also be cooked until you are in a person's body, perhaps a teacher, and you can play your role in the training of others."

"The bean, who heard these words of wisdom, said: 'Please take me to the deepest part of the pot so that I can be cooked. Then, crush me with the bottom of the ladle and mix me with others. Our strength is in becoming one with others.'"

After a few moments of silence, the wise old man realized that the listeners are still waiting for the rest of the story, and therefore said: "The end."

The king raised his cup to honor the wise old man, and the audience did the same. During his speech, the wise old man noticed the tears falling from Edith's eyes onto her cheeks. He glanced at Edith, a mature, beautiful woman whose aging had not yet been able to dim the glow of her eyes. The wise old man was not alone in his assessment; many saw Edith with her smooth skin as much more attractive than her daughters. As he was telling the story, the old man found mysteries that he was eager to discover in Edith's tearful eyes.

Lot's face had steadily turned red after drinking several bowls of mead, and his eyes showed drunkenness. Lot had become so impressed by the ceremony and the ambiance that he started speaking words that surprised even his wife and daughters. Seeing drunken Lot, King Bera said, "You can't find the quality of mead we make here anywhere else. It was made of the best-stored honey and water. What is your opinion?"

Lot, who felt that his manner of speaking was slower than usual, replied, "I don't have much experience to distinguish good mead from bad. My noble uncle considered drinking mead a disgraceful behavior, and we obeyed him as a sign of respect. But I have no doubt that this mead, like other things in your city, is unrivaled throughout this region. My uncle has told us about the special features of this city." After completing his last sentence, Lot gulped up the rest of the mead in his bowl and kept his head up toward the ceiling when he finished drinking.

The king repositioned himself in his seat when he heard Lot's comment and said, "I thought you had no idea where you have arrived."

Lot turned his head back to the king, and in a drunken tone said, "Of course we did not know, and my uncle did not know either. We had only heard about it. We separated from our uncle's tribe; he gave us the right to choose our path and said, 'If you go to the right, we will go to the left, and if you go to the left and that path, we'll be on our way to the right.' And I'm glad that we have stepped on a right path."

King Bera said nothing and looked at Lot's drunken face. Everyone in the palace drank, ate, and celebrated all night long.

# Chapter 26 – Trans in the Military

*San Francisco – LGBTQ Public Hall*

The LGBTQ Coordinating Association's meeting hall in the Castro District was only half-full: a lot of seats were unoccupied. Most people were sitting in the first five rows or standing in front of the hall, close to the stage. In each row, single unattached chairs were arranged in a classroom style. In front of the hall, a simple podium stood on the stage with an adjustable microphone. The exterior of the podium, facing the crowd, was decorated with a poster of the association logo. On the right side of the podium, there was table covered with a red tablecloth with four chairs facing the audience. There were about 40 people standing below the stage and waiting.

A man with a short red beard passed through the crowd, walked up the steps to the stage, and stood behind the podium. He adjusted the microphone's height. He seemed to be around forty to forty-five years old. The shade of his thick and upright hair was a little darker than his beard. His tight T-shirt and jeans showed his fit and healthy physique. He tapped on the mic and paused, waiting to hear feedback from the crowd, but only the crowd's hum could be heard in the hall.

As they waited, people were talking to each other, either one on one or in small groups. The excitement was felt in audience's tone, as they were trying to keep their voice level under control. The man behind the podium kept tapping the mic to no avail.

Looking at the back of the microphone, the man, tired of trying, turned to the audience and with a louder voice said, "I don't think we need a mic today."

When he started talking, the hum sank to silence. He said, "Thank you for your quick response to LGBTQ Coordinating's urgent call to convene with short notice." He then added, "Of course, we could also review the subject we're discussing here now, at our monthly meeting. You must have heard the news. It has been published all over the place today. The media announced Trump's executive order to ban transgender individuals from the military and expel those who are already in the military. Thank you for getting here so quickly. Today, in his latest tweets, Trump has officially attacked several decades of LGBTQ achievement."

Earlier that morning, as his usual daily habits, in three consecutive tweets, President Trump wrote, "After consultation with my Generals and military experts, please be advised that the United States Government will not accept or allow...Transgender individuals to serve in any capacity in the U.S. Military. Our military must be focused on decisive and overwhelming... Victory and cannot be burdened with the tremendous medical costs and disruption that transgender in the military would entail. Thank you."

For the LGTBQ community, Trump's military on the transgender ban was worse than the "don't ask, don't tell" policy (DADT) of the Clinton administration in 1994. DADT was a compromise for Bill Clinton's campaign promise of lifting the ban on homosexuals in the military, which had been instituted since World War II. Under DADT, homosexuals in the military were not allowed to express their sexual orientation, and commanding officers were not allowed to ask service members about their sexual orientation.

The law was interpreted by Virginia A. Phillips, a Riverside District judge in 2010 as a violation of fundamental rights such as freedom of expression and privacy. The judge granted an injunction prohibiting the Department of Defense to enforce DADT. Later, the Ninth Circuit Court of Appeals reinstated Judge Phillips' injunction. And eventually, U.S. Congress, at that time under the liberals' control, ended DATA for good. It was never reviewed by the Supreme Court.

One person in the crowd shouted, "Al, we have to give a proper answer to Trump's audacity. He's gone too far."

"Exactly. That's why we gathered here to see what reaction we should plan. This attack is to take away our legal rights. They're not going to stop here," said Al at the podium, nodding in agreement. "If we remain silent, be sure that opponents of our rights will attack our other legal and established rights also."

A young girl, sitting in the front row, stood up and shouted, "This tweet is not acceptable at all, and we have to give them a response that will shake the White House."

While she was addressing the audience, the girl's long, blond braid was hitting her neck with every turn of her head and body. She continued, "From the beginning, it was clear that the policies of this crazy guy are against us. The problem was our wishful thinking and our hopes of getting something from waiving a wrinkled handwritten rainbow flag in the convention of idiots' party along with some other empty promises."

To control the meeting, Al jumped in to interrupt the young girl whose fervor was becoming more intensified by the second and said, "Thank you, Rachel, that's exactly why we're here—to figure out what to do. Let's look at the matter calmly and see what must be done peacefully."

Disappointed by the interruption, Rachel, who was standing in the front row, shouted, "Why are you talking so much about calmness? Don't you realize that our peaceful attitude made them more aggressive? They dared to attack our legal rights. If we continue like this, they will regain the Supreme Court, and will push us back to the '50s and '60s."

Rachel's harsh words, despite her mid-20s age and somewhat innocent look, revealed her knowledge and involvement in LGBTQ activities. She never missed attending any meeting or protest in San Francisco. No matter what kind of protest was going on in the LGBTQ community, Rachel Blair was always there. She was proud of her family history, especially of her grandfather, who was a trade unionist. She had one foot in Berkeley and one in the Castro neighborhood to organize or attend protests. Rachel was present almost everywhere.

A middle-aged woman, three rows behind Rachel, said, "You're right, but we have to see what we can do. I think it's critical that we react tonight. It's three o'clock in the afternoon; it will be good if we can arrange a quick rally by seven o'clock."

"Right, there are a lot of more necessary steps that we need to take in the next couple of weeks," said Al from the podium. "I agree with Margi. We will talk about legal actions against the White House during our regular meeting. Since this morning, many lawmakers in Congress have shown their dissatisfaction with Trump's tweets. Even the military commanders have made comments against him, and we should not miss the opportunity. Now, let's contact as many people as we can because we have to show muscle tonight. Reach out to your contacts and inform everyone."

Then, Al addressed Rachel and said, "Rachel, I promise you we'll continue this discussion later. But now I know you are an expert in social media marketing. Let's create a wave in the plaza tonight."

Rachel nodded in a sign of agreement, and although she was a bit disappointed by not being able to continue her rant, she felt pleased to hear Al's statement regarding her ability to organize. Rachel pulled the phone out of her pocket and started.

***

Hours later, a massive crowd had gathered at Harvey Milk Plaza. Placards and banners were erected everywhere stating, "Trans people are not a burden. Trans rights are human rights." They all chanted, "Get up and fight!"

The protesters were waving rainbow flags throughout. Several television networks had sent their reporters and cameramen to Harvey Milk Plaza to broadcast the event. Next to the large television trucks and their equipment, reporters were interviewing the demonstrators in the plaza.

Rachel was being interviewed by a TV network. She had a handheld loudspeaker in one hand and was holding a rainbow flag up to her face in front of the camera with her other hand.

"Today, the majority of LGBTQ groups, individuals, lawyers, veterans, teachers, and students have come here to tell Trump that if anyone is a burden, it is him," she responded to a reporter's question who asked about the purpose of the gathering. "Until trans' rights are not respected everywhere, including the military, we will not be silent."

Rachel noticed how fast she was speaking, so she continued more slowly, "The only reason for the military transgender ban is Trump's bigotry."

The reporter went on to interview someone else, and Rachel moved to another part of the plaza, with the loudspeaker and flag in her hands. She was shouting a few more slogans through the loudspeaker. She had recently formed a small group called Radical Girls and was seeking an excuse to announce the existence of her group with a big bang. She was contemplating taking advantage of the current situation.

The sky was turning dark. She saw Al standing in a corner next to the gas station and talking to another man. She walked toward them but stood a few feet away. Al noticed Rachel's presence waiting for him to finish. Al was tired and not wanting to engage in a conversation with Rachel or respond to her criticism, but he had no choice. He knew Rachel would not go anywhere until she spoke to him. Al ended his conversation with the man and walked to Rachel and said, "It was a terrific rally. I didn't expect to mobilize so many people in a few hours. I heard that there were protests in the New York's Times Square and Hollywood. Thank you; you did a good job."

Rachel saw the fatigue in Al's face and backed off her decision to debut her group in the large event in the coming days. She said only, "We made a small group with friends and ..."

Al relived and asked, "Great, what's your group's name?"

"Radical Girls," Rachel replied.

"Okay ... send me a website link if you set it up, and I'll post it on the general coordinating site."

Rachel did not want to be connected with groups she called conservative LGBTQ, as she did not care much about them. With no emotion, she replied, "Okay, but what I wanted to tell you is that we have a meeting in the next few days, and we are going to decide what effective actions we should take to oppose Trump's ban. If at the general meeting, we see that the coordinating organization is going to be soft, we will go our own way."

He stared at Rachel's eyes. Al could not recognize if he had to take her words as a threat or just a notice. Al was well aware of Rachel's passion, energy, and capability. But he was not sure if Rachel's claim about launching a radical group was real. After Rachel stopped talking, he said, "I agree with you on the effectiveness of the response, but I don't get what you mean by soft. I mean, I see what you're trying to say, but I'm not sure if you can see the bigger picture." Al could feel that his words were about to enrage Rachel and immediately corrected himself, "I don't mean that you don't know, but let's talk about it at the general meeting and hear different opinions. I'm sure that your comments will give everyone enough motivation to do something un-soft."

Then, for not giving Rachel a chance to continue the same discussion, Al tried to change the subject completely, "Oh, are you reading the series in the *Bay Area Chronicle*? There is a column about visiting Sodom and Gomorrah."

Rachel realized that Al was trying to change the subject. She did not mind because the new subject was attractive to her. She had read them online. Rachel asked, "I saw and read most of them. What is it that the writer is trying to say, what does he mean?"

"Timothy is the columnist," Al said. "I saw him on the other side of the street a few minutes ago. I wanted to talk to him about it. I'm so eager to know what he meant by these stories too. He's touching a sensitive subject. It seems like a nice and interesting fiction. I've also heard that two websites close to the Baptodist church reacted to it. As far as I know, nobody has ever touched this issue."

Al saw that Rachel had fallen into her thoughts again. He did not know if Rachel's silence was due to her thinking about his words on the newspaper article or whether she was planning a new dispute. Or maybe both—cooking up a plan about stories of Sodom and Gomorrah? When Rachel found the silence awkward, she asked, "Can you introduce me to the author of those stories?"

"Sure, let's go across the street, he might still be standing there," Al answered.

They walked in the direction that Al had pointed. It was completely dark now. The crowd was scattering. Most of the giant TV equipment had gone, and a few crews were busy collecting their wires and cameras. Al was glad to direct Rachel's interest toward another matter altogether. Midway across Castro Street, Al saw Tim, standing on the stairs next to the Solcickle store. Al raised his hand and called him in a loud voice, "Tim!"

When Rachel saw Tim that responded to Al, she started to walk faster so she could keep up.

# Chapter 27 – Achan

"Hey, buddy, can I take a look at your paper?" Michael asked the man sitting at the counter searching through his newspaper.

"I need the sports section," the man replied to Michael.

It was still a few hours from the evening busy time at the bar. In the past few days, Michael had had a strong inclination to read the contents of Tim's stories in the newspaper, but he found ways to contain his desire. Michael knew that the stories were not Tim's, and he believed that his former partner did not deserve credit for materials that Art, his current partner, was providing. Despite Michael's objection, David and Essie had decided to add Tim to their group, and he complied, especially after his last visit to the bar. Michael could not say no to Art. He accepted Art's insistence after he kissed Michael on his cheek.

Now, when Michael saw the newspaper in the customer's hand, the temptation to read the last part of the story was too strong.

"Actually, I don't really want sports section. It's slow here, and I thought I'd see what's going on around the world," said Michael. The man took a long chug of his beer. Then he handed the paper to Michael after removing the sports section. Michael placed the newspaper on the counter and leafed through the pages. When Michael saw the title, he folded the rest of the paper and began to read the column …

****

## *Elam – Chedorlaomer's Palace*

In a large indoor courtyard, Chedorlaomer was sitting on a soft cushioned pillow, watching the games, and shouting and laughing at his men, each of whom was surrounded by two or three alluring women. Occasionally, in the center of the courtyard, a slave would display acrobatic skill in addition to blowing fire; this was followed by the audience's cheers. And the dance of the swords by two entertainers, showing their intense fighting skills, thrilled the already excited audience.

In the king's section, Chedorlaomer was sitting in the middle surrounded by his wife and two girls. Tabitha, the king's lawful wife, the queen of Elam, was sitting motionless on his left, while the two enticing young girls were sitting on his right. Two tall and sturdy guards stood just behind Chedorlaomer's two young girls, and a giant guard was right behind the queen. The queen's special guard, Arshum, was present almost everywhere she went.

Tabitha, with a straight, long black hair reaching to her waist, and shiny black eyes decorated by long, thick eyelashes, was watching the show without paying attention to the girls on the other side who were busy tempting the king. Tabitha's thin face and high cheekbones made it difficult for others to guess her age; her face also concealed her emotions. But in general, the queen seemed to be sad at all times. On that night, as usual, Tabitha was watching the show indifferently as she sat beside her husband, the king of Elam.

Chedorlaomer's first-rank warriors were sitting in rows that extended from where the king and the queen sat to the center of the courtyard. The feast was held by order of the king as a reward for his warriors' loyalties and good fights on behalf of Elam's kingdom.

The horn declared the beginning of a one-on-one knife battle in the center of the courtyard. With his hand on Tabitha's thighs and his face toward the other two women, Chedorlaomer turned back to the game. Two muscular, topless slaves with daggers began to circle each other. One of them would attack the other, causing his opponent to retreat, and the other man with a similar move would spark the excitement in the audience. With a quick move, one of the slaves tripped the other using his foot. As the man fell to the ground, his rival jumped onto him and slit his throat with his dagger. The crowd exploded into cheers. The victorious slave was dancing to the cheers, lifting his hands, jumping around the field, and causing more excitement in the crowd while the defeated man was lying on the ground in his blood, trembling through his last breaths.

Chedorlaomer took his hand off Tabitha's legs and held up his hand as an order to the crowd to be silent. Then he reached behind his head to receive a small bag from one of his guards and threw it to the winner. The slave snatched the bag in the air, bowed and left the field. Two men came in, lifted the corpse, moved it away, and washed the blood off the ground to make it ready for the next fight.

Another horn announced the arrival of two other slaves. Both bowed to the king, waiting for Chedorlaomer's sign to start their death match, from which only one would walk out alive.

Chedorlaomer placed his hand between Tabitha's legs again and watched the fight while grabbing the neck of the girl on his right and pulling her toward his lap. The two fighters locked their horns, looking for an opportunity to attack one another. Suddenly, one of them inflicted a wound on his rival's chest. The wounded man looked at his chest calmly, then stepped furiously toward his foe who evidently was frightened, as he retreated backward. The fearful man now was running away from the angry, aggressive, and wounded fighter as the fight turned into a cat-and-mouse race. The crowd, was half laughing and half booing. The wounded slave paused and waved his hand to protest the crowd. The crowd's anger grew louder. The man threw his dagger on the ground and looked at his opponent. The frightened man seized the moment and attacked his unarmed rival who was standing still. The wounded, unarmed man grabbed and twisted his opponent's wrist, removed the dagger from his hand, and quickly slit his throat. Clapping and yelling "Hooray!" the crowd cheered the triumphant man deafeningly. Moving his arms up and down, the winner went on bragging about his power, calling the crowd for more cheers.

The king raised his hand to quiet the crowd. Ignoring the king's call, the fighter was pounding his chest as a clear sign of defiance. The crowd became silent upon the king's order, but the slave was still dancing victoriously, challenging Chedorlaomer's authority. The slave showed his back to the king and asked the crowd to cheer on. With a gesture from the king, the field guard threw a dagger which pierced the defying man's temple. He kneeled and tumbled on top of the corpse. The arena became dead silent as Chedorlaomer, standing in anger, looked at the crowd. The king stretched out his arm with an open hand to receive the bag of coins from his guard. He pulled the coins out of the bag and threw it among the crowd sitting before him. The crowd burst into applause. Girls darted around the warriors to collect the valuable coins.

A security guard appeared from a corner and approached the king. The guard whispered something in Chedorlaomer's ear. The king pointed to the messenger, and he returned to the same direction he had come from. Chedorlaomer turned to Tabitha, grabbed her face, and kissed his wife on the lips forcefully. Then the king signaled the queen to follow him.

When the king entered the room, he saw two guards holding Achan's arms whose hands were tied behind his back. Achan's eyes were covered by a piece of white cloth. Wounds were seen on his chest and abdomen. The wounds seemed fresh. Tabitha, along with her guard, followed the king inside the room and saw the scene.

Chedorlaomer approached the guards that were holding Achan's arms and commanded, "Remove his blindfold."

One of the guards obeyed the order. Achan blinked a few times, as his eyes were hurt by the light of torches hanging on the wall and the middle pillar in the room.

The king said, "Beautiful Achan, love of Birsha. Sorry that we had to welcome you like this."

The king then slowly rubbed his index finger on Achan's chest's wounds and tasted the blood by sticking his finger in his mouth. He turned to the same guard and ordered, "Untie his hands and get out of the room, all of you." Then he slowly walked around Achan.

The guards went out. Achan, standing in silence, looked at Tabitha and said, "What do you want from me? Why did you bring me here?"

Chedorlaomer, who now stood right in front of him, squeezed and turned Achan's face using his mighty hand. Staring into his eyes, and said, "Ask me; here, I am the one who orders."

The king stood face to face with Achan, so that the tip of Achan's nose touched his. The king stepped back and continued, "I don't want anything from you. I would have liked to see you personally, as I've heard much about Birsha's abundant love for you. I wanted to see for myself who is the person who has conquered the heart of the king of Gomorrah. Here, you are not a hostage; you're my guest."

Tabitha, who had not spoken until then, came forward and stood behind the king and said, "But my king, what if they hear the news of Achan's kidnapping? Have you thought about its consequences?"

The king, as he still was staring at Achan's eyes, suddenly hit Tabitha in the face with the back of his hand. If Arshum did not hold her back, the queen would have landed on the floor. Without looking back, Chedorlaomer stepped forward, stood in front of Achan, put his hand on his wounded skin, and stared into his eyes, saying, "Here, no one dares to question my actions and authorities. In Elam, I am the decision maker, and everyone else has to obey me."

The shine of pleasure sparked in Achan's eyes. Achan gazed at Tabitha, who now regained her balance. A broad smile appeared on Achan's lips. Quickly, Chedorlaomer held Achan's back and put his other arm under his knees, scooping up the skinny man like a lightweight child. Holding him in his arms, the king moved to the door where the guards had left. Achan stayed motionless in Chedorlaomer's arms, like a chick trapped in an eagle's beak. The tired, skinny boy threw his right arm around the king's neck and took a satisfactory look at Tabitha over his captor's shoulder. Achan saw the blood on the corner of the queen's lips and smiled.

# Chapter 28 – Rachel

Once the concept of "nature" had been opposed to the concept of "God," the word "natural" necessarily took on the meaning of "abominable"—the whole of that fictitious world has its sources in hatred of the natural. —Nietzsche

*San Francisco – Roma Skincare Office*

The door was opened, and a young girl entered the Roma Skincare office. Behind the reception desk, Simone looked at the newcomer and asked, "How can I help you?"

"I wanted to see Ms. Johnson," she said casually.

Looking carefully at the girl, Simone asked, "Your name?"

"Rachel Blair," the girl replied.

At this moment, Melody came out of her room with a smile on her face and without looking at Simone said, "Rachel? Come in!"

The girl followed Melody into the room. Looking at the girl's black trousers, paired with a dark gray jacket over a white shirt, Simone had no doubt that the girl was there for an interview. But what made

Simone worried was that she was not called in to join them in Melody's office. From the beginning of her career at Roma, Simone, as employee number one, was present for all the applicants' interviews. This time she did not even know that an interviewee was coming. Simone guessed that because of her relationship with Essie, Melody no longer treated her the same as before.

Melody looked at the beautiful girl on the other side of her desk. She could have guessed that the highlight in the girl's hair was natural. Rachel was a delicate, elegant young woman with a small, upright nose and full lips, with a smile that multiplied her beauty, a girl who at first glance would make her innocently lovable. The girl's face was just like the doll that Melody had wished for as a child, but like so many other wishes had been ignored by her mother.

"Rachel Blair, I looked at your resume. You just graduated…majoring in the trade union… interesting. How did you became interested in this field?" asked Melody.

Rachel answered, "For generations, my family was very supportive of labor union activities in San Francisco. And my grandfather was an active member of the longshore strike in 1934. He was one of the first to establish the first trade unions in this city. I also had a great interest in the history of these activities."

"These things should be alarming for any employer, but I do not know why somehow when you're saying it, that is not too threatening," said Melody, who liked the excitement in the girl.

After explaining her idea, Melody felt that she was too honest and quick to share her opinion with someone whom she just met for an interview. To wrap up her unprofessional comment, Melody smiled and continued, "It does not mean that the answer to your job application is positive. Also, speaking about strikes and labor unions are not something you want to talk about in your first interview."

Melody immediately regretted her last statement too. She thought, "It's not my business to guide her to say or not say anything. I'm not her mother to give her advice." She remembered David's recommendation about interviewing applicants: that one must be ready in advance and work on some questions about the applicant's resume. David always criticized her failure to designate time on details. Despite Melody's displeasure with David's criticism, her husband would always express his opinion.

To add something to her previous comment, Melody said quickly, "Tell me about your strengths and the relevance to our line of work here. I see you did few volunteering jobs for non-profit organizations."

"I'm a lesbian. I needed to say this first and foremost," Rachel said without hesitation in a challenging and proud tone.

Melody froze in reaction to Rachel's unexpected response. She did not realize the relevance of Rachel's answer to the question about her strength. Apparently, everything went wrong from the beginning. She was going to get worried when Rachel continued, "Of course, I don't want to say that this is my strength ... although it is a strong point for my personality ... that it's positive to say it ... I'm just trying to be honest from the get-go if I am to be accepted... I just wanted to be clear about everything."

"Well, of course, this is not anybody's business, and it has nothing to do with me and others," Melody said in response to Rachel, who now was babbling. Melody felt relieved to see she was not the only one starting the meeting on the wrong foot.

"Yes, I know. I'm just saying to get it out of the way. It's like being in the closet if we're too late to say this…"

"We?" asked Melody.

"I'm involved in a lot of activities in LGBTQ organizations in the city. I mean, we believe that those who are still hesitant or afraid to come out to their families, friends, people in their work environment and elsewhere … it's better to come out sooner. Coming out is an ongoing process."

Melody observed the pretty girl across the desk. She was not offended by young girl's comments. She remembered herself at a younger age, when she also was a source of energy, power, and activity. Although Melody still had no complaint about her own inner energy after crossing the 50-year milestone, the moment brought her the melancholy feeling of a wasted life. She thought about all her energy and happiness which was ruined by two men in two marriages, and what had been left was an illness in the form of emotional attacks, and a cold husband that would not deal with his own anger issues, let alone help her.

For a moment, she compared herself with Rachel. Her own skin was not as firm as before, especially in the neck area. The body was not the same. Like the air that takes away the shine on silver, time had done its damage on Melody, no matter how careful she was to watch her diet and work out. Using special treatments to shine the silver would work only for a period, just like plastic surgery. And Melody knew it. She recently was experiencing menopausal symptoms and was not happy about it. And always at that point, Melody would blame herself for thinking about having a child too late.

Suddenly, Melody saw Rachel there, moving in her seat uneasily as the silence was prolonged. To prevent herself from falling into the whirlpool of the child issue, Melody said with a sigh, "Well, yes, of course ..."

Melody was absorbed in her thoughts, which caused to forget why she had said those words. She did not know if Rachel had understood her state of mind, which was totally somewhere else at the moment.

Melody was trying to focus on her last comment when Simone knocked on the door and came in. "Essie is here and says you should be going somewhere."

That was the best news. Melody did not have to talk any longer to the girl who was watching her from across the desk. She had forgotten entirely about Essie's arrangement. The day before, Melody had asked

Essie to come to the office to go to the airport with her to pick up her friend's daughter who was coming from Chicago. And now Essie was a way out of this impasse with Rachel. Essie saved her from this awkward interview. Melody informed Rachel, "I'll review your resume and let you know. I will call you if there is a question."

Rachel's gesture indicated that she knew there was no chance of being hired and replied reluctantly, "Sure." She rose and walked to the door.

Outside, Essie was chatting with Simone. Simone was clearly unhappy about a surprise visit, about not knowing in advance about the arrangement with her boss. Melody walked out of the room at a fast pace. In the waiting room, she rushed toward Essie, grabbed his arm, pulled him toward the door, and said, "That was good you showed up. I'd totally forgotten the flight arrival was in an hour."

She kept pulling Essie into the hall. They reached the elevator where Rachel was. At the last moment of exiting the office, Melody took a half look at Simone's face but did not notice her dissatisfaction. They entered the elevator and Melody introduced Rachel and Essie to each other.

"Essie, one of my best friends, and this is Rachel, our possible future employee," said Melody.

Essie glanced at Rachel and stretched out his hand to her. He was shocked to feel such a firm and tight handshake from a tiny girl. On the sidewalk, Melody asked Essie, "Where did you park the car?"

"Next street, not a long walk." Essie pointed to the street on the right.

Melody turned to Rachel and asked, "Where is your car? Did you come here with a car?"

"I took the bus," answered Rachel.

"We're going to the airport. If you're going the same direction, you don't have to take the bus; you can just come with us." Melody suggested.

Rachel thought about it, and then said, "Okay, I am also going in that direction."

Melody said happily, "So, let's go; we can finish the interview in the car."

All three walked to the car. On the way, Melody started the conversation and said, "Essie, Rachel has just graduated with the master's degree and wants to work on her PhD thesis. Her major is in line with what you've been doing throughout your life."

Essie looked at Rachel and asked, "Study in what field?"

"Labor and trade union," Rachel responded.

He was surprised and asked "What? Is there such a major at a university called trade union?" he laughed loudly.

Melody was surprised by his laughter; she was worried that Rachel would be annoyed by that unusual reaction. So, she quickly asked, "What are you laughing at?"

From the main street where the office building was located, they turned to the adjacent street. It was obvious that she was slowing her pace to stay with her older companions.

Essie said, "I'm sorry, I didn't mean to offend anyone. It's very interesting to me that there is such a major at a university. In many countries, such as Iran, a discussion about trade union leads to imprisonment, torture, and possibly execution."

Rachel, who was two steps ahead, suddenly stopped and looked back at Essie. She thought that Essie was making fun of the subject after his weird laugh, but when Rachel saw he was serious, cautiously asked, "How can that be?"

Essie replied, "To be honest with you, the level of suppression is so high that this is the least of the worries there. In Iran, people are forced to comply with far worse atrocities."

They reached the car. It was Melody's. Essie never wanted to own a car. He would drive Melody or David's from time to time. Essie, Melody, and David were together most of the time. In the evening, Melody would go to David's office, then the three of them would go out or spend some time together. If David and Melody went home with a car, Essie would take Melody's. Things changed when Essie started dating Simone. Now, Essie spent most evenings with Simone and having a personal car was going to be a necessity.

Essie opened the front door for Melody. Melody climbed into the front seat quickly and sighed. Essie made her feel safe. Not just with Essie: she had the same sense of security and safety with David as well. The thought of not seeing them every day would make her sad. The two men, who despite being like-minded, differed in many aspects, like temperament, behavior, character, and speech. The sense of being with these two men gave Melody confidence and tranquility. And the opposite was the lack of all those feelings.

Before Essie could open the door for Rachel, the young girl quickly took charge, grabbed the door's handle and opened it herself. Drawn back and a little offended, Essie walked around and got into the car and sat behind the wheel. To change the atmosphere, Essie said, "Well, I hope traffic balances out our late start."

As usual, he checked the situation around him. He then glanced at the rearview mirror to see Rachel. She was looking down, checking her cellphone. Essie was happy that Rachel accompanied them. He did not want to talk to Melody about Simone, and in Rachel's presence that was improbable, which brought Essie a sense of relief and temporary joy. Essie felt he wanted to get into a discussion with Rachel.

"Well, Rachel, what do they teach you at the university about trade unions? Is it only the history of unions and how they've been founded, or events that took place at the time?" Essie asked while he was looking at Rachel through the rearview mirror.

Rachel grabbed the lead and began to speak. The discussion went beyond school curriculum and her study at the university. She talked about her family history, and the history of organizing unions in San Francisco, which was the launchpad for the LGBTQ movements. With short and pointed questions, Essie drove Rachel into a heated debate. Melody was listening in silence. She noticed that Essie became interested in the young girl's method of argument and gave all his attention to Rachel.

Getting involved in the debate, Essie missed many turns on the route and to correct his mistakes he made few U-turns. Melody seemed to feel better about Rachel compared with her first impression at the office.

"Do you think it's coincidental that the path of the Pride Parade every year is exactly what had been chosen for the funeral of the first slain union worker during the battle with employers and the police?" Rachel asked Essie, sounding a little louder than she had been a few minutes ago.

"Of course, it is not a coincidence. Of course, the LGBTQ movement had a close relationship with radical movements. What I want to say is that over time, none of those unions are the same. Workers don't have much interest in joining them. Besides the union that became conservative … in my opinion, the LGBTQ movement should stay away from the radical movements, some of which are really anarchist and crazy. Now, the time has changed, and in the 21st century, I think if not the majority, but a large part of the society, including mainstream, are more suitable allies for your movement. As I understand, following legal successes, especially in the context of same-sex marriage in the Supreme Court, LGBTQ has now been accepted in society… sort of," Essie replied.

Rachel realized that Essie was remarkably informed about relevant issues, and she was not talking to an ignorant man. She said, "Believe me; separating from radicalism is like emptying the spirit of a movement from within. This has happened to all other movements."

At the last moment, Essie realized he was missing the highway exit to the airport. With a very sharp turn, which caused Melody and Rachel to jerk in their seats, he said, "I'm sorry, I was distracted. I was missing the exit." Essie said that so coolly that it did not seem the car was about to roll over.

To conclude the conversation before arriving at the airport, Essie continued, "Believe me, once, I was too radical, but my point is something else. The cause of your anti-racism, anti-Trump, and countering alt-rights resurfacing in the society, is being abused by some groups such as Islamists. It is a grave mistake to embrace those groups. You know that in Islamic countries, gays are executed just for being gay? I myself witnessed my cellmate being executed because he was gay. It was horrific to see him hung. We were very close and the way he died left a big scar in my soul."

Melody realized that Essie remembered his past again. He had told many of those stories to Melody and David before. Terrible and sometimes exciting scenes were beyond the imagination of the couple. All those occurrences for a person were hard to believe.

"What I want to say is that I understand your tendencies toward the radical left and uniting with them against capitalism. But Islamic groups have no legitimacy. They are not progressive in the struggle against capitalism. Being on the same path with them is regressive."

Rachel had been silent. Essie thought he became too emotional and forced his opinion a little too hard. He glanced at the young girl through the mirror again, and in order to change the subject, said, "In two minutes we'll be there. I am so sorry I forgot to drop you off."

Melody laughed and said, "You guys were so much involved in your discussion that we didn't even feel the time. I only hope that we can find my friend's daughter. Her flight landed 15 minutes ago."

"It's okay; just drop me off on the way back," and to make a final statement, Rachel continued, "Let's go back to the subject. Suffice it to say that your position and stance is very much like the right wing. You claim that we are wrong to support Muslims, but the human rights debate is universal, and no exception can be made. If now, Trump in support of racism has dragged his sword against Muslims, we cannot just stand and watch, even though gays are being executed in the Islamic countries."

They reached the airport's parking lot. Rachel's last comment echoed in Essie's mind. Her statement "Your position and stance are very much like the right wing" hit Essie hard. Something inside Essie's head was boiling. He wanted to scream out loud, "I fought all my life as a leftist against a religious fundamentalist regime that executed all my friends. I know all the left classical texts that you believe in religiously. You have learned to be leftist in the university, I have learned in prison, under torture, with my flesh and bones. After spending a lifetime struggle for justice, you are accusing me of being right wing? You have no idea that this regime of Iran is abusing your cause and spending millions of dollars in the United States to help the same Ku Klux Klan groups whose demonstrations you line up against. They created a network of mosques in American cities to advance their reactionary intentions, and then you call me right wing?" Essie was about to burst out these arguments that were shaping and flaring up in his mind.

Melody, who saw Essie's face, realized that he was about to burst, and said quickly, "Oh, I'm afraid we're so late. Let's leave the rest of discussion for next time, please."

Essie came back to his senses and stayed quiet. After several moments passed, he thought that the whole thing was funny. The Middle Eastern man looked at Rachel again and saw a 24- to 25-year-old girl with whom he had been engaged in a polemical debate in the past hour. He was laughing at himself. "What am I doing?" he asked himself. "Why and to what end am I getting involved in discussing political issues with this kid who still has not experienced anything?" He felt embarrassed. After half a century of living under challenging conditions, his passion had led him to such emotional conversation, like when he was an adolescent.

Essie said, "Thank you, Rachel, it was a good talk, I enjoyed it very much. Let me just finish this discussion with a quote from Nietzsche: 'The process of evolution does not necessarily mean elevation, enhancement, strengthening.'"

Essie did not know why this sentence from Nietzsche came to his mind. It was not directly related to the discussion. He searched his mind. Perhaps with that quote he was telling himself that aging does not necessarily lead to maturity. His mind was in disarray, and he could not think right. The car had been stopped at the parking lot for a while, and Essie was deep in his thoughts, staring at the wheel, motionless, sitting silently.

Rachel did not say anything. She had heard of Nietzsche but did not know much about his ideas and writings. She also could not see a connection between the quote and the subject of their conversation.

Essie apparently was trapped in one of those states of the void. Melody held his hand and brought him back.

All three got out of the car. Inside the airport's waiting area, Essie walked into the men's room. He needed to put his face under cold water. There was no handle on the faucet. He held his hand underneath the automatic dispenser, and water poured into his hands. It was hot. He splashed a fistful of water onto his face few times and went out. Melody had found Jennifer, her friend's daughter, a teenager who had two cordless earbuds in her ears and a sign of disappointment on her face because of the long wait. Jennifer did not even bother to respond to Essie's greeting. Melody put her arm around Jennifer's shoulders and started walking toward the exit. Jennifer threw a glance at Rachel, who was walking alongside Melody. Essie followed them, walking a couple of steps behind.

## Chapter 29 – Edith

Melody was sitting on the bed, looking at her iPad. David walked in from the bathroom, slipped into the bed, craned his head to see what was on the iPad, and said, "What are you reading?"

Melody said, "A few days ago when Essie and I were going to the airport, we gave a ride to an applicant I interviewed."

Wondering, David asked, "Where did you take her, to the airport?"

"Yeah, I was late to pick Jennifer up, and I had to cut the interview short. When we went outside the building, she was standing there in need of a ride, so she tagged along with us," Melody replied.

David said with a laugh, "Let me guess. Essie engaged in a debate with her and everyone forgot she had to get out."

"Exactly as you said."

With the same laugh that now seemed to her to be a little insidious, David continued, "Recently, Essie has been more comfortable talking to women. I remember that he never talked to anyone at all, but now he connects to people easily, especially the opposite sex. It must be Simone's effect."

Displeased, Melody replied, "No, this was different. The girl, who was about 25, had challenged Essie."

"Well, my question was, what are you reading? How is all of this related to my question?" David asked.

"In their heated discussion, Essie talked about a German writer named Nietzsche, whom the girl had no knowledge of. I'm reading some passages from Nietzsche to see what his thoughts were. It's hard to read. It is very tiresome for me; I guess it's the translation problem," Melody responded.

"It's not the translation's fault. In general, it's not easy to read German philosophy texts. Oh, are you following Tim's stories? It's turning into a very interesting series. I think Tim has become an asset to the newspaper. It's impressive: Art sees, and Tim writes. Interesting characters are showing up in the story. Essie jokes about the wise old man and his similarity to me..."

***

### *Sodom – The House of Flowers*

The wise old man was observing the flower stem in a clay vase closely. He was in a large room that he named "the house of flowers." The ceiling had been made of straw and soil with built-in chambers through which sunlight could shine from dawn to dusk. The openings illuminated the length and width of the flower house, nourishing flowers as well as allowing gentle cool air throughout the house of flowers. Inside the house of flowers, the wise old man had collected a variety of herbs that he planted in different containers of various sizes. The wise old man would spend tireless long hours inside his house of flowers.

He heard someone call his name from the outside. For a moment, he stood up and tried to listen carefully. He cupped his right hand to his ear as though it would help him hear better, and he focused on the doorway. It was near noon but still early for lunch. The wise old man heard and recognized his name once again. Recently, he was not sure about the sounds and voices he heard. He opened the entrance door and immediately recognized Edith, Lot's wife, who was standing beside a guard. Edith was relieved to see the wise old man's smile and said, "Greetings to you, wise old man. This morning, I saw Lady Leah outside the gate and asked her if I could come and visit you."

The wise old man opened the door and told the guard, "You can go." Then he spoke to Edith with a welcoming gesture, "What a splendid decision you made. It was my duty to invite you here."

As Edith entered the house of flowers, she instantly froze and looked at the flowers astonishingly. With a deep breath, she inhaled the aromatic air into her lungs. She heard the wise old man's voice from behind, "As you know, your husband's request for living in Sodom is still under review, and that's why I had postponed my invitation. But of course, you did a good deed coming here today."

The wise old man was standing close beside Edith now, looking at her from the side. Edith was still dazzled by the unusual, different species of herbs in the house of flower. They were standing shoulder to shoulder, on a narrow path in the middle of the house of flowers. On both sides of the path, jars and containers were carefully arranged so that the shorter plants were out of the shadow of the tall ones. Edith turned to the wise old man. The old man saw in his guest's eyes a condition that he called "the impact of the house of flowers." Like any other person who entered this magical space for the first time, Edith would look for words to express her sense of the whimsical passion at this moment. The wise old man, knowing that his guest was struggling to find right words, said, "Yes, I know, breathing here is like finding the meaning of life. You feel that air goes smoothly into your body, like you have never experienced it before. I must also admit that when I am here, I feel I am alive. I don't have the same feeling outside this room at all."

"I feel that I am complete here. What I wanted from life outside this room disappeared into me entirely after I entered. I have never felt as safe as now at this moment next to you," responded Edith.

Edith stayed quiet. She realized that she might have gone too far. Indeed, she did not know if her sense of security was a product of the amazing scented atmosphere or the presence of the wise old man. Edith suddenly turned around, walked two steps forward, and bent her knees and stretched out her right arm to touch a plant's leaf.

She had said what was on her mind, and it was out now. To relieve her from embarrassment, the wise old man said, "So am I. Sometimes, I think if I'm here and there is a ferocious animal out there, as long as I breathe this air, I am secure. I do not know why, but I do. Spending time here is more pleasant than anything else."

The wise old man then noticed what Edith was doing and said, "Do not touch the leaves of that bush. It brings a rash to your skin."

Edith quickly pulled her hand away from the plant's leaf and stood straight. The wise old man continued, "The powder on top of the other flower's petal, on the other side of the bush, eliminates itching. Flowers are like thoughts: some harm and others soothe. It's important to learn which one you should grow in the flower house of your mind and which one to isolate, so you don't get hurt."

Standing in the same spot, showing her back to the old man, while closing her eyes, Edith breathed deeply but kept her silence for a moment. The old man broke the silence and asked, "Tell me now, which of your thoughts bothers you the most in the flower house of your mind?"

Edith turned to the wise old man. Tears were forming in her eyes. She came closer to him and stared at him. Two big teardrops rolled onto Edith's cheeks. She put her arms around the wise old man's neck and hugged him. The wise old man, who did not expect this move, stood motionless. It had been a few decades since a woman had been this close to him. Fighting this pleasant but unknown sensation sweeping through his body, the wise old man touched Edith's shoulders and gently pushed her back slightly and said, "Speak. Sometimes speaking is the greatest cure of all. First it heals the human's soul, and then the body. Tell me, what are you suffering from?"

Edith pulled herself together and said, "I'm not happy. I never was, even when I went to my husband's house, even when I bore a child. Abraham, my husband's uncle, always thought that I was a sad person, spreading sorrow around."

The wise old man said, "I have heard so much about Abraham. Tell me about him; I want to know more."

"I was a little girl when Abraham took me from my father's tribe and gave me to his nephew," Edith said. "I did not have anyone in the new place, and I was never accepted as a member of the tribe. I have always been looked at as a stranger by everyone in that tribe, even by my own daughters. Abraham shared secrets with my daughters. But he did not share them with me. I know that he did not tell even Lot about them either."

"Like what? What secrets? Wasn't Lot from the same tribe?" he asked.

Edith said, "Lot is a simple man: a child can trick him. Our daughters decide for him. Even when he was separated from his uncle's tribe, our daughters were the ones who brought Lot where Abraham wanted. Abraham separated my daughters, Paltith and Pultith, from me …"

The wise old man jumped in and asked, "Hold on for a moment. What do you mean by Abraham led Lot in the desired direction? How?"

Edith babbled a little and then replied, "I heard with my own ears. The night before our group was separated from them, Abraham went to the girls' tent and told them what they should do the next day."

The wise old man asked again, "And what did they do the next day?"

Edith said, "The next day, when we arrived at a place where our tribes should go different ways, Abraham told Lot, "Whatever you choose, I will go to the opposite. Our resources will not be enough for the survival of our people, our flocks, and our sheep. If you choose to go to the right, I will choose to go to the left. And the girls forced their father to go to the right as Abraham guided them earlier.""

The wise old man said, "And that was toward Sodom. What do you think the purpose was for Abraham to do this? Did he really know that the way to the right, the one that Lot picked because of your daughters, would've led to Sodom?"

Edith responded, "I do not know. I really don't know. Abraham is a strange man. People talk about the power he has."

The wise old man thought for a moment and demanded, "As you claim, your husband is a simple-minded man, so what is the reason that you are not happy with him?"

Edith lowered her head and said, "He has no interest in me. I know it," Edith answered.

The wise old man asked, "How, is there another woman?"

Edith blushed in embarrassment and responded, "He doesn't like women in general. I know that."

Both were silent. The wise old man did not know what to say or how to change the subject. At this moment, to his relief, the sound of the horn, announcing lunchtime, came from the school. "According to one of our students, this is the most beautiful music that is heard every day at noon," the wise old man said quickly. "Let's go to lunch."

Edith, hesitating to leave, said, "I wish I could stay in this house forever."

"Same here, but in a period in which ignorance is the most distinctive feature among people, those who think always prefer to be alone than to be with others. But the remedy is not in solitude. The solution is the propagation of thinking," he said in a calm tone.

Edith said, "I'm sorry, wise man. I do not understand the meaning of your words. Perhaps, I am part of that general ignorance into which I was born and grew up."

"We are all the same. We all come from darkness, and it is not known where we are heading. But in the meanwhile, everyone, by his or her thoughts and connection to superior forces, inside or elsewhere, moves toward the brightness. This brightness is relative—reaching absolute brightness will be realized when everyone moves together collectively and harmoniously. You and I in this house of flowers are now part of the tranquility and vitality. We feel the happiness, which resembles moving toward the brightness. But the only way that it is possible to achieve perfection is to be alongside our community. Not only our friends in this city, but all humans, including our enemies, outside and everywhere," said the wise old man, feeling excited about his lecture.

Edith, now very confused, asked, "So, this is nothing but a dream. Is it possible for all the bad people to get along with good and ordinary people?"

The wise old man responded, "No, not now. These bad people, whom you and I know, like Chedorlaomer, will die one day without any realization of their bad deeds. It is not possible to reach this dreamy goal in our lifetime. Future men will crawl toward perfection slowly. It's a process, a collective move toward excellence."

# Chapter 30 – Berkeley

## *Berkeley, Civic Center Park*

Rachel arrived precisely at the time she had promised to meet Tim. They were supposed to meet at a coffee shop on Center Avenue, close to Martin Street in Berkeley. Crowds were gathering at Berkeley, and scattered groups of people, mostly young, were approaching the center square.

The day before, a large number of people had held a big demonstration in Crissy Field, in San Francisco, in opposition to a previously announced radical right-wing rally. The alt-right rally was canceled in San Francisco, but the news of the gathering in Berkeley the next day had drawn many people and groups such as Antifa and Black Cascade to downtown Berkeley. Different LGBTQ groups were also participating in the anti-alt-right rally. The police had already announced a ban on carrying any weapon and threatened any offenders with a harsh response.

Rachel checked the time. There was no sign of Tim. She had told her young friends in her radical girls' group to wait for her at the south corner of the MLK Civic Center Park. She had come to the cafe alone to meet Tim. Rachel had not been able to meet Tim in Harvey Milk Plaza the night of protesting the trans ban in the military. Apparently, Tim had a previous engagement and was in a hurry to leave that night. But she met Tim accidentally the day before at the demonstration in San Francisco and immediately introduced herself, referring to Al as a mutual friend. Tim promised to meet with her at Berkeley the next day so they could talk. Rachel was not happy with the fact that Tim was running her around on the pretext of having no time. Rachel felt that Tim, despite a slight age difference, was a snob who by pretending to be busy, tried to depict himself as an important professional person.

However, the interest in Tim's writing about Sodom had forced Rachel to bite the bullet and wait for him. Rachel was keen to know more about the person who was telling the stories that were being published by Tim. She was uncertain whether the narrator, who saw dreams in his trips, was a real person. However, Rachel was determined to dig up the truth. The second reason Rachel tolerated Tim's arrogant manner was that she wanted to use the newspaper for which Tim was working to introduce her newly formed group.

Rachel saw Tim from afar, approaching her with a fast pace and carrying a small briefcase. To show her frustration for the long wait, she pretended to check the time repeatedly and not notice Tim's arrival. When Tim got closer to Rachel, she said: "Oh, finally, you're here; I thought you were busy again and couldn't waste your precious time talking to me for a few minutes."

Tim just replied with a smile, "I'm sorry that I'm late. All roads to the field were closed, and the cops are inspecting everyone."

"No worries. Would you like to go to the coffee shop or the field? My friends are there," said Rachel.

Tim said, "It's better to be where the action is. What do you want to talk to me about?"

"Your series of stories about Sodom. I wanted to know more about it," responded Rachel.

Tim, guiding Rachel with his body gesture on their way to the square, paused and said, "I told Al, too. I cannot identify the person who gave me these stories."

Rachel replied immediately, "So, definitely what you are writing is not your imagination? Or is it?"

"No, but I don't know whether they are the imagination of the narrator," Tim replied.

"Certainly it's a fantasy, either yours or someone else's. Whatever it is, it's interesting," said Rachel with a grin.

Rachel's petite body was walking briskly to keep up with Tim's fast pace. Together, they strolled toward the field. Tim was not sure what to say in response. It was one of those moments that bore the contradiction.

*Moments that demand silence, while the weight of silence itself calls for the interruption.*

Tim did not understand why he was walking next to this girl. Rachel had requested to see him without presenting a specific question. Analyzing Rachel, Tim thought about what else she could want. He forced himself to say something and was upset about the awkwardness of his position. He thought, "She's the one who should ask questions. Basically, why should such young girl create this weird feeling in me?" Tim broke the silence, asking "What did you want to talk about?"

Now the ball was in Rachel's court, and she was forced to say, "I wanted to know if I could meet that person."

Tim had clearly answered the question a few minutes ago. He realized that Rachel did not have anything else to say. He knew from the first few minutes of their acquaintance that he was dealing with a very smart person. In fact, they had many similarities. Both were very energetic, talkative, and highly active in the LGBTQ community. Tim did not immediately try to remind her that the answer was already given, so he asked, "Why do you want to see him? Why are you curious about the source?"

"It's an interesting subject to me; I wanted to see how realistic it is," Rachel answered.

Tim turned to Rachel with a surprised look and said, "But just a few moments ago, you said that you know for sure that they're imaginary."

Tim understood Rachel's question, but he was playing with her. He knew that she wanted to know if Art had made up his stories, or whether he saw the whole thing in meditation. Tim was getting tired of the game. He was there to produce a report for the newspaper, and so far all he had done was talk to this young girl. At the intersection, they bumped into Art and Essie.

Tim was shocked for a moment and became disoriented. He did not know why he was so surprised. Tim looked at Rachel quickly, as if the very secret that he was trying to hide appeared right in front of them and it was about to be revealed. Indeed, it was. Art was the subject of their conversation, and at the very moment he was playing with Rachel by concealing Art's identity, everything had come to light. Of course, it was important Rachel did not know Art was the same person—yet.

Rachel, who was suspicious of Tim's babbling, recognized Essie and said, "What are you doing here?"

Essie, acting like he had seen an old friend, replied, "How's it going, Rachel? What a wonderful coincidence. How are you?"

Art gazed at all three and wondered whether something was going on between them that he did not know anything about. He felt a strange feeling of being in the dark. The crowd grew larger around them, and occasionally loud noises were heard from the other side of the field, the sound of booing someone or something by a group of people.

Tim asked Essie and Rachel, "How do you two know each other?"

"We had a long, incomplete discussion on the subject of trade unions," Essie replied and then turned to Art and introduced the two of them: "Art, Rachel; Rachel, Art."

Rachel waved her left hand, greeting Art. Rachel, pleased to hear Essie tell Tim about their discussion, turned to Tim with a winning look. Their presence on the sidewalk was becoming a problem, as they were blocking people passing by. Essie was carefully eyeing everyone, as usual.

Tim, addressing Essie and Art, asked, "What are you guys doing here?"

Art replied, "The same thing that everyone else has come here for today."

Art did not tell the truth. There was another reason that Art and Essie were there. Essie had received urgent news from his Iranian friends in Southern California three days ago. His friends, affiliated with an Iranian opposition group who monitored the movements of the Iranian regime, warned him about an imminent threat that might have been taking place in Northern California. In consultation with the group, Essie discussed the issue at the meeting three days earlier, a meeting Tim was absent from.

*** 

David's Office -Three days ago:

David demanded, "Essie, tell them what you told me."

Essie said, "One of my friends sent me a message from Iran's infiltrated network in the United States that I thought it best to share with you guys. Most likely, the Islamic regime's agents plan to launch an operation in San Francisco in the coming days."

Michael asked, "Who are these people and how did your friends know about that? Is this news credible?"

"My friends are cautious not ever to send me any wrong news. This time, they didn't say with certainty that something is going to happen, but they gave a high probability," Essie responded.

David looked at Essie and said, "You didn't say who they are. Until now, we were witnessing terrorist acts in the U.S. by white supremacists or ISIS, but Iran has not had such a record."

Essie answered promptly, "Yes, they have had many terrorist acts, but didn't receive much coverage in the media. One of the Iranians living in Texas, Mansour Arbab Sayar, intended to assassinate Saudi Arabia's ambassador in Washington, now the country's foreign minister. The FBI arrested him. He, who was in direct contact with Tehran, went to Mexico with the intention of taking logistical and operational assistance from drug cartels. There, by mistake, he contacted a U.S. informer, and he was exposed. It was officially revealed by the attorney general, Eric Holder, in a press conference. The guy confessed to his crime, and now he is in prison."

"Wow, I did not hear anything at all about that," said Michael, startled.

"Me too," said Melody, looking at David in surprise.

David said, "Well, how did your friends find out about this attack now?"

Before Essie had a chance to speak, Melody asked, "Well, why don't you call the police?"

Essie said, "The Iranian regime has created a widespread network of influence in many countries around the world, called the Al-Mustafa community. This network, whose center is in the religious city of Qom in Iran, exports mullahs and builds mosques in all countries, including the United States, as a propaganda method for the regime. Now, at least as far as I know, they have centers in the five cities in the United States, to advance their plans."

"Well, how come the FBI and Homeland Security don't have the info that you do?" asked Art, who was silent until that moment.

Essie said, "Of course they do. Al-Mustafa's community centers and mosques are legally operating, licensed by the previous administration under the authority of the State Department. This was a sign from the U.S. government's goodwill to Iran in nuclear talks."

"My friends infiltrated their network as Iranians who are interested in Islamic values, and sometimes they have more news than intelligence agencies do."

Art asked, "What exactly are their intentions?"

Essie replied, "I'm not sure. As my friends told me, the director of the Islamic Mosque in Houston receives orders directly from Tehran. He has recently given instructions to a zealot in the mosque to conduct an operation in San Francisco. Our friend, who is infiltrated, had become close to the zealot. Although the hardheaded guy in the mosque did not tell everything, he talked about a plan to travel to San Francisco and do a great act. They sent me a photo of this person. There is still no concrete evidence that we could submit to the police."

Michael asked, "Why do they do that? What is the interest for Iran in this?"

Essie answered, "I'm sure you all know that the leader of Ku Klux Klan is David Dunck. But perhaps, you guys had no idea that he's been in contact with the Iranian government and he regularly travels to Tehran? Dunck was first contacted by the Houston imam via Press TV, Iranian Television Network in English. Iranian authorities provided him with great financial assistance through the Interests Section of Iran in the Pakistan embassy in DC."

"Following Trump's victory in the election and the resurfacing of the radical right wing, it was now time to repay some of the past generous aid. Probably the mosque's imam is using the alt-right's network. Why? It's likely they want to respond to Trump, threatening the regime in his election campaign and rallies. The last few years were the golden age for the Iranian regime. Their lobby had access to the State Department and the White House. And all this was due to the illusion of previous politicians to strengthen the position of reformists in Iran. Secondly, the Iranian regime, in essence, seeks to undermine the Western world to prove its position among Muslims in the Middle East as a dominant Islamic power. The alt-right is so bold as to rally and clash with their opponents openly. Therefore, now is the best chance for the sworn enemies of the United States to take advantage of the situation. Meanwhile, guess who would be the suspect if, for example, an explosion occurs? ISIS, as simple as that."

Michael said, "It sounds like a conspiracy theory. I think nobody brought as many changes in favor of LGBTQ as Obama did. I still prefer Obama over anyone else."

Essie responded, "Of course, I'm not talking about Obama's policies on LGBTQ status. Don't get me wrong. I fully agree with the last part of your comment, but Obama was a disaster in foreign policy, particularly in the Middle East, and especially in Syria, with the rise of ISIS. Empowering Putin in the Middle East was a direct result of Obama's policies."

David jumped in and said, "My friends, we're getting distracted. We're not here to compare Obama with Trump. We're here to discuss serious news that Essie received about three days ago."

Melody said, "I still believe we have to inform the police and just clear the way for them to act. I don't think the intelligence community is so weak that we have to sit here and decide on this issue."

Art said, "What can we say to the police? We don't have concrete evidence, except a picture showing a face of the guy sent by Essie's friends. What would we tell the police?"

Melody answered, "We can tell them what we know."

Essie said, "Then I have to be interviewed by them and identify my friends to the police, etc. I won't do it."

David suggested, "Maybe I can talk to Detective Smith without getting too much into details. I've talked to him a few times on the phone. He's a smart guy." With a sneer he added, "He has followed us in the past, he seems to like us dearly." David continued with a solemn look: "Essie, you and Art go to the crowd tomorrow, and when you see the suspect, the one whose picture is on your phone, you can quickly inform the police. Or, if it's too late, Art will decide what to do."

Surprised, Melody interjected, "David, I can't believe you're suggesting this. What does it mean 'decide how to deal with the issue'? How could you forgive yourself if something happens to Art and Essie?"

David said nothing and only looked at Essie. Then, to ease the atmosphere, Art said, "David is right. We will go and search as much as we can. We'll just look around to find that person, and then we will alert the police. The whole thing may not be real anyway, but even if there is the slightest chance, we should do it, just to prevent a tiny possibility of any threat. David, can you see how you can make detective Smith aware by implying a possible imminent incident?"

***

David: "Hello, Detective Smith, I'm David. Yes, Johnson. Do you have few minutes?"

Smith: "Yes, where do you want us to meet?"

David: "I mean, for a conversation over the phone."

Smith was using every opportunity to visit David's office at Tech2AI. He wasn't looking to find something special, but he knew about the adventures that were taking place at David's office and that David's presence could help answer the questions the detective had percolating in his mind. Smith responded, "Yes, How can I help you. Anything happen lately?"

"You know that tomorrow there will be a big gathering in Crissy Field. I was wondering if you have prepared any special security arrangements," replied David.

After a few seconds of silence, Smith said, "I don't follow. Of course, we have. The police always are ready and follow a specific protocol."

David had already thought a lot about how to discuss the subject with Smith. But at this particular moment, all those thoughts had vanished, and David hesitated. After a long pause, he said, "Yes, I understand, of course. I wanted to tell you that ... Through an anonymous message, a photo was sent to me that a man might create disturbances in tomorrow's gathering. No additional explanation has been given in that regard."

Smith: "Did you get an email? If yes, you know better than me that the sender can be tracked easily."

David intended to say that the sender sent the photo through the snail mail but Smith's suggestion had created a technical challenge in his mind and he said, "Not necessarily. It's not always the case that the source is tracked. You know, these days using multiple proxies, emails go around the world to reach their destination."

To avoid getting involved in technical discussions with David, Smith said, "We usually receive a lot of these anonymous tips; almost 99% of them are baseless. Now, before you send it to me, describe the picture to me. Is he white or black, looks like a foreigner or anything stands out about him that you can recognize?"

David refused to tell Smith that the suspect looked like a Middle Eastern man. He knew that Smith would immediately bring Essie into their conversation. "I cannot tell any specifics, I'll send you the picture, and you'll see for yourself," David said, in a very formal manner, replying to Smith.

Smith: "Okay, but before you hang up, there's another thing I wanted to ask you about. Is it true that your house was burgled?"

David: "Why? Why are you asking me this?"

Smith: "In the night of ... now I don't have the record in front of me. Several phone calls came to the police station, saying that screaming and crying were heard in your house. Also, our search in your neighbors suggests that someone broke into your house, but you have never filed a complaint officially to the police. Why?"

David stumbled what to say in response. "Yes, it was a small incident. When we arrived at the home in the middle of the night, the window was broken, and my wife screamed in horror. I did not have time to inform the police formally, and I continued postponing it every day until I forgot about it."

"In any case, you know that the police are the protector of all citizens, and in such cases we are the ones that you can count on," Smith's tone showed that he did not believe David, and then he continued, "If, of course, that citizen trusts and respects the law." And he hung up the phone.

*** 

Nothing happened in San Francisco the previous day, and the alt-right announcement set the stage for the next day in Berkeley, the very day Rachel and Tim ran into Art and Essie. Rachel was standing on the sidewalk, staring into Art's eyes, along with three men whom she had not seen nor known until recently. She knew they were hiding something from her. Rachel suspected Essie's presence, along with a young man with whom he did not have anything in common. Essie and Art could not have the same reason as Rachel and Tim to be in Berkeley that day. Essie suggested moving toward the grassy field. They all started to walk together. Essie and Art were in front, followed by Rachel and Tim. Essie was carefully staring at faces of the people and at all those who were passing them by. They approached the crowd. In the center of the field, police were trying to keep the two groups apart. Rival groups stood face to face, screaming at each other, causing chaos. Sometimes slogans were unclear, and a bunch of different people would shout a slogan toward their opponents.

Essie guessed that the suspect would probably carry explosives or weapons in a backpack or a bag. As they were moving along, Essie and Art's eyes quickly slid from one bystander's face to the next. Essie was checking back and forth every few seconds. Tim and Rachel were walking a few steps behind them. The number of anti-racist and anti-alt-right groups was much larger than their rivals—the alt-rights were completely outnumbered. Some white youths from the isolated right-wing extremists, standing shoulder to shoulder, formed a circle, making it difficult for others to pass. Essie walked up to the line and Art followed him. Tim started talking to a man, writing something in his notebook. Rachel followed Art and Essie. The crowd on both sides were pushing each other near the line by which the alt-rights were separated from the rest of the people. The atmosphere was tense. The police were trying to separate the two lines by their continuous incursions. Everyone was recording the scene by video and taking photos of individuals in the other camp. Essie came to the front but was thrown backward by one of the skinheads who pushed him on his chest. Art held Essie, preventing his fall. Art stood motionless for a moment, as he gazed beyond the alt-rights' row. After regaining his balance, Essie noticed Art had focused on a person across from him and said, "Did you see anything?"

Art was staring deep into the circle of skinheads and told Essie, "May I see the photo again?"

Essie quickly pulled his phone out of his pocket and showed its screen to Art. "I think the person we're looking for is sitting on the ground and searching for something inside his backpack," Art said.

"Let's show him to the police," Essie suggested.

"I think it's too late," Art said and moved to the opposite side.

Essie followed Art. He looked back and saw that Rachel was stepping forward fast. He turned to Rachel and said, "Get out of here quickly, please." And when he saw that Rachel continued to follow him, Essie stopped and grabbed her shoulders and commanded, "Did you not hear me? I said get away from here, now. You are in imminent danger."

Essie saw the spark of excitement in Rachel's eyes and became certain she would not leave. As if injected with a high dose of energy, Rachel turned back, called her friends by a long whistle, pulled her shoulders out of Essie's hands, and followed Art. Art now stood face to face with a white man. His shining head indicated that he had shaved it no more than a few hours before. The skinhead pointed his phone to record Art. When Art, who was looking at the suspect over the man's shoulder, saw him filming, he grasped his phone, clutched his hand and crushed it. The skinhead, sporting a swastika tattoo on his neck, grabbed Art's wrist. Art made him kneel down by twisting his hand and kicking him in the nose by his knee. The skinhead rolled back onto the ground. Two of his friends, standing beside the skinhead, attacked Art. At this moment, Rachel, reaching the right side of Art, kicked one of the attackers in the groin and forced him to sit. Another girl, on the left side, tackled the other attacker, causing him to fall over the man on the ground.

The crowd booed, and the police tried to run toward where the brawl happened. The mass prevented the police from moving quickly. Detective Smith, in his T-shirt and jeans, was looking at Art from a few steps behind. Upon Detective Smith's request, a joint undercover force team was formed from San Francisco PD and Berkeley's police department in a very short time to help Berkeley police. Smith followed Art's gaze to inside the circle of the alt-right crowd. Smith realized that Art's target was the same person he had seen in the picture that David had sent him earlier. Art removed the attackers on his way toward the suspect one by one; each of them was thrown several feet. Art reached his target. The man looked at Art, drew his gun from his waist, and pointed it at Art. Smith, pushing aside the crowd in front of his path, opened a way to the spot where Art was standing. Art, moving his wrist from a few feet away, removed the gun from the hand of the terrorist who was still sitting on the ground. The terrorist, astounded by what happened before his eyes, looked at Art and reached his hand into the backpack.

Art stretched out his arm toward the terrorist, his palm showing him to stop. The man was frozen—he did not have the power to move. Smith fired two shot in the air with his gun. The crowd, screaming and running, scattered away from him. Then, Art took the backpack from his lap slowly and looked inside. The terrorist, totally paralyzed, was still sitting on the ground. Smith and Rachel had come near Art and the man. The detective took the backpack from Art, looked inside, and immediately placed it gently on the ground. Then Smith showed his badge to a number of Berkeley policemen who were approaching. He shouted, "Quickly evacuate the area."

Two officers forced the terrorist face down to the ground and handcuffed him. The police also removed Rachel from the area. Smith turned to Art and asked, "How did you know that he had a bomb in the backpack?"

Looking for Essie with searching eyes, Art said, "I didn't know. I think you've got his picture too, haven't you?"

Smith, seeing Art leaving the scene requested, "Please come with me. I have a few questions that I need to ask you."

While walking away, Art encountered Hun and several other policemen, blocking his way. "Detective, I need to leave, I've got to be somewhere. I will be talking with you tomorrow, wherever you want," Art said while thrusting ahead, causing a few policemen to fall to the ground.

When Smith saw policemen on the ground and considered Art's power, he looked at Hun and said, "Don't forget, tomorrow we have to talk."

Smith saw Art disappear after he walked toward Essie and the young girl next to him. Sirens were approaching, louder by the second. Smith ordered Hun, "Quick—request a bomb-neutralizing robot."

# Chapter 31 – Chedorlaomer

Staring at the darkness ahead, Detective Smith sat in the passenger seat. Hun was driving the car on the way back from Berkeley. The day had turned into night, but Smith was unable to figure out what happened before his own eyes on the green field in downtown Berkeley. He had thousands of unanswered questions but did not bother sharing his thoughts with Hun. He knew that his partner had no interest in talking to him at that time, either. Art's extraordinary, quick moves to arrest the terrorist and then to knock down several members of the alt-right group with such ease had spun Smith's head. He thought, "The key to unlocking the mystery must lie somewhere."

Detective Smith pulled his phone out of his pocket and logged on to the *Bay Area Chronicle* website. He began reading when he found the last published story by Tim…

***

*Elam Territory – Chedorlaomer's Palace*

"My king, a messenger has arrived from Abraham. He has requested permission to enter," the guard said to Chedorlaomer, who was sitting on his throne, staring into the void. Prior to guard's entrance, the king's chamber was in absolute silence. Only the light of torches mounted on the pillars in the middle of the chamber was illuminating the king's muscular face. The reflection of light was shimmering in the king's big eyes. His large jaw was not in harmony with other features of his face, but the king's black, thick, full set of hair would distract a viewer from the overall disharmony of his look.

Chedorlaomer flinched on his throne, and while he remained seated asked, "Who is Abraham?"

"We do not know, my king. He says he has an important message from Canaan about Sodom," the guard said cautiously.

Chedorlaomer stood up and began to walk after he ordered the guard to bring in the messenger. The messenger was escorted by two guards and bowed to Chedorlaomer.

"First of all, tell us who Abraham is that has sent us a message," said the king without looking at Abraham's messenger. He was showing his back to the man.

The man, trembling, started talking in a lower voice: "Abraham is the head of the great tribe of Abraham. His location is far from here. Lot, his nephew, with his own tribe, was separated from the great tribe of Abraham, and now they are waiting behind Sodom's gate. Abraham's tribe is larger than all the cities we've seen so far."

Chedorlaomer, still walking back and forth, asked, "Well, why should this matter to us? We have no interest in the punishment of Abraham's defectors."

The man replied, "The people who are loyal to Abraham have a great number of sheep. My great king, Abraham knows that you do not have the land to graze livestock. You live in the mountains, so you cannot accept sheep that are offered by Abraham."

The king, confused and impatient, said, "What are these absurdities you're telling us? They are all nonsense. Of course, if we had flat land, my people would have sheep too. No one asked your master to send us sheep. So if you are here to inform us about that, you are observing the obvious. Take him away," the king commanded the guard as signs of irritation gradually appeared on his face.

Before leaving, the messenger said hurriedly, "Great king, please accept my apology; I could not convey the message correctly. Please let me say only the last part of the message. My master acknowledges that you have something far more valuable. The water of all regions passes through your territory. Abraham believes that with the control of the water that flows into the plain and the cities in the valley, you have absolute power, and you can receive imposition from all the territories that are benefitting from the water. Sodom and Gomorrah are the two cities that are benefitting the most. So, they need to pay the most. Abraham said he could cooperate with you on this matter."

King Chedorlaomer ordered the guards to leave the man alone. Then, he went to one of the pillars and removed a torch from its base. He stood in front of the messenger and held the torch near his face. Panicked, the man pulled his neck back to save his face from the heat, but he did not step back. Moving the torch side to side by the man's face, the king said, "Where does your lord get all this information from?"

"Abraham is aware of everything. He knows all the regions, including territories in the valley of Siddim," answered the messenger while drops of sweat rolled down his forehead.

Chedorlaomer, who kept the torch close to the man's face, asked: "Why is Abraham the enemy of our enemies? He is not residing in this area—why is he hostile to the people of the plain?"

"Hostility is not his motive, great king. Abraham is willing to deal and trade with you only for the mutual benefits that your region and people of his tribe will receive," continued the man, still sweating hard.

The king noticed the man's frightened eyes and the drops of sweat on his face as he was talking. Chedorlaomer stepped back and moved the torch away from the messenger's face. After a few moments of thinking, the king asked, "What is the deal? What is Abraham's specific offer? Go and tell your lord that if he has a plan in mind it is better to come here and see me personally. I will not enter into any deal with anyone whom I have not met."

The messenger bowed and left the chamber while two guards held him tightly.

# Chapter 32 – Leah

Now Sarai, Abram's wife, bore him no children. She had an Egyptian slave-girl whose name was Hagar, Sarai said to Abram, "You see that the LORD has prevented me from bearing children; go into my slave-girl; it may be that I shall obtain children by her." And Abram listened to the voice of Sarai.

So, after Abram had lived ten years in the land of Canaan, Sarai, Abram's wife, took Hagar the Egyptian, her slave-girl, and gave her to her husband Abram as a wife.

He went in to Hagar, and she conceived; and when she saw that she had conceived, she looked with contempt on her mistress. – Book of Genesis [16:1-4]

Rachel was shocked by the incident at Berkeley. Like others at the scene, she was seeking an answer to explain Art's phenomenon. She was just a few steps away from Art and what she saw had shaken her beliefs. "Who are they and what kind of experiment was that? Is Art's power related to Tim's stories in the *Bay Area Chronicle*?"

She did not like Tim's arrogance. She was also not comfortable around that mustachioed Middle Eastern guy. She consider Melody only as a sweet lady. "Could Melody's husband be the mastermind behind all of this? Was it David who would run a secret project, like those in sci-fi movies?"

Rachel had heard David's name, but she had never seen him. Whoever David was, he was somehow linked to Tim's published stories. Rachel guessed that all those characters could not have been created by Tim's imagination. It was probably Art who traveled to those places and met people at those historical events. But how? She had to read Sodom's stories. The answer could be found there. Among the characters, Rachel connected with Leah, especially in the last episode she had read that day...

****

## *Canaan Region – Shur Spring*

Riding horses, Leah, along with four of Sodom's fighters and a refugee from Lot's tribe, were approaching the water well that the refugee promised would be found nearby. After two full days of riding, Leah, like the warriors, was weary.

Like her horse's black shiny mane and tail flickering under the sun, Leah's braided black hair hanging on her shoulders jolted with every trot. From the early morning of that day, after spending the night camping by a well, everyone in the group had been on horseback without rest, yet to find any sign of a living creature. The thirst had made their mouths sticky and dry. Despite being hungry, they had no desire to bite on pieces of bread they had brought from Sodom. Like their riders, the horses were exhausted, lifting their legs heavily and pounding forward hard. Storm, Leah's horse, was trotting behind the guide's horse uneasily and acting irritable. Leah did not know that biting the front horse's tail was the result of fatigue in Storm or was the effect of being forced to stay behind the lead. Storm never used to be the second horse.

Leah laughed at her horse's disobedience and asked the guide, "Were you not already in this area, or did you forget where the spring of water in the wilderness was? What was its name?"

The guide turned his face back and answered, "Shur, my lady."

"Yes, Shur. Where is that spring you've been promising since noon? Soon the sun will disappear behind the sand. Are you sure you guided us through the right path?" asked Leah.

Without turning his head, the guide pointed his finger and said, "There, Shur spring is there!" Then he pulled the harness to stop the horse.

Leah looked carefully toward the spot where the guide pointed and said, "Okay, let's go."

New energy had fluttered in Leah's horse, as if she understood the guide pointing to that spot. Hoofing on the ground, Storm was ready to sprint, fixing her big dark eyes in the pointed direction. Her nostrils devoured the moisture nearby. Storm raised her neck and neighed. The mare was snorting hard by pushing air out of her lung through her nostrils. No longer could she endure staying behind another horse. Upon Leah's squeezing her calves into horse's sides, Storm jumped forward like a thunderbolt. Leah pulled the harness and said, "Calm down Storm, what is it with you? Calm ... shush."

The trees and lush greens near the pond were growing larger as the eager group approached the promised point. A hill on the back of the pond appeared like a tall, semi-long wall. Even from a distance, Leah could feel the softened air and the freshness created by the trees and the water. When they reached the pond, all the men with their horses rode into the water and floated off the horses' backs. Leah was still sitting on her horse, watching the thirsty and thrilled fighters and the guide's excitement and joy. The mare under her hips, like her master, chose to restrain herself and refused to follow the others. Leah dismounted, took the saddle off the back of the mare, and said: "Go and saturate yourself."

Leah would always talk to Storm in the language of mankind. And the mare, who had become more and more like a companion to Leah, seemed to understand her fully. Storm, unhurriedly and gently, went to a point on the edge of the pond, away from the men and their horses, and while quenching her thirst, kept an eye on Leah. Leah looked around. She gazed behind the trees, bent over and examined the ground, and touched the soil surface. She stood and stared at the direction toward the trees. Leah moved to the side of the pond where several trees were growing closely. She cast a glance at the warriors on her left. In the distance between the trees and the hill behind the pond, she saw a moving shadow. Someone who had been hidden behind a tree started to run up the hill. Leah took off from where she stood and dashed toward the hill. Leah caught the fleeing one and with a strike to the back of the escapee's heel, ended the race. Falling on the escapee, Leah turned the person over. She saw a young girl, shaking in fear. Leah quickly stood up.

Leah shouted, "Who are you and what are you doing here?"

The girl did not answer; she curled herself up on the ground. Leah shouted louder, "Is there anyone else with you here?"

The girl kept her silence and only shook her head. The guide and the warriors had now reached them. The guide said, "I know her. Her name is Hagar. She is from Egypt and works in Abraham's household."

Leah looked at the girl, squinting her eyes to see better. There were bruises on the left side of her face and neck below the right ear. Leah extended her arm and offered to help the girl up. The girl grabbed Leah's hand cautiously, stood up, and began to dust the sand and dirt off her clothes.

Leah looked at her belly; she was pregnant. "What are you doing here? Why did you come here alone?" Leah demanded, then turned to the guide.

The guide shrugged his shoulders slightly to show he was clueless. Hagar lowered her head, looked down, and said slowly: "I escaped from home and I never want to go back there again."

Leah commanded her men to go back to the pond, "We'll stay here tonight. Set the fire; see if you can catch something to eat to regain our strength. If you cannot find anything, then prepare what we have brought from Sodom to eat. Then we can rest."

Men walked toward the pond. Storm came near and stayed close to the women. Leah caressed her mane while talking to Hagar, "Apparently, you are not alone as you claimed. You carry a child in you. What is going on? Why did you run away? Why do you have bruises on your face and neck?"

Hagar, shyly, touched her bruised neck and said, "I was working at Abraham's house. He bought me from my family in Egypt. Lady Sarai was kind to me at first. But one day, they told me that I have to bring a boy for Abraham. Lady Sarai is barren, and she cannot bring an heir for him. Abraham is a powerful man. All the people in our tribe are under his control, but Abraham was sad because no seed of him would be fertile, and without an heir, all his wealth would disappear. Lady Sarai could not endure her husband's sadness, so she offered me to Abraham. She told me that Abraham sleeps with me only until I have a child inside me, only for that purpose. Abraham agreed ..."

Hagar timidly looked down and rubbed her belly with the palm of her right hand. "... At first, everyone was happy, so was I. But Lady Sarai began to feel sad; she started to beat me for unjust excuses. I could not stand it, so I ran away."

Leah sighed and said, "Why did you not tell Abraham?"

Hagar said, "I did. I complained to him about the lady Sarai on the nights that he was with me. But nothing changed. Lady Sarai beat me even more. I felt that she would no longer want me to bear a son for Abraham. I felt she wanted to kill my baby. Every time I complained more, I was beaten more."

Leah asked, "How do you know it's a boy?"

"I know. I'm sure," replied Hagar.

The girl stepped forward to Leah, who was now standing in front of her and threw herself into Leah's arms. Hagar plunged her head in Leah's shoulder and cried. Leah hugged her gently.

"What are you going to name him? Have you chosen any name yet?" said Leah in order to calm the girl.

With her tearful eyes, Hagar raised her head and stared at Leah. Shaking her head while still sobbing, Hagar implied that she had not yet chosen a name. Leah wiped the tears from the girl's cheeks with her finger. It was almost twilight. The area was fading slowly into dark, as if suddenly everything became opaque, covered by layers of darkness. But Leah could still discern the spark of life in Hagar's eyes. She took a look toward the pond. Tiny flames could be seen where the men were present.

"Name him Ishmael." Leah put her arm on Hagar's shoulders to guide her forward. They walked toward the dazzling fire that now had grown bigger and brighter. "Think about your son, the future is bright," said Leah who was thinking about Damaris.

# Chapter 33 – Scent of Maria

> But the LORD God called to the man, and said to him, "Where are you?"
> He said, "I heard the sound of you in the garden, and I was afraid because I was naked; and I hid myself."
> He said, "Who told you that you were naked? Have you eaten from the tree of which I commanded you not to eat?"
> The man said, "The woman whom you gave to be with me, she gave me fruit from the tree, and I ate." – Book of Genesis [3:9-12]

*Georgia – Atlanta*

His Excellency touched the red, soft, velvety petal of a lively rose flower that had risen to the sun. Walking in the backyard garden released extreme joviality into his being when he grew tired of his enclosed office on the third floor. At that moment, with a deep breath, His Excellency inhaled the aroma of a newly mowed lawn into his lungs. In addition to the grass, he discerned a peculiar odor of freshness but could not determine which flower or plant was the source. The droplets of water on the leaves of trees always inspired a feeling of youth in him. Another deep breath with closed eyes shook His Excellency with mirth.

Decades earlier, at the age of 32, His Excellency, ambitious and energetic, could not stop spreading the word of Christ, not even for a second. In addition to the weekly sermon, preaching to a crowd of thousands at the church, he was a successful televangelist, performing three live TV shows every week. It seemed that Christ was speaking through him, words flowing from his tongue to reside in the hearts and minds of his audience.

*God's love and Lord's mercy are everywhere at all time. As the radio frequency can be adjusted with waves in the air, a human being needs only to adjust his heart frequency with the ever-living abundant flowing wave to connect with God.*

From the beginning, even when he was a newly appointed pastor, for His Excellency, only the love of the Lord and of his son was real. He always believed it was that love that made him succeed in every single moment of his life.

His Excellency saw Maria, the head maid, walking toward him. The movement of Maria's breasts flared in him the fire of vitality that had been sparked moments earlier by walking in the greenery. Maria's large breasts bounced as she took quick steps while approaching him. It was a long time since the head of bishops had found himself so youthful and alive.

Avoiding direct eye contact, Maria walked within a few steps from His Excellency, and with a timid and a unique accent said, "I'm sorry, Your Excellency. Peter Jr. is here. He says there is an urgent matter he needs to discuss with you. He called you several times, but you were not available."

Maria was from Argentina. She had a small private room on the first floor of the mansion. Maria recently requested leave to celebrate her fortieth birthday with her family. She had two grown children. Her mother, whom she visited once a year, was living in Argentina. Unlucky in her marriage, she had been separated from her alcoholic husband for several years now. Maria had suffered physical and emotional abuse from her husband, but she tried to live with him for the kids' sake and because of her beliefs. Finally, she could no longer tolerate the abuse and filed for divorce. When Maria told His Excellency that her church considered divorce a sin, he counseled her. Despite the fact that she remained silent about his occasional sermons, His Excellency knew that Maria had never stopped believing in Catholicism.

Nevertheless, her aroma was something else. That scent would drive His Excellency mad. Although Maria was just turning forty, to His Excellency, she had the freshness and tenderness of a thirty-year-old woman. Her two rosy cheeks would blush with shyness. They would grow even rosier with more rush of blood when she received minimal attention from the opposite sex. His Excellency adored this feature; Maria's shyness was beautifully displayed on her face. Her light colored, curly hair with carefully cut bangs made her look even more innocent. Despite her age, His Excellency saw her as a raw fruit about to become ripe. *A Woman of Thirty*, the famous work of the French author Balzac—His Excellency had read it years ago. At that time, the novel portrayed a unique perspective in the mind of His Excellency. Recently, he tried to reread the book, only to find he had lost its original feeling, so he put it aside altogether. He did not want to ruin the feelings that he had before.

*Books transmit a variety of feelings, depending on the reader's age, that don't always reappear upon a second reading. A book that was read in the past that had its mark on a soul is a unique imprint on emotions. Those feelings will never reappear.*

But that aroma, the scent of Maria. It could not have been from those precious perfumes. It was more like scented soaps. "But no," His Excellency thought, "it's not that either. It is her skin that makes a unique scent. Perhaps it's just the smell of her skin."

*Every skin has its specific odor. Only a sharp sense of olfaction distinguishes the difference.*

His Excellency never asked her if she used perfume or soap, or whether that heavenly scent came from her skin. This feeling would happen to His Excellency when he just passed by Maria, or when she was around.

For a short moment, his eyes fell on Maria's cleavage. In a blink of an eye, the same devil was embodied in his mind, sitting upon him. His Excellency took his gaze away from Maria's breasts quickly and said, "Tell him to come here. The weather is perfect today, isn't it Maria?"

Maria replied, "Yes" and stepped back quickly to send in Peter Jr. His Excellency closed his eyes and filled his chest with air, which was a mixture of Maria's scent, the unknown plant, and the freshly mowed lawn. He thought of Sara. He missed his wife dearly. For a moment, he was saddened. He opened his eyes and saw Peter Jr. and was startled.

"How long have you been standing there?" His Excellency asked.

Peter Jr. replied, "Not long, a few seconds. I didn't want to disturb you. What a good aroma! Which one of these flowers is the source?"

"I think it's coming from roses. What's going on?" said His Excellency casually. He was not willing to share the heavenly aroma with Peter Jr., the one that was a mixture of Maria and that unknown flower in the garden.

"Bad news and a strange story," Peter Jr. said. "It's strange that an Iranian was arrested in Berkeley in collaboration with the alt-right groups. He was going to detonate a bomb. Details are not completely out yet. But we've been informed by our sources in the San Francisco police department that the suspect was connected to a mosque in Houston."

His Excellency scratched his pointy chin slowly with the tip of his nail and said: "It's bizarre. What's their plan?"

Peter Jr. said, "The interesting part is that the people who work with Sam in the same company were involved in the arrest."

His Excellency asked, "Sodom's people?"

Peter Jr. nodded and added, "We received this info from our guys in the police station as I said, and Sam did not yet send us a report on this."

His Excellency: "Well, what's the bad news?"

Peter Jr. cautiously said, "There are some allegations against you that are published on the Post Evangelicals website. Apparently, in an interview with your spouse, somehow your son's condition was exposed along with allegations about the way you treated your son. I have already contacted them and even requested to their admin to delete the article as soon as possible. But it's there." Peter Jr. tried to find the article on his phone.

His Excellency's face turned pale before Peter Jr. finished his sentence. The pleasant blush turned the color of the yellow rose grown in the corner of the garden. For a moment, he felt the weakness in his knees. It was just seconds ago that the thought of Sara saddened His Excellency, and now the sorrow was turning into anger and fear.

Three years ago, after Sara found out her husband sought to treat John, she suffered a nervous breakdown which led to her hospitalization. After she was released from the hospital, His Excellency forbade her to see John. When Sara realized that she could not see her son, she set her room on fire. The fire spread quickly to engulf part of the mansion. After that day, she was forced to leave the house. Sara was arrested several times attempting to get into the house to see John. His Excellency's lawyers filed a restraining order against Sara, so she could not be within 500 feet of the house. When Sara broke the law repeatedly it led to her defeat at the family court and His Excellency was granted full custody.

Without financial support, Sara found herself hopeless. Almost all her friends left her entirely to support her husband. His Excellency remotely managed Sara's basic needs. He provided her with a place to live and arranged a monthly allowance through church acquaintances. Unbeknownst to her, Sara was under His Excellency's total control. Receiving regular reports on his wife's condition would give His Excellency peace of mind about Sara's possible unexpected moves. His Excellency was aware of the potential power of the anger of a mother separated from her child. So, he was careful to know as much as possible about his wife's deeds.

The head of bishops knew that Abraham's Sarai had experienced the same when God commanded Abraham to sacrifice Isaac. The command of God is something that must be carried out without any objections, even at the expense of everyone's destruction. However, he knew that Abraham also could not calm Sarai. Sarai begged Abraham until the last minute. For both, Abraham and His Excellency, an order had been sent from God, and it had to be executed. In His Excellency's opinion, Abraham was in a better position. What Abraham was ordered to do was easier than what he had to accomplish. Unlike him, for Abraham, the period for completing the work was not indefinite. Abraham only had to put a knife on his child's throat, and then ... God's command was done. But His Excellency felt he needed to put the knife on John's throat every day, and bit by bit cut his boy's beautiful skin. Only love of God would have made the impossible possible. How could he endure this child's torture? As Sarai had taken Abraham's hand to prevent the execution of God's command, now his Sara, too, wanted to fight God's order. His Excellency's permanent nightmare was becoming a reality. The fear that Sara would publicize the issue was a nightmare that came to him in his sleep. Mostly, the nightmare would come to him at dawn:

He sees Sara, lively and energetic, with a larger body than an ordinary human can have. She approaches his bed, and reaching with her hand grasps his throat with her muscular arms. In this condition, His Excellency is neither able to move nor shake any of his limbs. In Sara's powerful claws, he is taken from the bed, like a piece of meat, pulled toward the door, and dragged down to the stairs. On the first floor, everyone is gathered: the chauffeur, the servants, Peter Jr., and all. While His Excellency hangs from his neck in Sara's hands, he sees James and other leaders of the church. Maria also is there, standing with tearful eyes, making the sign of the cross. They all look at him with pity. His Excellency is waiting for Sara to decapitate him at any moment, but instead, she throws His Excellency on the ground and places her foot on his chest. That is when he cannot breathe and wakes up with a loud cry.

At that moment, he stared at the ground and remembered the nightmare. His Excellency heard Peter Jr.'s voice saying something he vaguely could understand. He raised his head. Stretching out his arm, Peter Jr. showed him the screen of his phone. It was the published story that he mentioned earlier. His Excellency grabbed the phone with one hand and rubbed his neck with his other hand. The sun was burning hot. No scent of any kind was coming to His Excellency's olfactory sense. Slowly and trembling, he held Peter Jr.'s hand, and they both went into the building.

# Chapter 34 – Edna

Sam had been beset by excessive pressure from Peter Jr. who was continuously requesting reports, more photos, and videos. It was as if Peter Jr. no longer paid attention to the risk that Sam could lose his job. But Sam was not aware of the critical situation with which Peter Jr. and his boss were struggling. Since he was recruited, Sam had never been contacted by the church's liaison to this extent. Peter Jr. told Sam that he as the project manager at Tech2AI was now in a critical position, so the elders of the church had their eyes on his activities. His Excellency's right hand kept emphasizing the degree of sensitivity and the responsibility that Sam was carrying. What else could Sam have done? He was tired of all those pressures. How much more should he have recorded from people he saw every day? His exhaustion was not just physical. Sam's spirit was no longer capable of bearing the loneliness in his life. The regret of not having a mate, being with someone he could talk to, someone to caress him, had penetrated deep into his soul like a sharp knife, tormenting him. He had no social life; Sam had no one to call, and no one who would call him.

Melody's short daily visit to the office became consoling moments for Sam. He had a new image for his nighttime fantasy. Recently, Sam ordered a female sex doll, designed with the latest technology in the making of dummies under an alias name. This way, he could minimize the stress caused by loneliness. Of course, his new companion's name was Melody. In the evenings, Sam was no longer a lonely wanderer; he knew where to go. After seeing Melody in the office, he would head home with enthusiasm.

Alongside his new companion, who had eased his loneliness, he would also read Tim's stories with interest. Theater and TV were no longer the kind of entertainment that satisfied him. He would count the days before he'd see a new episode of Sodom's story. Sam liked Edna's character, though she did not have many similarities to Melody. Notably, in the last part of the series, Edna was on the rise in the circle of ruling powers…

*Gomorrah Territory – King Birsha's Palace*

Edna told King Birsha the news in the morning, and since learning, the king had been in agony, twisting like a wounded leopard. She did not want anyone else to tell the king about Achan's kidnapping. Edna was aware of the king's love for Achan. Edna knew that although she had been Birsha's mistress, Achan was always the king's favorite. Edna recalled the day when the king's eyes were locked onto Achan's. Since then, Birsha became a different man.

One look was enough. Edna and King Birsha were passing through the city inside a royal chariot. People were standing on both sides of the path, expressing their emotions toward their king. Achan was standing there too, among the crowd. Inside the chariot, the little curtain was closed all the way. The king was returning from Sodom, where he had visited King Bera. In the middle of the city, the king opened the curtain on his side of the chariot. It was as if an unknown force compelled him to look outside. Old and young, men and women, stood around the path, waving at the royal chariot and cheering their king. In the crowd, Birsha saw a dark, young, skinny man with black curly hair and big eyes. His eyes caught the young man's eyes. The king released the curtain and placed his hand on his chest as if he was struck by lightning. Only Edna was inside the chariot. She realized that the king saw something that affected him deeply. Edna ordered the charioteer to stop, and she opened the curtain close to Birsha. She looked at the crowd outside. The people, standing next to each other, were thrilled. She saw a slender young man, standing still in his spot, looking at her. The king looked out again. Edna followed the direction of Birsha's gaze. It was the same slender young man who was standing and looking back at the king. Edna ordered the charioteer to move on.

The king was silent for a few days afterward. Edna knew what happened to Birsha during the exchange of looks with the young man. King Birsha became indifferent to her as if he was possessed. Edna ordered servants to find the boy and to bring him to the palace. When the king saw the young man in the palace, his face opened up like a blossoming flower. Birsha saw the same young man he had seen in the street, but now he was present with him in the palace. In addition to Achan's eyes that had been carved on king's mind, now his thick round lips fascinated the king. Birsha came back to life. Edna realized that with Achan in the palace, the king's enthusiasm would be restored not only to life but to her as well. To her surprise, she saw that because of Achan, Birsha's passion doubled in intensity. And that was why Edna decided to arrange the transfer of Achan, an underprivileged boy, to the palace to be King Birsha's companion.

But now someone had abducted Achan. Edna tried to calm Birsha without success. King Birsha was pounding on the wall, shouting, "How did they take him? Are they going to hurt him?"

Edna, with a calm voice, replied, "Witnesses said that a couple of men abducted him when he was coming to the palace from the city late at night."

Edna had never seen such wrath on the king's face. Crossing back and forth and punching his left fist into his right hand, Birsha asked with a threatening voice, "Who are they?"

Edna responded, "Evidence suggests that they were Chedorlaomer people."

The king said, "Of course it's him ... Achan had no enemies..." The king paused and continued furiously, addressing Edna, "and you ... you were also his enemy. I remember several times Achan said you didn't let him into the palace."

Edna grabbed and shook the king's shoulders with two hands and asked, "What are you trying to say? I've never been Achan's enemy. I did not like him as much as you did but the thought of hurting him had never crossed my mind. I love what you love. Do not forget."

The king slowly started to calm down, but he shouted again after a few moments, "Alert the army. Make them ready, all the forces. We must attack Elam and bring Achan back home."

Edna had sent the guards out of the chamber, so she was the only one who heard the king's command. Edna stood in front of the king and with a firm yet calm voice, said, "Look at me. If you want to see Achan safe and sound, you should control your emotions. We need to consult with our allies. If we prove that Chedorlaomer is involved in Achan's disappearance, it would be a declaration of war. We have a pact with our allies. Any attack on one of the five regions is an incursion on all. I have already sent messengers to our sister cities. But first, we have to make sure that it was, in fact, Chedorlaomer who abducted Achan, and we should be able to prove it to our allies with enough evidence. I heard that Sichra and Amim returned to Sodom, but Leah is still on a mission. Our best practice at this moment is to be calm and thoughtful. I have received reports of subversive actions by Chedorlaomer people in our sister regions, Admah, Zeboiim, and Bella."

The king was calmer now than before. He did not say anything and turned his face so that Edna could not see his tearful eyes. Every time Birsha imagined Achan's face, his heart was squeezed in his chest. Birsha did not know what condition Achan was in, and what they were doing to him. Was he under torture or injured and bleeding, lying chained in a dungeon? Maybe he was dead. These thoughts created an endless agony in Birsha's mind and controlling them seemed to be extremely difficult. Now, his only hope was Edna.

In fact, Edna was the king's hope all the time. It was Edna who had all of Gomorrah's important affairs under control. Birsha himself knew that Edna had practically been managing all matters of the kingdom. She was not so beautiful, but she was an attractive woman. Edna's attraction was the result of her self-confidence, manners, and her managerial skills, rather than the product of her beauty and body features. A woman whose intelligence, acuteness, and resoluteness in approaching challenges had stolen King Birsha's heart. In every single matter, Edna would quickly find her place in the command position.

Edna, in fact, did not hate Achan, but it was his lack of discipline and self-restraint that was troubling her. Achan was not important enough for her to engage her emotions about him. However, she could see the effect of his childish behavior on the king's character. For this reason, she decided to punish him without the king's involvement. Edna knew that the king would not approve any restrictions on Achan. Hence, occasionally she ordered that the palace gate be shut on him, as he would take the liberty of going out without permission. She could not let Achan's chaotic behavior damage the very order that Edna had worked hard to create with diligence and care in the palace.

But Edna did not know the height of the king's dependence on Achan. And now, with his disappearance, Edna was seeing dark clouds approaching, which undoubtedly were going to spread their shadow over all the cities in the valley of Siddim.

# Chapter 35 – Pamela

*Atlanta – His Excellency's Office*

Descending the stairs, His Excellency bumped into Peter Jr. and said, "Come with me, we'll talk in the car. I have to go and see few people."

Peter Jr. was on his way up to visit His Excellency when he saw his boss leaving the second floor. Together, they walked down the stairs. His Excellency was touching the shiny oak of the railing with the tip of his fingers. He liked the stair's wooden railings in his house, which lined the staircase from the first floor to the third on both sides. It was more a sign of luxury and beauty than a handle to assist him ascending or descending. John the Third was very sensitive about the polishing of all wood materials in the house, such as cabinets, library shelves, and especially the railing. He had specifically assigned one of the servants to carefully polish every wooden item in the house with special lemon oil. While Peter was talking, His Excellency's sharp focus was on the railing, seeking any possible crack or spot.

They reached the ground floor and walked toward the main entrance. Teddy, His Excellency's chauffeur, brought the car to the front of the mansion. There was a circle driveway, with a beautiful fountain in the center. As the chauffeur noticed his boss exiting the building, he opened the back door of a black Lincoln MKT. His Excellency had always owned a Town Car, but he ordered an MKT after the manufacturer replaced its legendary car in 2011. His Excellency and then Peter Jr. climbed into the car's backseat. The car drove around the driveway and turned into a roadway, still on the property. It would take two minutes to reach the property's main gate, which separated the estate from the city streets. The green shrubs were trimmed carefully on both sides of the road; it was lined with trees that created a pleasant shade on that hot, sunny summer day.

His Excellency had been staring through his side window since they entered in the car. He turned his face to Peter Jr. and said, "Make Arthur Stevenson's name, place of residence, and workplace public. We have to increase the pressure on him."

"He is not alone," said Peter Jr., after he wrote something in his notebook. "Sam, our guy, told us that he has a circle of friends with whom he is constantly holding meetings."

"Where do they hold their meetings?" asked His Excellency.

"At work, usually in the evenings," replied Peter Jr.

The head of bishops shook his head twice and looked out again. Peter Jr. asked, "Do you want to release the video clip that Sam has sent us?"

"Not for now. We shouldn't make a superhero out of this guy. His name must be disclosed as a source of nonsense published in the *Bay Area Chronicle* and not more than that."

Peter Jr. responded, "One or two YouTube videos show his involvement during the brawl at Berkeley. It demonstrates the strange way that this guy knocked a few people down."

Again, His Excellency nodded twice. After a few seconds of silence, he asked, "What happened to the person whom I told you to contact in Houston?"

"Yes, I was just going to tell you about him. As you instructed, I warned him about their interferences here. He made a request."

Surprised, His Excellency asked, "Request?"

"Yes, they want the arrested person in Berkeley eliminated. I asked him, 'Do you think we are running a killing squad here?' He was anxious about their guy's confession. He was in a state of panic. I don't know how he trusted to tell me all that he said. It was a confession itself."

His Excellency immediately said, "Actually, not a bad idea."

Peter Jr.'s jaw dropped in disbelief. He thought he had not heard his boss correctly, but when he saw the His Excellency's serious look, just asked, "Why should we engage in this mess? There is nothing in this for us but the possibility of harming ourselves."

"We will need them. Besides, having them under our control, we'll make them indebted. They'll owe us a great deal after that. At the same time, don't forget: they have significant power in Latin America and are gaining ground in Africa."

The car pulled over. His Excellency looked out and said, "I have to get out here. I instructed Teddy to give you a ride. Anything else?"

Peter Jr. paused. He wanted to say something, but he was hesitant how to start. Teddy opened the door, waiting for his boss to step out. Finally, Peter Jr. said, "It's about your wife, Mrs. Sara."

His Excellency pointed to Teddy to close the door and wait outside. "What happened? Any new publication?" he asked.

Although he wanted to show that he was in control, His Excellency felt a sharp pain in his heart, and he was gasping for air. His doctor had assured him weeks ago that he had no particular problem after seeing a normal EKG result. However, recently he was feeling a painful cringe within his chest upon hearing bad news. Since he had found out they had used Sara against him, the anxiety would attack him the way that he had not experienced before. Every news about Sara would bring him the same feeling that he had heard the first time about his wife's rebellion. Peter Jr. noticed a little twitching under His Excellency's left eye. Peter Jr. realized that this must be a nerve attack.

By nodding, His Excellency responded to his subordinate's concern about his condition. Although the head of bishops was playing it down, he was anxious to hear Peter Jr.'s report about Sara. Peter Jr. continued, "Pamela Lang had an interview with your wife and published it on her university portal as part of her research."

His Excellency's face turned pale like the car's beige interior color. The story of Sara was going in the worst possible direction, and Pamela Lang's appearance at the scene made the bishop's concern grow tenfold.

"The so-called Evangelical Left wants to run a smear campaign against us, huh? They think they found the best angle to attack the real church and me," said His Excellency. The anger now was reaching his hands.

He knocked on the window twice. His shaking fingers were an indication of high emotional turbulence. Teddy opened the door, and his Excellency got out of the car without saying any words. He did not show any interest in the content of Sara's interview that Peter Jr. had printed. Surprised, Peter Jr. said nothing, and with his eyes chasing his boss who left the car, sat back.

Peter Jr. was still holding the documents in his hand. He had taken them out of his bag and intended to show his boss Sara's interview with Pamela Long. He had quickly printed the interview before rushing to the mansion. Teddy entered the car and sat behind the wheel. Waiting for the car to move, Peter Jr. saw Teddy was still sitting motionless, staring ahead. After a few moments, Peter Jr. asked, "Teddy, why are we staying here? Aren't you going to move?"

"His Excellency told me to wait here for him to come back," responded Teddy.

Peter Jr. realized that His Excellency was terribly upset. "He must've been stung," he thought. There was no other option but to sit and wait. He pulled Sara's interview by Pamela Lang out of his briefcase again.

Pamela Lang was the first lesbian black pastor in the church of Evangelicals. She taught at Boston University as an assistant professor of theology. She was a member of the Post-Evangelical Church which was a member of the United Baptodist Church, the same but broader alliance among Evangelical churches that His Excellency represented, its dominant conservative branch. The Post Evangelical, sometimes called liberal or Evangelical Left, despite the slight differences, in general was created to counter the mainstream conservative Evangelicals. A liberal interpretation of religious scriptures made them popular among youth, especially in the last two decades of the twentieth century. The Liberal Evangelicals' success forced the conservatives to think of new schemes in light of the new wave of heresy. Among the Post Evangelicals, in particular, the tendency toward acceptance of homosexuality as an internal sexual desire, with which the human being is born, contrasted with the most basic tenets of the Church of Evangelicals, such as the concept of man and family.

Of course, homosexuality was not the only danger. Promoting subjects such as Jesus versus Paul in the Evangelical Church would condone skepticism of all the biblical stories. Doubting biblical stories helped the Post Evangelicals introduce concepts beyond what was previously taught in the church. Those concepts fueled the tension between the dogmatism in the church and religious pluralism. However, undoubtedly, one of the most critical factors contributing to the Post Evangelicals' advancement in the heart of the conservative church was the role of women in the church and society. Not only in the mainstream Evangelical Church but also other major branches, such as the Catholic and Orthodox churches, women were always deprived of holding high rank. At the Church of Conservative Evangelicals, women were never nominated as bishops or members of the Church Council. This deprivation was the most potent weapon for Post-Evangelicals to shake up the pillars of fundamentalism and conservative thinking. The attacks from the left, even ostensibly forced conservatives to retreat on the role of women in the church.

Peter Jr.'s eyes were slipping on the interview's text, and sometimes he would stop to re-read parts of it:

Pamela: "How can the chairman of the council of the Baptodist Church do such a thing to you?"

Sara: "This is a fact; the chairman of this council was my husband. He kicked me out of my house and placed my son under harsh medical treatment on the pretext of being gay. I'm not lying; I'm not mad. He wants to keep his prestige intact by discrediting me, and he calls me a crazy person."

Pamela: "Why did you wait so long to bring up this matter, about three years?"

Sara: "My ex-husband took advantage of my anger and put me in prison. Then, because it looked bad for them, the go-between church people placed me in a house where I was under their total control. I was dependent on them. I neither had resources nor money to live. Even people whom I knew gave me medication and kept me emotionally numb. At the same time, I lost full legal and physical custody of my son. They didn't even permit me to see my son. Among those caring acquaintances, there were doctors who came to visit me who later testified against me in the court of law as an unstable person. I haven't seen my son for three years."

Pamela: "Well, how did you figure out all of this and what did you do next?"

Sara: "The son of my ex's colleague who was affiliated with the Liberal Evangelicals helped me get out of the house. I'm now looking to reopen the custody case. Let me tell you, and let me tell everyone, my ex-husband and his church are very powerful, they are everywhere; they have people in police departments, in the court, in the army. But I will fight them all, I don't care how powerful they are, because of my son. I don't care about anything else. What they did to my son and me aren't fabricated. They're trying to say that I'm crazy, but I will prove them wrong because I'm not crazy. They're going to see that I am not."

Pamela: "Don't you think that God will help you? Trust in Jesus Christ. Isn't this help that you received from the Post Evangelicals God and His Son's Mercy?"

Sara: "You are a good person, your friends too. You helped me, but I no longer believe in anything. God, who gave my ex-husband power to make millions follow him, is cruel."

Pamela: "Sara, look at me, I am a woman; I am a black woman and a lesbian. I am also a pastor. Everyone has his own interpretation of the gospel. While the message of Christ was love, in South America hundreds of thousands of people became the victims of the murder and plunder of the church, in the name of Christ. However, people received the message of love, and they still love Jesus. Only love can raise man to the sublimity. The love that is Christ-like."

Peter Jr. raised his head. He thought for an instant. He looked at Teddy, who was still staring somewhere beyond the windshield. Peter Jr. looked at his watch. Almost an hour passed. They were in the car, waiting in a quiet suburban street. Several cars had been parked on the opposite side of a narrow street. He did not see which house exactly His Excellency went into. Feeling unpleasant, Peter Jr. thought that this was the first time His Excellency kept him waiting for such a long time without any notice. Now, Peter Jr. guessed that the impact of Sara's news, which shocked His Excellency, was the reason for the long delay. It must have been related to his ex-wife's situation and the interview that led his boss to think about a solution. Peter Jr. tried to go back to the text, to read more, but he had lost interest. He was bored and tired of checking the news on his phone. The car's enclosure was smothering him. Peter Jr. wanted to get out of the car, but he did not know what the nature of His Excellency's business was. Deciding to stay, he leaned back and closed his eyes.

When the door opened and his boss entered the car, Peter Jr. did not know how much time had passed. He looked at Teddy who was sitting in the same position and looking in front of him. His Excellency was apparently in a better mood than when he left the car.

"Teddy, go out till I call you," said His Excellency.

Teddy went out, and His Excellency turned to his subordinate and said with a relaxed voice, "Don't worry about my wife. I will solve it myself."

Peter jumped in and asked: "Don't you want to see the interview? What she said is not good at all for the church's image in public opinion."

His Excellency frowned at being interrupted. Peter Jr. realized that he had gone too far and that his boss certainly knew better about the importance of the issue than he did. For this reason, he remained silent and waited for his boss to continue to speak.

"Review the list of right-wing and extremist groups that directly or indirectly are connected to us. See which of them are more powerful in Northern California. We need to arrange a gathering at UC Berkeley. Now that they attack us from within, we'll send their own kind to attack them. What was this clown's name, Mylos? It's a strange name. Arrange a speech for him at UC Berkeley. Gather all the information that you can and bring it to me by this afternoon at five. We also have a guest."

His Excellency knocked on the window to call Teddy after finishing his order. He paused a moment and turned to Peter Jr. again and said, "Do one more thing. You mentioned that the group in San Francisco holds meetings regularly. We have to take away their security. Their devilish nest must be destroyed."

With a confused look on his face, Peter Jr. demonstrated that he did not understand his boss's order and said, "What can I do, what should be done?"

"Find your own way, destroy it. This way, they realize that no subject is a joke. Sticking fingers in any hole might have the consequence of being stung by a serpent."

Gazing at his boss's eyes, Peter Jr. could not believe he understood him well. His Excellency, who was tired of Peter Jr.'s idiotic look, continued, "Yes, you got it right. Through your contact in there ... What was his name? ... Sam, yes, smash them, even if it takes sending them all to hell."

Peter Jr. grasped that his wife's interview must have really hurt his boss. "I don't think Sam is willing to do that," he said cautiously. "The final report that he sent to me was about a party held in the owner's house, and it suggested Sam's positive feelings, especially about the guy's spouse. I'm not sure if it's a good idea now..."

When Peter Jr. saw His Excellency's angry look, his tongue ceased to move. He swallowed the rest of his words and sat back quietly. They both remained silent, and His Excellency stared out the left window, turning his back to Peter Jr.

# Chapter 36 – Alt-rights

*Atlanta – His Excellency's Mansion*

At five o'clock sharp in the afternoon, Peter Jr. arrived at the mansion. He had gathered as much information requested by His Excellency as he could. Climbing the stairs, Peter Jr. had the list in his briefcase. Now that Peter Jr. had read Sara's interview, he would look differently at John's room on the second floor as he passed it heading up the stairs. Particularly since His Excellency's wife had started talking against the church publicly, Peter Jr. had a strange feeling about the direction the course of events might go. On one hand, he was worried about the controversy surrounding the issue, and on the other hand, he did not understand His Excellency's inaction in solving his wife's problem. Peter Jr. could comprehend the emotional challenges his boss was going through, but he was afraid that allowing too much emotion in this episode would put everyone in a dangerous situation.

Peter Jr. stepped in front of His Excellency's office door on the third floor. He knocked on the door and went inside. His boss was not alone. Someone else was sitting on the same seat from which Peter Jr. always used to gaze up at John Wesley's painting. His Excellency was apparently in a superb mood, with a smile on his face that Peter Jr. had rarely seen before. His Excellency said, "Oh, you are finally here. We have a guest today."

From the moment of entrance into his boss's office, Peter Jr. tried to remember where he had seen the guest's face. The guest was very familiar to him, but apparently, his mind was blocked and he could not place him.

"I'm sure you know Stephen Michel?" said His Excellency with a comfortable air.

Suddenly, Peter Jr. recognized the man in the suit and blamed himself for his lack of fast processing. Stretching out his hand, Peter Jr. said: "Of course, who would not know the president's senior adviser?"

Stephen was on his feet. His skinny face, small build, and thinning hair made him look older than his real age. Peter Jr. had frequently seen photos and videos of the president's adviser in the paper and on the TV, but now seeing him in person, Michel looked older than his photos portrayed.

"We were talking about the recent developments in the White House," His Excellency said, looking at his guest. "I told Stephen that with Steve's departure from the White House, things would be progressing toward calm and recovery. Incidentally, it won't be far from Steve's views. Of course, if Steve doesn't decide to take irrational actions."

Steve Baton was a controversial right-wing figure who joined the Trump campaign in 2016 as a senior advisor. Many saw him as a factor in mobilizing dissatisfied whites in the middle states in favor of Trump, an assessment that would infuriate the president.

Stephen Michel was from a Jewish family, residing in one of the most liberal cities of Southern California. His conservative ideology, which was formed during high school, put him in an alliance with Steve Baton at the White House. Steve's resignation, or in other words, the pressure to leave his alliance at the White House, was a product of the dominant generals' rising power. Despite his young age and limited experience compared with Washington politicians, Stephen Michel had been able to maintain his position in the power struggles surrounding President Trump.

Stephen was quietly listening. It was not clear what he wanted to say. Was it merely to respond vaguely to the speaker or did he indeed agree? His Excellency continued, "We will always be supporting the president, as we have done so far. Steve must also know that he will have our support, even outside the White House. But his stand in Alabama and campaign against the president will hurt the feelings of the loyal supporters who were the agent of victory for us all. The liberals' failure was the result of an alliance among many groups and movements that might differ significantly in their views, but we should not forget that we are all moving in the same direction."

"I agree with your opinion," said Stephen, who was silent until that moment. "And precisely, I came here to discuss the same subject, after consultation with the president, of course. Your talent and intelligence to see the reality are admirable. Early surveys on the GOP primary for the U.S. Senate seat in Alabama show that the president's position is weakening, which is not good."

His Excellency listened to the young man sitting on the other side of the desk, and said with his penetrating gaze, "Well, we all agree, so the problem was solved."

The head of the bishop's council of the Baptodist Church knew that the president had sent his adviser to him to request something. He wanted to hear it from him directly.

"The president is so eager for you to use your influence and set things up," said Stephen.

Although Stephen did not name Steve explicitly, it was enough for His Excellency to hear the president's direct request to intervene. That was the reason His Excellency had asked Peter Jr. to bring a list of groups that directly and indirectly were influenced by the Church of Baptodist to be read in the presence of Stephen to show off his strength.

"Oh, Peter, what a coincidence, do you have that list we talked about a while ago?"

Suddenly everything made sense to Peter Jr. His boss's whole plan was clarified. He answered, "Yes, it happens to be in my briefcase." He pulled out a sheet of paper, leaned over, and handed it to His Excellency.

His boss took the sheet, put his glasses on, and said: "You know, Stephen, what some need to know is that they are not the only ones who have influence and power among certain groups. In other words, there is no monopoly dealing with those groups. Sometimes they must understand that ideas and thoughts aside, what Steve likes to call the alt-right are mostly followers of Christ and the church, and nothing else. This is Jesus Christ who has an absolute monopoly."

His Excellency was well aware of Stephen's religious background and enjoyed his silence on this claim. Then he began reading the names of different groups on the sheet he held.

"Southern Nationalists, the League of the South, the Identity Europa, the US Liberation Party, the American Guard, Traditional Workers Party, Ku Klux Klan, Vanguard America, Proud Boys, American Nazi Party, Aryan Brotherhood of Texas, Aryan Nations, Euro, National Alliance, Nationalist Socialist Party, American Plugin, Neo-Confederates, Christian Identity…"

His Excellency had reached the end of the page but continued, "This is a long list. I do not want to spend time reading these names. Many of these groups are nothing but clowns, but we try to keep them in line with the church and punish them when needed. Horrible incidents like Charlottesville could've been prevented by managing them better."

His Excellency turned to Peter Jr. and said, "One of these groups has great strength in Oakland, California. Arrange a speech for Mylos at UC Berkeley through these guys. There is also a Republican club in the university. We will talk more about this later."

Then he addressed Stephen and continued, "This young man, I'm talking about Mylos, has incredible contradictions that disrupt all boundaries within him. He is a homosexual and opposed to homosexuality at the same time. He promotes the alt-right's views while he has a Jewish background, inherited from one of his parents. Ultimately, he gets what he's after: controversy. All of these groups need to know that these boundaries are worthless. Only Christ's path is worth following, nothing else."

His Excellency looked directly into the faces of Stephen and Peter Jr. They both were looking down. This is the way that His Excellency wished for all mankind: naught against the word of God.

# Chapter 37 – Tabitha

Peter Jr. was relatively satisfied with himself and his life at age 59. He was receiving a decent salary from the Baptodist Church for valuable services that he was performing directly under His Excellency's supervision. Sometimes, being away from the house, his wife, and children for his missions were inconvenient, but in general, he thought of himself as Jesus Christ's blessed servant for the prosperity he had received in connection with the church and His Excellency. What really would vex Peter Jr. was his boss's humiliating attitude. Peter Jr. had great respect for His Excellency, but he knew that the feeling was not mutual. He realized that his boss did not fully appreciate his intellectual and managerial capabilities. Peter Jr. had a feeling that his superior would not care for the thoughts and analysis of the very person who handles practically all of his projects. What Peter Jr. sought from His Excellency was not more wealth or promotion, but a bit of respect.

Peter Jr. had arrived a few hours early at the airport. He had to fly to San Francisco for the mission his boss assigned him to accomplish. To kill time, Peter Jr. immersed himself in his thoughts. He thought if he were His Excellency, he would solve Sara's issue more competently.

But alas, he was never asked, not even once. In his mind, Peter Jr. had repeatedly imagined His Excellency, while sitting in his third-floor office at his mansion, asking him, "Peter, what would you do if you were in my position?" It was a question that had never been uttered.

Deep in his thoughts, Peter Jr. heard a notification sound from his phone. The *Bay Area Chronicle*'s app informed subscribers about the release of the new installment in the Sodom stories. With his index finger, he tabbed on the text that appeared on his phone's screen. The story came up, and Peter Jr. started reading...

***

*Elam region – King's Palace*

Contrary to King Birsha's imagination, Achan was not in captivity. Neither was he fretful in the new place nor had his new masters a reason to harass him. Achan was not interested in taking risks or playing with danger. Chedorlaomer had provided all means of comfort for him. In Elam, they wanted information which Achan provided willingly, especially information related to Edna and her affairs.

More than Chedorlaomer, it was the king's wife who had made life easy for Achan. After a long time, Tabitha had found a companion to make her dreary life exciting again. As Elam's official queen, Tabitha had always played a ceremonial role in celebrations and feasts. In private, Tabitha would receive little attention from Chedorlaomer. Only for a short period, after marrying the king, life had shown its bright side to the queen of Elam. But the excitement was extinguished from Tabitha's life quickly, like a sandstorm in the desert. And now, after five years of living in Elam's kingdom, Achan's arrival had spread excitement and joy to Tabitha's life.

Initially, Tabitha and Achan were sharing a mutual feeling of discontent in the presence of each other. In the beginning of his involuntary stay in Elam, Achan assumed Tabitha, like Edna, would do nothing but curtail his activities. And Tabitha would see the skinny, weird guy to be intrusive like other men of Chedorlaomer. But soon, they became fond of each other and inseparable as if they had been created for one another's companionship. Wearing women's clothes, Achan was entertaining ladies in the palace by performing daily theatrical scenes he had seen in the cities of Siddim. Achan would bring joy to women by putting makeup on his eyes, lips, and cheeks, once playing the role of a queen, and the next day, a maid who had become a victim of his unscrupulous master. Achan's popularity grew among the women's circle. He became the talk of the palace; no one looked at him as that little skinny man again. He was a rather beautiful woman in colorful clothing with colorful makeup, and everyone seemed to love him the way he was. Achan's external appearance seemed normal to anyone who knew him.

Before living in Elam, Achan used to put on beautiful and colorful garments in the presence of Birsha, but he had never caught the king of Gomorrah's attention. But now, among these women, Achan, like a young girl, had grown so cheerful that he needed neither alcohol nor lovemaking to satisfy his inner desires. And among the women in the palace, Tabitha became his closest friend. For Elam's women, the only excitement was sleeping with famous men in the palace. For those who had never experienced life in Siddim's territories, Achan was like fresh air in a dry, hot desert. In the male-dominated culture, Elam's women had never benefited from entertainment, fun, or excitement. With Tabitha's generous help, Achan was organizing various entertaining shows, either a one-man show or sometimes multi-player performances. Achan also forgot his past life, King Birsha's joyful companionship, and Edna's harsh pressures and imposed limitations.

For Achan and Tabitha, the days were passing so fast and pleasantly in each other's company that at night both could not wait for the sun to rise so they could return to their childish games. Chasing each other, they would run from one place to another, yelling and screaming, expressing excitements that they had never experienced before.

One day, Achan put on a long red piece of cloth and a yellow scarf around his shoulder that he had found in the palace's ornamental fabrics storage. The colorful boy was running to surprise Tabitha by a loud scream in the next room, unaware that the king was meeting with Abraham's messenger who visited the palace. Tabitha, trying to escape from Achan, had run to face the king who became angry at the interruption. Tabitha realized that she had entered an unauthorized area, but Achan continued to scream into Chedorlaomer's chamber.

The king first looked at the guest and then to Achan, whose funny appearance made Chedorlaomer calm. The king said, "You two should end this madness," then he turned to the guard and said, "So what are you doing here?"

When the guard was guiding the uninvited intruders out, Chedorlaomer commanded, "Bring the creature to me. You can guide the queen out," pointing to Tabitha.

Seeing Achan's face with its excessive feminine makeup brought a wide smile to the king's face. Abraham's messenger, standing straight, was watching the scene and the king on his royal throne. Chedorlaomer put Achan on his lap and asked the messenger, "Have you ever seen such a creature?"

Abraham's messenger, who was not sure what the appropriate response would be to please the king, bowed slightly as a sign of respect. The king, who had now completely shrugged off his anger, caressed Achan's curly hair which had grown longer since he came to Elam. Chedorlaomer looked at the messenger with his curious eyes.

The guest rubbed his black beard and cautiously said, "Abraham does not regard these acts as desirable for men. He considers it unacceptable."

Bursting into loud laughter, which was a sign of Chedorlaomer's good mood, the king shifted Achan on his thighs and said, "So you've seen it before?"

The messenger bowed again and said, "If my king allows, I will go back to the subject that we were discussing before," and looked at Achan, who had curled onto the king's lap like an adorable cat.

The king said, "There is no problem; you can continue," and put his hand on the leg of Achan, who had been squeezing himself onto Chedorlaomer's massive body.

"As I said, my lord told us that he could offer you about three hundred skillful warriors to fight against them," said the messenger.

Chedorlaomer demanded, "What does your lord want in return?"

The man responded firmly but slowly, "He wants the city of Sodom. Abraham has already sent his people there as refugees. Abraham's nephew is the head of that tribe. They will remain in the city if the fight begins. Abraham wants only the great king to leave everyone and everything that belongs to his nephew's tribe untouched. Instead, Gomorrah, Admah, Zeboiim, and Bella, with all their people and wealth, will belong to the king of Elam."

A little tremor, like a wince, passed through Achan's entire body as he was resting in the king's arms. When Chedorlaomer noticed the tremor in Achan's body, he pushed him off his lap and ordered him to leave the chamber. Achan did what Chedorlaomer asked. Then, the king turned to the messenger and said, "It's not a bad plan, but I have two conditions: firstly, your fighters must come under my command, and secondly, after the victory, my warriors enter Sodom's territory, taking any woman they want. They will not do anything to your nephew's tribe. I promise."

"I will deliver the great king's message. As far as commanding the fighters, I can assure the great king of Elam that you can count on us more than you think."

# Chapter 38 – Coffee shop

*San Francisco*

"I'm so sorry, Simone. I didn't think Melody would do this. I mean, I guessed, but I did not expect it," said Essie.

Simone was sitting in front of Essie inside the coffee shop, staring at her cup of coffee. She did not say anything. The line at the cash register nearly reached their table. The loud noise of the cappuccino machine was forcing the girl behind the counter to call every name several times. The cheerful colors on the walls, tables, and chairs had made the atmosphere joyful, but Simone was not feeling any joy at that moment.

Simone said, "I didn't expect it either. It's ridiculous. It's not her business that we are together."

Essie lifted his cup of coffee and took a sip. There was nothing to say to Simone. What could he say? Essie wanted to ask, just to say something, "Are you sure that was the only reason?" But he changed his mind. Of course it was. Of course, it was the result of Melody's jealousy. What else could it be? Essie chose to be silent. The coffee shop was becoming too crowded. Essie thought about suggesting that they leave the place and go out. But outside it was too hot.

"The heat in August, it's unusual." Finally, he broke the silence and spoke about the weather. Everyone knows that talking about the weather is usually an excuse to change the subject. But the weather in San Francisco was indeed at a record high, so Simone also engaged in talking about the strange weather. She even went further and talked about climate change. Essie was very interested in leading the conversation about human effects on global warming. However, Simone quickly returned to the first subject, "You know that I can sue Melody for wrongful termination of my employment."

Essie became pale and said quickly, "Please, what are you talking about? Don't even think about it."

Simone continued with more energy when she saw the effect of her comment on Essie. "Why not? You know, everyone knows that Melody just fired me because we started to date." Trying to test Essie, she continued, "You can be my witness in case we go to court."

Essie stared at Simone's eyes. He tried to find out whether Simone was serious or was just teasing him. Whatever it was, Essie did not like it. Experience had taught him that everything starts with a talk and after some time, it turns into reality. There would always be a possibility of creating an issue by entertaining the concept first, even expressing it as humor. And Essie felt uneasy that Simone even had such a thought in her head. Being in such a stalemate would be a nightmare for Essie. He knew he would never testify against Melody, although Simone was right in this case. He was upset with himself. Why should he testify against the truth or keep silent if Simone would bring a lawsuit just because he met Melody and David before Simone and had a long friendship with them?

Essie liked Simone although he felt she did not understand most of his arguments. Most of the time, Simone was just a good listener. Essie was surprised by her attentiveness. There was no pretention on her side. She was focusing on his points during conversations as if she wanted to remember them.

Essie did not care about the reason a girl like Simone wanted to be with him. Somewhere in his heart, he knew that he wanted Simone's attention no matter how irrational it may look. Simone's presence was tickling and twisting somewhere inside Essie, slightly above his heart. A sense of youth. It was Simone's liveliness that like a river's current was flowing in Essie's soul. And Essie embraced it with all his being, like the dry, cracked ground in a drought absorbing the flow of a river on its surface for the first time. The fervor of being with Simone was felt not through the logic of his mind, not even through the beat of his heart. But it was felt through his lips moving on her soft, vibrant skin and her body taking in the joy of life in its entirety. And all this was going to end by Melody's silly reaction. "What if Simone actually files a lawsuit against Melody?" he thought.

Essie raised his head and saw that Tim was standing next to their table. Essie saw the sweat drops on his forehead from the heat outside. Tim had on his usual light, comfortable clothes—cotton pants and white shirt with rolled-up sleeves. The handbag strap was around his neck, over one shoulder. Without hesitation, he pulled a chair from under another table where two boys were sitting and sat down at Essie's table. Tim ignored the young men's dissatisfaction with his rudeness in not asking their permission.

Tim turned to Essie and said, "Did you hear the news?"

Essie had not heard any news that day. Since dating Simone, he had spent less time reading the news. He used to be addicted to it, but lately, after dating Simone, he had somehow changed his habit. He replied with a vague answer that sent neither positive nor negative confirmation: "There is a lot of news everywhere, depends on which you are referring to."

"All the papers and news agencies reported that an ISIS member was arrested in Berkeley before he could detonate a bomb. It's a total lie. You know that well," said Tim, and then showed Essie the paper and several videos that were uploaded onto YouTube that morning.

"Well, you were there, why didn't you report it in your newspaper?" asked Essie.

Tim responded, "My report on the Berkeley incident wasn't approved to be published. My boss said I don't have any specific evidence to prove my allegation. Do you have anything that would help me prove it so I can submit it to my boss?"

Essie's reaction to the news was not what Tim expected. Apparently, he did not care much at all. Essie's mind was still trapped between two women, and Tim was trying to bring him back to the real world: war, conflict, and politics—the same world that Essie had been struggling to deal with for the at least the last forty years. At that moment, it was difficult for Essie to return to the real world of rough politics from Simone's soft feminine atmosphere. In the past, if someone brought him this kind of news, he would burst into anger and immediately react. But now he was dealing with a different kind of commotion. Obviously, Essie was not dissatisfied to be wrapped within a world of ladies only. In an unconscious or self-conscious manner, he asked himself, "What kind of man hates to be liked by two beautiful women?"

Essie said, "I don't have a specific proof. It's just a picture that doesn't look like what you showed me in the paper. Instead, the YouTube videos confirm the Baptodist church's website's claim in exposing Art's identity."

Tim replied restlessly, "That is not my concern now. Can't you get some documents from your friends to prove the person arrested has a connection to the Houston mosque?"

Essie said emphatically, "As I said before, I do not want to be involved in this matter with the police. Because if I do, I have to answer many questions about who my friends are and where they found that evidence. What about that detective, does he know who's who?"

At that very moment, Rachel came into the coffee shop. Approaching their table, she said, "Hey, you guys all are here."

Tim frowned and said sulkily, "I'm getting suspicious that you are constantly following me."

Rachel, who was holding Simone's hand, told Tim, "Don't keep your hopes too high. You're not that important for me to follow you. I came here to see Essie."

Rachel had heard the news about Simone's dismissal, but she had actually come to the coffee shop to talk to Essie.

"Wait a minute." Essie asked surprisingly, "Tim, how did you find me here? "

Tim answered, "I went to your office. David told me you usually come to this coffee shop."

Essie turned to Rachel and asked, "And you?"

Rachel responded, "I asked Melody. I told her that I have a critical issue to discuss with you. She also said that you usually come to this coffee shop."

"That easy, really? My close friends let the cat out of the bag about my whereabouts," Essie said, laughing. "I need to change the coffee shop that I go to every day."

Essie noticed the grimace on Simone's face when he mentioned "close friends." In the midst of a mounting security crisis, such clashes would not benefit anyone in the friendship circle. He could guess Simone knew that one of those "friends" was Melody. Essie was puzzled what to do about the tension between Melody and Simone.

*Being pulled between two ladies is pleasant only to some extent. But where is the boundary? He who knows this edge is undoubtedly succeeding not only in a love crisis but in other life struggles.*

Contrary to the field of politics, philosophy, and survival, the world of women was not turf that Essie could claim to be a master of. That was the reason that in his first marriage, Essie had lost everything, like a child facing a professional poker player, despite his illusion of being an intelligent person. He believed that his defeat in love was an onset of failure in other battles later in his life.

Essie asked Rachel, "What's up, how can I help you?"

"I want to speak with you alone," Rachel replied.

Simone moved from her seat after she heard Rachel's request and said, "I have to go."

Tim also stood up and said, "I have to go too." Tim had realized that he would not get anything from Essie.

Unhappy to see Simone's reaction, Essie told Rachel, "You can say it in front of them. They're not strangers." Then he turned to Simone and continued, "Are you okay? When can I see you?"

Simone grabbed her purse and said, "I'll call you."

Essie looked at Simone's body. She had denim pants with a sports tank top that highlighted her firm, mid-sized breasts. Simone and Tim said goodbye and left.

Essie turned to Rachel and said: "Well, what's up? I heard you got hired by Melody's firm."

"Yup, I'll start next week. But I don't know, I was thinking about postponing my start day a little," said Rachel.

"You tried really hard to get the job. Why do you want to postpone? Melody needs help too as you know Simone is not working there any longer," Essie said in his giving-advice tone.

Neither Melody's company nor Simone's job situation was important to Rachel. After what happened in Berkeley, Rachel's energy had been multiplied. That was the reason she came to see Essie. Rachel was present when Art fought the skinheads in the alt-right group and the terrorist. "I want to join your group. I saw everything. I saw how capable Art is. I want to help you guys."

"What group? What do you mean, where did you hear that we have a group?" said Essie, his eyes bigger than usual.

Rachel was acting in a way to show Essie that she knew more than he thought. "I spoke with Melody. She told me that you hold meditation sessions, and Art is in the meetings. I asked her if I can attend. She said to ask you or David."

Essie had no idea how much Rachel knew, or how much info Melody had given her. So he did not want to promise Rachel anything before speaking with Melody. "Let me talk with my friend David, who is directing the meditation sessions. Also, you should know because of serious events these days we decided to not get together for a while to hold sessions."

Using her inherent ingenuity, Rachel realized that Essie might be one of the leading decision makers. To convince Essie and show her worthiness, Rachel added, "So you know that I'm in contact with large groups in the LGBTQ community. Also, I know that Art is gay. I can mobilize a significant force in the short term if anything threatens Art."

As he looked at the little girl, mixed feeling rushed to Essie's mind about Rachel. This was the third time that they met and Essie had a conversation with her. It was interesting to him that this young girl was showing off her potential to mobilize social forces. On the other hand, Essie did not know her well enough to trust such a genius. Rachel's social power could hurt the group if she succumbed to her youthful, hasty mistakes. Essie just said, "I'll let you know through Melody."

The man behind the counter called out a name that attracted Essie's attention: "Muhammad, double espresso cappuccino."

Rachel noticed that all of Essie's senses were focused on the counter to see who would pick up the order. She said, "Don't worry, if he is a dangerous person, he will not place an order under his real name."

Essie really enjoyed Rachel's interesting point, but at the same time, he could not take his eyes off the counter.

# Chapter 39 – Terrorist

*San Francisco – Police Department*

Detective Smith was not allowed to visit the man who was arrested in Berkeley. His request to his superiors was rejected. The detainee was placed in a category that Detective Smith did not have clearance for. Besides, the prisoner had been transferred to another facility sooner than usual. Smith was very eager to confirm the information that David had transmitted to him. The detective was alarmed that he was not able to even check the nationality of the detainee. Until they transferred the man, Detective Smith had repeatedly asked if he was an Iranian. And he could not get any straight answers from those who supposedly had the information. The terrorist did not say anything.

The shocked expression on the face of the arrested man who refused to even give his name confused Detective Smith. Smith could not access transcripts of preliminary interrogations either. The morning newspapers added to Smith's perplexity. Although Detective Smith had told his colleagues the man was an Iranian, the newspapers identified him as a possible cell or loan wolf connected to ISIS. Smith had never been so stymied in any of his previous cases. His curiosity was the reason he was pursuing the subject, but he had no idea why he was so curious.

How was it possible that the FBI did not find the man's nationality? He doubted everything: David, the entire interrogation system, even his boss. On the same day, he knocked on every door to visit the captured person. Now, Smith was walking across his office with a slow pace trying to think and make sense of it all in his head. He did not even know where the man was transferred that day.

Smith thought about pressuring David to expose his source of information but changed his mind. He knew that David and his friends were already under pressure from other parties and they were unlikely to say anything. Detective Smith thought, "Apparently, the only people who are in the dark about what is happening in this case are the police department and me."

Within a few hours, he had searched whatever he could find on Wikipedia and studied the history of ISIS, Islamic fundamentalism, and its various branches. He was unable to sort out many contradictions in his mind. He read about the differences between Shia and Sunni sects of the Islamic faith. He was baffled by the fact that if the detained person was Iranian, then he could not be an ISIS member. The picture David sent him was supposed to be of an Iranian, so the terrorist's connection to ISIS could not be accurate. The mass media reports on the suspect's affiliation to ISIS could not bear any truth. Hun's response also did not lessen the contradiction in the detective's mind. Hun told him, "Maybe he is an Iranian, and at the same time he was in touch with ISIS. Or it's possible that media were reporting hastily to beat their rivals, without verifying accuracy and the rest were copying from one another," and so on.

But no, Smith had gone through many cases during the 38 years of his service, and he had solved them successfully. He had faced many murder and theft cases, but in each case he had come to a logical conclusion and was able to unravel it. In those cases, Smith also recognized all sides including the motive as well as the killer or killers or thieves. This time, he saw himself as dumb and ignorant. In his mind, Detective Smith could not take even a step toward the conjecture and probabilities. Various questions were piling up in his mind without any answer or clue. Some of the questions that Smith wrote in his notebook were, "Who is attacking David and his friends? What is the motivation to invade David's house and his employee's apartment? Why did they leave a religious mark in the gospel for Stevenson? Was the verse a homophobic message that was left in Art's apartment? Was it a warning? But why did the company owner and his wife became a target, as they are not gay? Why Stevenson, where there are hundreds of known LGBTQ activists in San Francisco? How relevant is the company's relationship to published articles in the *Bay Area Chronicle*? Why do David and his friends hide their information from the police? What is the role of David's Middle Eastern friend in this regard? There is no doubt that the Middle Eastern guy is the source of the photo sent by David, but why has he not directly told the police? ..."

The more he added to his questions on the notebook, the more pressure he felt to solve this very challenging mystery. He was not able to answer even one question on that list. Smith had processed a complete background check on David and his people. No flag was raised on any of them, except Rachel. Rachel, who had recently been seen with them, had several misdemeanors for protests and disturbing the public order. The rest of them were clear. In the case of Essie, Detective Smith had not much to search on. He did not have a family, except a brother who had been working in an electronic chain store in Southern California. There was not enough information on Essie. Smith's inquiries showed that Essie had various jobs in Southern California, including working in a casino, buying and selling computer parts, and working other low-level jobs until he started working for David. Essie had only one case at the San Diego Police Department, in which he was not an offender. Detective Smith did not manage to review details of Essie's connection to that case due to its confidential nature, but he sent a request for permission to review the incident that

Essie had allegedly been involved in. After that, Essie was always associated with David and his businesses. During the last couple of months, Smith and his team had David's group under surveillance. It became apparent to Smith that Essie was trained in affairs of counter-vigilance and pursuit. In Smith's opinion, Essie was the key to solving the problem, but how could he extract the needed information out of him?

Moreover, what about the good-looking young man who had practically trapped the terrorist in the park? He had no outstanding record anywhere. He studied at UC Berkeley and immediately started working after graduation for tech companies. But the other day, his actions had spun Smith's head. His extraordinary power was unexplainable. The way he pushed obstacles aside to reach his target frightened Smith to his core. The man, sitting on the ground, froze just from looking into Art's eyes. He became paralyzed. The more Smith was thinking about that event, the more he became agitated and angry. He felt exhausted, especially in his legs when he was walking into his office. Smith did not report anything to the FBI about David's tip. The detective made a decision. He had to talk to David and all of his friends, individually and as a group. He knew that unnecessary force would not be effective. Detective Smith decided to approach them as a friend.

***

Hossein was still in shock 24 hours after being arrested at the Berkeley Civic Center Park. He could not comprehend why he was unable to do anything on the grass field the previous day. A day before the moment of truth, he had repeatedly reviewed different possibilities in his mind and was ready to act accordingly. But that day, the presence of that young tall man had paralyzed him. He felt his heart beat in his chest, without the ability to move his hand. "What happened to me?" The question was pounding in his head repeatedly, a question that he had no answer for. The young man's image showing in his head, standing on the field, would make Hossein angrier. Art's image would appear as Jesus Christ, precisely like images he had seen in the movies and in pictures.

They had taken him directly to solitary confinement. Hossein was surprised to see an undercover policeman at the scene, asking about his nationality. Before being transferred to the next location, the policeman was kept asking if he were an Iranian. How did he know? Hossein could not believe it when he saw his own picture in the officer's hand. How could they obtain accurate information on him? He did not see many details of the photo well enough, but he recognized the inside of Houston Mosque in the photo's backdrop. Hossein was upset at the fact that the black policeman was repeatedly asking questions to confirm his Iranian nationality. Then, he was moved to another unknown facility. He did not go through legal process. They did not even take him to court to appear before a judge. They only told him that he could not be released on bail. Hossein knew that no one would come forward to pay for bail anyhow. So far, he stayed mum. Hossein did not go under a severe interrogation at that point. He was delivered to the FBI, and they handed him over to the NSA after a few similar procedures. The questions from both agencies were alike.

Hossein considered committing suicide from the moment he stepped into the solitary confinement cell. He looked around for a way to accomplish his goal. Nothing was there. He did not want his action to fail. Hossein knew that if he did not complete the task, he would be in a worse situation. Most likely, they would strap him to a bed and deny him any movement, like the immobile condition he had suffered on the day of his arrest. Thinking of that condition sent a wave of tremor through his entire body.

Hossein had been pacing back and forth since he was thrown into the new cell. He looked around to find a way to end his life while contemplating different methods in his head. He was not afraid of death. Hossein had dealt with the fear of death a long time ago. However, the look of that young man kept coming back. What was the penetrating gaze of the young man that froze him stone cold? For the first time in life, he felt fear deep down inside his being. Hossein knew that the horror was not the result of the arrest, interrogation, and imprisonment. "Was it not?" For a fraction of a second, doubt came into his mind, but it was gone as quickly as it had appeared. Rubbing his face, he touched his cheeks and the stubble that had grown in the last couple of days. He shook his head and said, "No." He was not afraid of anything

He was ready to be martyred long ago. Nothing could have impeded the decision to sacrifice himself for God, his prophet Muhammad, and 12 Shia imams, especially to Aqha Hussain, the third Shia imam for whom he had special respect and he was named after. Hussain, too, stood and fought alone against the enemy's army and became a martyr. "Ah Allah, accept my martyrdom," he thought.

Hossein stopped and closed his eyes for seconds. Standing with closed eyes, the thought of being martyred soon brought a grin to his face. He reviewed in his mind, "What's sweeter than reaching Allah's throne by fighting for his cause?" He tasted the sweetness of heaven on his tongue. But suddenly those two eyes reappeared, the pair of bright blue eyes that made him paralyzed. He started pacing again. The faster he walked, the more anxious he became. Hopeless, he shouted: "Ya Allah, you help me. Take me to your kingdom. Help me get rid of these demons. Let me have my reward. I did not fail to do my duty to you."

Hossein felt pressure in his bladder. Looking at the corner of the cell, he saw the little toilet and walked to it. While he was urinating, he observed the toilet's metal body. The change on his face reflected the appearance of an idea in his mind. It would be all over if he could find a way to slam his head with all his might into the sharp corner of the bowl. He could collapse his head easily with the help of Allah. When Hossein was done urinating, he stood up and examined the various parts of the toilet bowl. He identified the best point on which he could hit his head. It would have been better if he were able to run and throw himself on that spot. He knew human weakness. Hossein knew it was possible his human weakness would ease the impact unconsciously, at the moment of the slam. So, a few steps run-up and a dive, like a dive to catch a ball as a goalie, could help him achieve his goal. Before the revolution, he used to be a goalkeeper in a soccer team. He loved playing soccer before he knew the real Islam. Afterward, he had no time for a hobby. Islam had called for him, and now he had to perform his last dive. Hossein had to pass beyond the human barrier. He was on the verge of crossing that border. It was time to be in the angels' companionship. "Oh, dear Allah, accept this sacrifice. To follow in your footsteps, I closed my eyes on physical pleasures. I have always lived in the memory of Ashura, and I ignored deceptive joy in this world. Take the fear off of my soul. Give me strength and courage to act upon my last duty. You know better that I never had an eye on paradise's promises although I know they are real. You are the truth. Take me to your kingdom."

He got up and stepped back. He measured the distance: three steps and a half. He thought, to jump start, it would be better if he pushed his hand back against the wall behind him. To test, he pressed the wall few times. The uncertainty came over him again. It was not because of the fear of dying, but the doubt of reaching the perfect outcome: death. It would be a disaster if he did this without success. He focused. He had to succeed. Being alive in captivity was not an option.

Hossein thought that the news of his martyrdom would create a reverberation in Muslims' hearts around the world. Not those Muslims who were just like American infidels. Not those who have been falsified under the name of ISIS as the symbol of Islam. With his blood, he would restore Islam. The world must know that only 12 Shia imams represent true Islam. He continued thinking in his mind that when Mahdi, the last hidden Shia imam, emerges, he will take his sword under his command and will perish all infidels altogether with divine power. But now first, "I must reach the doorstep of Allah's kingdom."

Hossein found himself at the farthest distance from the toilet, sticking to the wall. He stood on his side, with his right hand on the wall, ready to push himself with all his strength. After a couple of steps, with a horizontal dive, he smashed his head into the metal corner of the toilet bowl.

A few hours later, when the guard took a look through the window, he found Hossein on the floor in a pool of blood. The warden opened the door and faced a disgusting and disgraceful scene. Hossein's head had been split over his eyebrow to the top of his head. The toilet bowl was broken off its base, and feces were blended with his blood, encircling his head and half his body. The guard took a step back. He pressed the radio button on his shoulder and repeated it several times: "Emergency situation in cell number twelve."

# Chapter 40 – Return From Canaan

Since Mark Stevenson was paid a visit by the lawyer of J & J firm, which was hired by a company called Lord L.L.C., he had started receiving Lord News magazine regularly. It was a weekly publication of the Baptodist Church, covering political and scientific news, in addition to Christians' activities around the world. A large part of the semi-colored, illustrated magazine was usually on the influence and power of the Baptodist Church in more than 120 countries, including many in Africa and Asia.

What shocked Mark in the last issue was the photo of an individual named Arthur Stevenson. When Mark saw Art's face, his heart almost stopped beating inside his chest. After many years, he was seeing Art's face. But he could not understand what the article was trying to reveal about the person in the photographs. Wherever Art's name was mentioned, it was in connection with Sodom and Gomorrah. Mark could not believe what he was reading. His son was named as a member of a Sodom group, but why and what was a Sodom group? A question was constantly bugging him: "Despite the existence of so many gay people in the nation, why had his son had become a flagrant symbol of biblical reference against gays? Was it a dirty joke that targeted him?"

Using his limited access to the library and a computer, Mark searched and read the stories published in the *Bay Area Chronicle*. He caught up with all the stories, but he was still confused about the connection. Another name was listed as the author of the series. How could all these have been related to Art? And in other news, which apparently was a report on real events, the magazine unveiled Arthur's devilish power. Mark decided to ask his lawyer all the questions during their next visit, which was scheduled that same week. His lawyer had told Mark the court's proceedings to reopen the case was coming earlier than expected. Now, Mark was more interested in the story of his son, Arthur, than in his case. He began reading the next part of the story on the computer monitor screen in the library…

***

*Sodom Territory – King Bera's Palace*

"Thank you for accepting my request for a visit," said Lot, standing in front of King Bera who was sitting on his throne.

The king pointed to the chair next to him, the one Amim used to sit on, and said, "Have a seat."

Lot obeyed and sat down where King Bera ordered him. It was obvious on Lot's face that he was hesitating to say what he had come to say. Staring at Lot's eyes, the king noticed the indecision on Lot's look but said nothing, instead waiting for Lot to speak. Lot repositioned himself in his chair and looked at his trembling hands nervously. After a moment, Lot said, "I wanted to bring up an issue … How can I say it … It is about my wife, Edith."

Curious, but still looking at Lot's face, the king silently waited for him to continue. Lot said, "Since we have arrived at the city gate, my wife spends most of her time in the city, visiting the wise old man although we are still awaiting your decision."

The smirk on the king's face was an indication that he understood Lot's concern, but in jest, Bera said, "And your complaint now is why everyone is not allowed inside the city or why your wife is?"

Lot, who seemed obviously unhappy that he was obligated to speak about his wife, replied, "It's been a while since I noticed Edith has changed. Apparently, conversations with the wise old man have affected her."

"What kind of change?" asked King Bera.

"How can I put it? She looks so cheerful and lively," responded Lot.

With a loud laugh, the king said, "Are you upset that your wife is happy?

Feeling trapped, Lot replied, "Absolutely not, but she's not attentive to the girls and me anymore. It seems she does not care for her family and the people she belongs to. She cannot wait to go back to the city when she comes home."

King Bera said instantly, "Is this a bad thing? Are you and your people not eager to be allowed to live in Sodom? All my advisers have agreed to grant your wife lasting permission to live in Sodom, but I will postpone it until the final decision for all. At your wife's request and the approval of the city council, she has been allowed to enter any time she wishes. As I've been told, Edith has already started working in a school, and as a useful member of the community she is playing a positive role."

Lot remained silent. There was nothing that he could say. He could not complain about the compliment his wife was receiving from Sodom's ruler. What could he ask him: "Put my wife under pressure"? Besides, he had no evidence for his claim that Edith was doing something against her tribal traditions. If he could point to anything, it undoubtedly was a norm, practiced by city residents as their rights. The same rights that Lot and his daughters would call immorality.

The king changed the subject and asked, "Now that you are here let me inform you about the possibility of dividing your people into different territories. This is one of the conditions that will speed the process of deciding on your tribe's situation."

Lot replied reluctantly, "We would prefer all to stay in Sodom; my daughters, especially, insist on this matter. However, if your condition is mandatory, please at least divide us among the territories of Sodom and Gomorrah so that families are able to see each other more often."

Meanwhile, the guard informed the king that Leah had arrived. To end the conversation, King Bera said, "Your request will be reviewed, but you should know that your entire tribe cannot live in Sodom. Now, you're dismissed."

Lot stood up. While the guard was guiding him out, Leah came and passed by Lot. Lot tried to attract the attention of Sodom's most powerful person after King Bera. But Leah, staring ahead, passed by Lot as if she had not seen him. The king, still sitting on his throne, grasped Leah's hand and said, "Welcome back. All the people of Sodom feel safer when you are in the city. Tell me how your trip was and what happened. I wish other members of the council were here— Sichra and Amim came back recently. Tell me, what did you find on this journey of yours?"

Leah rubbed her forehead and face and said, "I did not see the old man himself, that person's uncle," pointing to the way that Lot went out. "They said he has gone to the desert with no definite time of return. There were many people living in tents and under Abraham's control. As far as eyes could see, there were sheep and men. I had a strange feeling that I could not trust anyone or anything. On our way to Canaan, we found a girl carrying the old man's child in her womb. She was afraid of Abraham's wife more than the tribe's leader himself. But stranger than anything else was the military exercises. They practice fighting every day in a different area of their territory. It is unclear why Abraham needs that many warriors."

The king interrupted Leah's words and asked, "You had gone to verify Lot's words. Are these people behind our city gate honest in their claims? Apparently, what most attracted your attention was the character of Lot's uncle whom you could not meet."

Leah replied, "Yes, Lot was separated from his uncle to direct his people, but I did not find the reason behind it. Yes, I became interested in Abraham, without seeing him. I think I know Abraham well now. Perhaps seeing Abraham would not have been as fruitful as listening to the stories about him. Many in the tribe consider him a powerful man who takes his might from non-conventional sources; some also consider him a sorcerer whose magic lies in his words. Whoever he is, when the desert calls for him, Abraham goes alone into the depths, and when he returns, he comes back stronger. Perhaps all of this is an exaggeration of crazy people who need to be led by a charismatic leader who has a supernatural power. I regret that I could not see Abraham personally."

The king was losing patience from hearing too much about a man named Abraham. There were a lot of other vital issues that Leah should have been informed about. The amount of water flowing into the plain was significantly reduced. In Leah's absence, King Bera had received reports indicating the urgency of the water issue. In the king's view, the scarcity of water, which the sister territories were also suffering from, along with other events such as the kidnapping of Achan, were not all coincident. A creative mind like King Bera's could not easily ignore those facts.

"Leah, arrange a meeting with our allies to be held in Gomorrah, all of them. As I look more closely at these events, I see Chedorlaomer's role more clearly in this. You and I are going to Gomorrah. The wise old man also will accompany us. Sichra and Amim will stay in Sodom," said the king in a serious tone.

"What is the decision on Lot and his people?" Leah asked.

"I have not made a definite decision yet. The wise old man is not optimistic. He believes that Lot and his daughters and half of their people should not be admitted to our city. The wise old man does not have a good feeling about them. He does not trust Lot's daughters. But I think, rejecting Lot and his daughters means declining their request as a whole. We need to admit half of them into our city without granting complete inhabitancy privileges. The rest will be distributed among the sister territories. Gradually, we can approve their full privileges in Sodom based on their acts and behavior."

# Chapter 41 – Arshum

The phone on Tim's nightstand began to vibrate and woke him up. Tim opened his eyes and looked at the clock on the stand. It was 2:15 a.m. He grabbed the phone and saw his boss's name on the screen.

"Hello?"

"Did you hear the news, Tim? Sorry to wake you up at this time," asked Larry, Tim's boss.

Tim, somnolent and dizzy, thought it must have been certainly very important news for his boss to call him at this time of night. Tim asked, "No, what happened?"

Larry's next question puzzled Tim even more, "Are you okay?"

Tim replied, "I'm okay; I was asleep, why?"

"A huge explosion destroyed everything at the office," Larry answered.

Tim's heart started palpitating and he jolted awake. He remembered he had heard a big bang in his sleep, but he ignored it and went back to sleep. Tim asked, "Did anyone get hurt?"

"I don't think so. I'm on my way there right now. I just wanted to check if you're okay and to ask if you had anything valuable at the office."

Tim responded, "All my stuff is on my laptop…"

His boss interrupted Tim and said that he had to take another call and hung up. Already on his feet, Tim was pacing the living room of his apartment now. He could no longer sleep. In his mind was the question of whether the explosion might have been related to Art's stories published in the *Bay Area Chronicle*. Fear encompassed his entire being. He opened his laptop to check the most recent part of the story that he had written the day before and was supposed to upload on the server in the morning...

***

## *Elam Territory – Outside the Palace*

Sitting on a flat stone by the river, Achan put his right hand into a narrow tributary of the river coming down from the mountain. Although it was high summer in the mountains, the weather was cold, and Achan's fingers became red and numb after being submerged for too long in the freezing water. He pulled his hand out of the water and held his shaking fingers in front of Tabitha's eyes. Tabitha grabbed Achan's hand and put it on her chest.

"Staying here in Elam has numbed my soul as the freezing water did to my fingers," said Achan, while wiping his tears off his cheeks with the palm of his left hand. "How did I suddenly forget Birsha with all his kindness? And now this monster is planning to murder the man who showed me the most love in my life. And here I am, busy playing and enjoying myself. Shame on me."

Tabitha embraced Achan. She became as sad as the person in her arms, someone she was not sure whether to call a man or woman. Achan's volcanic yet soft emotional eruption brought tears to Tabitha's eyes. They laid their heads on one another's shoulders and stayed in the same position for several moments. Achan raised his head, stood up, and said, "Now, I understand the plan of refugees whom Sichra and Amim were talking about. I have to go back to reveal their plot to Birsha. I cannot wait any longer."

A heavy sorrow fell on Tabitha's heart. Achan noticed the grief on Tabitha's face. He had shared the greatest joy of his life with the queen of Elam. For Tabitha, his departure was the end of a happy life, a sweet but short dream. Achan held Tabitha's hands, staring into her eyes for few moments, and said, "Tabitha, you must understand why I cannot stay here anymore, not that I'm bored and tired. Even for this short period, I experienced the best moments of my life. And you were one of the main reasons for my happiness."

Tabitha could not hold back the tears from flowing down her cheeks. Her sobbing kept Achan silent for few moments, but then he continued. "I'm telling you this story wholeheartedly. I was nobody until Birsha took me into his palace. The king of Gomorrah fell in love with me, and I was interested in him, too. But what I experienced here with you was different. I became myself. Before coming here, I always had the same inner tendency to express myself. But here, by performing and buffoonery, I found my real self. Here, I found out that my inner essence is a joy. Maybe playing and entertaining allowed me to be me. I had a comfortable life in Gomorrah, but I was not what I wanted to be, although the king had chosen me as his first love. Don't make a mistake; I enjoyed the king, his love, and his lovemaking. But I would rather stay here and enjoy being me even for one day than be with Birsha with all that he offers me. Yes, I would rather stay here, be a buffoon, with no lovemaking forever."

Tabitha calmed down and listened to Achan's words. She never expected to hear such profound words from someone who, in his own words, called buffoonery his chief characteristic. Tabitha now considered Achan wiser than anyone else she knew, but Achan's words added to her heartache and sadness. To Tabitha, Achan was like a jewel that she had found in a hazy river and held for a while. And now, the pressure of the current in the same polluted river was forcing the gem out of her grip.

"Tabitha, listen to me. The joy I have, the happiness you and I are experiencing now, will go away if I fail to do what I have to do. It won't be the same if I stay. When your inner voice tells you to do something, you must act. I cannot see the ruin of those who have been so good to me and offered so much love. My action may save them."

Tabitha was receiving energy from Achan who was standing in front of her, talking with his big heart. Still holding Tabitha's hand, Achan sensed a tidal wave under Tabitha's skin. At that very moment, a passing sparkle shone in Tabitha's eyes, and then she said, "I'll come with you. I have nothing worthy of living here. Who am I and what do I have here? I am only a ceremony embellishment, an ornamental chair, nothing but an elegant frame."

For some moments, Achan remained uncertain what to say. Mixed emotions rushed through Achan's mind. Under increasing pressure from Tabitha's gaze, Achan became uneasy about not being able to give her a quick and appropriate answer. Was he in love with Tabitha? No; he was not in love with Birsha either, despite the king of Gomorrah's passionate and one-sided love for him. Achan never experienced love. Now he felt love in the free expression of his appearance and the liberty of being whatever he wanted to be. But his new experience and joy could dissipate fast if he did not act to help Birsha.

Achan knew that he was able to freely express himself in Elam, living in a situation that had been created by Tabitha. More than Tabitha's role, it was Achan's new appearance that made him free of the restraint. Achan was not really restricted to what he wanted to wear in Gomorrah. He was free with Birsha to wear anything he desired. However, Tabitha's encouragement to fill his inner vacuum made a different person out of him, a character that Achan was looking for all his life without knowing it.

Once again, Achan reviewed the whole situation. Was he in love with Tabitha? The answer was no. So, the reason for his long delay in responding was clear to himself now, especially the fact that he did not want to put Tabitha in jeopardy.

"No, absolutely not," Achan could only say these three words.

"Why?" she asked. "I can be so helpful in your escape."

"I will never forgive myself if something happens to you," replied Achan.

Tabitha had made up her mind; it was too late. Achan's denial did not affect her. All they needed to do was to go first out of the palace and then out of the city. Yet a great number of guards in the vicinity of the palace entrance and the city gate would make their escape difficult. After leaving the city, they needed two horses. Being on foot would not get them far. Neither of them had endured any hardship in their lives. And Achan had entirely forgotten the difficulties of his life prior to living in the Gomorrah palace. Tabitha, the daughter of Amraphel, the ruler of Shinar, was born and grew up in the palace. Her marriage to Chedorlaomer had helped unify four kingdoms in the region: Elam, Shinar, Tidal, and Arloch.

Tabitha could not trust anyone to help them. They both could perish if their plan or even their intention was revealed. Tabitha had serious rivals in the palace among Chedorlaomer's mistresses. Many of them sought to seize her position as Elam's official queen. Each of those women could function as an enemy against Tabitha. Her personal guard was the only one she could trust to some extent. As the queen of the Elam, Tabitha had been assigned her own guard since her first day in the palace. She had seen in many cases that his guard overlooked the king's orders calmly if the queen did not like them. The guard would have done anything that Tabitha requested, no question asked. He never refused to fulfill the queen's wishes.

Arshum, the king's most loyal guard, was apportioned to protect the queen from the very first. Watching Arshum's gigantic figure, stiff muscles, sturdy chest, neck, and arms, would give Tabitha a sense of security. Except in the bedroom, when Tabitha demanded to be alone, or when there was no threat, Arshum would follow the queen like a shadow. To Tabitha, Arshum's face was like a fixed, hard stone tablet. The pupils in his eyes were immobile. Tabitha never had any eye contact with her guard. In fact, Arshum had no eye contact with anyone; he looked nowhere but ahead of him. Even when Tabitha spoke to Arshum, looking directly into his eyes, the guard would avoid looking at the queen's eyes. He just would fulfill his duties without looking at her or talking. Tabitha never heard a word out of Arshum's mouth.

Two days after talking with Achan by the river, Tabitha called Arshum into her bedroom. Achan was already present. The bedroom was the only safe place for them to speak without any threat of being overheard. Only her husband and Achan were allowed to enter the queen's private room. It was the first time that Arshum was entering the queen's most private space. Arshum's nasal cavities were trembling. His hyperventilation was the sign of his excitement about being in the queen's bedroom. Wearing Tabitha's most beautiful dress, Achan was sitting on the bed with heavy makeup on his face. Tabitha stood up to face Arshum and demanded, "Arshum, look at me."

The guard did not move, only stared over Tabitha's head. The queen grabbed Arshum's arms and repeated, "Arshum, I said, look at me. That's an order."

Despite his usual habit, Arshum lowered his head and looked at Tabitha. He had an ongoing, formidable battle inside his mind and body. Small droplets of sweat were merging on his flaring face into larger drops. He could look for only a few moments at Tabitha's eyes. Arshum closed his eyes for a moment. Tears dropped from the corner of his eyes when he opened them. Tabitha doubted for a moment whether she should say anything. She could not figure out what was going on inside her guard's mind.

"Achan and I want to travel outside the city for a short period. We do not want anyone to know about it," said the queen.

Arshum took his eyes away from Tabitha's face and looked ahead again. Tabitha shook Arshum's arms, which were still in her hands and said, "Arshum, look at me. I want you to prepare two horses outside the city gate for us, three nights from now. No one should find out about what I just told you. Do you understand?"

Arshum apparently was looking at Tabitha, but he clearly was somewhere else. Achan rose off the bed, came close to Arshum, touched the guard's arm and back, and said, "Darling, are you sure he understands you?"

Tabitha shook Arshum and said, "Say something, don't you have a tongue?"

Arshum opened his mouth and kept it that way. With a short scream, Tabitha took her eyes from the guard's mouth and turned her back to him. "What happened?" said Achan, in a frightening tone.

"There is no tongue in his mouth, it is cut," said Tabitha, while still covering her face with both hands. The queen looked at Arshum's face again. She touched the face of the strong man standing in front of her, like a vulnerable, weak, fragile child, and said: "I'm sorry."

Arshum closed his eyes when the queen touched his face. Tabitha said again, "Promise me nobody knows about my request. Then, you can leave."

The giant guard nodded and headed back to the door. On his way out, Arshum sent an angry look at Achan, who had Tabitha's favorite dress on. Now the dress was covering someone who was pretending to be a woman. Achan's entire body shivered so hard that he crawled into the queen's arms.

When the guard left the room and closed the door, Achan said, "My dear, are you absolutely sure, I mean do you have trust in this monster?"

Tabitha replied: "Since I arrived in this city and this palace, he is the one I have trusted the most."

Outside, Arshum had put his ear on the door. He heard the queen's last words and closed his eyes again.

# Chapter 42 – Tech2AI

*San Francisco – Tech2AI's Office*

David was leaning on the desk in his office, reviewing a list of items on a single paper. He walked toward the door, opened it, and called Sam who was busy in the main coding area. Then he went back to his seat and waited for the project manager to come in. David asked, "Hey Sam, this report doesn't look good. I see deadlines were missed and some are approaching, and we're behind on almost all projects."

With a serious face ready for objection, Sam said, "Well, we've had some problems recently. Art has not been working for a while, and Essie is not here at all. You've been absent too."

"Essie and I weren't part of production anyway. Has Art been that effective? Really? Is he a game changer in the final release?" David asked.

Sam, who was careful not to give much credit to Art, answered, "It's not just that. There were other problems. There was a series of bugs showing up on test results. For a week, all the tests failed on three of our important projects. I myself had to do testing and couldn't oversee several other projects."

David raised his head from the report he was studying, looked at Sam, and said: "I'm sorry to hear this. Probably I needed to get more involved with some of them. You should've told me that you needed help."

"I didn't want to bother you; I knew you were involved with more important issues," Sam replied.

With a puff, David stated, "In any case, this company is the source of income for all of us. We're now working on two of our developing AI software, and we have five projects ordered by others that need to be released soon. I know that our software projects need further architectural work, but for other projects, we already have working templates. They just need to be tweaked based on each customer's criteria and their user needs. What are the problems that we can't release them on time? "

At this moment, the main doorbell rang in the hall and on David's phone. After the blast in the *Bay Area Chronicle*'s building, David urged everyone not to leave the main door open during working hours. Also, he asked Sam not to let in anyone who is not a Tech2AI employee without an appointment.

David and Sam both checked their phones to see who had rung the doorbell. Detective Smith was behind the door, waiting and looking into the camera. "What does he want now?" said David with a face that showed he was not happy to see Smith's face on his screen.

He said to Sam, "Send him here. We'll need to talk about this later. If we continue like this, we will all lose our jobs."

David pressed the icon on the phone app. Sam walked out of the office, and after a few moments, the sound of knocking on the door was heard. David said loudly: "Come in."

Detective Smith came into the office. His gray pants, a white shirt without a tie, and a blue baseball cap indicated that he was not working that day. His Martin Luther King lookalike face appeared somewhat tired. As he took off his baseball cap, his thin, short, kinky salt-and-pepper hair partially showed the skin on his scalp. David raised his head and saw the detective, and said, "Hello detective. What happened that you thought of me today?" David discerned an unhappy and dull look on Detective Smith's face. David guessed his look meant he was starting a bad day.

Smith said, "Hi," walked slowly forward, and squeezed David's hand. He sat down in the chair that David pointed to on the opposite side of the desk. After a brief pause, he said, "I don't know how to start. There are many unanswered questions in my mind that I need your help with."

"Of course. How can I help you, detective?" David asked.

Smith began to talk in an annoying voice, "I'm not sure whether you're hiding things from me willingly or by force. But I know that you're concealing some facts from me. Why do you want to keep me in the dark?"

David looked at him and said, "I did not tell you some stuff, like the night that they broke into our house. But you must know that there was no particular reason."

Detective Smith, who found an excellent angle to dig into, pressed more, "Your home is not that important to me ... well, it is important but is not my concern now. You know that I'm talking about other incidents, the story of Berkeley and the photo you sent me. Tell me more about that."

David responded calmly, "There is nothing complicated to go over. One of my friends, who received information from his friends, saw this risk. Because my friend was not willing to risk disclosing his source, I forwarded the information to you, because I had your card. It turned out to be a real danger. I am happy we did. As simple as that."

Smith, who was not satisfied by David's explanation, sensed some degree of honesty in David's tone. "You said that the man in the photo was an Iranian national, but reports say something else. Also, our investigation has shown that a different party has threatened you. Many facts and documents do not match."

David looked at Smith with astonishment. In his mind, he was evaluating Smith's argument. After a few moments, David said, "Did you not interrogate the person captured at Berkeley? Have you not determined his nationality yet? I never said that we were the target of the person in the picture. Besides, I don't know about other parties that you mentioned. Is there something that we should know? "

Smith did not want David to know that not only did he not extract any information from the arrested person, but that person had already committed suicide. He found out about the suicide in a confidential report that he wasn't supposed to have accessed. Smith had no choice. His trust in his colleagues at the police department was less than that of David and his friends who had hid everything from him since the beginning. Several documents about the break-in at Art's apartment and intrusion at David's house had mysteriously disappeared from his desk drawer. Smith found the situation very unusual. The detective started feeling sympathetic toward David and his friends. Among his colleagues, the only person whom Smith still trusted was Hun. At that moment, Smith decided to give David some information and ask him to reciprocate.

"The suspect committed suicide in the first week of his arrest. He was transferred to an unknown location soon after he arrived at the police station. As far as I know, even during interrogations by other teams, he did not mention his nationality. He was officially announced a member of the Islamic State."

With a dizzying look, David said, "It's impossible. I can assure you that person is an Iranian ... I mean, he was."

"But I gathered documents showing you and your friends were being attacked by religious conservative people connected to a church. I also found out that the same footprints found at Stevenson's apartment were found in the explosion of the *Bay Area Chronicle*'s building," said detective Smith with confidence in his tone.

David, who was surprised, asked, "What religion, domestic or foreign?" Apparently he did not hear the word "church."

Smith replied, "Oh, I didn't mention. It's a conservative church called Baptodist in Atlanta."

Puzzled, David demanded, "So, why don't you act? Why don't you arrest them? What are you waiting for?"

"It's not that simple," said Smith calmly.

Smith had nothing else to say in response to David's questions. He could not mention the fact that evidence had disappeared from his desk, and that there were no other leads to continue pursuing the case. Smith continued, "What is Stevenson's story? He was supposed to meet me the day the terrorist was arrested in Berkeley ... And I must admit we got the guy only because of Mr. Stevenson's timely action. Who is he, what's going on with him?"

Smith's friendly approach grew on David. David decided to share some issues with Smith as far as he could. Melody, from the beginning, believed in involving the police, especially Detective Smith. She insisted on informing the authorities but could not convince others in the group. Mocking her husband and other men, Melody attributed men's reluctance to accept facts to the influence of testosterone on their characters. Now David had come to a point where he felt he should have told Smith more. He felt the group needed help, as pressure was increasing on them.

"You must have read stories published in the *Bay Area Chronicle* recently. I have to tell you that those stories are not fiction." David began to explain the situation with an introduction.

Curious, Smith said, "What does it mean? Does he own a time machine to go back and forth?"

At this moment, the doorbell rang again. As David continued talking, he looked at his phone quickly and pushed the open icon on his phone, "I mean ... no, not a time machine..." he paused as he saw on the phone that the delivery man gave a package to Sam and went away. While his eyes were on Sam through the window behind the detective, David continued, "... I mean, Art can travel to the past through meditation ... he also can visit places at different times and see things."

David had an eye on Smith and an eye on Sam, who put the package on the big table. At the same time, the project manager was answering a coder who came to him with a question.

"I do not understand," Smith said. "You mean ... what you're saying is that he'd really gone to the place mentioned in the Chronicle ... Sodom?"

"Not personally ... or physically ... excuse me for a second, detective. Apparently, I have a package. Let me grab it quickly. I'll be right back."

David stood up and passed by the desk and then the chair on which Smith was sitting. The detective grabbed David's elbow and stopped him. He said, "You're kidding me, right? I'm not in a joking mood today at all."

"I kid you not at all," said David, who was astounded by Smith's move. "If I'm allowed, I should go and get my package. I was waiting for it. Will be right back."

Smith let David's elbow go with an apologetic gesture. David smiled and looked at Sam who was opening the package. At that very moment, the window between David's office and the main work hall smashed with sound of an explosion. The wave of the blast first lifted and threw David on the desk, then on the wall behind his desk. Smith was pushed under the desk with his forehead on the ground. The chair that Smith was sitting on fell on his back.

A few moments passed. Smith shook himself a little and tried to get out from under the desk. He raised his head and saw David, in front of him close to the wall, lying on his side unconscious. There were wounds on David's face, and blood was spreading on the ground. Smith got up slowly and stumbled toward David. He then carefully flattened David on his back and raised his head slightly. He checked David's pulse, both on his wrist and his neck. Smith shook him a few times. David did not move. Detective Smith called his name without any results, then opened David's eyelid.

The detective stood up and slowly went back toward the door. The glass of the entire window had been blown out. Only small shards of glass in the corners and on top were sticking out of the bare aluminum frame. Woozy, Smith slowly slipped through the frame without touching the sharp edges of the glass.

An immense explosion had destroyed everything on the floor. The long desk in the hall which used to be a work station was broken into many pieces. Computers and monitors were thrown around. Blood and pieces of meat were splashed, clinging on the walls. A few pieces of body organs had fallen in places. In the center of the hall, there was a three- or four-foot hole. A small part of the lower level of the building appeared through rough edges of broken wood and wires. Dust and smoke were still in the air, making it difficult to see the whole scene. There was no sign of Sam or any living person. Everything was torn into pieces: glass, wood, and metal mixed with pieces of human flesh, blood, and crushed bones. Smith could not hear anything but the shrill sound of a whistle in his ear.

A hand was placed on his shoulders. He jumped in fright, turned back, and saw a firefighter. He watched the man's mouth and lips move without a sound. Smith had no idea what the firefighter was saying to him. Two officers helped Smith walk toward the exit door, holding him under his arms. After a few steps, Smith stopped and pointed to

David's office with his finger. One of the firefighters ran into the office. Smith looked out from the far. David was moving. Dust and smoke were still in the air, making it hard to breathe. After taking few unsteady steps, Detective Smith fell on the ground.

# Chapter 43 – Clouds of War

As usual, His Excellency walked into his office at 8 a.m. He could not remember starting his day at the office later than that. He did not have a good sleep the night before. The same damned dream came to him with more sour flavors at dawn. He could no longer sleep after he woke up from the nightmare. Recently, there was not a day that he started without the nightmare, as the frequency of the bad dreams was increasing. His Excellency did not get used to it. He would find the dream as real and uncomfortable as if he was awake.

John Wesley the Third sat behind his desk. In a few moments, the room would fill with the aroma of coffee and Maria. A few minutes after he entered his office, Maria would bring his coffee. And that was when His Excellency could start easing off the bad mood and forgetting the pain in his joints. It was Friday morning, and the head of bishops had another reason to replace his unpleasant mood with passion. His Excellency was expecting to follow the next part of the Sodom stories. It was not because he was fascinated with the stories, though it was one of the reasons for his enthusiasm. His Excellency intended to write a comprehensive critique, and therefore he carefully examined the characters and narratives.

On that morning, however, immediately after sitting in his comfortable chair, His Excellency did not wait for Maria, the coffee, and the scent of Paradise, as he named the combination of the two aromas. He pulled out an iPad from his desk drawer and began reading the latest episode of Sodom's stories…

***

## *Gomorrah Region – King Birsha's Palace*

King Birsha's sullen and fuzzy face was reflecting his emotional condition. He was sitting in a room along with the kings and their companions from sister territories who had gathered to coordinate and assess the critical situation. Chedorlaomer and his allies had practically shut off the water to the cities in the valley of Siddim, creating a situation that even the wise old man did not remember from the driest years in the past. Contrary to the king of Gomorrah, Edna, in a perky, high-spirited mood, was sitting next to Birsha and talking the most on behalf of their kingdom. On the other side of the large rectangular table, King Bera was sitting along with Leah and the wise old man, on his left and right respectively. Three other kings—King Shinab of Admah, King Shemeber of Zeboiim, and King Zoar of Bella—were sitting in the middle on both sides of the table, along with their war advisers.

"We are in a situation that has been unprecedented hitherto," King Bera said. "Chedorlaomer's action, blocking the water flow to our lands, is an obvious declaration of war."

The king of Bella interjected, "Are we sure that Chedorlaomer is the cause of this drought? He had the power of water blockage in the past. We never had a good relationship with him before, but the question is why now if he is the cause?"

The king of Sodom replied, "The fact that he has not done it in the past does not prove his innocence. He may not have done it before, but he is certainly behind the blockage. Leah has collected many pieces of evidence from our people in the upper regions, especially in Elam. All of them indicate the closure or rerouting of rivers leading to Siddim's plain. We have no doubt."

Before anyone else started talking, Edna said, "Achan's kidnapping is also another reason to prove Chedorlaomer's hatred against us. We are sure that Achan has been kidnapped by them and is now in Elam."

With a smirk on his face, the king of Admah responded, "We have also heard about the news on Achan's performance in Elam. Our people also brought to our attention Achan's very close relationship with the queen of Elam."

King Birsha threw an angry look at King Shinab before he finished his words. The wise old man jumped in and said, "With all due respect, performing entertainments and being close to a queen of Elam will not justify the flagrancy of abducting a person."

The wise old man had seen the angry look of King Birsha and interjected to prevent Birsha from unleashing his rage on King Shinab and his bitter joke. But what the wise old man intended to say to his audience was something else. To understand the current circumstances, the old man used a metaphor:

"We all know what spark stone is and how it works. When two spark stones hit or rub against each other, it creates a spark, which can set fire on kindling or the sulfur in our torches. Now, imagine if one of those stones is missing or wet: the other will be useless. Doubting Chedorlaomer's motive in hostility toward us is the same as the wet spark stone. If one of us, like a stone, gets wet, the other stones will be useless. No matter how rough and strong we are as a single territory, we cannot create fire to defend ourselves without the help of our allies. The war is fire. Those who don't have a fire will be the ones who lose."

The king of Admah looked at the surface of the table and did not say anything. Everyone was silently listening.

The wise old man continued, "Our power is in our alliance. The reason Chedorlaomer has not declared war against us until now was his fear of our alliance. Why now? I do not know. He certainly counts on other forces. Your war advisers must know better than me." Then, the old man turned to Leah and looked into her eyes.

The king of Sodom restrained himself from praising the wise old man in the presence of the other kings. King Bera knew that brandishing the wisdom of his counselor in the face of other kings might spark a sense of rivalry and jealousy among his allies. Therefore, without referring to the wise old man's aphorism, King Bera said, "Even if we ignore the shutdown of the water stream, we have to react to Chedorlaomer's atrocities like sabotage in our cities and kidnapping and enslaving of our people. He has always tested our reactions in the past. When we did not respond appropriately to his insolence, he stepped up in his impudence."

Edna asked for permission to speak and said, "If I may, what the king of Elam did this time was more than a test. He has aimed to uproot us. This is not simply sabotaging; he has targeted the main element of our livelihood. Without water, our people cannot live. The discussion is far beyond ordinary sabotage or the kidnapping of one of our loved ones."

Edna realized that she went a bit too far, as her words might have played down Achan's situation. She glanced at King Birsha quickly, who was still lost in his thought. Edna continued, "Now there is only one option: an unwanted war with Chedorlaomer and his allies. We need to assess the strength of our forces. We need to talk about how many fighters each of our regions can contribute to our allied army in this crucial battle."

The king of Zeboiim moved in his seat and said calmly, "My question is if Chedorlaomer wanted to start the war, why he needed a pretext such as water closure or kidnapping? Why did he not start the attack unexpectedly? Did Achan have any information that could help Chedorlaomer win the war? Gomorrah is just one of our allies."

Leah looked at King Bera and with his approval said, "Chedorlaomer wants to pretend he is defending himself against our invasion. Slavery is customary in Elam and its allies' territories. Their slaves escape from their areas every day and come to us as refugees. Our enemies need to defend themselves in their kingdoms; otherwise, they may face an uprising among slaves. We should do the opposite, taking them out of their areas and making their cities vulnerable to possible domestic uprisings. I have a plan on this matter which I will share with Edna and my other war advisers."

Edna, frowning, did not seem pleased at being called a counterpart to Leah and a war advisor. Edna considered herself the real ruler of Gomorrah, and indeed she was. Especially after the disappearance of Achan, King Birsha did not even have the same level of efficiency before the abduction. It was Edna who had all the details of Gomorrah's affairs under her control. By taking over full authority from Birsha to issue various orders, she was the de facto ruler of Gomorrah. The wise old man realized Edna's state of mind and said, "I am not an expert in military practices, but aside from balance of power, planning is important in confronting the enemy. As Leah said, it is vital to pull the enemy forces out of their areas..."

The King of Admah interrupted the wise old man's comment and said, "Before we jump into any war plan, let us examine the matter a bit more calmly and with fewer emotions. If Chedorlaomer is responsible for sabotages and Achan's abduction (according to reports he's apparently having a good time in wherever he is), and if the water shortages are due to the closure or redirecting of the stream by the king of Elam, we must first pursue a policy of dialogue with them. Let's see what they have to say against our charges. Secondly, if they accept responsibility, we have to know why and what their requests are. Speaking of war is easy sitting in this room and behind a closed door. But we must know that many will die in a war. Besides, what if we lose? And then what will happen to our cities, our people?"

The king of Sodom slammed the table with his hand, but he quickly controlled himself and calmly said, "Your Excellency, Shinab, the king of Admah, what you said about the nature of any war is real. Casualties and destruction are the minimum results of any war. None of us likes to pursue a confrontation. All these years, we owe our good life and well-being to peace and stability. We even devote part of our mind-connection ceremony to peace permanence, the peace that we have been protecting with vigilance. Leah and her under-commands were able to prolong the peace with their day-to-day work on countering Chedorlaomer's plots. But we have reached the point that without water, life is not possible for us. I know this is the same for Gomorrah. I have heard that your people and the beloved people of Bella have seen little changes in the amount of water coming to your lands. We are not able to survive in this situation; we must fight. You can continue to live for now, but you should know that if we are defeated in war, Chedorlaomer's destroying you will be a very simple task unless you decide to join his community of slaves."

King Shinab, in a defensive position, replied hastily, "King Bera, I understand your situation and want you to know that we will always remain in this alliance. But what I am trying to express is that before we go to the last stage, let us send a convoy to Elam and find out what Chedorlaomer's response and demands are."

Looking at the wise old man who was nodding as a gesture of agreement, King Bera said, "Very well, I accept it. Let me send a delegation to Elam for dialogue to show that we are not the ones who seek the war. But beware of Chedorlaomer's divisive acts. As the old man said at the beginning of this meeting, the secret of our success lies in our alliance. Our current problem is the vital element of life that has been taken from us. "

Angry and frustrated, King Birsha stood on his feet, banged on the table with his both fists, and shouted at the king of Admah, "If your closest person were kidnapped, would you still be seeking negotiation with the aggressor? If any of you who are sitting here do not participate in this battle, we will fight them on our own. This is my final decision."

King Birsha then left the room. A few moments passed. Edna, impatiently, was sitting in her seat. All eyes were on her now. Looking down, Edna was evaluating her very next words and moves. She did not expect such a reaction from Birsha. King Birsha had not only announced the end of the meeting but had placed himself in a deadlock position. If she did follow her king in leaving the room, it would be an insult to the other kings, ruining the possibility of keeping an alliance. If Edna stayed and continued to speak, it would be overruling the king of Gomorrah's final decision, discrediting him. Moreover, King Birsha's reaction to her decision to counter him would be unknown; possibly she would lose her position forever. It was a dangerous gamble when King Birsha's mental stability was under question. She also could not sit there forever without any words forever.

It was not only Edna who had been surprised. All the kings present at the meeting, especially King Bera, were in a similar situation. The king of Sodom needed three other allies in the battle with Chedorlaomer. Without adding their fighters to the allied army of Siddim's plain, the defeat in the war with Chedorlaomer and his allies was certain. King Bera, looking at the wise old man, was searching for a way out of the ever-intensifying situation. Staring at a point in the distance, the wise old man did not even turn his face to King Bera. The king of Sodom, who was desperate to seek help from the wise old man, broke his silence, addressing Edna, "We all are aware of King Birsha's harsh condition and share his grief. Edna, it is best to be with your king at this moment. We will be setting up a delegation to send to Elam for the final talks or, better to say, warning."

Edna, who seemed as if a heavy load was taken off her shoulders, quickly got up, bowed as a sign of respect, and left the room. The task of making a right decision before leaving the room was one of the most significant challenges of her life.

Without any representative from Gomorrah, the King of Sodom arranged a delegation to be sent to Elam to visit Chedorlaomer. King Bera named Amim to be in the delegation and asked other kings to assign the most reliable and closest advisors to be involved in the negotiation. After completing the session, King Bera did not accept Edna's request to attend the convoy. The king of Sodom considered her role essential at the top of Gomorrah's affairs when his close friend, King Birsha, was in an unsuitable emotional state. Edna found King Bera's proposal logical and agreed immediately. The plan was to send a messenger instantly to Elam to ask Chedorlaomer's opinion to receive a delegation from territories in the valley of Siddim soon.

***

On the way back to Sodom, King Bera requested that the wise old man join him in the royal carriage in the caravan. On their way to Gomorrah to attend the meeting, Leah, who was in charge of the caravan's security, had placed key figures in separate carriages. But now the king asked to consult with the old man about various issues. It did not take long for King Bera to get his question off his chest. The king demanded the old man's opinion on decisions in the meeting. The old man replied, "I have always believed in your ability and wisdom, and now I became certain of what I thought. I am not saying this to please you. After King Birsha's exit and Edna's poor performance, I noticed your look. But I did not say anything intentionally. I was not worried about King Birsha's anger and his exit. On the contrary, I found that the best opportunity could happen at the moment."

The puzzled king asked, "Opportunity? Birsha's immature reaction almost disintegrated the alliance and put an end to the longtime cooperation among kingdoms in the valley of Siddim."

The wise old man nodded and said, "That was one possibility but unlikely. The other three kings also know that they are vulnerable without us. In fact, Birsha's action was a timely pressure that weakened their position. King Shinab understood that he needs to get close to you as a point of gravity. Otherwise, other options, including irrational decisions, were on the table. You should know that they also understand Chedorlaomer's danger, but lack of courage has deprived them of making the right decision. In other words, fear has been paralyzing them. They are afraid to lose the status quo if they take the risk and lose. It is unclear how long they can continue living in fear. That is why I say Birsha's emotional outburst can push them toward you and take the right decision."

King Bera nodded and admired the wise old man for his brilliant thinking. The jolting of the carriage on the path had made Bera exhausted. He looked out the small window. The sky was getting dark. He thought about the upcoming events and the war that was now imminent. At a turn in the pathway, he saw Leah, riding her horse and giving commands to the caravan's forefront forces. From a distance, fires were flickering in Sodom and becoming bigger at any moment. King Bera took another look at the old man. His head had fallen on his chest. His wisdom was a product of a lifetime travels, studies, and thoughts. He knew that such trips were difficult for an old man in his age, though the king did not hear any complaints during the trip from him. He had passed out from fatigue. The king of Sodom felt proud to be surrounded by such people. He gazed out again. The sky was completely dark. Sodom was glimmering, brighter than ever, a city that was shining like a bright gem on the apex of the regions and perhaps the whole world.

# Chapter 44 – UC Berkeley

*Berkeley – UC Berkeley*

"UC Berkeley is not just a university. It is a culture, a history, a home to all those who care for humanity and progress. You cannot be indifferent, especially at this time of crisis," said Rachel, while walking along with Art on that sunny day in mid-September. Rachel had been desperately looking for Art the past few days, and now she had found him. Nobody would have given her a concrete answer when she asked Art's whereabouts.

Art looked over his right shoulder to look at this agile petite girl who was walking swiftly. With a smile, Art asked, "What do you want? What can I do for you?"

Rachel replied, "You've probably heard that during Free Expression Week they have arranged a speech at UC Berkeley for that clown, Mylos. The issue is fundamental. The alt-right plans to start the violence."

"How did you get this information? How reliable is your source?" asked Art with a look that showed his seriousness and disbelief.

"I have my own sources, and so far they've never been false," Rachel replied with a somewhat thoughtful look.

When Rachel saw Art's sarcastic look and his mockery in disbelief, she grabbed his arm and stopped him. Art was startled; he turned to her while looking at the girl's hand on his right arm. "What's wrong?" Rachel said. "Am I not good enough to have my own sources?"

Art was getting tired of Rachel who came out of nowhere in the street and caught him by surprise. "How did she find me?" He thought, "What she says might not be farfetched."

"What is their plan?" asked Art.

Rachel continued, "They plan to break out in violence by bringing rocks, sticks, brass knuckles, and razors when the opposition and leftists start to protest. This is a serious matter."

Art questioned, "Who's the opposition?"

Rachel was amazed by his lack of information about current issues. "Yeah, a large protest is now emerging from different groups. In an announcement, more than seventy UC Berkeley professors called for canceling the speech. But the alt-right counts on Antifa to start a fight. They know that the members of Antifa are a good stimulus to begin violence. Then, they expect Trump to blame both sides, probably denouncing the left more."

Art said quickly, "Well, tell the Antifa members not to provoke them."

"I don't influence Antifa or other similar groups," Rachel objected with a grin. "I'm persuading different LGBTQ groups to participate in the protest. My own group will be there too."

Art responded, "Well, what is it that you want me to do? Like you, I don't know any members of Antifa."

Rachel said, "Please don't play innocent with me. I saw you in downtown Berkeley. I don't know how you did what you did, but I saw you take control of the scene. You have to do that at UC Berkeley."

Art did not like Rachel's tone, ordering him around, so he said, "I have to go now. Need to do something. Give me your number."

Art took Rachel's phone, entered his number, then pressed the call button. He returned the phone and asked: "When is the speech, date and time?"

"In two days, the day after tomorrow at 11 a.m.," replied Rachel.

While walking away, Art said, "Call me tomorrow."

After a few steps, Art's phone rang. He looked at his phone screen to check what number was calling him. Art heard Rachel's voice from behind, "It's me, just wanna make sure."

When Rachel found out that several sites connected to radical right-wing groups had published Art's name, photo, profile, and address, she realized that tracking him would not be an easy task. But Rachel was more persistent: she called Art while he was still in her sight to make sure she was in possession of the right number.

Art walked through a few streets without having a definite destination. Before Rachel showed up in front of him, he was going to Michael's apartment, but now he did not want to disclose his hideout by going there directly.

***

One hour before the encounter between Art and Rachel, David had held a meeting in Melody's office. Art, Essie, Melody, Simone, Michael, and Tim were sitting in a circle. Remnants of wounds still were showing on David's face and neck. David warned about the audacity of those who exposed Art's information. A powerful explosion had destroyed Tech2AI, and six people, including Sam, were killed; the rest were critically injured. Melody was holding David's hand throughout the session as if transferring energy to him. But what David was most concerned about at that moment was Art's published pictures online. In addition to not so explicit photos in Berkeley's central park, some vivid shots were showing Art without a background.

The background in the pictures was removed entirely. It was not precisely clear where and when the photos were taken. Considering his outfits and the angle at which the photos were taken, Art believed that someone shot them in the workplace. David urged everyone, especially Art, to be very careful. All agreed that until further notice, Art would stay away from his apartment and limit his appearance in public places. He didn't need to go anywhere for work. They all were affected deeply, especially David, who apparently was not the same person anymore.

Essie mentioned Rachel's request to attend the group meetings, but it was unanimously rejected. Essie saw Rachel's addition as somehow positive. He believed that Rachel's connection to diverse crowds, especially at LGBTQ events, would strengthen the group's overall position. David was against the continuation of group's meetings in general and said, "We ourselves should not hold any meetings. The conditions are very dangerous. Essie, you can be in touch with Rachel."

While avoiding Simone's look, Melody immediately volunteered to stay in touch with Rachel and proposed, "Rachel is about to get started working with me. I can be her link to our group."

David and Essie simultaneously said, "No," and then when each of them realized that their opposition loud and clear might offend Melody, each let the other speak. They both became silent, and Melody, who did not understand their position, retreated from her proposal.

To change the subject, Tim said, "Now that Art's been identified as the one who narrates the Sodom stories, can I mention his name?"

This time, Essie and Michael simultaneously said, "No." Without giving Michael a chance to speak, Essie said, "There is no need to confirm their allegation and give them credit. Right now it's just a claim. I personally think that a powerful church is leading the attacks against us. I'm sure they're behind everything. The sign they left in Art's apartment is proof."

After being discharged from the hospital, David had completely forgotten to share the latest information that detective Smith had given him before the explosion. He remembered Smith was talking about the Baptodist Church's involvement in breaking into Art's apartment. All that stuff had been erased from his mind. Now that Essie spoke about his speculation, David remembered everything and shared it with the group.

At this moment, Essie's phone vibrated. He first looked at the phone and then turned to Tim, and said, "Is it you, did you send me something just now?"

Tim immediately said, "Look at this link; I guess it is relevant to what you said."

Tim had sent Essie the link to Pamela Lang's interview with Sara. Essie started to read, and everyone became awkwardly quiet. David started talking again and said, "I think, if you all agree, as of right now, Essie will contact each of us individually in a way that he himself determines. This is the last meeting we all are attending in person. Essie will consult with me on every issue. And, Art, I do not know if I stressed enough that you need to be careful to protect yourself. Don't go out if you don't have to. If nobody has anything else to say, let's leave."

Essie quickly interjected and said, "Tim, make an appointment with this lady, Pamela. Maybe you and I will have to go on a trip to Boston. We might be able to take care of things over the phone too. Tell her that you are the author of the Sodom stories. Now you're an important figure and can meet with anyone you want."

Essie caught David's curious eyes and told him he would explain it later. They all stood up. Simone kissed Essie goodbye in front of Melody and went out. While typing on his phone, Tim took a peep at Art and Michael who were talking in the corner of the room. Indifferent to Simone, Melody walked to her desk and started to work on her computer. Michael said goodbye to Art with a kiss and left the room.

***

Earlier in the morning, Rachel had asked Melody if she could come to the office. Melody told her that she had an important meeting and it would be better to come in the afternoon. Outside the building, when Rachel saw Simone, and then Michael leaving, she figured out she surely would find Art soon.

***

People exalt the 150-year history of UC Berkeley with over 90 Nobel prizes, 13 field medals, and dozens of major historical events, but Art's keen sense of attachment to the university was due to more than just its high academic achievement and historic importance. The UC Berkeley campus and its surroundings always gave Art a good feeling. Art could even breathe more easily there. Trees and greenery were factors in creating a clement air, but for Art, it went beyond atmospheric and environmental aspects; he tasted the sweetness in every inhalation and exhalation when he was walking around the campus. The tranquil environs created by the architecture of large, rugged brick buildings were so personal that Art could not describe them to anyone. For Art, UC Berkeley was a castle in which he felt secure. Every building in this fortified stronghold was a fort against a possible attack by the enemy. Looking at Wheeler Hall, from every angle, would take Art back to historical films in ancient Rome and its coverture protecting the inhabitants against barbarians. Wellman Hall was a group of castles, arranged around the central building so that it was impossible to infiltrate the heart without suffering a high number of casualties.

And passing by the famous Sproul Hall would remind him of Mario Savio's image, which he had seen many times, standing on the police car, giving the well-known speech in 1964. The Free Speech Movement in the '60s coincided with the beginning of civil rights movements, Vietnam War protests, and many others. The very first steps of the march to freedom, which were not easily achieved, had mostly been sparked at UC Berkeley, a place that Art loved and cherished. And just down from the Sproul Hall was Strawberry Creek, a limpid stream of water alongside old trees. When Art was studying at UC Berkeley, he would sit by the creek for hours, thinking about everything and nothing. In his comeback visit to the UC Berkeley, even now, Strawberry Creek was one of his favorite places to spend peaceful time. And in the past two years, UC Berkeley, the symbol of freedom, had been attacked by the most prominent right-wing figures and groups.

That day, Art had come to prevent violence at Rachel's request. "Preventing violence" echoed in his mind, a phrase that gave Art a sense of pride, like a medal worn on the chest. He was supposed to meet Rachel at Sather Gate. As Art approached Sather Gate, the number of people in the crowd was growing. Art saw Rachel who was standing under the gate's arc, looking around. Her serious look indicated she had important news. Art raised his hand from afar. Rachel did not wait for Art to reach the gate and moved toward him. Grabbing Art's arm, Rachel tried to guide him in a direction she had in mind. This was the second time Art felt offended by Rachel's holding his arm and pushing him around. He resisted moving in the direction that Rachel was leading him and asked, "What's up, anything new?"

Rachel said, "Let's go toward the creek, I'll tell you on the way. Apparently, it's worse than what I thought. Mylos's speech is just a cover; there won't be any speech at all. They didn't even go through applying for the permit and haven't paid the required fee for today's event. It's not clear whether Mylos is coming."

Art said with astonishment, "Well, then, the problem is solved. So why is the crowd still coming here?"

The sound of the crowd's booing and whistling came from the distance. Rachel seemed very nervous. She said, "They know there won't be a speech, but their force is already ready to strike. They know that the Antifa is here. I've heard that they have already brought and placed sharp objects, rocks, and other things near here. The police were searching everyone. They come to Sproul Hall with no weapons and their logistical team will be arming them later."

Rumbling and booing rose again from the same direction. Rachel exclaimed, "Let's go. Apparently, everyone is here."

Art followed Rachel, and after a few steps said, "Well, why you don't give this info to the police?"

Speeding up by taking small but rapid steps, Rachel responded, "The problem is that we don't know where exactly they placed their weapons."

When Rachel and Art arrived in the front of the famous Sproul Hall, they saw a person on the steps of the building, strolling among several police officers. He was posing in front of the camera and taking pictures. There were between two and three hundred people in the front of the building, booing him. Rachel turned to Arthur and said, "It's him, Mylos."

Art scanned the scene and looked at the person whom Rachel pointed to in the distance. His shoulder was covered by the American flag, giving him an outlandish look. Suddenly, Art noticed a group of twenty men approaching the crowd from the eastern side of the field. Art patted Rachel's shoulder and ran without hesitation to the group that was now running toward the crowd in front of Sproul Hall. Police were lined up to separate protesters from Mylos, close to the stairs. Art noticed that the attackers from the east were armed with baseball bats, some made of metal, plus sticks and knives. The crowd in front of the building noticed the group of invaders, armed with a knife and clubs, approaching them. Now Art was running toward them as well. Rachel saw Art knock down two, three men when he reached the first line of attackers and was swallowed by their crowd. A chill went through Rachel's body when she saw Art's disappearance. She let out a frightened gasp. After a while, several hands rose, holding clubs and sticks, to attack Art, but before going down, people were thrown around in every direction. Rachel knew that Art was in the center where the skirmish was going on. Rachel saw several men, who were focusing on the person involved with them, thrown and stacked up one by one on each other. Abruptly, for a few moments—Rachel did not exactly know how long it lasted—the whole group, whether standing or lying on the ground, froze in their spots. Art quickly moved among them and collected their weapons and piled them up far away from the group.

Police and protesters were moving toward the frozen attackers. Rachel did not move. She turned a white bucket that belonged to maintenance upside down and stood on top of it to have a better view. The group of attackers, surrounded by the police and protestors, were unfrozen now. The police quickly made a circle between the invaders and protesters. Some officers also lay the invaders on their abdomens and handcuffed them.

Farther away, Rachel could hardly see the location, on which all weapons, knives, and sticks were piled up. The reflection of the sun shining on metallic weapons hurt Rachel's eyes. Art was missing. Rachel could not spot Art in the crowd. She jumped down and ran toward the crowd to find Art. She reached the front where protesters and police were pushing each other. The police had created a barricade to prevent more clashes between the two groups. Rachel looked behind the police line. Several people were seriously injured on the head and face. Rachel did not find Art on the other side among the defeated crowd. It was so hot. She felt droplets of sweat running down her face. Protesters were still booing and chanting. Rachel thought, "Art is not just the hope for LGBTQ; he is the hope for everyone and the only chance for humanity."

# Chapter 45 – Escape

After the mayhem at the UC Berkeley, Rachel concluded that she was not the same angry, petite 24-year-old girl anymore. At least, she imagined it that way. It was as if the event at UC Berkeley had added years to her age. Any adventure in the past would make her feel like she had changed, but she believed that the event at UC Berkeley was something else. Rachel could not wait to gain more experience. In the last few weeks, she had many thoughts on how to work with her newly founded Radical Girls group.

In the past few days, Rachel had been bugging Al, the member of the LGBTQ Coordinating Association and the one who introduced her to Tim. Rachel was insisting on holding an event for Art to give a speech to the community. Given the fast pace of events in the country, especially in Northern California, and explosions at the newspaper's office as well as at Tech2AI, she believed that the time was ripe for Art to address the community and the nation explicitly. Rachel convinced Al to discuss the issue at the next board meeting, and she ensured him that she would handle and the obstacles to holding such an event with the help of her group.

Rachel borrowed the key to the coordination room from Al and in the evenings met with members of her group on a daily basis. In addition to talking about holding a public event for Art's speech, in the meetings Rachel compelled her group to read the Sodom stories.

Only a week had remained at the big public gathering. In the group meeting, Rachel removed her tablet from her bag and brought up the newspaper's website. She encountered an error message showing high traffic on the newspaper's server. Rachel did not know whether it was the result of a DDoS attack, a distributed denial-of-service caused by opponents of Sodom's stories, or if the excessive popularity of these stories put high loads on the newspaper's server, or both—especially after the publication of paper ceased, which led all readers to read it on the internet. After several attempts, she finally managed to go to the website and find the latest installment of the story. Once the story appeared on the tablet, Rachel began to read for the group of five in an excited voice…

***

## Elam Territory – Chedorlaomer Palace – Tabitha's Room

Tabitha held Achan's trembling hand, and with their eyes closed, they touched their foreheads together. It was the moment of truth. Arrangements had already been made, and now it was time to move. The room in which Tabitha had lived for the past five years now seemed too small. This was the most significant event in the life of a woman who had not experienced anything other than boredom. She was transferred from her father's royal palace to live in her husband's court. Despite all the ceremonies, feasts, and celebrations, Tabitha never felt excitement. It was just a relocation from one palace to another; her position changed from princess to queen, celebrated by a few days' period of music, dance, and noise. And then quiescence again. When she saw Chedorlaomer for the first time, she felt the excitement and exultation within her. At first, everything seemed colorful, but soon after, the colors lost their luminance, as if a thin gray curtain fell on everything and made the air gloomy. From then on, a sigh of boredom would come out of her chest. Hatred was the only thing that kept a place inside the queen's heart for many years. She often wondered, "Is this going to be my life? How long do I have to endure such cold and boring days? Is it this until the end of my life, and then everything will be over?"

That was her life until she saw Achan for the first time, in the room next to the palace chamber in which the stinking warriors' celebration took place. She saw a young tawny man whose hatred was emanating from his face. Tabitha compared the kind of hatred she saw from Achan's eyes with her own disgust with Chedorlaomer. It must have been different. Later on, she asked Achan about his feelings about herself that night.

"I do not know what it was; a combination of the confusion, exhaustion, and hatred that was stored in me. I had found Edna again standing in front of me, but this time in another palace. I said to myself, 'Why there should always be an Edna in every court that sacrifices happiness to acquire power?' However, later I realized that I was wrong," Achan replied plainly.

And now Tabitha was preparing herself to fly along with Achan. She had no idea where the destination would be and what expectation she could have. "Whatever it is, at least its excitement supersedes the tedious life that is waiting for me in this castle," thought Tabitha at that moment she was silent, attached to Achan by forehead and hands.

Achan opened his eyes, looked at Tabitha's, and said: "You look very beautiful tonight."

"You too. I never saw your eyes shine like this." She continued after a brief pause: "Let's go over the plan again. We will go to the city through a secret path that leads us outside the castle. Then, we go near the gate and find somewhere to hide until Arshum takes us out of the city through the guards he knows. He said he has prepared two horses in a place that can get us to Gomorrah."

With a smile on his face that showed he was feeling happier, Achan asked, "Are you sure of this secret path that goes outside the castle? Is it still there?"

"Yes, I found out about it a few years ago from one of the kitchen crew whom I caught stealing food and taking it outside," she said with a confident look. "A few days ago, I went all the way to the end again with Arshum. Arshum knows it too well. I told him to bring you out after me."

The horror appeared on Achan's face. "Why aren't we going together? I do not feel good about this monster."

Tabitha replied, "Don't worry; if we go alone, we draw less attention, just until we reach outside the palace. We will go to the city gate together when we step outside the palace. I'm quite confident in Arshum. I feel he loves me so much that he'll do anything for me. If I ask, he will even kill Chedorlaomer for me."

Tabitha looked out of the window. It was dark outside. She said, "We have to go now."

She hugged Achan and went to the exit door. Before leaving the room, she turned and looked at Achan again. The light from the torch that was mounted on different spots in the room gave a pale red color to Achan's face. Despite his desire, Achan was wearing a boyish black garment. At the very moment that Achan blew a kiss to her, Tabitha stepped out.

The entrance door to the secret way was in the kitchen basement. To reach it, Tabitha had to walk through several passageways to the kitchen and from there to the basement cellar. It had been a few years since Chedorlaomer was spending nights in the queen's bed, but the queen's appearance at that time and in that place could have raised the guards' suspicions. From the time Tabitha shut the door and entered the hall, she saw herself at the start of a thrilling journey, the details of which had been playing out in her mind for the past few days. The light of the torches mounted on the walls illuminated the corridors. The queen felt a strange, fast heartbeat as if her heart was jumping out of her chest, as soon as she walked in the hallway. Before going out, and even moments before that, standing in the room with Achan to say goodbye, she felt the thrill, but it was not as intense as now. Tabitha quickly and very quietly tiptoed to the end of the corridor. She stretched her head forward and looked right and then left. After making sure no one was present, the queen continued to the left with the same cautious steps. Tabitha heard something, but she could not figure out which side it came from. Tabitha was in front of the kitchen door and had no idea how she got there. She opened the door and slowly slipped inside. Tabitha had been practicing what to say if someone showed up inside the kitchen. It was not possible to poke her nose in first; if a crew member were still there, she would look suspicious. She exhaled hard, as if she had held her breath all the way to the kitchen. Once inside the kitchen, the queen rushed directly to the other side, where there was a large trapdoor in the floor. She grabbed the door handle, but it was heavier than she expected. A few days ago, when the queen had practiced her escape, Arshum was with her and lifted the door from the floor easily. But now she realized this simple detail of how to open the door was totally forgotten in the plan. Arshum was waiting for her at the end of the secret path. Then her guard was supposed to go back and bring Achan with him. Now, the door was closed, and the secret, zigzag path was too long for Arshum to hear her voice from where he was. All she had to do was to lift the door and enter the secret passage before anyone would catch her there. Tabitha gathered all her strength again, grabbed the handle with two hands, and lifted it. The heavy door came up a bit but fell back down as the queen's hands failed to hold on.

Tabitha sat on the door in the back corner of the kitchen. The whole plan was about to be ruined. If she could not find a way into the hidden passage and someone saw her there, rumors would spread, and they would have to abandon their plan for now. Her eyes fell on a few sticks with different sizes and length that were next to each other alongside the opposite wall. She had no idea what those sticks were there for or how they should be used. Tabitha hurried to the other side to check them. If she could put one of them under the door when it was raised slightly, then she would be able to use it as a lever to lift the door. She picked up the thickest and tallest stick and set it close to the door's edge on the ground so that she could push it under with her foot when the door was lifted a little. With two hands, Tabitha gripped the door handle again and tried to lift the door with all her might. She lifted the door slightly. Putting her weight on the left leg, she shoved the stick with her right foot. Her power was waning, and the stick stuck to the edge of the door, refusing to go under. Once again, she struggled hard as a sigh came out of her throat. She kicked the stick again and finally pushed it under the door. She fell flat onto the floor. Sweat was pouring out of her entire body. She felt a severe hunger in her stomach. Tabitha remembered she had not eaten anything since that morning. The subject of food barely came up when she was with Achan. Since Achan arrived in Elam, the queen had lost weight and became thinner, just like her new playmate.

She stood up and pressed on the outer end of the stick, which was raised slightly above the ground. Nothing happened. Tabitha ran to the other end of the kitchen, grabbed another stick, brought it back, and put into the slot. Tabitha jumped in the air and landed on the sticks. The door moved slightly. Again, she gripped the door handle and pulled it with her remaining power. The door moved a bit farther. She sat beside the gap that had become wider now and pushed the door's edge with both legs. The door opened more. Now, Tabitha had enough clearance to slide into the basement.

Quickly, she placed her foot in the dark on the steps she knew were there. Thinking about closing the door on top of her head was out of the question. Tabitha descended slowly down the stairs in the basement. Flickering light through the door gap from the above illuminated the way to the place where she knew there was ingress into the secret path. The queen entered the secret path by moving a few sacks of beans and dry wheat, which were covering a narrow opening. Arshum had already put several torches to light the pathway for her.

After walking through the winding path, Tabitha felt she was close to the end of the secret way. She saw a tall silhouette a few steps away. It was Arshum. The queen felt like she was seeing an old acquaintance who could calm and protect her after a long journey of passing through dangerous obstacles. She ran the last few steps and threw herself into Arshum's arms. Arshum embraced the tiny queen and took a deep breath while putting his head on the Tabitha's, exhaling out of relief. A few moments passed. It would seem that both were gaining energy. Arshum was taking the queen's sweaty aroma deeply into his chest, and Tabitha as if in a solid fortress, was resting peacefully. Suddenly, the queen parted from Arshum and shouted, "Arshum, go back to the palace and bring Achan here, fast."

The giant guard did not make any move. He stood at his spot and only looked at the queen. Tabitha said firmly, "Why are you standing here? Go to Achan; he is waiting for you. Also, I could not put the cellar door back in its place. If someone comes to the kitchen and sees the displaced door on the floor, they will find us here."

Arshum stood still, like a stone. Tabitha approached Arshum angrily and banged on his chest with two fists, "Why don't you go? Have you lost your mind?"

Arshum grasped Tabitha's hands by her wrists and placed them on his heart. Then, he hinted by the intimation that the queen should choose him to run away from Elam. Tabitha first looked at the guard's gesture with patience, not understanding what he was trying to convey. But when Tabitha realized what the mute guard meant, she shouted while laughing nervously "Arshum, I do not know what you've been creating in your mind, but know that I have to go somewhere with Achan. My departure is not because of what you think. I command you to go back to my room and bring Achan here to me now."

After the last command, she went behind Arshum and pushed him forward from the back as if he was a bull stuck in mud. Arshum took two steps forward and turned back and gazed at the queen. Tabitha noticed that a few drops of tears rolled down on Arshum's cheeks. She could not understand why he was crying. "Go, please go. Don't stop; it will be too late."

Arshum disappeared into the hidden path toward the palace. Tabitha no longer could see him in the dark, but she could hear the heavy footstep that were moving away from her and toward the palace. The fatigue from entire day's struggle conquered the queen's body. Exhaustion from the challenge of opening the massive trapdoor, as well as all the emotional ups and downs on an empty stomach, seized her, and she could not resist the need to lie down on the ground. She lay on that spot; there was nothing but rock, soil, and gravel. Tabitha cleared the area around her with her hands, tossing the large pebbles a few feet away, and lay on her back. For a moment, the whole situation became too strange for her, being in such a place at the end of the palace's underground passage way. A girl who from the day of her birth to that very moment had all benefits of a prosperous life by birthright and somewhat by force, now chose to follow an uncertain future voluntarily. On the other side of a large wooden door, out of the palace, was an unknown world waiting for her where she might not be able to survive a day. A chill passed under her skin and shook her entire body. She was cold. The torch that Arshum had brought her to light the path was dying. She turned to her side and lay in a fetal position. She decided to go back and dissuade Achan from the whole thing. Shadows of doubt clouded her mind. She thought of Achan, waiting for Arshum with fear in her room. The image of Arshum also popped into Tabitha's mind with his heavy steps, going to Achan. She remembered tears on Arshum's face and his reluctance to bring Achan. Her guard's reaction had surprised her. Suddenly, Tabitha felt something was crawling on her leg. She froze. The illusion of a snake on her foot paralyzed her. The darkness and lack of her usual comfort had multiplied her horror.

She jumped up from her spot, like a just-released bent bamboo pole. She stood and looked around in the dark. She saw the shadow of a scared mouse, running away under her feet. She jumped out of fear again and screamed. She felt nauseated. Tabitha decided to go back to the palace. The midway torches were all burned out. Touching the wall of the secret passageway, she slowly crept toward the cellar. Tabitha hoped she could convince Achan not to run away for now. She was feeling uneasy. The queen knew that Achan would be angry at her. There was no other way. She could not bear any more pressure. After walking for a while, she saw the dim light coming from the kitchen basement, through the hidden gap leading to the passage. Her worries doubled. "How could Arshum leave the kitchen door to the basement open?" The speculation added to her speed and worries. She entered the cellar and looked at the wooden door to the kitchen. Arshum had left it completely open. She stopped for a moment, then darted up the stairs and jumped into the kitchen.

Her face was red as if blood had rushed up to her head. She was running toward her room with long steps fearlessly. It seemed the number of corridors and halls had multiplied. "Was this the way I came?" Tabitha did not even want to remember what she had thought in the kitchen a few moments ago. A scary force was pushing her forward. She reached the door and stopped in front of her room. No one was around at that time, not in the kitchen nor in the halls. "Arshum and Achan must have come from the same way," she thought, then pressed the door with two hands to open it.

Tabitha's brain could not process what her eyes were seeing. Arshum was standing in the middle of the room, pulling Achan's throat from behind with one arm and holding the young man's mouth with the other hand. The queen was paralyzed. Everything seemed to stop. The scene was unimaginable. Tabitha thought that this was all a nightmare and she was still lying on the ground at the end of the secret passage. At that very moment, Achan's last struggle came to an end, and he let out his last breath. Achan's eyes were bulging out of his purple face. Arshum released the lifeless body of the young man, which fell to the ground. Tabitha ran to Achan with a loud scream, embracing him. But then something in Tabitha's throat was chocking her, preventing more shrieks coming out. What came out of the queen was the sound of howling, like a wounded dog. Holding Achan's head in her hands, Tabitha looked up at Arshum, standing above her and Achan. Arshum was just standing and crying silently with large drops of tears falling on his face. Guards arrived to the room and saw the scene. She continued sobbing and shouting Achan's name, occasionally calling out to Arshum, asking, "Why?"

After a moment, Chedorlaomer appeared at the door along with his personal guards. The guards who had come earlier opened the way and paid tribute to the king. "What's going on? I see you have some private entertainment," said Chedorlaomer, who himself could not understand what was happening. "How come we are not invited to this blood feast? The sound of your celebration is echoing all over the palace."

# Chapter 46 – LGBTQ

*San Francisco – Market Street*

There was not even one empty seat available in the LGBTQ Coordinating Association auditorium. People were standing on the left and right sides of the hall, blocking the exit ways. The turnout in the auditorium was so high that the line of people reached the lobby outside the hall and even farther to the main entrance. Al was on the stage behind the podium. He was busy adjusting the microphone while talking on the phone and sometimes waving at the person at the back of the hall working the lights.

The crowd's general hum in the public room had made the damp air more cumbersome. The crowd was getting restless—they wanted the program to start. A large rainbow banner was mounted on the wall behind the podium as were rainbow strips on both side walls. Several television cameras were setting up equipment below the stage to broadcast the live event that was supposed to start in a few minutes. Well-known names appeared among these networks. Next to each camera, two people were standing, one who seemed to be a cameraperson and the other a correspondent. Rachel had played a significant role in organizing the event, and she was busy around the podium, going up and down on the stage.

Art was sitting quietly on a chair in the first row, staring ahead and holding Michael's hand. David and Melody were sitting next to Art on the right, talking to each other. Michael, Essie, Simone, and Tim were sitting on the left and waiting impatiently. More than the heat, Art was bothered by the anxiety of giving a speech that was supposed to start in few minutes. At first, Art had resisted Rachel's proposal of going on the stage to speak to the massive audience. But with her insistence and the rest of the group's agreement, Art was convinced that he should overcome his fear of public speaking and play his role at this critical time.

What made Art doubtful about public speaking was his emergence as a leader or a hero. Art was not comfortable to speak to a big crowd. Also, his modesty was preventing him from giving speech to those who were more active and had more experience in LGBTQ issues. He believed many activists who fought for the rights of the community for years would be more qualified to speak than him. Art also knew that the crowd that night in the room was not just the LGBTQ community. Tim's stories had drawn many people who were interested in the topic, regardless of their sexual orientation.

Art, however, was not the same after the blast in the company that killed many of his colleagues. Of course, he was not happy to be the center of the attention, but the issue was no longer a private matter. He had to share his opinion about the current state of affairs and concerns about common future that had learned through his vision, discoveries, and his power.

Al was supposed to begin the event, followed by Rachel's short introduction. Before Art, Tim had to deliver a short speech, then it was time for Art to tell the people what was in his heart and mind. Art had prepared his speech with the help of Tim and Rachel. It was only five days ago that Art found out the event's date. Each day passing was like a countdown for Art. Although Tim and Rachel had helped him prepare the speech, he was the one who was supposed to deliver it. Art was not comfortable about that at all. He had never done such a thing before, and now Art was about to stand in front of a crowd so large it made his head spin to look at it. What would happen if he lost his train of thought during the speech? Art repeatedly practiced his speech before Michael and the mirror. He had his notes ready on a piece of paper, but even now the note was blurred. David had suggested meditation as the only solution to overcome his nervousness. Art closed his eyes but calming the mind was not as easy as David advised. He needed to hear David's voice to get rid of complex thoughts in his mind. Group meditation or trying only with David was not possible at that time. However, Art closed his eyes and when he opened them, he saw Rachel notifying him that Al was going to start now.

Art did not hear anything at all when Al, Rachel, and Tim went behind the podium and gave their short speeches. He just saw them on the stage behind the microphone for a few moments. Art did not even hear folks' cheering and clapping after each speaker. He only heard his name.

"And now here the source of my stories that I wrote in the *Bay Area Chronicle*, ladies and gentlemen, Arthur Stevenson," Tim announced, as he finished his short speech on the stories in the *Bay Area Chronicle*.

Art looked at David and saw a smile of confidence on his face. Art just realized that he had been holding Michael's hand all this time. He kissed Michael, squeezed Melody's hand, and passed in front of Essie who briefly touched his elbow. After passing by Tim who was coming down the stage, Art walked up and stood behind the podium. Two bright lights in the ceiling hit his eyes. He could not see the crowd well. From where Art was standing, he could see only shadows of people through a halo of light in the first few rows. He felt his heart beat in his throat. Art was happy that he could not look at people in the eye, though he tried to find Michael in the first row. But he couldn't keep looking. He just had to start. Art knew that many eyes were staring at him behind the lights that limited his vision, eyes of people who came there in that evening to see what he had to say. He looked at his watch. It showed 7:25 p.m. "I have to start," he thought. The hum died down, and Art felt the pressure of the heavy sound of silence. He remembered his colleagues who were killed or injured by the blast. He forgot about himself and the people who were sitting and waiting in the hall for him to start. Art swallowed the last sound of his heartbeat in his throat and began with a trembling voice:

"Our history has been full of ups and downs. We have come a long way; we passed through many harsh barriers, the unjust laws that were completely legal imposed on us. But we crossed the barriers. We overcame obstacles and broke down walls by our collective efforts."

After the first few seconds, Art started to feel calmer. His heartbeat slowed, and he regained his confidence. He realized that had forgotten to greet the crowd. It was too late now. He just had to continue:

"As Frank Kameny said, political movements are a collective effort, which requires a large number of individuals to reach a specific goal. In addition to collective efforts, these movements require smart leaders, and Frank was one of them. Frank showed us that when all the laws from bottom to top, all the way up to the Supreme Court, are against us, other ways are needed to break through. Frank and others found ways of moving forward and broke those walls. They took the movement onto the streets."

Art looked at the paper on the podium, but he could not find the next line after what he said. He felt much better than at the beginning of his speech. He looked at the first row again and saw Michael's face. Art recognized Michael's romantic look for a second as if he were proud of him. He took a look at his notes again. Knowing that he did not have to start from where he finished, Art chose a line, raised his voice, and continued:

"We are the yardstick and barometer of justice in the society. Yes, we, the LGBTQ. We are the representation of the rainbow. Of course, there are other measurements: anti-racism, inequality between women and men, and anti-immigrant laws. But we must know that without respecting LGBTQ rights in a society, justice and freedom are futile."

The sound of continuous applause interrupted Art's speech. After a while, Art continued, "And right here in the United States of America, we were able to institutionalize our rights to some degree. We have not achieved these rights easily. We fought hard. We moved forward inch by inch. Sometimes there were advancements and sometimes retreats. But as a group of people whose existence is undeniable, we gained our rights. However, now these rights are under attack again.

"After decades, we have been able to achieve our legal rights. We were able to break the tall walls of injustice. Yes, we smashed them, all the way to the Supreme Court. And now they want to retake our achievements, the result of an endless endeavor of thousands of LGBTQ activists. They could not then, and they cannot now. They cannot defeat us."

The crowd was now on their feet applauding, and it was hard for him to continue, so Art waited for a while, and then, as people realized his respect for their excitement, they became quiet. Art continued:

"That is why they choose to go through illegal channels. That's why they seek to create chaos to stir the social balance, sometimes through the White House executive orders and sometimes by creating an environment where the alt-right can create chaos. They want to create an environment to push the children of the rainbow back into the darkness and to the age of fear and horror. But let's not forget that we are the representatives of the rainbow, of every gender, race, and religion, even the very same genders, races, and religions that repressed us throughout history or justified our suppression. We have gained our strength from our struggles and the concept of the rainbow. We are vigorously continuing to maintain our civil and social achievements and preserve our rights. Rest assured that they are no match for us."

People cheered again as Art's voice strengthen in his last sentence. The applause was so loud that the podium was shaking. Art continued:

"We have secured our rights in ballot boxes and through legislatures, thanks to the tireless struggle of our activists over the past decades. The Mattachine Society and Daughters of Bilitis formed the foundations of movements within the depths of society, and our massive movements were able to convince lawmakers to abide by our human rights. And now the defeated forces, those who have been buried in the cemetery of history for many years, then resurrected like zombies, want to take away our rights by violence and bombs."

Many in the audience stood up and applauded passionately. Art was forced to stop his speech. He waited for the audience to calm down, and continued from where he had paused:

"Over the last century, we passed through times during which homosexuality was introduced as a type of disease. We forced the American Medical Association to change that concept. We changed it through our efforts. By order of President Eisenhower, we were deprived of all government jobs, but after two, three decades we changed it, and we regained the right to be hired in government offices. Initially, freedom movements, the trade unions, and civil society were ashamed to stand beside us. They were running away from us, but we declared our existence with pride and made them acknowledge the reality. We took the slogan "Gay is good" to the masses. We made it a norm that it is not possible for a civil or labor movement to fight for human or civil rights without us. We have defied discrimination and changed the laws with the politics of fighting tooth and nail.

"Let me give another example to people of my generation, who have not witnessed real street protests and legal fighting. Do you remember that not too long ago in July of this year, President Trump banned the presence of transgender members of the military and their rights by his executive order? You took the protest to Harvey Milk Square on the same day. In New York and Los Angeles, and in a few other cities, people did the same. But we didn't stop there. We filed a lawsuit. And now the federal judge in Washington, D.C., Colleen Kollar-Kotelly, blocked this executive order." Cheers and loud applauses prevented Art's voice from being heard. After the crowd's fervor calmed down, Art went on, "This is the dual way of protesting on the street and in the court."

Again the audience burst into applause and cheered the speaker by continuous clapping. Art immediately and more loudly continued:

"We fought only to be accepted as we are; we want to feel good about ourselves. We struggled to be free, so we could dance freely with our partners. So we can hold the hand of the one we love and walk in public places. We fought for the kiss, yes, kissing the one whom we love freely, yes, for dancing and kissing. For us, for young people in my age, talking about these rights, the right to have good feelings might sound ridiculous, but these obvious rights once were considered legal violations and crimes that by law deserved severe punishments.

"Finding the power to be one's self and having identity depended on the participation of more people and activists in the cause. Therefore, laws were legislated and imposed so we would not be able to show our identity freely. As Harvey Milk proved during a legal and electoral challenge, the phenomenon of coming out was beneficial not only regarding individuality, personality, and mental health but also as a shift in the balance of power. Our numbers grew, and we have been able to attract the attention of other movements' activists to align our forces with them. We have evolved our revolution peacefully."

At this moment, Art paused and then lowered his voice:

"We should remember that if we could not have danced with our loved ones freely, freedom and victories would not have been conceivable for us. The annual Pride Parade reminds us of that successful revolution, which was not achieved easily. Frank Kameny had rightly said that Stonewall happened at the right time, and Stonewall happened because it was the time to take place."

The hall burst again into applause, cheering and excitement. Art silenced the crowd by continuing his speech:

"The creator or creators of those stories about Sodom and Gomorrah in the Old Testament and afterward are a testimony to my claim. The writer or writers, who recorded their grudge against LGBTQ with their imaginary fire gods burning queers, fed people fiction generation after generation. But they could not succeed in denying one fact in their fictional stories: that Sodom and Gomorrah along with three other cities in the Valley of Siddim lived happily in freedom and prosperity. Has any believer from Abrahamic religions ever asked why? Some have pointed to climatic conditions as the cause, but there were many territories with the right climatic conditions over the course of history, and they were not happy and prosperous. But according to the Old Testament, Sodom and Gomorrah experienced prosperity, happiness, and freedom. You know why? Let me tell you why. Because no one there had to be in the closet. It means there was an environment in which no one needed to hide her or his sexual orientation. The power was in the hands of those who did not discriminate against anyone."

The audience could not stop interrupting the speaker by applause. When he was writing his speech, Art was uncertain how much he should address the adventures of Sodom and Gomorrah that he had intimately experienced. He did not want to put a question mark over rational logic in his speech by mentioning stories that only he had witnessed. He decided to leave it to the people to judge his stories that had been published as Tim's series in the newspaper. For that reason, when he talked about Sodom, he left the details untouched on his observations during meditations. After calming the crowd, Art continued:

"The same evil that had sent their imaginary angels of destruction to rain fire on Sodom have sent their agents to explode my workplace. They murdered my colleagues and destroyed the company that I used to work for."

Art stopped talking for a few seconds. He remembered his burned friends in Tech2AI, and the rage came alive within him. He raised his head and looked up at the ceiling to control his fury with deep breaths. Then, he stared at one of the cameras under the stage that was zoomed at him and said with a firm voice, "I, Arthur of Sodom, tell all you evil forces that your time is up. The good and pure forces in history have now risen in us to uproot you and to wipe your filth off the face of humanity."

He paused again. For a few moments, a heavy silence reigned over the crowd. No sound was heard from anyone, and a few seconds felt like hours. Rachel ended the silence by clapping, first slowly and then faster, which eventually propelled the audience to their feet. A thought passed through Art's mind that he might have gone too far. He decided to back his claim with facts and reasons:

"According to unofficial police reports, the source of the explosions and some of the alt-right attacks has been determined. They are connected to one of the conservative churches in our country. We are all familiar with thoughts of conservatives and fundamentalists in every religion and cult. They see themselves as representatives of God on earth, and they regard any illegal and illegitimate act permissible for them."

Art stared at television cameras again and said, "I declare that your era has come to an end. We will not allow you to take humanity back to the dark times of history. You think, like Abraham, you can put the knife on the throat of your Isaac and sacrifice him. But you must know that the time of barbarism has passed. Now Sarai is on our side and will fight against you."

After saying his last words, as Art pointed his finger at the camera, he continued to gaze at the camera confidently, despite the cheering and applause. He knew that the message would reach the right party. He would like them, whoever they were, to see the seriousness in his eyes:

"Let me state this also. At this podium I declare that, in addition to being a thermometer of justice in society, we are the messengers and heralds of peace that will make a society in which dynamic forces can be fruitful. Peaceful societies had the most achievements throughout the history. However, we will not sit quietly against disruptors of peace. We will take them back to where they belong: to the depth of history.

"We live in a city that happens to be the center of advanced technology in America and perhaps the whole world. These days, we are talking about artificial intelligence and the dangers that may threaten humanity. I believe what threatens humanity at this period of time is not AI but fundamentalism in every form and shape. Even if AI, or even if, in the future, extra-terrestrial creatures pose a threat to us, humanity cannot fight them victoriously without first shaking the heavy weight of conservatism and religious fundamentalism off its shoulders. Humanity must first get rid of the fundamentalism in every form so that it can confront future challenges and problems to open its way forward. You can be sure that we, in San Francisco, will use our greatest strength in both technology and justice, and we will put the muzzle on ferocious fundamentalists and will move forward. Humanity on our planet cannot stop behind your walls of reactionary ideas. On this path, all progressive and forward-looking forces in our society, even moderate religious forces, are on our side. If you want to test your chance, give it a try. The battlefield is our planet earth. Bring it on: we're ready."

Upon Art's last word, the crowd exploded with emotional cheers. Art felt that he had just warmed up and could continue for hours. For the first time, he held his hand above his eyes to see past the bright lights. Art glanced over the entire hall and saw the whole vibrant audience. He looked at his friends' faces, sitting in the first row. Art felt the joy and enthusiasm within himself. He ended the speech with the words "Thank you."

In one of the last rows of the hall, Detective Smith was carefully listening to Art's speech and monitoring the audience reaction. Skin abrasions were still fresh on Smith's face as a result of the blast in David's office. Although Smith was still on sick leave, he asked to come to the event and lead the police department security team directly. Hun and several undercover policemen were patrolling inside and outside the gathering and watching every suspicious movement.

Most of the people were standing and walking inside and only a few were intending to leave. A number of people went to the front to chat with Art and the event organizers. Detective Smith sent a message to Hun, asking him to go to the front with a few officers and be careful. Smith, who now felt closer ties to the group, was worried about a threat. He had listened to Art's speech while paying attention to his team and the security of the building. An unpleasant feeling was stewing in his heart and mind. An instinctive sensation was telling Smith that this was just the beginning of bigger adventures.

# Chapter 47 – Abraham's Men

> So the men turned from there, and went toward Sodom, while Abraham remained standing before the LORD. —Book of Genesis [18:22]

Smith settled in at his desk. In their small room at the police station, Smith and Hun were sitting across from each other at the same desk. Two years ago, when Hun was transferred to the San Francisco Police Department, there were talks about promoting Smith to a lieutenant position, but it had yet to happen. If Detective Smith was promoted before retirement, he would have better pension benefits. His wife had been ill recently, and his son who had studied in NYU stayed on the East Coast after graduation and started working for a financial institution. Since then, he had been visiting his parents less frequently.

Thomas Smith was born and raised in a relatively religious family. Everyone called him by his surname. Once, Hun became very surprised when he heard a colleague called his partner Tom at the station. The recent events caused Smith's calm soul so much turmoil that he needed to talk to someone. Detective Smith could understand if David and his friends treated him as an outsider. He also did not want to share work-related problems with his sick wife. But Smith could not understand why his partner was acting aloof after two years of them spending most hours of the week together. Hun was an antisocial young man, and Smith never felt a close connection with him, as if a hidden obstacle had always prevented Hun from approaching Smith. During his 38 years of service with the police department, Smith never had experienced such coldness with his partners before, even with those who had odd personalities. A 33-year-old man who was born into a Korean family in Southern California, Hun joined the police force after graduating from high school and a short period of helping his father run a grocery store. To avoid any disagreement, Hun would not engage even in work-related arguments with Smith.

The recent incidents within the police department increased Detective Smith's reluctance in sharing his point of view with other colleagues. Thus, Tim's writings in the *Bay Area Chronicle* were the only reference he could use to decode actions by Art, David, and the circle around them. As a result of the blast in Tech2AI's office, the last conversation between Smith and David was wiped out of the detective's memory. Sometimes, Smith would remember David's scattered words like a dream, but he could not fully comprehend what intuition was flashing in his mind.

After settling into his chair behind the desk and turning on his computer, Smith began to read the last part of the Sodom story…

***

*Sodom Territory – Leah's Work Site*

Damaris sat on the desk at the end of Leah's workroom and crossed her legs. There was nothing else in the room except the same desk and two chairs, each on a different side of the large, wooden desk. Drowning in her thoughts, Leah was walking across the room slowly. She had received a report that two unidentified men were arrested planning to enter the city illegally the night before. Leah was reviewing probable scenarios in her mind before she interrogated them personally. She was not paying attention to what Damaris was saying.

Damaris, bored and impatient, asked, "Have you noticed that we have not gone on a picnic at the river for a long time? We have not even gone out together for a walk recently."

Damaris, who did not receive any response from Leah, looked at her lover who was still pacing back and forth thinking. "Leah, Leah, did you hear what I just said?" asked Damaris angrily.

Leah looked up and saw Damaris sitting on her desk and waiting for a response. Leah replied, "Damaris, I told you before, we are in an emergency situation. Why don't you understand? We are under lots of pressures from all sides. I expect more support from you. Ordinary people in our city are worried about this situation, yet you say things like this."

"You do not even listen to me anymore," said Damaris stubbornly.

"Do you see these problems surrounding us? I can never remember a time in my life that our city has been at such a high risk, the city where we were born, where we are prosperous and happy in. Soon, we won't have water to drink or to irrigate our crops. There is no river anymore to walk along."

Damaris, whose attention was drawn to Leah's words, sat upright and said, "Is there anything I can do? What happened to the city's water reservoir?"

"The least you can do is not put pressure on me. Please understand the conditions around here."

Annoyed, Damaris jumped off the table, walked toward the exit door, and left the room with the door open. Leah sat down on the chair behind her desk and held her head with both hands. Outside the room, a guard appeared behind the door. Leah looked at the guards. The guard said, "My lady, they are here."

"Bring them in," Leah ordered.

The guard in the hallway pointed to his right, and the three guards brought two prisoners inside. They forced the men to kneel, facing Leah, in the middle of the room. Leah looked at the two kneeling men and said, "Where did you come from and why did you want to enter the city stealthily?"

One of the men said: "We came from Canaan and we wanted to meet our acquaintances."

"Did you come from Elam or Canaan? For what purpose has Chedorlaomer sent you here?" Leah asked firmly.

One of the prisoners looked at the other and said, "We are from Abraham's tribe, and we came from Canaan. We do not know who Chedorlaomer is."

Leah turned to one of the guards and said, "Go get Lot and bring him here." Then she asked the same man who had responded to her question, "How do I know that you're telling me the truth? Why did you want to enter the city overnight, without permission?"

"We saw you coming to Canaan a while ago when you entered the city with Hagar," the same man said.

Leah stared into the suspect's eyes and asked, "You did not say why you tried to enter the city secretly at night. Why didn't you go to the guards at the gate?" Her tone showed that she was convinced the men were from Canaan.

At this moment, the guard appeared at the door, then Lot entered the room. After bowing to Leah, Lot said, "Greetings to Lady Leah. Thank you again for permitting my people to live in the great city of Sodom. I had come to the palace to pay my respect to you and King Bera personally. The guard found me and said that you needed me." At the same time, his eyes fell on the two kneeling men in the room.

"My lady, what are they doing here and why are their hands in shackles?" asked Lot.

With her own surprised look at Lot, Leah asked, "Do you know these men?"

"Yes, these men are close to my uncle, Abraham. What are they doing here?" replied Lot.

Looking away from Lot, staring at the men, Leah asked, "This is exactly my question too: why did you come here; did you come to visit Lot?"

"Not you," Leah interrupted the man who had spoken before. She asked the other man, "You, I want you to answer me this time."

The man who was ordered by Leah to speak lowered his head and kept silent. After a few moments in the same condition, the man replied, "No, we have not come to see Lot. We came to see others. We did not know that they had already been transferred to the city."

"Is it the first time you have come to meet your acquaintance, either here or behind the gate?" asked Leah quickly.

Both men remained silent. Leah stood up and walked toward them. She stopped in front of the men, looked at them, and repeated her question. The prisoners did not answer. "Who did you want to visit here? What is the name of the person you wanted to meet?" asked Leah again.

Heads down, both men stayed motionless and silent.

Suddenly, Leah kicked the first man hard in the face. The man fell on his back to the ground and blood splashed out of his nose. Lot panicked and took a step back, while a strange sound came out from his throat involuntary. Leah shouted to prisoners as she stood in her place, "Until you answer my questions, you will stay in the dungeon."

"Take them," Leah ordered the guards.

The guards raised the man who was still on his back and took both prisoners out of the room. Lot, shaken and stunned, standing in his spot, was trying to avoid eye contact with Leah. Leah came close, stared at Lot's eyes, and asked, "What do you know about these men, Lot?

Despite the fact that you were sheltered in Sodom, we can reverse the process at any time. You must now consider yourself part of Sodom and bound to protect the city's interests and security. Tell me all you know about these men."

Leah recognized the muddle in Lot's eyes. She knew that his answer would most likely be truthful. Lot controlled his mind and said, "Of course, we feel that all of us belong to this beautiful city. You can count on any help that we can provide. I do not know these people closely, but I have seen them before. They were trusted by my uncle. My uncle usually uses these men as messengers and envoys."

Leah listened carefully to Lot's words and asked him in a friendlier manner, "Lot, I visited Canaan a while ago to decide for you and the status of your people. I met several people in Canaan. I noticed that many men were engaged in military exercises every day. What is the reason for training those fighters? Has Abraham ever been involved in any war? Has he ever engaged in any conflict with other territories and kings?"

"As far as I remember, we never engaged in any war before. And I must say that until the time I separated from my uncle, our tribes had been living together." Lot continued, "I asked my uncle the same question many times."

"Well, what was his answer?" Leah asked curiously.

"My uncle believed, in addition to protecting people, sheep, and the security of the tribe, men folk should not be idle. He believed sloth is like a disease, like a plague that can destroy everyone. We were more of a wandering tribe; we worked the land little. We used to go from one region to another. For this reason, my uncle always tried to force the tribal men to work all the time, either to make something or to practice fighting. If they had nothing else to do, my uncle would make them dig holes in the ground from morning to noon, and fill them up in the afternoon. Sometimes, he forced them to bring the rocks off the hills and move them around."

At this moment, Lot's daughters stopped at the door and entered the room without permission. Paltith said, "Hello my lady," then she turned to Lot and said, "Father, we heard two of our relatives were arrested at the city gate last night."

Leah showed her back to Lot and his daughters, walked away from them a few steps in the room, and said, "Who allowed you to enter the room? Here, there are rules that differ from the tribe you used to live in before."

The guard came in and grabbed one of the girl's hands gently to take them out. "That's okay," Leah said, pointing to the guard. She walked back to Lot and the girls and continued, "Now that you are here, I have a few questions for you two. Do you know these men?"

Paltith turned to her sister and responded, "Yes, they are our relatives."

"They were arrested last night outside of the city trying to get in without permission. You have not seen them yet, so how do you know who they are?" asked Leah.

Paltith responded immediately, "We have heard who came to meet the relatives."

"Since the time of their arrest, nobody has seen them. Whom did you hear that from? Your father just saw prisoners a moment ago, and he had no chance of informing you about their identities. Besides, Lot himself did not know them well. How come you call them relatives?"

Lot looked at his daughters as the two sisters stayed quiet. Leah continued, "Have you had any other visitors from Canaan outside the city before your father and his tribe were granted shelter for living in this city?"

The girls and Lot continued to be silent. Lot said, "My children if you know something, we are now a member of this great city and have a duty to cooperate with Lady Leah."

Paltith stared furiously at her father briefly and stayed quiet, looking down again. Leah shouted angrily, "If I find out that you hide something from me, I will send you back to Canaan. Guard, they all can leave."

Leah then walked back and sat behind her desk. First Lot, then Paltith stepped out. Pultith stood still inside the room and asked Leah, "Can we see our relatives?"

Leah shouted to the guard with a ghastly look, "Take her out of here."

After they all left the room, Leah laid her elbows on the table and covered her ears with both hands.

# Chapter 48 – Sara

*San Francisco*

It had been only a few days since the group had decided not to gather in one place due to the dangerous situation surrounding all of them. As everyone agreed at the last meeting, each one had to be in touch with Essie individually. Essie, as the coordinator, now was spending most of his time at Simone's apartment, where he was connected to everyone through a secure and encrypted app that had been created in the Tech2AI lab. Through Rachel, Essie heard the news about Art's involvement in the melee at UC Berkeley. Essie became very upset about Art's imprudence. Not only had Art not consulted with Essie before deciding to go to UC Berkeley, but also he kept quiet about it afterward. Art simply told Essie that he had to go there. Essie had learned about UC Berkeley in the media but had no idea Art was part of that havoc. Several people had been arrested, and some of the detainees provided police with information about their weapons.

Like any other citizen in the United States, Essie had had trouble trusting the news the past few years. He learned to doubt the accuracy of news. How could he trust anything when sometimes fake news was finding its way to even the most prestigious press and news sources? Over the past two years, the news media in the West, especially social media, had become so overwhelmingly chaotic. Any news, albeit straightforward and noncontroversial, needed to be carefully examined for its accuracy. Progress in retouching technology—Photoshop, video editing—had helped spread fake news tremendously. No online video clip or photo could initially be trustworthy. They used voice-over video skills widely to spread fake news for specific purposes.

In Essie's opinion, any news could have had a Russian source. Essie remembered a detailed report by a famous magazine two years before which revealed the existence of an agency in Russia generating fake news for specific political goals. The report named the agency and shed light on the activities of the center, which were manipulating political, economic, and social events in the West. The report was a warning about a troll center in the city of St. Petersburg in Russia as one source of spreading fake news. After two years of producing fake materials nonstop and meddling in the crucial U.S. presidential election, these troll machines were still polluting social media and the internet's digital environment, so Facebook was forced to report it to the U.S. Congress. Now, any news about San Francisco's events and any incident of alt-right activism were not immune to this chaotic environment in media.

During this period, the word "fake news" had also been used for other purposes. The confusion about the definition of fake news became a tool in the hands of people in charge of U.S. government offices and Trump, who used the phrase for any news and analysis critical of him. This phenomenon had added to the deterioration of the situation in the circulation of real news. Now newspapers in New York, Washington, and Los Angeles, which had gained their credibility over a decade of relatively healthy journalism, were also depicted by the White House as news fakers. Of course, Essie knew that newspapers and other media had their own share of mistakes as well as a history of promoting specific political interests, such as the echo chamber of the previous administration regarding the Iran nuclear deal. But the

Russian trolls were excluded from these titles by the White House, unlike the U.S. mainstream media.

After the major explosion in the building of the *Bay Area Chronicle* in the middle of the night, which shook a large area in San Francisco, Tim and other newspaper staff did not have a specific place for their daily work. The newspaper, however, was still visible and updated online. Despite hackers' efforts to penetrate it, the newspaper server was able to survive. Two days after the explosion, the newspaper management succeeded to update its daily content without having a physical location for its employees. The buildings, fixtures, and computers were all destroyed by the blast, but by 2017 there were fewer companies in Silicon Valley and elsewhere in the country that kept their data and content on local servers.

In recent months, Tim was participating in a regular gathering at David's office and interacting with others closely. However, since joining the group, Tim had been particularly interested in Essie. He initially considered Essie to be an odd-looking, tight-lipped, standoffish, and reserved foreigner, who when he spoke had something to say. Tim could never see himself as congenial with such a person, let alone looking forward to seeing him. Tim was not a racist man, but he did not expect to ever work with an individual like Essie before. And now, Essie's comments sometimes sparked such admiration in Tim for pointing to hidden logic and ideas behind the issues that Tim could not refrain from praising the mustache guy.

At first, Tim had joined the group to be around Michael. Of course, satisfying his curiosity about Art and his stories was part of his eagerness to join the crowd. Art's original stories were unique, and Tim was devouring them to be written later in his feuilleton. After a few sessions, Tim thought that he alone could continue the stories that Art was narrating, using his writing skills and creativity. But after a while, Tim found that it was far beyond his imagination. Initially, Tim assumed that Art's stories were fictitious, and what he was hearing and then publishing in the paper in the form of feuilleton were all products of Art's creativity as a talented storyteller. But the stories' simplicity and their enticing nature brought the notion to Tim's mind that they could be real. Art would send stories to Tim frequently, mostly in writing and occasionally through phone calls. In Tim's opinion, it seemed unlikely that an individual like Art could make up such details by himself.

After the Berkeley incident and seeing Art in action at the park with his own eyes, Tim became sure that something was going on beyond his imagination and knowledge. All of these events now brought Tim closer to Essie, an occurrence that Tim embraced willfully.

Although Tim was not alien to technology, he was not fond of spending time with nerds and coders. He used the benefits of the latest innovations and smart devices without any interest in the function of computer codes and the algorithms behind the technology. Tim was in love with discussions, debates, and polemics. In the group he had joined, Essie was the only person who shared those characteristics. In fact, Essie had character traits that Tim had long sought in sources for his reporting. He was astounded by Essie's accurate information and analysis on current and past events. Tim could not believe the amount of Essie's knowledge about different cultures and countries. After Essie told Tim about his adventures, the rising star at the *Bay Area Chronicle* considered writing a series of stories about the Middle Eastern man. Essie welcomed the idea, with a condition for working together on the stories or a novel: when completed, his name would be listed as a co-author.

Following the explosion in the newspaper's building, Tim was looking forward to visiting Essie on a daily basis in Simone's apartment. Being in her apartment was much better than spending time at the coffee shop or wherever Tim could accomplish his day-to-day work. Tim had a luxury apartment himself, but he hated staying at home. He had to get out every morning. After the explosion in his workplace, in the early days when there was no place to go to work, Tim was like a lost bird, flapping here and there. The few times that

Tim had visited Essie, he did not want to leave the place. Tim finally overcame his hesitation and said, "Hey, I don't know how to say ... can I ..."

"Whatever ... if you like," Essie replied immediately. Essie knew Tim's interest in staying longer and more often in Simone's place. He also knew that the young man was uncomfortable asking. Essie did not see Tim as a shy person and liked to hear the request from the horse's mouth. So, with a silenced laugh, Essie watched his departure every time. Essie's laugh was neither because of his mischievous character nor because he disliked Tim. He just wanted to play with or perhaps outsmart this bright young journalist.

Essie liked Tim's style of writing better than most current journalists'. He liked it not just in the Sodom stories, but when he wrote about other issues as well. Essie had found and read most of Tim's other pieces, even the older ones. He kept his reading of the works a secret. Essie had read them with pleasure. More than the content, Essie was enjoying Tim's style. Tim played well with words, animating, dancing, and using them in different forms. Tim knew the words' actual concept, their weight, and positions. Verbosity was not his style, nor was using big words unnecessarily. There were, of course, some opinions that Essie wanted to point out, but he was waiting for a right time to discuss them with him. Essie regarded Tim's writing as close to ideal, not the content, but its style and flow.

Essie wished he could write like him. Of course, Essie too was a good writer; perhaps better than Tim but in Persian. English was Essie's second language. Although the Middle Eastern man was good at writing, he knew that he would run out of words and phrases to express his ideas. Essie might have been much better than other native writers, but he was not happy with himself compared with Tim. Tim's articles had been improving over the years, but there were still some weaknesses in substance and subject matter. It would be better if Tim had enough knowledge of the main subject of his articles. Essie often fantasied about the possibility of combining their skills. If they could work together, they could have produced ideal work, both in form and content.

Tim finally mentioned his wish, "Can I come here and work with you every day?"

And Essie had replied, "You know that this is not my apartment. It's Simone's, and I am a guest myself here. You certainly can ask her. I have no problem, you know, as a guest."

Simone did not like Tim, but she agreed to his request.

Essie realized who could be behind all the attacks after reading Pamela Lang's interview with Sara and Detective Smith's findings of the conservative church's role in recent attacks. Connecting the dots, excluding the downtown Berkeley event, led Essie to the bishop of the Baptodist church, John Wesley the Third. He shared his finding with others in the group.

Essie asked Tim to call Pamela Lang and arrange an interview with Sara. Pastor Lang recognized Tim. She was up to date on reading the Sodom stories. In fact, most of Lang's friends at the university and the Post-Evangelical Church were also reading Tim's series. They all had mixed feelings. Pamela, at least, had her own contradictory thoughts. Pamela was not sure whether she should have liked or challenged it. She liked the series in the newspaper as a work of fiction. She felt they were exciting stories written in a superb style. But Pamela should have stopped there. Tim's stories were an explicit abjuration of Old Testament narratives. She had been discussing this with colleagues at the university. If the *Bay Area Chronicle* stories were fiction, why should the Old Testament narrative be interpreted as non-fiction? There was no logical answer to Pamela's question, like many other questions she had been facing, which alienated her to the point of dichotomy. Pamela was running away from the conservative church. That was why she joined and became one of the most active members of the Post-Evangelical Church of Baptodist.

Now, Pamela faced a question: How far should she distance herself from the conservative ideas? Particularly after publishing her interview with Sara, there had been many unusual pressures on her from various directions.

Pamela found out that most of the pressure was being coordinated against her by conservatives and a person called Peter Jr., but she did not have enough evidence to expose them. Even If she had enough evidence, Pamela was not sure she would want to make them public yet. So far, her friends at the church believed that she had stepped out of line. But she did not know where that line was. Pamela was repeatedly confronted with this question in her mind but was hopeless to find an answer. The damn line that existed everywhere, not just about Tim's stories against the gospel, the line between her and the conservative church, was the same. A church that not only would condemn gays but also would not allow women to be in a pastor position. So, where would Pamela's place be as a black lesbian in a church where His Excellency was head of the bishops' council? How far should Pamela distance herself from the conservative church, considering her intellectual capacity? Some might say as much as possible, but Pamela had to draw the line in just the right place, considering her religious beliefs as the cornerstone of her life.

If the conservative church claimed that there is no place for homosexuality in Christianity, then where should Pamela stand if she loved the Father and His Son Jesus Christ? And she was a true believer of the Trinity.

No, Pamela considered her existence as a lesbian to be a fact, and this fact must have had a place in the throne of Christ and the infinite love of God for his servants. The same servants whom God had sent his son on earth to guide and show love through sacrificing himself. Pamela knew that if someone and something was not supposed to be a part of this circle of creation, it was the rotten reactionary thoughts of the conservative church that had nothing to do with Christianity.

But what should she do now with Tim and his friends who, according to Tim, were systematically under attack by the Baptodist Church? This was another line Pamela needed to draw. Without confirming or rejecting Tim's claims, Pamela knew that the young journalist was not exaggerating about attacks when she thought about the pressure on her in recent weeks.

The pressure on Boston University's board of directors to oust Pamela from the associate professorship position was immeasurable. His Excellency's church was coercing many of the wealthy donors who had been contributing sizable amounts of money to the university regularly in the past to cut off their financial assistance. Pamela was being accused of slander and defamation by the head of the bishops' council because she interviewed his ex-wife. The prospect of losing her job was a massive stress for Pamela. The board was resisting. However, rumors were not optimistic.

*Discontinuing large-scale charitable donations on reputable universities is similar to an earthquake with a magnitude of 8.0 on the Richter scale on a poorly constructed building. If the earthquake does not collapse the building entirely, its foundation will be damaged profoundly. The building facade might look normal, but nobody can safely live or work in it anymore.*

Sara was almost under the same kind of pressures. Church members were insisting that Sara return to the arms of Jesus Christ by condemning Pamela Lang as a liar. Creating terrifying scenes by unknown individuals at night had made Sara extremely nervous and ill.

Tim had asked Pamela if he could contact Sara. Pamela was contemplating, "For what purpose? What would Tim and his friends want from Sara? Would covering Sara's condition on a wider scale promote their main agenda?" Using Sara and her issues was openly a declaration of war against the conservative Church of Baptodist. By opening the can of worms, it was unclear what consequences would follow. Pamela herself had already begun the controversy, and now she had to decide in which direction the whole issue needed to move. Pamela was not a revengeful person. If she were, much more could have happened to ruin His Excellency's reputation. Pamela was on the verge of being fired and knew that His Excellency and his followers were behind all these conspiracies. She saw herself as a victim of politics that had no resemblance to Christ and Christianity. And the Sodom group, as she would call them, were victims of the same plots. Pamela made her decision based on her conscience, not because of vengeance or retaliation. The guide was a call from her heart. If she was a true believer in Christ, no other option was conceivable.

In a conversation with Tim and his friend with the strange accent, Pamela offered to relocate Sara to San Francisco. Not only for an interview: Pamela also asked the Sodom group to settle Sara in San Francisco temporarily so that the trial for the custody of her son could be moved from Atlanta to San Francisco. Pamela believed Sara would be more secure anywhere besides Atlanta. Pamela feared that living among members of the conservative church, who were entirely under His Excellency's influence, Sara would end up in a mental hospital. Although Sara's lawyer had accepted the custody case as pro bono, he could argue the case without her presence in the court. If agreed, Pamela would put Sara on a plane to San Francisco, and Tim and friends would take care of her until further notice. Tim told Pamela that he would discuss the matter with his friends and inform her as soon as possible.

An in-person meeting could not be convened to discuss Sara's issue. They could gather in a place if they wanted, but the group had decided not to. Instead, Essie was supposed to coordinate the decision-making process and take actions. Essie himself believed that bringing Sara to San Francisco was a good idea. Sara's presence could always be used as leverage against the enemy.

Tim was not sure which legal consequences would follow, especially since Pamela's primary contact was himself. He was aware of the power of the Baptodist Church. In particular, Tim witnessed the tremendous amount of pressure the same church was imposing on the newspaper's management to stop publishing the Sodom stories. And now, a group consisting of gays and lesbians and a Middle Eastern man hosting a bishop's wife could trigger many backlashes.

Art agreed without any hesitation. Art's motives were not based on politics, not even logic or reason. Art thought with his heart and conscience. For him, there were humanitarian reasons for helping a person in Sara's condition that did not require deliberation, especially after Pamela updated Tim with the new information.

Michael had no particular idea and agreed more with Art. Michael had been very quiet in the last few months. He had never been a talkative man, but after recent incidents and Art's overwhelming involvement in the events, he was distraught.

Melody, like Art, did not hesitate to help the bishop's wife. In fact, she was ready to keep Sara in her home. David agreed but believed Sara's situation was a problem that needed careful assessment. Essie would not see a security threat to Sara. Essie wrote to David, "If the bishop had any intention to harm his wife, he would've already done it. Apart from a consideration of the church's reputation, they would probably prefer a harmless, ill Sara under their control. Of course, there are always risks, especially given the fact that Sara will not be in their proximity to control."

David missed chatting with Essie as they could not see each other like before. For years, David had been spending almost every day with Essie. They would bicker over any topic from politics to philosophy and anything else that could have been a subject of a two-person conversation. In the past few weeks, David had no appetite for anything and anyone; he seemed to have lost something. David knew that the cause of his boredom was Essie's absence. Once, he sent a message to Essie, "I missed when you were talking my head off, buddy." And Essie replied, "Same here, really."

They all agreed that Essie should decide where Sara should stay while living in San Francisco and that they wouldn't reveal it to anyone.

Essie sent a message to Melody and Tim: "You two will go to the airport to pick up Sara, and then take her to the parking lot. On your way bringing her to me, tell her that I will take over and she'll come to my car. I will send you detailed instructions later."

Meanwhile, Essie had asked Rachel to arrange a place for Sara's housing. Essie had a plan to deliver Sara to Rachel at a location outside the airport, after receiving her from Melody and Tim. No one would know Sara's whereabouts but Rachel and Essie.

Essie, who was excited and disciplined about playing this kind of secretive game, did not even tell Simone, who was asking him about Sara's future residence in San Francisco.

After many years, Essie was back in the middle of a chase and a counter-surveillance game like he had experienced in his 20s. The useless paranoia that he had carried all these years was vigorously reborn in him. Once, David told Essie, "You know, this habit of yours is a sickness. You check your surroundings when you arrive in a place, trying to know who's who and what's what."

In fact, Essie's constant vigilance was a sickness, a mental disorder that was the result of his past full of pursuit and counter-surveillance for survival. However, this characteristic was now considered an asset for the group. In addition to that, Essie himself felt young and alive again by returning to a condition similar to his youth.

Essie knew how influential the Baptodist Church was and did not underestimate his opponents. Essie learned not to underestimate his enemy when he had been involved in the struggle against the Iranian regime. He would use the word "enemy" to call those who were responsible for the explosion at Tech2AI.

*Misjudging an enemy who goes so far as to kill innocent people, directly or indirectly, is the zenith of stupidity, and in such a battle for survival, one must avoid foolishness as far as possible.*

Simone realized that Essie had not left the apartment for the past few days. Essie was rejecting Simone's suggestions to go outside for a walk to get fresh air. After the explosion at the office, which left six people killed and others in a coma, Essie went to the hospital once to visit David. The only other time was to go back to his apartment to pack some clothes and pick up other personal stuff. Essie said to Simone, "If for any reason you are not comfortable with my staying here, please be straight with me. I won't be offended at all."

Simone did not mind. In the last few days, all Essie had done was pace in Simone's apartment or sit behind his laptop and send messages through his phone. When Simone was home, Essie would try to keep her company. But when he was alone again in that small place, he was pacing for hours trying to think.

The living room was connected to a part of the kitchen. On the other side of the kitchen was a narrow hallway that would lead to the bedroom and bathroom. The main entrance opened to the junction of the kitchen and the hallway. Essie had pushed the coffee table away from the couch so there was enough space for him to walk through from the living room, where he could see the entire street through the full window, to the kitchen. From there, he would turn to the left, going into the hallway and walking back the same path to the end of the living room to watch the street again.

Simone had used cheerful colors in the decoration of her living room, including various paintings. It created a pleasant atmosphere for Essie to spend hours and days in the apartment. Essie was not happy with the new circumstances, but he had been in much worse situations in the past. Once, he had spent two weeks in the basement of a small mud house on a hillside on the border between Iran and Iraqi Kurdistan. There was only a hole to see the valley outside.

Although Essie had lived in a calm and comfortable environment since then, the comparison between the present desirable environment of Simone's apartment and the past, which had never been erased from Essie's mind, made his life acceptable. Essie was mostly worried about his friends, especially David and Melody whom he could not be around to defend against threats.

Before contacting Pamela and making the decision to transfer Sara to San Francisco, the news of the referendum in Iraqi Kurdistan had unleashed the lariat of Essie's memoirs from the time when he had lived in that area. He narrated those stories for Tim who was taking notes as eagerly and rapidly as a thirsty wanderer in a desert who had reached a spring of cold water. Tim was slaking his thirst with the cold water, which he knew was not a mirage. Tim became more and more interested in Essie's tales than in the Sodom adventures.

For a journalist like Tim, Essie was a winning lottery ticket. Tim sought to gain a journalistic reputation, entering as a heavyweight figure into the world of press. And Essie was the best opportunity to stabilize his professional career.

"Oh, after the end of these adventures, let's write a book together on the background of current affairs," said Tim.

"I have no objection, but my name should be published as the co-author. In addition to Kurdish issues, I have stories, documents, and information that can cover the relation between Iran and the U.S. in the past 40 years, from the time of the Colt, cake, and gospel event until the Obama administration last year."

Tim had not heard some of the phrases that Essie mentioned, "What is the Colt, cake, and gospel event?"

Essie replied, "Probably it's beyond your age. You might have heard of Iran Gate, or Iran Contra. To deal with Khomeini, President Reagan had sent a cake, a handgun, and a gospel literally to show good faith."

"I had not heard about it, but Iran Gate was familiar," said Tim.

Conversations with Tim about various issues distracted Essie from his primary responsibility and the original plan for some time. Essie, who was fascinated with complex debates, sometimes would forget about the crisis and chaos surrounding them.

Except for Tim, until the day Sara arrived at the airport, Art was the only person who came to visit Essie. Essie told Tim not to come to the apartment the day that Art was supposed to be at Simone's apartment. Essie had planned to be alone with Art and persuaded Simone to leave them alone. When Essie realized that Simone had not honored his request, he directly asked her to go out for a couple of hours. Essie was not a brazen person. He was embarrassed to ask Simone to get out of her own apartment, but there was no other way. He had to maintain his discipline. Simone went out despite her wish. Her face was showing discontent with the current situation and no end in sight.

The big day arrived, the moment of truth. A winter evening in San Francisco, seventy-seven degree Fahrenheit, was so delightful that Essie wished he could be with his friends, drinking beer, in new places that he and Simone had discovered lately. The smell of smoke was in the air. It was said that the fire in Napa Valley was the source, but Essie believed it must have been much closer. He now terribly missed spending happy days with his friends. Essie hoped to see those unwanted episodes end soon, that series of events that had dragged down everything bit by bit like a swamp into itself. Despite the excitement of the early days after the adventures began, Essie realized that he was no longer the same young person who was capable of those types of actions like before. He adapted to the peace and comfort in his life. He often asked himself, "Who would prefer an adventurous uneasy life simply because of its excitement over a peaceful and tranquil life?" Essie thought that many might choose the former, but he felt that he was about to reach the end of his life's thrilling path.

Tired but determined, Essie was driving to the airport. Driving on the 101 freeway, a flood of thoughts was creating waves of uneasiness in his mind. He tried to focus. Essie had no time to examine the past adventures and experiences at that moment. The plane was supposed to land at 7 o'clock. He had told Tim and Melody that he would wait in the Park and Fly structure to take Sara with him. Essie had thought that the safest way from the terminal to the parking lot, where he was waiting, was passing through the crowd. Essie had chosen a parking lot that usually had more available spots than other parking structures. He knew the San Francisco parking lot at the airport like the palm of his hand. During the time he lived in San Francisco, Essie had picked up many guests at the airport, most of whom were David and Melody's.

At 7 o'clock sharp, Essie was at the spot he planned to be. He estimated if the flight had no delay, it would take at least half an hour for Melody and Tim to bring Sara to his parking lot. In a quick patrol inside the parking structure, Essie found no unusual activity. He hoped the enemy would not interfere with Sara's flight from Atlanta. Essie thought if they were after Sara, at the most, they would know the flight's number. Essie was hopeful that the enemy had no knowledge of who would pick her up. Of course, it was wishful thinking. All possible occurrences were calculated quickly in his mind, "Certainly, they don't know that I am waiting here at this particular parking lot. But if they follow Tim and Melody here..." He reviewed the worst possible cases that might happen and concluded, "If there were a possibility of violence, it would happen right here, where I am."

The clock was ticking. Essie was looking at every passing car carefully. His heart was beating faster now. He sent a text to Tim and Melody, informing them of the exact location of his car in the lot. Forty-five minutes passed, and Essie heard nothing. He had requested Melody to keep him updated with the text messages. The anxiety was growing in Essie who believed in himself as a seasoned warrior. Essie believed in his plan as he thought it was flawlessly designed. He had thought of everything. It was impossible for the enemy to commit an act of stupidity in the airport terminal. It was almost an hour now. At that moment, Essie heard a buzz. It was a text from Melody. He cupped his hand over the screen to block the light. He could barely read the message. Melody had written, "You were right. They had filed a complaint with the police that we're trying to kidnap Sara as a confused person. We were detained in the security room all this time. We are out now and coming."

Essie had guessed that their first trick would be the same as mentioned in Melody's text. Essie had asked Tim to get help from his father to contact Pamela to provide all legal documents to refute such an allegation. Sara had a health certificate from a doctor proving her sanity. Furthermore, Pamela gave her an official letter with Boston University's letterhead, confirming the identity of those at the airport who would pick her up. In addition to that, Tim's father was ready to intervene quickly as a lawyer, in case of any complication. Tim was glad that his father's involvement was not necessary that time of the evening.

The second text came from Melody indicating their arrival at the Park and Fly structure. Essie said to himself, "Show time." After a few minutes that seemed like a few hours, Essie recognized Tim's SUV slowly approaching where he had parked. Following Tim's SUV, a black van was moving a few feet on his tail. Essie sent a text quickly, "Be alert and ready."

When Tim stopped behind Essie's car, Melody opened the door on her side. Two men immediately came out of the black van and moved toward Tim's SUV. It was too late for Melody to return to the SUV so Tim could drive away. Essie quickly got out of his car and walked toward them. Two masked men with their guns equipped with silencers had almost reached Tim's SUV. One of them pointed his weapon toward Melody, and the other walked toward the driver's seat where Tim was still sitting.

Out of nowhere, Art appeared from the back of the armed man whose gun was pointed at Melody and knocked him down, using his elbow to hit the upper part of the man's ear and temple. Art then went to the other man who turned back after he heard what happened. With a few quick strokes, Art confined him to the ground first, then lifted his unconscious body up and threw it on top the other man. Everything happened so fast. Essie collected their weapons and searched their pockets. He found nothing. Melody, trembling, hugged Essie. Art opened the SUV's rear door and said to Sara, "Welcome to our city, San Francisco."

Art then went toward the unconscious men. Tim was still sitting in the car. Essie opened the front passenger door for Melody as she was regaining her composure. Essie told Tim, "Get out of here quickly."

Essie was going to tell Art to get away from there but in his astonishment saw he was already dragging the second man into the van. Holding the door, Essie was waiting for Sara, who was not in a hurry to leave the SUV. Essie looked at Art, who was at that moment behind the van's wheel, taking off slowly. A smile of contentment formed on Essie's lips. He knew that Art's presence would be critical to the operation. Even if nothing happened, Art would add to the security factor at the scene. He had reviewed the whole plan with Art the day he refused to accept Tim and asked Simone to leave her apartment for a couple of hours. When Essie had seen the van tailing Tim's SUV in the parking lot, he sent the "Be alert and ready" text to Art who was already at the scene.

Essie had never experienced such sense of satisfaction before. The plan went flawlessly. He was mumbling, "Arthur of Sodom, the savior of all."

# Chapter 49 – Amim

When Hun was hired by the San Francisco police department, he had no idea he would have to work with a black detective. It took a long time for him to be speak with his partner, Detective Smith, let alone comfortably connect with him on a somewhat personal level.

Hun remembered his childhood. He was eight years old when the Los Angeles riot known as Rodney King riot—or as the Koreans called it "Sa-I-Gu," meaning "four-two-nine"—took place in Korean Town. On April 29, 1992, four white policemen were acquitted on charges of beating Rodney King, an African-American taxi driver in Los Angeles. African Americans and Latinos took to the street to protest the acquittal of the policemen. During the riot, some protesters created chaos in the south part of the city, looted shops, and set businesses on fire. On the second day, the riot and insecurity spread to the Korean Town. Because of the extent of the clashes and the limits of the police force, police units left some areas, including Korean neighborhoods, to protect more important commercial areas in Los Angeles, such as Beverly Hills and other high echelon neighborhoods. Koreans, who became the target of attacks by plunderers, armed themselves to protect their businesses and places of residence. The riot took more than dozens of lives from both sides and left many more injured.

Hun recalled that second day of the riots vividly when his family's small shop was looted in Korean Town, and his father and brother rushed to help his uncle and cousins. On the third day, one of his cousins was killed by an armed robber, but the invaders were forced to retreat due to the resistance of self-organized members of the Korean community. Scary scenes of armed conflict, sometimes one-on-one fights, were engraved in Hun's mind. On the fourth and fifth days, the intensity of the clashes was reduced by the arrival of the National Guard and the army; finally, security was restored in Korean Town. The riot increased mistrust between Asians in general, and the Korean communities in particular, and African Americans in the Los Angeles area.

Hun felt a kind of sympathy toward his partner's fragmentary nagging about the Sodom group. Especially after the explosion at the Tech2AI office, Hun found Smith in a condition that he had never seen him in before. Hun was not unhappy or ashamed to be happy to see his senior partner in a mentally weak position. Hun's childhood memory of the riot filled his mind and soul with a pessimistic view of black people and in this case his partner, Detective Smith.

The young Asian detective saw printed-out Sodom stories on his colleague's desk. He picked up the sheets of pages, sat behind his desk, and took a look at the last segment of the story. Unlike his partner, Hun had no compassion for the members of the Sodom group. He had moved to San Francisco with the help and assistance of the most powerful Korean Church to study at the University of Ulivet. Until now, he had not read anything from the series that was the talk of the town and the nation. Only out of curiosity, Hun held the papers that he had picked up from Smith's desk and began to read...

   ***

*Elam Territory – Chedorlaomer's Chamber*

With a mocking smile, Chedorlaomer looked at the members of the expedition, representing the valley of Siddim's territories, standing before him. Three men, on behalf of Admah, Zeboiim, and Bella, were accompanying Amim who was sent by the king of Sodom. Among the four, only Amim was Chedorlaomer's interlocutor. An overwhelming number of armed guards, whose hands were on their swords, were standing behind them. The guards' presence caught the delegates' attention.

With the smile that was left on the corner of his lip, the king of Elam said, "I do not see anyone from Gomorrah among you. Maybe Birsha thought that Achan would represent him in here?"

"Your Excellency, we are here for other issues," replied Amim. "If you are willing to talk about them…"

The king stopped Amim and said, "You want to say that the fate of Achan is not important to any of you?"

"Of course it is important, but we are representing …" said Amim.

Chedorlaomer interjected, "How important is it to you? I heard that Birsha has not slept since Achan left Gomorrah and came to Elam."

"Perhaps Your Excellency is referring to Achan's abduction. We all know that Achan never left Gomorrah willingly," Amim said.

The king stood up furiously and shouted to Amim's face, "How dare you accuse us of kidnapping people?"

"We will be very pleased to hear from Achan if he can tell us about life in Elam," Amim responded calmly in a low tone.

Chedorlaomer kept silent for a moment. He sat down on his throne with a long chuckle. At the end of his laugh, the king said, "I have a question for you about men who sleep with other men. I do not know when men sleep together which one is right; do they become braver or more stupid? I want to hear from the love of King Bera."

Amim first said nothing, but after the king of Elam raised the same question, he replied, "Your Excellency, we came here for other matters. Our leaders have sent us here to submit some questions for you. If I may, I would like to present them now."

The king shouted again, "You are disrespecting me. Answer my question. I am your master now. Know that what Bera can give you, I have too." With a loud and hysterical laugh, Chedorlaomer put his hand between his legs and showed Amim his genitalia.

Amim moved slightly from where he was standing. The three guards, who stood behind him, took their swords halfway out of their sheaths. The king pointed to the guards and said, "Be calm. Amim is not that stupid to make any mistake here. Are you, Amim? Let's go back to the same question: Has your personal relationship with your master made you more courageous or more stupid?"

"I do not have a problem in answering your question. But the question is wrong because stupidity is not the opposite of courage; cowardice is. It would have been better if you asked, Does it make one cowardly or brave?" Then Amim glanced at the guards and continued, "Maybe those men who possess different women in the palace can answer the question better—of course, the correct question."

Amim's companions looked at their counterparts with worry on their faces, waiting for Chedorlaomer's reaction. The king kept silent for some moments. His facial expression did not reveal anything. Then Chedorlaomer again laughed uproariously and pointed his finger at Amim and asked, "Do you want to say that you are brave? Well done. I admit that you are brave, but let's see how your relationship with King Bera made you courageous. Are you willing to swap places with Achan? We will let Achan go with them, and you stay here. Are you that brave?"

"Your Excellency had said that Achan came here willingly. Freedom is the opposite of captivity," responded Amim immediately.

"Think as you wish. Give me the answer: Are you ready to stay here so Achan can leave?" the king asked again.

Amim paused and looked at Admah's representative, whose fear was apparent on his face. Then he replied, "We have come here to negotiate with you. I will answer this after completing the talks and what we have come here for."

Chedorlaomer rose from his throne. He stepped forward and stood face to face with Amim without any words. The guards who stood behind Amim took a step forward. Amim glanced around.

"There will be no negotiation," the king said. "Everything depends on your answer to my question." Then Chedorlaomer shouted at Amim's face, "Are you ready to exchange your place with Achan? Answer me."

At the same time, Tabitha entered from the side of the chamber and screamed, "They killed Achan. This is a trap. Achan was killed."

Following her, Arshum entered and grabbed Tabitha's hands, trying to pull her out. Tabitha resisted and shouted several times, "They killed Achan."

The guards, who were behind Amim and the rest of the delegation, jumped from behind and placed their swords on each of the four delegates' necks. The king said to other guards, "Take this mad woman out of here."

The three guards moved toward Tabitha and Arshum. When the guard struck Tabitha in the face with the hilt, Arshum thrust his sword into the guard's chest. Another guard stabbed a dagger into Arshum's heart, and the other struck his sword on his neck. The queen's personal guard fell to the ground. Then the guards went to Tabitha and grabbed her hand to take her out of the chamber. Chedorlaomer shouted, "Hold it. Let the delegates hear how Achan was killed. Bring the queen here."

The guards brought Tabitha to Chedorlaomer. The king squeezed Tabitha's face in his big hand and asked, "Tell them who killed Achan. It is shameful for Chedorlaomer to kill a man who is really not a man but a woman." Then, the king went to Amim and asked, "Tell me, who is the woman in bed, you or Bera? If you are a woman when sleeping with the king of Sodom, you can leave. Otherwise, I will kill you here myself." The king approached Amim, shouting into his face, "Tell me."

Amim spat on the king's face and said, "Are you trying to scare me with death? Tell your guards to let me go, and then you will get your answer."

Chedorlaomer replied coldly, "So, you are not afraid of death. I have something far worse than death for you. Open his mouth. He has a big tongue; it needs to be trimmed." The king then pointed to Arshum and said to Amim, "You see that monster? I, myself, pulled his tongue out of his throat."

The four guards held Amim on his back on the ground. Two guards sat on Amim's chest holding down his hands, and two other guards opened his mouth. Chedorlaomer pulled out his dagger from the sheath and approached Amim. Tabitha screamed, "No, no…"

The king threw Tabitha on the ground, punching her in the face. He continued stepping toward Amim while addressing his wife. The king said, "Do not be afraid, I won't kill him. I told you before that I will not kill a woman in a man's body."

Three other representatives of the delegation were standing quietly in a corner with the two guards watching them. One of them could not control his trembling body, and the floor under the other man's feet was wet. The third representative's knees were slackened, and he sat down at the same spot. The king, upon reaching Amim, noticed the three other delegates and said, "Do not worry. I will send you back home to inform your masters about the outcome of our negotiations."

# Chapter 50 – Church and State

*Atlanta – Church of Baptodist*

"Dear colleagues, please accept my gratitude. Thank you for responding to my urgent call for this meeting," said His Excellency at the conference hall of Baptodist Church in Atlanta, addressing the conservative church's bishops' council.

Confidence was glinting in His Excellency's words. He gently continued, "We usually meet to handle the highest levels of church administration and resolve issues that determine our role in the great community of believers in the country and all around the world. But today, I want to consult you on matters far beyond and more important than our usual concerns. I have talked with you both individually and in group meetings about issues that need the church's special attention. But now, the crisis has surrounded us. Weapons were openly pointed to us by hands that are no longer invisible. We must make serious decisions."

After that last word, His Excellency fell silent and stared at the nine bishops around the large wooden table that had dignified the conference room. The head of the Baptodist Church was waiting for someone to challenge him. His Excellency had convened the meeting to bring the leaders of the conservative church in line with his agenda. In his opinion, hesitation was no longer permissible. He could no longer quietly witness the strengthening of enemies and the escalation of attacks in the mass media against his church. His eyes were slipping from one face to another, but he was not able to make any of his audience respond.

After a while, His Excellency reiterated, "Your vote and the opinion of this council can change the fate of the conservative church in the new era."

He paused again and gazed into the eyes of those who were considered the elders of the church. Finally, James broke the silence and said, "John, I'm still waiting to find out what is the urgency of this meeting. Please tell us what are you talking about; what type of decision have we gathered here to make that, as you claim, can change the fate of our religion?"

His Excellency, laden with anger, heard James's brief question and saw his smirk. James had worn a brown three-piece suit, decorated with a dark brown striped tie, matching the dark gray color of his coat. In almost all of the similar meetings, James would challenge His Excellency, particularly in the presence of other bishops. Today, however, he tried not to reveal his annoyance with the person who introduced himself everywhere as the head of the bishops' council of the conservative church. But when James heard about the fate of the church from the mouth of His Excellency, he could no longer remain silent. James threw his question gently, like a softball, toward his old friend and rival.

His Excellency was waiting for James to speak. However, John Wesley the Third was nettled when he heard his usual rival's question. His Excellency knew that the bishops, and particularly James, never wanted to address him by the title he preferred. But this time James called his name in a manner as if his primary goal was to belittle him in front of others.

His Excellency tried to respond in a softest possible tone to have the most effect on his listeners. "James, you and I have often disagreed on different issues. Although you mostly have been dealing with the church's administrative affairs, I was contemplating strategic approaches to advance imperative affairs and countering dangers that would have threatened us. Nevertheless, we understood each other after each discussion. But today, despite all the reports that Peter Jr. has sent everyone here, you are telling me that you don't see the momentous conditions that we are in?"

James blushed but did not say anything immediately. He did not want to start a two-person debate. James knew that other bishops first tried to show their impartiality, but ultimately, they would offer acquiescence to John's demands under pressure. So James chose silence, hoping someone else would speak up. James's prediction came true as a bishop sitting next to him said, "Of course we came here for consultation. Although I receive your reports on a regular basis, in fact, like James, I do not know what you meant exactly by making the decision."

"Apparently, none of you read the press..." His Excellency knew that he should not give his audience the smallest room to breathe. Otherwise, he could not reach his goal. "The amount of attacks on us has been multiplied since that Sodom guy gave a speech. A day does not go by in which we don't receive a flood of requests by people and church members who call for an appropriate response. I'm sure that you're receiving them as well."

James interjected His Excellency's words, "Again, about Sodom? Why do we have to take a position on this? Let them tell stories about whatever they want."

"I'm surprised; we apparently considered ourselves as the most faithful Abrahamic religion, but we have been left far behind others.

In the last few days, three announcements have been published by the three major religious centers in Russia, Iran, and Israel, and we are still silent. The Orthodox Church of Russia, the Iranian foreign ministry, and a well-known rabbi in Jerusalem have strongly condemned the material contained in the *Bay Area Chronicle*. I have heard that the Catholic Church is also preparing a response to the fictions published in the city of sinners. Only Saudi Arabia has not raised its voice because it is said that the son of the new king has a very close relationship with tech companies in Silicon Valley. Over the past few months this person, the so-called the future king, who is also known as MBS, has actually taken over power in his country. Trying to show off, he has been pretending to bring many reforms that have been taboo in their religious traditions, such as women's driving, women singing in public, and allowing fatwa by women. His reforms have been confronted by strong opposition from religious scholars in the country. And I have heard that MBS is going to invest heavily in AI technology in Silicon Valley. Except Saudis and us, virtually the rest of the religious centers, who claim to follow Abraham, have responded and attacked our enemies, enemies who have announced our church as their first target. It's an embarrassment for us."

While His Excellency was busy talking, Peter Jr., who was sitting beside him, provided the bishops with publications of the religious centers that his boss just mentioned. Another bishop said, "Well, we can write a few lines and express our opinion on the alleged devilish attack on the credibility of the gospel. If by making a decision you meant this, I have no objection and agree with it."

"Of course, that's not the case," said His Excellency, using a softer voice. "We have been the main target of their attacks, and our reaction cannot be like them. We must certainly do more than what they have done. Otherwise, what would be the difference between them and us?"

James interrupted him again and interjected mockingly, "So what else can we do other than condemn them on paper? We cannot punish them."

"But condemnation without punishment is meaningless. It will be like letting a murderer who received a death sentence free at the end of his trial, saying, 'Goodbye,' and 'Go home,' only to see him kill again," said His Excellency calmly.

"I cannot believe what I hear," James said with a surprised look. "Your analogy is not real at all. Our condemnation is different from the condemnation of a judge in the court of law. Of course, we do not have the executive power. And we are also subject to obey civil law. Centuries have passed since the church had absolute power. It seems you do not believe in the separation of church and state."

Again, His Excellency said calmly, "Of course I don't. A true follower of Christ cannot see the power of God and Christ only among the four walls of the church or only in the minds of Christian believers. Of course, God and church are true power and absolute authority, both in this world and in the next. If the church does not already have this power, it does not mean that it will not seek it in the future. The state must belong to the church. If the church was not supposed to be the ruling power on earth and if it were meant only to be the authority in heaven, why did Jesus Christ establish the church on earth? It is not the church that should be allowed to exist from the generosity of the state. This is the church that should give the state a small portion to manage people's civic and municipal affairs."

Practically, as usual, the discussion turned into a two-person debate between His Excellency and James. In addition to the red color from the rush of blood on James's well-groomed face, his jugular veins were also raised with anger. James responded again, "Didn't the church once possess absolute power over religion and the government combined? So what happened then? Why did the church have to accept separation from the state? With your logic, all of Silicon Valley and San Francisco, like Sodom and Gomorrah, must be burned in the divine fire." James sneered after his last word.

His Excellency stared directly at James's eyes and said in a commanding tone, "James, I wonder how you are in such an important position. Firstly, the church that had abused its power once is not the same church that found its proper direction and position after the seventeenth century. Secondly, the current compromise by the church is just a temporary solution to abandon ruling the state for full control of the state of affairs in the future. About your last comment, no one knows; if that is the will of God, everything is possible, even the destruction of a city as large as San Francisco. Hasn't it happened in Sodom and Gomorrah before? Unless you, like those infidels, believe that the gospel has lied, or perhaps sediments of the so-called post-Evangelicals have penetrated into your mind."

Despite the fact that James was an eighty-one-year-old man, he stood up briskly. Anger and excitement made the old man, whose slow movements normally showed his age at meetings, in the blink of an eye stand at the conference room's exit door. Before leaving, James turned back and said to His Excellency, "You're brewing dangerous thoughts in your head. I cannot ever be a part of the responsibility for the events in the real world as the reflection of your perilous views." Then he went out.

His Excellency, with a loud voice aiming to reach James out of the room, shouted: "If it were up to you, the followers of Jesus Christ would be persecuted in this country, like in some parts of the world, but fortunately our influence is undeniable, even in the White House. Our power is comparable to no time in contemporary history."

The head of bishops stood silent. He knew that no one else was outside the conference room. However, he whispered something in Peter Jr.'s ear. Peter got up and went out and returned after a while and said, "The building door is locked, and no one is inside."

His Excellency was content with his two-party debate with James. He was hoping for it from the beginning. First, he pushed James out, and then he saw clear fear and obedience in the eyes of the remaining bishops in the room. From this moment on, it was easy for His Excellency to push his agenda. He only had to provide the necessary evidence to gain the bishops' agreement. He appointed two bishops in charge of drafting a response on behalf of the conservative Baptodist Church. It did not matter to His Excellency what kind of response would be given to the *Bay Area Chronicle*'s trifles. A word without action for His Excellency was like an insult in the air, devoid of importance.

What John Wesley the Third anticipated was action to strike at the enemy. Just as the enemies of God did not remain silent, they warded off the church's attacks now had Sara in their grip. His Excellency was sure that Sara would return to his arms someday, like Ibrahim's Sarai, who had been in the pharaoh's captivity for some time. He did not doubt God's command and the divine verdict. He had experienced it many times in his life. Why should the decree of the divine be otherwise this time? All that needed to be done was to listen to God and his son's command. Who cares about cowards like James, who would prefer to escape instead of staying and fighting at this crucial moment? In his view, if these eight lower servants of God who were now sitting in front of him had left the scene, as James did, he would be prepared to execute God's command single-handedly. His Excellency had always done so. He always thanked God for having provided so much wealth and resources, with which he could do anything in the church's interest and dignity.

His Excellency won the permission from the bishops who were present at the meeting to contact members of other Abrahamic religions. He knew that, in the event of an acute situation and higher level of locking horns with the enemy, the Baptodist Church could not see its condemnation by other religions. By engaging with other religious representatives directly in this matter, not only would such danger be prevented, but His Excellency could easily reach his goals in a coordinated chorus with those who have plenty of resources at their disposal besides claiming to follow Abraham. It was imperative to use the powers and resources of other religions in the event of a rare partnership. The Baptodist Church could easily defeat its enemies in harmony with other religions and display a show of patience and tolerance in cooperation with so-called religious rivals. From His

Excellency's point of view, as the ripe fruit begs to be picked, the time was right in every possible way.

The conservative church now had people in all small and large, private and public institutions, as well as the army and the police. Most importantly, there was nothing comparable to the Trump-Pence power in the White House. By pressing the psychological buttons in the personality of this narcissistic, egoistic president, it could obtain any assistance from him. And, of course, the priority for Trump would be to see the church members as reliable voters for his re-election campaign. In the case of impeachment, Mike Pence was church's favored candidate in the first place.

A week ago, by His Excellency's signal to the White House, the U.S. Ambassador to the United Nations voted against the resolution proposed by the United Nations Commission on Human Rights (UNCHR). The UNCHR in the resolution had objected to the death sentences of homosexuals in other countries, in particular the Middle East. The United States vote corresponded with the governments of Middle Eastern countries. With this vote, the church sent two messages to the LGBTQ community. One was the warning of the death penalty for committing such a sin, and the other was demonstrating the church's might.

Now, by referring to the influence of the church in the White House, His Excellency had subdued the bishops, and he quickly could gain whatever he wanted. The head of bishops told them he was planning to invite a representative of the Orthodox Church of Russia to visit the United States. He was a rising star who with the help of Vladimir Putin became the number one figure in the Orthodox Church of Russia. Reading some of Anthony Raspusky's writings, His Excellency felt a sense of affinity toward the new Rasputin in Russia. Even before the issue was raised at the bishops' meeting, Peter Jr. was asked by his boss to contact Raspusky.

In order to contact other religious representatives, Peter Jr. sent a message to the Shia religious authorities in Iran through the imam of the Houston mosque. Contacting the Catholic Church in Rome, the conservative rabbis in Jerusalem, and the Sunni authorities in Mecca was a bit more difficult. As for the Sunni religious representative of Islam, His Excellency had no trust in the country's prince crown. John Wesley the Third was afraid the whole plan would be exposed to the enemy due to the prince's ties to Silicon Valley. In the case of Israel, His Excellency did not want to contact government officials, although he knew that nothing could be hidden from the eyes of the Mossad agents.

His Excellency was very sensitive about the Catholic Church and especially Pope Francis. He was not happy with the actions and opinions of the new pope. Given the pope's friendly gesture toward LGBTQ people, His Excellency did not know what position he would take if he was informed about the current rift with the Sodom promoters. For this reason, Peter Jr. had been instructed to find the right person in the Vatican's circle of power and test the subject first. His Excellency had heard news about the power struggle in the Vatican recently.

In addition to all these actions that were merely communicated with the bishops, and receiving their tacit agreement, His Excellency also was talking about the sort of punishment that had not been clearly defined as to its method and nature. His Excellency was surprised that the bishops who were present at the meeting did not react negatively to the issue of the sinner's punishment. His Excellency attributed this phenomenon to his proper management of the session. In the end, John Wesley the Third thanked the other bishops and asked them to consider the subject extremely secret. He requested that no one to share any of this, not even a word with James.

# Chapter 51 – Doubts

"Hey, Tim, the stories of Sodom are getting better and better. How does Art tell you these stories?" asked Essie, sipping a glass of red wine and lounging on the sofa in Simone's apartment.

Sitting on the other side of an L-shaped sofa, holding a glass of red wine as well, Tim responded, "We use the app that you guys made in Tech2AI. Art clears some of my questions by phone, but in general, that app is our main line of communication."

"I was not a part of making that app," said Essie. "David himself wrote the algorithm. It's a total secure file sharing and messaging application that is capable of end-to-end encryption. No one, not even David, has the key to encrypt. There is no encryption key at all. I'm glad that you guys don't take a chance of being in one place. All of us have to be cautious and limit our visitation as much as possible."

Essie stopped talking. He did not know if he had been able to convey his intent to Tim tacitly. Tim had his eyes on his phone and did not react to Essie's last comment, but the message was received. Tim lifted his glass and took a sip. He became heavyhearted. Recently, Tim had no other joys except talking to Essie, writing, and reading fans or critics' comments about his column. He had never experienced this level of loneliness. Tim was no longer in the mood to go to parties or to meet his friends. He was surprised to see such behavioral changes in himself. Tim was deep in his thoughts when he finally heard Essie's voice asking, "Tim, I have a question: How much of Art's input goes into details narrating his observations to you? In some parts, I see descriptions that make me wonder if these are his words. Or did it come from the power of your writing?"

Tim paused for a few seconds. In the past, he would not hesitate to claim credit for a piece, but now, in response to Essie, he said: "It's mostly his. I don't know if Art went to every place or if he is just quoting King Bera. Sometimes I change the sequence of the stories, but I write almost all the details that Art tells me, which makes me wonder how he comes up with all of these details. Occasionally, I do minor corrections though."

Tim noticed that Essie was all ears. To increase the joy for Essie, he said, "I've prepared a few parts for upcoming issues that will be published soon, but I haven't submitted them yet. Do you want to take a look?"

Seeing Essie's reaction, Tim's hope was boosted for future visits with Essie. Tim pulled a small laptop computer from his bag, turned it on, and brought up the piece. A sense of pride grew in Tim as he saw Essie devour his article. Tim got busy with his phone and Essie started reading...

***

*Sodom Territory – Outside the City*

The horse soldiers and foot warriors in rows and columns covered a vast area on the outskirts of the city. Leah was riding Storm, her shiny black mare, trotting shoulder to shoulder alongside King Bera who was on horseback. They were heading toward the exercise field where the queue of warriors was awaiting their arrival. Despite the cool breeze, sweat droplets were apparent on the king's forehead from the heat of a sunny autumn day at noon. Twenty guards were riding horses around and behind the king and Leah. King Bera watched the rows of well-ordered warriors from afar, and told Leah, "We are witnessing a good discipline. Today, our fighters have to demonstrate their abilities, carrying it to the end of war game. The heads of other territories will join us to witness a showdown of our fighting power. Sichra informed me that everyone responded positively to our invitation."

The king apparently had forgotten Leah herself had arranged the entire exercise plan. Leah did not say anything. Part of Leah's attention was focused on controlling her mare. Storm could not endure the king's horse overtaking her. Leah pulled the horse's bit to hold her back a little. Storm became angry with her rider's move and pounded her hoofs on the ground, raising the dust. "Since early morning, everyone was deployed and prepared in a specific position," Leah said.

The king was still staring at the soldiers on the horizon. "It is also good for us to practice as the field commander," the king said. "I will be on the battlefield myself when the day comes. Taking Amim's revenge is now more important than everything else for me, but the soldiers and warriors are accustomed to your commands. You will be next to me on that day."

They arrived at the exercise field. The whole field stood in attention by order of a shouted command. King Bera looked over the soldiers from a higher level. The soldiers' queues were endless. At every row of fighters, a leader was standing outside. In the right corner of the field, the horses quietly waited to obey their riders' commands. Some horses were pulling their necks; however, on a broader scene, small moves were not so visible. At the beginning of the field, several tents were encamped to cater to the kings of other regions. Warmer air at noontime had attracted insects to the water and food inside the tents.

The first caravan of guests appeared from afar. King Bera dismounted and handed his horse to one of the guards. Leah dismounted as well, but she still was in possession of Storm's bit. She knew her mare would not accept someone else's hand. Leah had to take care of walking and strapping Storm's bridle herself. She followed the king into the tent after securing Strom. The king was sitting on an extended bench in the back of the tent. He was deep in his thoughts. As soon as the king saw Leah, he asked: "Don't you think we put everything in jeopardy by fighting Chedorlaomer, everything that we have built so far? What is your opinion?"

Leah was surprised. She did not expect to hear such a question immediately after stepping inside the tent.

"Sometimes it's not our choice; we have to fight. It's as if a force against our will pushes us toward a direction. And if we do not obey that force and refuse to face the enemy, we'll meet a pitiable destiny." Leah continued after a pause, "I have thought about this too. Indeed, what we have built in this city is unique. Now we have to prepare to defend this beautiful city with all our power to keep it safe."

King Bera had received a significant blow after representatives of the sister territories told him what had happened to Amim. The wise old man's consolations made King Bera calm a little, but he could not forgive himself for sending Amim to a deathtrap. The king had underestimated Chedorlaomer's turpitude, and for this reason, he constantly blamed himself. But now, as the sole supporter and promoter of the war against Elam, King Bera was wrestling with his doubts. In recent days, the king of Sodom had repeatedly asked in the council of advisers meeting, "Should I push into a war because of my vengeance? Are we rushing? Is it Amim's fate that forces me to start the war?"

The wise old man, Sichra, and Leah assured King Bera many times that engaging in the war was indeed not the decision of King Bera, but the result of atrocities by the king of Elam. They told Bera that the war had begun before what happened to Amim. Blocking the waterway to the valley of Siddim, especially Sodom and Gomorrah, had nothing to do with the king's revenge for his love.

However, before Bera would go to war with Chedorlaomer, he had engaged in a battle with himself. And on that day, the king knew that if he could not eliminate this doubt, he would not be able to persuade his guests, including the kings of Admah, Zeboiim, and Bella to participate in the war. Without joining the forces of other territories, such a critical war doubtlessly would lead to a defeat. Bera had been asking his advisers about his doubt in the last several days, and every time he heard the same answer, the king would fall into silence again. It was as if by asking his advisers, King Bera would get something off his chest, but then after listening to the responses, the doubt would enter his deep thoughts again.

Leah now was sitting in front of her beloved king, witnessing his deterioration, a king who was destroying himself by battling an internal fight. On his way back from visiting kings in Gomorrah, during which the decision was made to send an envoy to Elam, King Bera was surprised at Birsha's emotional behavior. And now he was demonstrating the same emotions differently. Doubtfulness was gnawing at him from the inside, this king whose reputation had resounded everywhere as a powerful yet gracious ruler. A leader whose name was the equivalent of justice both among his own people and others. A king whose quick yet sound decision was valued by people everywhere now had to make the most significant decision of his entire life under these particular circumstances.

Leah, the second most powerful person of Sodom after the king, hesitated to judge King Bera. She had seen how Bera was encountering the same curse Birsha did. In a short period, if not precisely like Birsha, King Bera had become frail. Leah was not afraid of the same fate, but she was so preoccupied with the complexity of the situation that she did not want to engage in futile thoughts. Leah thought about her responsibilities. At that crucial time, she knew that her job was more than just advising the king of Sodom. Leah knew that she was not only responsible for the control and security of Sodom; she knew that her role was more than just commanding warriors in the upcoming war. Leah knew the lives of all of Sodom's citizens, as well as people living in the valley of Siddim, depended on her leadership. Looking at the king sitting on the bench in the tent and thinking, Leah realized that in preparation for the upcoming battle, she could only rely on the wise old man and Sichra.

For a moment, she thought about Damaris. Leah had not seen her love for several days. Many tasks prevented her from visiting her. And when these pressures reached their highest point, she felt the need to be in the vicinity of Damaris badly. In those moments of loneliness, like when she was in Canaan or in Gomorrah attending the meeting of the kings, only being with her love would calm and energize Leah. But Damaris's very existence depended on Leah's leadership to save the whole kingdom.

Leah sat down on the bench next to the king. She put her left hand on the right hand of the king. King Bera raised his head and stared into Leah's eyes. It was as if he noticed for the first time that someone was sitting next to him. The king saw the peace in Leah's eyes.

"Leah, where do you get this peace from? You know we are gambling on everything. How can you be so calm?" asked Bera.

She pressed the king's hand. Leah wished she could have transferred some of her energy into the king's body by squeezing his hand. But she knew that the king needed more than her touch. After Amim, the king's soul was wounded. Chedorlaomer probably was aware of Amim's importance to Bera and hurt the king by hurting his love. What the king needed at that moment was an emotional treatment, which Leah was unable to give.

*Only two things cure the wounds caused by separation of two lovers: the return of the loved one and time,* neither of which was now possible for King Bera. There was no news from Amim, and Sodom had no time to wait, given the rapidly unfolding events.

After the return of the delegation from Elam, various stories were heard about Amim's fate. It was not clear where these stories were coming from. Leah tried to block rumors from reaching the king. The report, given by members of the delegation, about Chedorlaomer's severing Amim's tongue and the news of Achan's death had shaken Sodom and Gomorrah. The shock was so formidable that had broken the kings of two territories.

The wise old man and Sichra entered the tent. Bowing, they showed their respect to the king of Sodom. Staring at the void, Bera did not see the arrival and tribute of the newcomers. "Welcome, we are ready, and we are just waiting for the guests to get started," Leah said in order to draw the king's attention to the wise old man and Sichra who were looking at each other.

The king raised his head and smiled. "They are almost here," said Sichra.

The wise old man sat beside Bera, and Sichra sat down next to Leah. The wise old man first looked at the king and then into Leah's eyes. He immediately looked back at Bera's profile and said, "My king, it is vital for us to persuade other kingdoms to participate in this critical war. I would suggest you let Leah command the warriors in today's practice which is taking place in the presence of our guests, and you get a firm commitment from them to contribute their combat forces in the upcoming battle."

The king nodded in agreement. A guard appeared at the front of the tent and told Leah, "Several caravans are approaching in the distance."

Leah, Sichra, and the wise old man stood up and went outside the tent. The wise old man looked at the horizon from right to left. After the autumn's afternoon breeze caressed the old man's newly trimmed white beard, he realized that the air was stuffy inside the tent. He turned to two women standing beside him, and asked: "Are they all fighters that we can mobilize against Chedorlaomer?"

Leah replied, "Almost, plus some volunteers who are now in the city."

Sichra asked, "How about Lot's people? Are they among those we can use in the battle? They are now considered inhabitants of Sodom. It will be a good test to measure their loyalty."

Leah winced and said, "I do not trust them at all, especially Lot and his daughters. I sense mischievous intentions around them. I don't have a good feeling about them. On my visit to Canaan, the chief of their tribe avoided visiting me intentionally. They said that he had gone out to the desert to contact a powerful force that cannot be seen by anyone. I felt that even his wife had some untold secrets to tell me."

Listening to Leah's story, the wise old man rubbed his forehead and said, "I have also heard a lot about Abraham. As people say, he is a powerful man who influences all his people. This is also a kind of ruling method. Lot's wife says Abraham was very close to her daughters, much closer than to his nephew. Most likely, those men who were going to enter the city at night without permission had messages from Abraham for Lot's girls."

Leah looked at the old man with respect and praise. She said, "I guessed this too, but I'm not sure. They are all silent. What can we do in this situation? Everything is going on so fast, and addressing these issues will prevent us from our main problems, Chedorlaomer, and war."

"How about asking Abraham to send fighters to help us in this battle?" The wise old man asked. "His relatives would eventually be in danger if we are defeated."

Leah responded, "We do not have much time. The war is approaching fast. Our water reserve is limited. We cannot wait for more. I have a report indicating that Chedorlaomer has amassed his forces and met with his allies in Amraphel, Goiim, and Ellasar. All four territories entered into a war pact. But if our allies come to our aid with all their might, we can defeat them."

The first caravan belonging to King Birsha was approaching the top of the hill where the guests' tents encamped and where three of

Bera's advisers were waiting. Tents were set on top of the hill, overlooking the plain, where fighters and horse soldiers were organized in rows and columns. In the far back and to the left, a clump of trees separated the grassland from the small forest behind it. This was the grassland where the fighting exercise was about to begin.

Birsha's royal carriage arrived at the front of the tent where King Bera's advisers were standing to welcome the king of Gomorrah. The four panting horses that were pulling the carriage had foam at their mouths. Birsha and then Edna stepped out of the carriage and were welcomed by Bera's advisers. Sichra approached Eden, and everyone entered the tent. King Bera came forward and embraced Birsha. They stayed in the same hugging position for a few moments. The rest were silently watching the two kings. Birsha whispered something into Bera's ear. Sichra came close to the wise old man, stood next to him, and said, "This scene reminds me of the story that you asked me to tell King Birsha before."

Watching the two kings in front of him, still embracing in sorrow, the wise old man nodded in confirmation. Then he replied quietly, "What I purposely omitted from the story was that the stranger, who whispered into the king's ear, was himself a king in the past."

Sichra shivered. She looked at the wise old man and asked, "What is the ending? What happens to the two kings at the end?"

"We will see, we will see," replied the old man.

# Chapter 52 – Dungeon

Essie looked at Tim. Tim noticed and looked back at Essie. The young writer detected a looming question in the face of the man for whom he had great respect. For a moment, Tim hesitated to ask his opinion about the story. He could not read satisfaction or displeasure in Essie's look at all. Tim expected any question or interpretation except the one that Essie threw at him: "Do you know Rumi? Have you read any of his work? I guess you've heard his name, right?"

"The Persian poet, Rumi?" asked Tim.

"Yes. Of course, Rumi is far more than just a poet. His life story is amazing. He was a philosopher, thinker, and a Sufi," replied Essie.

Tim said, "My father once gave me a hardcopy of his book as a gift, designed with golden lines on its cover and miniature paintings on the inside pages. I read several lines of his poem and never touched it again. I don't think my dad had read it either. Why do you ask?"

As if Essie were warming up to his favorite discussion, he continued, "It's so weird. I saw a couple of plots in Art's ... well, your stories resembling Rumi's. Like that stranger who whispered something in the young king's ear, causing the king to give up his throne. It's somewhat similar to the story of Bera and Birsha. It's not quite the same though, as in Rumi's story the king and stranger go to towns with their mystical view of begging to follow the path of contentment. The more similar example is the story of the bean narrated by the wise old man. In Rumi's story it's a chickpea."

Tim replied, "Really? I didn't know. I never read anything from Rumi. I thought he was only a poet."

Toying with his mustache with his thumb and index finger, Essie said with a smirk on the corner of his lips, "He was a storyteller, expressing his stories in the form of poetry. In that era, poetry was the only form to express opinions or stories. He was also believed to be a gay man."

"Really?" wondered Tim.

Essie poured more wine to fill his glass, and continued, "There are many narratives in this regard, some countering this narrative. Rumi was an Islamic scholar and a well-known character of his time. However, when he meets a man named Shams, he falls in love with him instantly and madly. He even brings Shams to his home to live under the pretext of marrying his stepdaughter. It's rumored that Rumi's sons killed Shams to preserve the family's honor and told their father that Shams had left him. Rumi leaves home and, seeking Shams, he becomes a wanderer in towns, cities, and other countries for many years, but he never finds him."

Tim said, "Wow, so sad and utterly interesting! I never heard of it. In the last part of the series, I wrote about Birsha and Bera's fate. See how close it is to the Rumi story about the stranger and the king."

Essie put Tim's computer on his lap again and continued to read…

***

*Elam Territory – A Dungeon Underground*

For a few days, Tabitha did not know that in a hole next to the cell where she was locked up another person was breathing. On the third day, she heard a sound like moaning, indicating the feebleness of its source. At first, Tabitha thought that an animal was dying somewhere very close. Tabitha had no idea where she was and where the moaning was coming from.

After the queen had burst into the meeting during which Arshum was killed and her husband cut out Amim's tongue, guards brought Tabitha to the hole that she was now in and shut the door on her. It was a filthy place where the smell of urine, blood, and stench mixed with fear and created a dreadful atmosphere. Tabitha thought she would get used to the stink after a while, but she did not. After a few days, she was still disgusted by the reek of her surroundings. A little light from a distance was gleaming. The light, which barely illuminated the space in Tabitha's cell, was coming from a torch in the main hall where the guards were stationed. The guards brought the queen to the dungeon through a secret pathway that she had never seen before, one like the secret passage from the kitchen to the outside of the palace but with a different entry. Tabitha could not hear any sound except occasional voices from the guards and the animal that was moaning nonstop. She felt that she was kept imprisoned in a place hidden deep underground.

The groans were gradually turning into human cries. Suddenly, Tabitha thought of Amim. "No," she thought, "It cannot be him, the man whose tongue my husband severed."

The queen had seen everything with her eyes. To scare the queen, Chedorlaomer ordered the guards to force her to keep her eyes open and watch. Chedorlaomer suspected that the story of Achan and Queen Tabitha was more than what Arshum told him in his mumbling and gesturing language. Arshum had somehow explained to the king that Achan was going to kill the queen, and that was why he had to kill the young man immediately. Tabitha had said nothing to her husband about the incident. But the king's face showed his skepticism, that he never believed Arshum's story. After that, the only thing that Tabitha could do was to weep, on Achan's, Arshum's, and her own fate. She had cried more over Achan's doom for all his capability and feelings. Tabitha remembered Achan's face with his extruding eyes at the last moment of his life. He had a surprised look rather than the look of someone who was struggling for air. Every time she remembered that scene, it would make her weep to the point of exhaustion.

That day, Tabitha had overheard the negotiations between the delegation and her husband from outside the king's chamber. From Chedorlaomer's tone, she realized that her husband had no intention of negotiating with the delegation members. The queen had heard Amim from the adjacent room. She had no idea who Amim was. While listening to their conversation, Tabitha found out that Amim was the king of Sodom's lover. Behind the curtain, her mind depicted a human image like Achan who was courageously debating Chedorlaomer. But when she entered the chamber, Amim's impression was imprinted on her mind, despite what happened quickly. Tabitha saw that Amim was utterly different from Achan. Then, everything happened so fast: Arshum was killed, Chedorlaomer severed Amim's tongue, and she was transferred to the dungeon, where she was imprisoned now, searching for the source of the strange sound.

When Tabitha realized that the source of groaning was not an animal, she called the probable name, "Amim, Amim."

Apparently, every time Amim became conscious, he fainted after a few moments. Tabitha was thrilled when she found out that there was an unconscious man who was on the ground behind the wall. She thought, "Perhaps the guards beat him so hard he cannot move. Maybe another prisoner is there, and I called Amim's name in vain." She shouted again with a loud voice: "Hey, what's your name?"

After a while, Tabitha heard someone's mumbling, a mixture of groans and inaudible words behind the wall. Clearly, the person was responding to her now. She tried again, "Amim, are you there?"

Again an inaudible sound came back from behind the wall. She understood that Amim had responded. Suddenly, Tabitha also realized that Amim could not talk.

"I am Queen Tabitha, the one who interrupted your meeting that day and informed you that Achan was murdered."

Tabitha heard a voice on the other side of the wall. She heard something different from before. The queen sensed that Amim had acknowledged his identity. Tabitha heard the guard approaching and told Amim to be silent. The guard opened the door with a torch in his hand. He had brought a piece of bread and a bowl of water. Tabitha covered her eyes, which were irritated by the light of the torch, and said, "The other prisoner is in pain; give him a sip of water."

The guard did not say anything, and when he was about to exit, Tabitha said again, "Did you hear what I said? Give him water and bread. I do not want it, give it to him."

The guard stopped. Looking at Tabitha's uncleaned face, he replied, "It seems that you do not understand you are no longer the queen of Elam."

"I am still the queen of Elam and the daughter of Shinar, the king of Amraphel. Is anyone else standing outside?"

The guard stayed silent, and after a moment said in a lower voice, "No, no one is here."

"If you take me out of here, outside of the palace, and if I can reach Amraphel, I will make you a needless man in life."

The queen heard the heavy footfall of another guard approaching her cell. The first guard closed the door and left without saying anything. Tabitha heard the first guard order the approaching guard, "Bring water and a piece of bread for the other cell. The king wants him alive."

Tabitha realized that her promise had found its way into the guard's mind. She smiled and waited for the guards to leave, and then called

Amim. She did not hear any sound in return. Tabitha guessed that he fainted again. She was confident that he would regain consciousness. Amim's unstoppable groaning and his presence next to her revived the light of hope in Tabitha's heart in that dark and lonely dungeon. She remembered the guard's reaction to her request. A flash of joy sparked inside her. Tabitha had not felt that kind of joy since Achan had flown away from her life.

# Chapter 53 – Wandering Kings

> Then the king of Sodom, the king of Gomorrah, the king of Admah, the king of Zeboiim, and the king of Bela went out, and they joined battle in the Valley of Siddim.
> With King Chedorlaomer of Elam, King Tidal of Goiim, King Amraphel of Shinar, and King Arioch of Ellasar, four kings against five. —Book of Genesis [14:8–9]

*Valley of Siddim – Battlefield*

Panting hard, King Bera reached the hilltop and threw himself down. There were two deep wounds on his right arm and left thigh. The king had not noticed how and where he became injured. Bera felt an extreme burning sensation from his right shoulder to the elbow. He had slid down, and now looked up at the hilltop. There was no trace of Birsha. King Bera shouted, "Birsha, Birsha."

When he did not hear any response, Bera pulled himself back up toward the hilltop. The king's left leg was not complying with him, so he had to drag it in pain. At the peak, he looked down the other side: Birsha had fallen on his abdomen, not too far from the top. Bera crawled down the hill and, after reaching Birsha, tried to turn him over.

Grunting, the king of Gomorrah rolled over and lay on his back. Birsha saw King Bera's face looking at him from above. Bera grabbed Birsha's arm and said, "Only a few more steps left, get up."

Half-raised, Birsha tried to stand up but fell back on the slope and slid down a little lower. Bera grabbed his arm again and while pulling him up, said, "Try to move on your knees, like this."

King Bera looked down over the plain. The sun was fading through the dust raised in the air, sinking into an unclear line on the horizon. In the distance, the dust in the sky marked what happened or was still in progress on the battlefield. At that moment, King Bera did not want to think about what went wrong. Strange things had happened in the arena. Not only he had not anticipated them, but his mind could not process them.

Now, Bera only had to take Birsha to the hilltop. A trickle of blood was still observable on Birsha's neck. The dirt and the blood, coagulated around the wound, made it hard for Bera to find the exact depth of the injury. He rubbed the wound gently. The pain jittered Birsha. Bera examined the wound. It was not too deep. Again, he took Birsha's arm and pulled him up the hill to the top. After they reached the top, King Bera pushed Birsha to the other side. The distance to the bottom did not seem to be far. The sand dunes also did not pose a danger. But when King Bera pushed Birsha down and then skidded himself downward, he realized that contrary to what he thought it was not a short distance at all. At any moment Bera was expecting to reach the bottom only to roll down farther with no end in sight. Bera had shut his eyes and mouth to prevent the sand from entering. He opened his eyes only once and shut them instantly.

***

King Bera saw the battlefield. He did not comprehend where the blow came from. Since the early morning, the fog had fallen on the plains and surrounding areas, but the visibility was not obscured entirely. Around noon, his men, Sodom's warriors, attacked and split the enemy's front lines under the king and Leah's commands. Everything was going according to plan, as King Bera plotted with Leah, Edna, and Gomorrah's commanders. King Bera was in the middle of the battlefield. Suddenly, the king saw some of his men looking back, and he heard yelling from behind. Bera could not tell from where they were being struck. Sodom's forces were attacked from the rear and left side of the field. The enemy's fighters on horses had approached where Bera and Leah never thought possible. Before that ambush, Sodom and its allies had been advancing, and the war was about to be easily won. Sodom's army was hit from the area that had been secured by Admah and Bella's forces. The Sodom and Gomorrah fighters were responsible for attacking the enemy's front line to advance, and others were in charge of protecting the rear to prevent counterattacks by Chedorlaomer's forces. It was impossible for Elam and its allies to be positioned behind them. But the impossible happened. From the southwest, left and back of the field, enemy fighters pushed forward and struck Sodom and Gomorrah's forces.

The fog became thicker than before. The white curtain fell on the plain and covered everything. King Bera had seen Leah, who was riding on her shiny black mare, eradicating the enemy. He remembered that Storm, Leah's horse, bent its two front legs and threw her rider on the ground. Bera did not see Leah afterward. He dismounted his horse and tried to run toward Leah, but Elam's soldiers attacked him, and he fought back. After Bera subdued the attackers, dirt sprayed on his face and eyes from the hooves of a galloping horse. The king could not see anything for some moments. He sat on the ground. Bera had expected a poke or strike on his head or somewhere on his body at any moment. But it did not happen. He rubbed his eyes with two hands, trying to wipe the dirt off his face. When Bera opened his eyes again, he found that the combination of dust, thick fog, and mist in the air was such that it limited his visibility to only a few steps around him. At times, someone would suddenly appear from the fog, and the king would know how to react quickly. In the distance, King Bera could discern the sound of clanking swords, whining, and screaming. He tried to recognize the location of Leah by remembering the shadow of the sun's position in the sky when his top commander had fallen. Suddenly, a trotting horse appeared through the haze, dragging his unconscious rider whose foot was stuck in the stirrup. Bera went forward and recognized Birsha. He clutched the horse's reins. There was a blow to Birsha's neck and head. Bera shook Birsha, but he was unconscious. He released Birsha's foot from the stirrup. At this moment, an enemy's soldier approached from behind. King Bera raised the sword to the chest of the attacker, who threw himself on the kings. The offender was killed and fell on Bera. He shoved the bleeding enemy aside. The blood of the fallen man had warmed the king's neck. He lifted Birsha's arm and dragged him to the opposite side of the battlefield. As they got farther away from the battlefield, the screaming and the clanking of the swords was disappearing.

***

King Bera regained his consciousness. He had been lying at the bottom of the hill. Trying to lift his head to look around, the king felt a sharp pain from below his right ear to his shoulder. He found Birsha who had fallen on the ground the distance of a few spears away. The king scanned the path they had used to come down the hill. He found no stone or sharp objects that could have caused his pain. His sword was missing. It must have been lost somewhere in the midst of rolling down the hill.

King Bera could not guess how long he had been there. It was getting dark. He felt the cold air on his skin, through his armor and clothing. He went to Birsha and shook him again. The king of Gomorrah moved, opened his eyes slowly, and said, "What happened? Where are our guards?"

"I do not know yet. We will find out soon; we have to move," King Bera said with a determined voice, extending his hand to Birsha. He said, "You look much better than before."

Birsha held Bera's hand and got halfway up. He was shivering from the cold and exhaustion. They moved together in the direction Bera was guiding them. It was completely dark now. King Bera could barely drag his left foot. They both lost their swords and did not even know if their crown and throne were still at home. The king of Sodom had only a dagger on him.

"We have to go to the other side. I saw trees around there. We have to get ourselves to a safe place and spend the night," said Bera.

Falling and rising again, the two kings were on a path and neither knew where it ended. Sometimes, one would fall to be lifted by the other, and sometimes both would tumble and stay on the ground motionless. The clouds were gone, and there was no trace of the fog. The night had added to the nipping cold of autumn in the desert. Their survival depended on moving forward. Since they began moving on the hillside, when it became dark, they had fallen a hundred times or more. Sometimes a creature that was seen only as a shadowy animal figure would creep by. Several times, too, snakes had crawled by and quickly escaped from under their feet.

For some time, both kings were face down and passed out on the ground. In the darkest time of the world, these two kings had come a long way to find the light, not just in this plain, but swept across the universe. Sometimes, they would fall into sleep, and sometimes they were up and on the go, and still amid the darkness and the starry sky. And the only hope each had at that moment was the presence of the other on his side.

"Are you awake, Bera?" Birsha asked.

"Yes," replied Bera.

Birsha said, "I have never seen the sky like this. Stars seem to be falling on us, like sleek daggers."

Bera responded, "Yes, I see it; as if the only open and clear way is a path to the sky. I just remembered the connection of thoughts. Were all those connections in vain? Was there no connection at all?"

"This long night, no matter how long, will pass too," Birsha rose up on his elbows after saying that last word. Although King Bera could not see clearly Birsha, he found that his companion was half-raised.

"What happened, Birsha? Did you hear anything?" asked Bera.

"I just remembered a story that shook me to the core." Bera did not say anything and just waited for his friend to continue. "Your wise old man sent me a story through Sichra. I recall that day well. You sent Sichra and Amim to deliver information about the refugees who had arrived at Sodom's gate," said Birsha.

"I remember, and after Gomorrah, they both went to other territories," Bera said it fast to hear the rest of the story.

"Yes, that day, Achan was there too. Sichra narrated the wise old man's story, which impressed me, but it was an unfinished story," Birsha added.

"I remember that Sichra told me something about it; I do not recall the story," said Bera.

Birsha spoke enthusiastically, "In short, the wise old man told the story of a stranger who went to a kingdom and requested to meet with the king. As soon as the king accepted the stranger in his chamber, the man whispered something in the king's ear, and then the happy and wealthy king accompanied the stranger in wandering deserts and unknown places."

"Well, what happened at the end?" asked King Bera.

The king of Gomorrah stayed silent without any sound or movement. Bera asked again, "Where did they go, what happened next, are you up?"

"Yes, now everything makes sense to me. Do you remember a while ago when you had invited us and our allies to see the fighting practice? You encouraged Zoar and Shinab to participate in the battle?" responded Birsha.

"Yes, it was not a long time ago," Bera said.

"We came first, and when I arrived at the tent where you were, I whispered something to your ear, remember?"

Bera responded positively, waiting for Birsha to continue.

"Do you remember what I murmured into your ear?" Birsha said.

"No, not exactly, it just made me feel good about your presence there at that moment."

Birsha continued, "On the same day, the wise old man had a chance to remind me of the same story. He told me something that roused my curiosity. He told me that the stranger who went to the king's chamber and whispered in his ear was himself a king. I asked the wise old man what wisdom is behind this story, and he narrated the rest, and now I am enlightened about what that wisdom was. It sparked in me like a flash of lightning."

Bera whose eyes were half-closed, opened his eyelids and moved a bit with Birsha's last word. Then he asked, "What was that wisdom? I'm a little confused."

Birsha, as if liveliness had come back to him, continued, "The wise old man said that he had dreamed this story several times with variations, and in the last one he saw that the kings who had been lost in the desert would eventually be able to find themselves. Do you understand what it means?"

King Bera fell asleep again for a moment and jumped to Birsha's question, "Not much, I'm muddled."

Birsha said, "We are those wandering kings and we will eventually find ourselves."

"What do you mean by we find ourselves? Will we find our way back to our palaces?"

Birsha responded, "I do not know exactly myself what he meant by finding ourselves. But when I remembered that story again, suddenly something indescribable was ignited inside me."

A beam of light appeared on the horizon. Bera fell asleep completely, and Birsha sat where he was. Now he could recognize the outline of his friend's body asleep nearby. The brightness of the stars was fading quickly. Birsha looked around. They were close to the trees that Bera told him about before. It was not far. The king of Gomorrah closed his eyes where he sat. He felt as if something went out of his body, that part of his being was extracted. The feeling of unity with all that was around embraced him: unity with everything, the fading stars above and sands that he was sitting on, Bera who was sleeping there, the battlefield that they had fled from, and the pre-dawn light whose brightness he could sense with his closed eyes. He had no pain, no burnt skin, and no hunger. At that time, Birsha felt the most desirable sensation. He felt that he found himself. He had found himself. He did not know what it was, but he understood the concept of the wise old man's message. Birsha felt Achan at his side. Not just in his imagination; King Birsha could sense the presence of Achan very close. Birsha saw his love again. Achan's figure was so real that it would rule out any delusional thought. He wondered if it was all a dream. No, he was not asleep. He knew he was not asleep. The king of Gomorrah had spent the days and hours with Achan, and now he felt the same sensation.

A voice brought Birsha to his senses. He looked at Bera who still was asleep or may have fainted. He looked at the direction the sound came from. Two limping men were walking along the path to the trees, which was the kings' destination. He dragged himself to where Bera was and woke him up slowly. Birsha could not recognize the men's identity from afar. King Bera rubbed his eyes and squinted. They were warriors of Sodom. The newly arrived men had not yet seen the kings. Bera stood up and called them. The men approached and paid tribute to the kings after finding out who they were. King Bera asked, "What happened? Where are you going?"

One of the warriors glanced at the other and lowered his head. They both were injured. Their feet were bleeding. They were carrying their swords, and their faces were covered with dust and mud. One of the men raised his head and said, "We were defeated. We lost the battle." For a moment, he became silent and then continued, "Most of our men were killed, and the others were captured. And some of us were able to escape."

A sound was heard from the distance among the trees. Birsha said, "Let's go over to that forest, apparently more people are in that tiny forest."

# Chapter 54 – Last Supper

> When evening came, Jesus was reclining at the table with the Twelve. And while they were eating, he said, "Truly I tell you, one of you will betray me." —Matthew 26:20–21

*Atlanta and San Francisco – Various locations*

His Excellency had not been able to close his eyes the night before. He was in a pivotal moment in his life, when he had to make a critical decision. As usual, His Excellency followed through with obeying the Lord. There was no other choice but moving toward God's will. He had already submitted to God's order, putting the knife on his Isaac's throat. He passed that step and the commandment of God to start curing his son. Now, he had another hard decision to make. For this decision, dozens of people might perish. But His Excellency had no fear when the divine plan was at work, and the benefit is the benefit of God, not his servants.

The head bishop of the Baptodist Church had considered only love as the basis of such a great decision, not the worldly type of love, not the one that infected the impurity of contemporary humans. He would recognize only the words of Jesus who learned, experienced, and taught the love, the infinite love, the Lord's love. His Excellency believed that even among the highest rank of the Lord's servants, only a few came close to the true meaning of love, let alone understanding or experiencing it. Only Jesus Christ understood love and displayed it on the cross by sacrificing himself. After him, no one was born able to discover the deep secret of love. At these moments, the only thing His Excellency was thinking about was love.

John Wesley the Third did not comprehend the meaning of love during formal education from his religious instructors. It was even stranger to him that love had poked into his soul through someone whom he had not seen or heard. Just one poke, like a chicken pecking seed, was enough. Since then his soul was infested with love. His Excellency had found the whole mystery of love in a section of the book *The Brothers Karamazov*, in which a woman goes to Father Zosima, confessing to her sin. She had killed her husband in his sickbed, fearful that if he recovered he would start beating and oppressing her again.

At that moment, Father Zosima told her that God loves everyone, including sinners. A sinner who knows she has sinned in front of the Lord is closer to God than a faithful saint in heaven. His Excellency had written somewhere in his notebook, "The love creates the sin and love washes it all. Inside everyone, this is the love that creates the lowest and best qualities, the same love that Christ had presented to humanity and was sacrificed for its teaching. The son was sacrificed for the immortal love of the Father on earth." And His Excellency believed that he owed his unique understanding of love to Dostoevsky. Among all the branches of Christianity, after the Evangelical Church, His Excellency felt closest to the Eastern Orthodox Church.

Once, before John's incident, after which their family relationships disintegrated, Sara had challenged her husband in a conversation on this issue. She said, "You know that Father Zosima in the book, contrary to your presumption from his opinions, was a symbol of tolerance against the extreme and conservative views of the Orthodox Church." Proving her point, Sara found several quotes from the same book for her husband. His Excellency, angry and humiliated, never spoke to his wife about that topic again, and he continued to believe and preach his conviction about love.

For several weeks, John Wesley the Third had persuaded church leaders to act against the enemy. He had everyone on his side, either implied or by vote, except James. His Excellency did not understand James's insistence. His argument and opposition were obvious, but the head bishop believed that the motive behind James's persistence against the mainstream was his own personal interest. His Excellency had not revealed the details of his plan to the rest of the bishops. He said only that the enemy of the Lord must feel the pressure. There was no alternative; they could wait no longer. His Excellency had to order the start of the operation.

Peter Jr. had worked with his boss on the details of the project for the last several days. Everything was ready. They tried not to involve the church in the matter as much as possible. They sought help from one of the most trained right-wing groups and outsourced their work to prevent the Baptodist Church from taking any blame. Only Peter Jr. would be in touch with members of that group without showing any affiliation with His Excellency or the church. Individuals of each specific operation were instructed by their superiors about their duties. In addition to continuous contact with the leader of each group, Peter Jr. personally reviewed the details of each operation several times in advance to prevent any unexpected complications.

***

One of the four passengers in the blue 2013 Chevrolet Express van that was parked on the street looked at his watch. It was midnight. The man turned to the rest of the group and said, "Let's go, it's time."

Four tall, strong men, wearing black jumpsuits, got out of the van and walked to the building's main entrance to ascend to the third floor, where Simone's apartment was located. The car was parked a few steps from the building. One of the men was carrying a large sports bag.

Another man, walking faster, went to the building door and opened it quickly with the tools in his hand. The street was quiet. The last man waited to check the security of the area around the building, then he stepped inside. The stinging, cruel wind of the December night in San Francisco had cleared the street of all creatures, so the group was able to enter the building without being seen. After entering the building and before climbing the four steps leading to the ground floor, all of them donned fabric masks to cover their faces. Only two eyes and a mouth were visible behind the masks. On the first floor, similar to a hotel hallway layout, the doors were facing each other. At that time of night, the only sound was soft music coming from one of the apartments, but all the doors were closed. To their right, there was a doorway which led to the stairway.

They moved quickly to the right and entered the staircase. The man carrying the bag put it down, unzipped it, and took out several guns equipped with silencers. He handed them to the others one by one. Despite their heavy build, the men were taking agile steps quietly up the staircase. One was ahead, and two, walking alongside each other, were following his lead. The man on the left was checking the upper floors through the staircase gap. The fourth person was following the others five steps behind. They reached the third floor, and the man who was moving in front of the others opened the door. He peeked into the hall and, after ensuring that there was no one there, signaled the rest to follow him. They turned right and stopped in front of the fourth door on the right side. One of them used a special device to hear if there was any sound coming from the inside. He gestured with his hand to indicate there was no sound. The top part of the door was decorated with a golden metallic number, 304. The man who opened the downstairs door pulled out two sticks of metal from the side pocket of his pants and quickly started to unlock the door. The second man pulled out two cans and two syringes from the inside the bag. He kept one syringe and handed the other one to the third man. The person who was working on the lock opened the door slowly and all four men crept into the apartment.

They quietly closed the door. The kitchen was on the left side, and the living room was at a slight angle to the right. A small nightlight on the ceiling illuminated a little area in the kitchen. The light from the street shone through from behind the shutters and made the living room a bit visible. On the right was a small corridor leading to the bedroom which was across from the bathroom. One of the men went into the living room and the second stayed in the kitchen. The remaining two were ready to go into the corridor, planning to burst into the bedroom, when a toilet flush was heard from the bathroom. One of them signaled the other to stop and wait.

The door to the bathroom opened and Simone emerged, turned the light off, stepped across the corridor, and entered the bedroom, shutting the door behind her. The commander pointed to the others to move ahead. They stood in front of the bedroom. Two men were positioned on either side of the bedroom door. A slice of light was shining from underneath. Both men paused by the door. The other two men in the kitchen and living room stood in the corridor behind them, taking out items from inside the bag. By nodding, the commander received confirmation that everyone was ready to storm into the bedroom. On the count of four, using his fingers, the commander ordered the attack. One of the men kicked the door open, and all swarmed inside the bedroom.

Essie and Simone were in bed. Frightened, Simone screamed at the top of her lungs. Shocked, Essie, with his eyes popping, tried to jump out of bed. One of the attackers hurtled forward and hit Essie's face with the back of his gun. Essie fell back on the bed. Another man pointed his gun at Simone's forehead. Essie lifted his head and watched while holding his hand over his wounded face. The commander of the operation warned Essie, "If you say or do anything, we'll pop her brain out."

Essie looked at Simone's frightened face. The commander ordered one of his men, "Tie his hands."

Upon receiving the order, the man went to Essie, laid him face down on the bed, and tied his hands behind him with a white zip tie. The commander signaled to the person who pointed the gun toward Simone to stand down. The man lowered his gun. Essie stared at both the man and at Simone. Simone looked away and, lowering her head, stood up and said, "They promised me that you wouldn't hurt him and that nothing bad would happen to him."

The commander replied, "Depends on what the definitions of hurt and bad things are."

"You promised me," said Simone with a sad voice. She continued louder, avoiding Essie's look, "Your boss promised."

The commander responded, "Nothing happens to him now. We have orders to take him alive."

The way Essie was positioned on the bed, he could barely see half of Simone's face and body where she was talking to the man. Essie's mind could not process Simone's conversation with the invaders' commander. He had lost his ability to analyze what was unfolding in front of him. Essie did not believe what he was hearing. Expecting to wake up any second, Essie thought he was asleep and having a nightmare, or those people, including Simone, were performing a funny play for him. Other than that, what else could it be? He repeated in his mind, "No, it's impossible."

One of the men stood by Essie and poked the tip of a syringe into his neck, injecting its contents into him. As Essie faded into unconsciousness, he heard the commander's voice from behind saying, "We also have to inject you."

Essie passed out. The commander stepped toward the window and looked outside through the shutter. The man who gave Essie the injection went to Simone. Simone lifted her left arm and looked at the needle as it was inserted into her skin. Then she lay down on the bed and slept.

***

In another location, a big blue Chevy van was parked on the opposite side of the Get Cool Bar. A cartoon of a smiling plumber had been painted on the van's back door, showing off the size of his Stillson wrench. In large white letters, "Piping the sky" was written on both sides of the van. Inside, in the rear compartment, a man was holding a sniper rifle with a mounted scope on its top, targeting the door of the bar across the street. The man was monitoring the customer traffic through a sniper scope. He saw a few customers go into the bar; after a while, someone came out. Without taking his eye off the camera, the sniper, who was wearing black jumpsuit, dried his sweaty right palm on his chest. For a moment, the man took his eyes off the camera and looked at the photo that was placed next to him. It was Tim's picture. The sniper put his eyes back on the scope and focused its lens. The bar door opened, and Tim walked out. He pulled up the collar of his long coat to block the cold air on his face. Tim turned to the left and put his hands into his pockets. His head was the target of the sniper scope. When Tim's temple was at the intersection of the plus sign inside the lens of the sniper rifle, the sniper pulled the trigger. Tim fell to the ground. The gunman put the rifle on the van's floor, slid forward from inside, and climbed behind the wheel. Without any hesitation, the killer turned on the car and took off.

***

Melody's silver X5 SUV pulled into their driveway, and the garage door rolled up. David stepped out of the driver seat and walked around the front of the car to the other side where Melody was sitting. He opened the door and Melody stepped out and kissed his lips. Melody shuddered in the freezing wind of the late winter night, a chill that passed through layers of clothing and penetrated to the bone. David said, "Get in before you catch a cold. I'm coming."

Melody ran through the darkness and disappeared into the back of the garage to enter the house. After closing the passenger door, David went to the back, opened the door, and grabbed his briefcase. Then he walked to the driver side and picked up his phone from under the dashboard below the radio and control panel. He closed the door and went inside from where Melody had gone.

Across the street, a little distance from their house, a large blue van had parked. On both sides of the van's was written the same trademark, "Piping the sky." Two men in black jumpsuits were observing the arrival of the couple. The driver asked the man sitting next to him in the passenger seat, "Is it time?"

"No, wait. Not yet," replied the man who seemed to be a higher rank.

About 10 yards from where the Chevy had parked, the porch light of a house went on. Both men inside the van sank down into their seats. A teenage boy wearing sweatpants and a thin jacket came out of the house. He had a single cigarette and a lighter in his hand. Apparently, his body warmth prevented him from feeling the wintry chill outside. With the cigarette on his lip, he walked away from the house a little and came close to the street curb. The van's passengers could see in the spark of the lighter the boy's young face as well as the cigarette. The boy sucked a few quick puffs. He rubbed his hands and put them under his arms as if he had just felt the cold. After some more puffs, he put the cigarette out by stepping on it on the ground. The teenage boy coughed a few times and went back to the house.

Neither the boy, nor the van's passengers, nor David and Melody, had seen Rachel, who was in her Toyota Prius, the seat reclined all the way back. She was listening to her loud, favorite rock music band through the earpiece connected to her phone. She also had not noticed any of the activities around her. It had been almost an hour that Rachel was waiting for the couple to arrive. The petite yet energetic girl, who was in charge of handling Sara's needs, had tried to contact Essie since that afternoon without any success. As they had all agreed, everyone in the group had to resolve group issues with Essie. With Essie unavailable all day, Rachel did not know whom to turn to.

Upon Simone's instance, Essie had turned off his phone to spend a quiet evening with his love. Their alone time had been neglected recently by a series of unfortunate incidents. Essie accepted Simone's request to make up for his lack of attention, offering an exclusive romantic night together with a bottle of Merlot.

Sara was suffering from the flu, and Rachel did not want to take her to the clinic or hospital. The group's energetic girl had only Essie, Tim, and Melody's phone numbers. Art's number had been changed, and only Essie and Michael knew his new number. Tim would not answer Rachel's call, leaving just Melody to ask about the others. She managed a brief talk with Melody. David, along with Melody, was attending an important party thrown by a major tech company in Silicon Valley. Most owners, CEOs, and executives of giant tech organizations had been present at that party. Despite his lack of interest in attending, David had to be there to find a way to restart his business after the explosion. Some of the city's influential figures were attending the gathering as well. Melody could not figure out exactly what Rachel was saying on the phone. She told the young girl where they were at the moment and that they could not see her until the next morning.

Since that morning, Rachel had been restless. She was not showing interest in the Radical Girls organization, which she had founded as a counterweight to traditional LGTBQ groups. The events around Art and David had taken up all her time and attention. Rachel was not happy about the lack of action, at least the part she was responsible for.

Sara's flu was more an excuse to speak to Essie or someone else in the group about the real issue. What had brought Rachel in front of Melody's house that night wasn't just about sharing Sara's physical condition. She was simply dissatisfied. Rachel could not be content. A feverish girl whose inside energy was about to explode any minute, a girl who would stick her nose in everywhere and everything all day, a magnet to all kind of troubles, now only was in charge of an old woman's needs. Ironically, she was assigned to her responsibilities by the same mustache guy whose penchant for using big words in polemical debates she did not care much for. Not that she disliked Essie, but Rachel could not understand why he should be the sole decision maker. Of course, she knew that Art was at the center of everything and without him, nothing would matter at all. Rachel also knew that David's role was critical. The more she thought about it, the more she realized that each had an essential role in the confrontation with the enemy, except her. And that was bothering Rachel. She was a fidgety person. She could not stay only in charge of feeding an elderly woman. She did not grasp the importance of her role. Rachel did not know that His Excellency and Peter Jr. were willing to sacrifice much more to find out about her and where Sara was hidden. Rachel did not have Essie's address; if she had, she would undoubtedly have gone there and waited in front of his apartment. So the unhappy, dissatisfied girl decided to go to Melody and David's house and wait in the car. She made herself busy listening to her favorite music and daydreaming without noticing any of the activities around her. She neither noticed the van's passengers nor the arrival of David and Melody.

The light was turned off outside the house where the teenage boy had come out to smoke. The man sitting next to the driver in the van held the remote control that was as large as a handheld phone. He touched the red button, looked at the driver, and said, "Now, it's time."

They looked at each other, nodding in agreement. The commander pressed the red button on the remote. A ray of bright light accompanied by the sound of a formidable blast shook the entire neighborhood, shattering a few car windows and activating their alarms. The blue Chevy van started up and sped away from the scene.

Rachel jumped out of her seat. The blast had shattered her car's rear window. The earth under her had trembled. She thought she was sleeping and her car was moving like a cradle. But as Rachel gathered her thoughts, she discovered the depth and intensity of the explosion. It seemed as if a giant meteorite had landed in the middle of the street. She got out of the car. Several neighbors had rushed out of their houses to the street in their pajamas or underwear. Rachel looked at David and Melody's house. Smoke was coming out of their house. She walked toward the center of the explosion. Her mind was focused more as she was moving faster. After few steps, she noticed flames behind windows in Melody's house. First, Rachel walked faster, but now she was running toward the house as fast as possible. The garage door was dislodged and had fallen in front of Melody's car. She entered the house from the garage. Ambulance sirens were heard from a distance. After entering the building, she could not see anything. The curtain on top of the window opening to the backyard was in flames. Rachel went to the curtain, pulled it down, and tried to put the fire out. Nonstop coughing and the heavy smoke made breathing difficult for her. She recognized Melody on the kitchen floor. Bending herself to breathe more easily, Rachel walked over to her. Melody was unconscious. She put her hands under Melody's armpits, trying to pull her out of the house. Melody was heavier in that condition than Rachel could handle. Breathing was becoming more difficult, and Rachel felt pain in her lungs. She stooped down over Melody. The young girl could not determine whether the unconscious woman was alive. Melody was not breathing. Her pulse was barely felt. Rachel saw two firefighters at the building entrance who were watching the scene through the smoke. Rachel cried for help. Two firefighters ran toward Melody. Rachel shouted, "I don't see her husband. He must be at home too."

Then Rachel ran to the other rooms while the firemen were carrying Melody out. She entered the master bedroom and saw David who had been thrust into a corner, his head having hit the wall. She reached over to David. Rachel screamed, and four medics rushed into the room. One of them faced Rachel's resistance when he tried to take her away. But Rachel had no other choice, as she felt dizzy. The rescuer put an oxygen mask on her mouth as she was continually repeating Art's name.

   ***

For two days, two teams, each consisting of four men, had been working in a building where the LGBTQ community hall was located. The operation was carried out as repair work that the building management had permitted. The teams had set up enough explosives underneath the building and its key columns to destroy the entire block.

After the commander of the LGBTQ building explosion team received a text confirming the explosion at David's house, he realized that he was up next to perform his duty. A few seconds later, the group's commander, who had parked his blue van a block from the building, received the second message on his phone. He pushed the red button on the remote control that he was holding. It was as if a tremendous earthquake had shaken the ground. The likelihood of people's presence was rare in cold weather. In front of the commander's eyes, the very building at which Art had delivered his famous speech a few weeks before was leveled to the ground. The commander instructed the driver to get away from the scene as quickly as possible. The large van pulled away from its parking spot and turned to the left. As the blue van was moving away from the scene, he watched from the side mirror flames of fire rising on top of the smoke and dust.

***

Lolling on the sofa, Art was watching TV, stretching his legs out on the small table in front of the sofa. Indolence and sleep were taking over his body. He had spent the whole day with Michael in the city. Since that morning, a strange emotion had been occupying his mind. Art did not know what that feeling was, but he hugged and kissed Michael all day long, and he was surprised at the eruption of so much love in himself. Although Essie had told everyone to avoid going out as much as possible, Art decided to go to the city to show Michael all the places he had seen and liked or intended to visit but never could. They had a fantastic day together. Even in that cold winter weather, like two passionate tourists, they took a ferry around Alcatraz and under the Golden Gate Bridge. Art had asked Michael to take a day off so they could explore the city together. And they traversed the whole city together, including places where Art had good memories; he wanted to show them to his love. At sunset, they went to Michael's bar, where they had met each other for the first time.

Art had spent the day with his two loves: the one whom he loved dearly and the city he had fallen in love with since his first visit. And now he was sitting behind the same counter just like at the night he arrived at the Get Cool Bar. Michael went to the other side of the counter to make the same drink for Art. Like that night, Art did not ask for a specific drink. Michael poured them two mugs of beer and placed two shots of vodka beside each mug. Then both poured the vodka shot into each other's beer and gulped it at once with big cheers. They repeated the ritual a few more times. Then, like the first night, they clasped each other's hands and stared at one another in the eyes. Returning to Michael's apartment, they made flaming, exciting, and emotional love on the same couch that Art was now sitting on euphorically.

Art was still on the sofa in front of the TV waiting for Michael to come back from the other room. His eyelids were heavy and on the verge of being closed. He heard Michael's jaunty footsteps. Michael came with half-dry hair wearing a lime colored T-shirt which was magnifying the beauty of his dark skin tone, which Art was madly in love with. He sat next to Art. They embraced and kissed each other ever so tenderly.

A bang from the hallway behind the door separated them. The door's lock was smashed loudly, and two masked men stormed in with guns in hand. Michael and Art jumped up from the sofa and turned to the intruders. The invaders pointed their guns, equipped with the silencer, to Michael and Art and fired. Everything happened so fast. When Art realized the situation, he raised his right hand, showing his palm to the attackers. Both attackers were thrown back fiercely. Art looked at Michael on the ground; the blood on his T-shirt was spreading around his chest. Art sat next to his love and raised his head slightly. A smile appeared on Michael's lips. Art slowly lowered Michael's head and hurried to the table. He grabbed the phone and returned to Michael. He dialed 911 and said, "We need an ambulance immediately. Two gunmen broke into our apartment and shots were fired. My partner's been shot."

Art touched the hair on Michael's forehead. Michael's eyes were closed. Art's tears were dropping on Michael's arm. He placed Michael's head on his leg and while listening to the phone, he put his index and middle fingers on the left side of Michael's jugular and said, "I barely can feel the pulse ... it's very weak."

Art lay Michael's head down slowly, stood up, and went to the masked men, who were unconscious in the hallway outside. They were wearing jumpsuits. He went over to the one who was leaning against the wall and took off his mask. He was a white man in his thirties, and his left nostril was bleeding. Art turned to another man and removed his mask. The second attacker looked older, in his fifties with white hair, and like the other shooter was a heavily built muscleman. Art had never seen them before. One of the men still had a gun in his hand, and the other's gun was beside him on the floor. Two Asian male neighbors were looking at each other, hesitant to approach Art and the men on the floor. One of them pulled his phone out of his pocket and placed it on his ear after hitting three buttons. The sound of the police siren was heard from afar. Art kicked the man who leaned on the wall in the head, causing the gun to fall from his hand. Then he threw the weapon in the apartment. He did the same to the second intruder, returned to the room, and kneeled down beside Michael, who was in the same position. The blood had covered more of his T-shirt.

***

It was 3:50 in the morning in Atlanta. Since the night before, His Excellency was dealing with an overexcitement that he could not alleviate. The three-hour time difference from California and the lack of sleep exhausted his mind and body. His Excellency thought about his diminished physical power and remembered his youthful energy. In the last few hours, waiting for Peter Jr.'s phone call, he thought about many subjects. To kill time, John Wesley the Third had pulled everything from the back of his mind and played with them. From Sara to his son and all the current affairs of the church, he reviewed everything including encountering other bishops. His Excellency brushed up on plans and discussions with representatives of other religions and faiths. Subjects, one by one, appeared in his mind and left, but he received no news from Peter Jr. His excitement was being replaced by anxiety. Worries were finding their ways from His Excellency's mind down to his stomach, grasping his heart as well as his gut. The level of anxiety, however, was not so high to cause him a dysfunctional mind.

His Excellency tried to pray a few times without success. He closed his eyes. As always, he tried to depict the glorious, heavenly image of Jesus Christ in his mind. He could not understand why the image would not appear. With closed eyes, he tried to find lines and lights he could imagine to create the image. But those lines disappeared as soon as they emerged. His Excellency began to pray, but the words were fleeing from his mind and he could not finish sentences of prayer. Thoughts about various operations that were to be performed would replace the prayer. Pictures of the Sodom group members and their despised faces suddenly came into view, pushing words of prayer away. His Excellency had repeatedly reviewed all those pictures that he received from Peter Jr. Sam and Simone had been able to send explicit images of individuals to Peter Jr. in different situations. Peter Jr. had opened a separate file for each member of the Sodom group, files that should be closed tonight. He hoped everything would go as planned. And why wouldn't it? Peter Jr. had put the best-skilled operatives together and had trained soldiers whose motivations were not just money but the light of God that had illuminated their hearts. Or at least their acts indicated as much.

The phone rang and jolted His Excellency as he realized that he had dozed off in his chair. He did not know how long he was asleep.

He had tried to take a nap despite the excessive excitement, but anxiety had kept him up. The phone, however, made him aware that fatigue eventually took over the excitement. His Excellency picked up the phone. Peter Jr.'s voice was heard from the other end: "All five are done."

His Excellency did not say anything. He was afraid to ask Peter Jr. about the success or failure of the operations. Something was keeping him from asking further questions. He felt the pain on the side of his face as he was pressing the phone receiver to his ear. Peter Jr. did not say anything more. He did not want to break his boss's thread of thought.

His Excellency put the receiver on its black base and hung up. He leaned back in his chair and closed his eyes. In a flash of thought, he regretted why he had not questioned about the success of all the operations. He said to himself, "If something were wrong, Peter Jr. would have told me." With a deep sigh, he felt much better. His mind became clear of excitement and anxiety all at once. Finally, tranquility revealed its angelic face to him. He felt that his sacred relationship with his creator was being reestablished. A religious image came to his mind. First, he was not sure if it was Abraham, or Christ Himself, who came for him, but he had no doubt he was sensing the warmth and presence of a holy figure in his surroundings. Of course, to him, there was no difference between the two. Abraham was as supreme as Christ. Despite the existence of Christ's love in his entire body and soul, His Excellency knew that if Abraham did not exist, there would not have been Jesus. He was ashamed for a moment to compare these two symbols of God's light in his mind. All those prophets were messengers of God's commandment that, at a certain point, advanced the will of God on earth. The same way that His Excellency himself had carried on this will by inspiration from the Father, the Son, and the Holy Spirit.

When John focused more, he saw that it was Christ himself who came for him. The Son of God took His Excellency's hand and led him to a hall. Yes, he had no doubt. He knew the event: the Last Supper. His Excellency saw the apostles sitting there. There were only two seats unoccupied. Apostles of Jesus were sitting there, talking, eating, and drinking. He had seen different images of the apostles at the Last Supper, but they were never moving in those pictures. Now everyone was talking and moving in his seat. His Excellency and the other, the one who had held his hand, moved forward. At the dinner table, John did not see the Son of God. Just a few moments ago, Jesus took his hand and led him to this point. But now that they were in front of the table, His Excellency saw that he was holding someone else's hand. He sat down in his chair and placed the other person on his side. He looked at the others. The bishops were in their seats, drinking wine. John poured wine into a bowl and sank bread into it. He saw another hand sink bread in the same container at the same moment. His Excellency raised his head. Yes, everything became clear to him. James was sitting in Judas's seat. He only smiled without saying anything.

When his neck fell on his chest, His Excellency realized that he had fallen asleep for some time again. The smile still was on his lips. He stood up slowly and walked toward the exit door. Before turning the lights off, he paused and looked at the famous John Wesley's large image on the wall over his desk, with white hair over his shoulders. His Excellency felt he heard in his mind the songs composed by John Wesley. He stared at the picture for a few moments, then pressed the switch, turned off the lights, and stepped out.


End of book one.

487

## About the Author

Kayvan kaboli is an Iranian-American author. He is the co-founder of the Green Party of Iran. He has written a few short stories, many articles and produced several television programs and documentaries. Children of Stonewall is his first novel.

He earned his bachelor's in Economics and master's degree in Software Engineering. In addition to literature and film, he is interested in environmental issues.

@GetToSource